Out of the Loop

Also available by Katie Siegel

The Not a Detective Mysteries

Charlotte Illes Is Not a Teacher

Charlotte Illes Is Not a Detective

Out of the Loop

A MYSTERY

Katie Siegel

CROOKED LANE

NEW YORK

Books should be disposed of and recycled according to local requirements. All paper materials used are FSC compliant.

This is a work of fiction. All of the names, characters, organizations, places and events portrayed in this novel are either products of the author's imagination or are used fictitiously. Any resemblance to real or actual events, locales, or persons, living or dead, is entirely coincidental.

Published in the United States by Crooked Lane Books, an imprint of The Quick Brown Fox & Company LLC.

Crooked Lane Books and its logo are trademarks of The Quick Brown Fox & Company LLC.

Library of Congress Catalog-in-Publication data available upon request.

ISBN (hardcover): 979-8-89242-393-9
ISBN (paperback): 979-8-89242-394-6
ISBN (ebook): 979-8-89242-395-3

Cover design by Michel Vrana

Printed in the United States.

www.crookedlanebooks.com

Crooked Lane Books
34 West 27th St., 10th Floor
New York, NY 10001

First Edition: February 2026

The authorized representative in the EU for product safety and compliance is eucomply OÜPärnu mnt 139b-14, 11317 Tallinn, Estonia, hello@eucompliancepartner.com, +33757690241

10 9 8 7 6 5 4 3 2 1

To my parents, who have one (1)
book genre they both enjoy.
It's a mystery how I ended up like this.

And to all the wonderful booksellers.
(Based on my experience,
Savannah is an anomaly.)

Contents

Contents

Chapter Two
The Air Feels Different

It took Amie Teller all of twenty-three minutes to realize that she was no longer in a time loop.

In her defense, the morning of September 17 (which she had become supernaturally accustomed to waking up in) was fairly nondescript as far as Monday mornings go. It didn't begin with a radio alarm or a noisy neighbor or a partner bringing her coffee. She had a calendar on her wall, but never got into the habit of crossing off the days with a bright red marker. And she hadn't checked the date on her phone in a long time.

Because of that, for the first twenty-three minutes of Day 1 A.L. (After Loop), there was absolutely nothing to alert Amie to the fact that this wasn't the same day she'd relived for the past seven hundred and sixty-ish days of her life.

* * *

Day 1 After Loop (A.L.)

The morning began as it always did: with the gentle tones of her alarm going off at 8 AM. Most days Amie would simply tap the screen to stop the ringing. A few dozen times the device was silenced by being hurled at the wall, the floor, the ceiling, or, once, out the window. There had been one particularly dark day when Amie just let it ring and ring and ring and ring and ring, until the phone finally got the hint and died a couple of hours later.

A surprisingly healthy effect of being stuck in a time loop was that social media had swiftly lost its appeal. Before the loop, Amie would start her day by scrolling through multiple feeds. By Day 4 I.L., being greeted every morning by the same posts and photos had broken the habit.

So that was why, for the first twenty-three minutes of Day 1 A.L., Amie lay quietly in bed, doing her morning sudoku, oblivious that the needle had been moved on the skipping record of her life.

When the text came in, she instinctively swiped the notification away. The puzzle was almost complete; she'd look at the text when she finished. Just a few more—

Wait.

Sitting up in bed, she stared at the spot at the top of her screen where she'd seen the notification.

Did I imagine that? she thought, adrenaline shooting through her body.

Amie finally began taking in her surroundings, her heartbeat quickening at every new observation. The clothes she'd worn the day before were still sitting where they'd been tossed on top of the hamper, grass stains streaking her favorite pair of jeans.

She hadn't given it a second thought the day before when she'd dropped to her knees in the grass to "look" for the ring lost by Hallie From The Park. She'd known exactly where the ring was, having found it many times before. Some days, when Amie was feeling especially starved for company, she'd spend a few minutes on the lawn with Hallie From The Park, passively patting down the grass as she listened to the other woman talk about her sunrise yoga class and its stuck-up instructor. Amie would never let the charade go on for longer than five minutes—Hallie From The Park had dinner plans with her boyfriend, and was anxious that she'd lost the ring forever.

Amie hadn't been anxious about losing things for a long time. Similarly, she'd stopped caring about transient things like grass stains on jeans. The time loop was more effective than the strongest stain remover on the market.

The air feels different, Amie thought, tearing her gaze away from the dirty laundry as she looked to the window. There wasn't much of a perceivable difference, but for someone who had lived the same day seven hundred and sixty-ish times, the difference was there. Amie wouldn't have known how to put it into words. It was just *different*.

She didn't even remember jumping out of bed when she heard the truck beeping outside. Finding herself at the window, she threw back the curtains and looked down at the street. A tow truck was backing up toward a car parked along the yellow curb, which was maybe the most exciting thing Amie had seen in ages.

As she pushed open the window and stuck out her head, something cold and wet hit the top of it. Heart pounding, she twisted to look up.

It was raining.

It was *raining*.

She stared at the dark clouds until a large raindrop landed directly in her eye, startling her out of the almost hypnotic effect the overcast sky was having on her. She hadn't seen rain clouds in over two years.

Feeling overwhelmed, Amie retreated into her bedroom. She sat down on the floor before her legs could give out and send her there a lot faster than she would have preferred.

She was still clutching her phone, but it was a struggle to tear her eyes away from the open window, as if the new day might disappear if it was no longer being perceived.

Finally, she mustered up the courage to look back down at her phone, hand shaking as she read the new message.

Ziya: Hiya, feeling better this morning?

Amie stared at the text for a long, long time. To be exact, it was two minutes and eleven seconds, but it was definitely an excessive amount of time to spend staring at a six-word text message. Then again, Amie hadn't been familiar with the concept of "wasting time" in quite a bit of it.

Bubbles popped up on the screen as Ziya began typing again, and Amie almost dropped the phone in surprise. ("Being surprised" was also a concept she hadn't been familiar with in some time.)

Ziya: Lmk when you're free to reschedule our dinner
Ziya: Unless you're not ready. Totally fine!!

Amie winced. Ziya thought she'd canceled because she didn't want to go. In Amie's reality, she had gone on their "friend date" dozens of times. In *Ziya's* reality, Amie had texted her about a massive migraine, requesting they postpone their dinner.

The excuse was weak, of course. Amie didn't get migraines, and Ziya knew that. The weakness of the excuse never really mattered, though. She never thought she'd have to deal with the repercussions of Ziya not buying her lie.

Amie locked the phone. She'd reply sometime later, maybe. It didn't really matter.

No, she corrected herself. *It* does *matter. Things matter now.*

She was still sitting on the floor. Standing up felt both incredibly exciting and horribly intimidating.

Still having yet to reacquaint herself with the concept of wasting time, Amie sat on the floor for half an hour, trying to figure out what different and exciting thing she was going to do to celebrate this brand-new day.

Finally, as her stomach began to rumble, she gave up, put on her shoes, and headed for the café to get her long-awaited blueberry bagel.

Chapter One

Emotional Support Plastic Flamingo

Day 15 In Loop (I.L.)

After two weeks, Amie was ready to admit that she was stuck in a time loop.

In all honesty, this was probably something she could have acknowledged at *least* a week and a half earlier, if not sooner. Anyone is bound to notice such a life-altering temporal anomaly after a maximum of three days, unless they're living in a remote cabin in the woods with zero human contact. And even then, that person would have to eventually clock the same flock of birds landing in their yard every morning at 9:47 AM, or the thunderstorm that starts each day right after lunch, or the perpetual waxing crescent moon.

If Amie was being honest with herself, she had become aware of the loop within the reasonable window of time for someone not living in a remote cabin in the woods with zero human contact. It was the *acceptance* that took a little longer.

That's a normal thing to happen, she thought on Day 4 as she once again passed two men standing outside of her favorite coffee shop, Eons Café, having the same argument about baseball they'd had for the previous four days (she didn't count the Original Day as a part of the time loop). She walked past them and entered the shop.

This is the first time I've seen this happen, she lied to herself on Day 9 as the barista at Eons once again accidentally knocked a drink off of the counter. She headed for the front, napkins already in hand.

Maybe if I don't react to it, she thought on Day 11 when Eons was once again out of blueberry bagels, *then everything will continue as normal tomorrow.* She ordered a plain bagel instead.

There were other events throughout the day that were much more indicative of something being amiss than a repeated spilled drink and a bagel outage. Even so, for two weeks, Amie remained steadfast that if she just continued on living her life, her life would eventually continue on.

"Am I supposed to do something?" she asked out loud as she lay on her bed, staring at the ceiling. It was the morning of Day 15 I.L. She'd long since stopped clicking on the YouTube link her dad sent her at 9:27 every morning. She knew to avoid the main stairwell of her building between 5:10 and 5:55 after a couple of awkward run-ins with movers carrying a couch upstairs. She knew every lurid detail of Loud Sidewalk Woman's date that she would recount over the phone from 2:43 to 2:51 (unfortunately, LSW's ride would always pick her up before Amie could hear if the guy was purposefully catfishing her or had just recently got a haircut).

She had even stopped doing the dishes, which was strange for her. It was one of the few household chores she actually enjoyed doing. Washing the dishes was calming, almost therapeutic. And she could listen to her favorite podcasts while doing it.

But the feeling of accomplishment was lessened by the knowledge that whether or not she washed the dishes each day, they would still end up clean and stacked in the cabinets the next morning. Besides, it was difficult to experience true calm while feeling doomed to repeat the same day until the end of time. And she had caught up on all of her favorite podcasts by Day 6.

"What am I supposed to do?" she asked the ceiling, rephrasing her original question. Amie had never been a big believer in any particular higher power, although she acknowledged that she didn't feel it was her place to make a firm ruling on the subject. Regardless, if there *was* a chance that opening a dialogue with some omnipotent power could free her from this temporal prison, she was down to chat.

Unfortunately, if such an omnipotent power existed, they clearly weren't in the mood to reply. After about an hour of lying still, waiting for some sign, some direction, *any* instruction, Amie climbed out of bed.

So, after two weeks of being stuck in a time loop, Amie was ready to admit that she was stuck in a time loop.

Knock knock. Knock. Knock knock knock.

Amie rubbed her knuckles as she stepped back. David had long ago requested she use a very specific knock to differentiate herself from the countless salespeople he claimed to be avoiding (Amie lived a few doors down from him and never encountered any salespeople). She also knew that David was blasting his record player, both from previous visits and the fact that she could hear Ella Fitzgerald through the door.

Hence the loud, complicated knock, and her stinging knuckles.

After one more verse of "They Can't Take That Away from Me," Amie heard the music lower in volume. A moment later, the door swung open.

"Come in, watch your step." David was already walking away from the door, stepping carefully over a row of dominoes. Crouching down next to a low coffee table, he continued placing sections of a toy car track on its surface.

David Lenski was around fifty years old, with unkempt brown hair that was graying at the temples and dark-blue eyes that were laser-focused on his task. He was younger than Amie's actual father, but he and Amie looked similar enough that he had on more than one occasion been mistaken as such.

Stepping inside and shutting the door behind her, Amie surveyed the familiar scene. It was familiar in part because David's apartment usually looked like some variation of this: most of the furniture pushed to the edges of the room, with others acting as surfaces for different portions of one giant Rube Goldberg machine.

A large table stood on one side of the room, covered in a variety of items: kitchenware, mouse traps, rubber ducks, a small fan, and many more that could all be categorized as "etcetera." The wicker chest under the table stored even more miscellaneous objects, each having the potential to play some role in David's newest machine. The wall behind the chest was almost completely covered with pegboards, serving as an adaptable space to hang all sorts of tracks, ramps, pulleys—anything that could possibly help a small ball get from point A to point B.

It was a chaotic mess with no clear path. It almost never was, until David would finally drop the ball and let the machine do the rest of the work.

The scene was also familiar because—as it may have been mentioned—this was not the first time Amie had lived through this day. But although she had experienced that Monday sixteen times before, she had only visited David thrice in that time.

The two neighbors had met about a year before the time loop began, soon after Amie had moved into the building. She'd been working at a public relations firm for a few years post-college, living with a parade of roommates as she tried convincing herself that she was enjoying her work. Then Amie's employer and landlord came to a joint agreement to blow up her life, simultaneously laying her off and converting her place into a short-term rental. She was lucky to quickly find the writing job and a new place to live. Despite the low salary and the high rent, Amie enjoyed the peace and quiet of no longer having roommates. Most of the time.

One day, she'd come upon David struggling to open the front door while holding two cardboard boxes full of wooden blocks. After a good amount of cajoling, Amie had managed to wrest one of the boxes away from him and haul it up to his apartment. With the amount of time it took her to convince him to let her into his apartment with the box, she knew he either wasn't going to murder her, or didn't want her to see the bodies of the people he had already murdered. If the former situation was true, great. If the latter, she figured holding a heavy box of wooden blocks would prove to be useful.

David didn't murder her, and since then visiting her neighbor had become a regular occasion for Amie. At first she would show up under the guise of having baked too many cookies or scones or muffins. Eventually, she just started showing up. David seemed to enjoy having an audience as he tinkered with his machines, and Amie enjoyed having someone who enjoyed having her around.

She'd also found out that he'd managed to write a few bestselling books and was "semi-retired," which apparently meant that he spent most of his waking hours building Rube Goldberg machines, or acquiring objects for said machines, or cursing at the machines when they didn't do what he wanted them to. As for the books, Amie had long since given up on trying to get him to reveal their titles, or the pen name he wrote them under.

The first of her three September 17 visits to David was on the Original Day, when her only experience with time loops was watching *Groundhog Day* when she was twelve.

Her second visit was on Day 1 I.L., when she frantically dashed up the stairs, banged on the door, and froze as she heard Ella Fitzgerald's muffled crooning through the door once again.

She'd stayed for ten minutes, unwilling to say out loud what she thought was happening to her, as if outwardly acknowledging the loop would somehow give it permanence.

Her third visit was on Day 12 I.L. Although she didn't want to admit it to herself, Amie was steadily acclimating to her situation.

And even though he had no way of knowing, she felt bad for going so long without visiting David. She felt even worse when she learned that she'd woken him from his afternoon nap, and worse still when he told her to stay, saying, "Once I'm up, I'm up."

Despite feeling like an imposition, she ended up staying for over two hours, far longer than her usual visits. And even though she couldn't bring herself to say the words "time loop" to David that day, she'd left his apartment feeling a little less alone.

And now, on Day 15 I.L., Amie was ready to say the words out loud.

"Is this a judgment-free zone?" she asked, picking up a lawn flamingo that had been lying on the couch and taking its seat.

"No," David replied bluntly, not looking up from his work.

Amie's jaw dropped. That was not the response she'd expected. "Why not?"

"Yesterday you judged me for not knowing that 'SMH' meant 'shaking my head.'" David connected two track pieces together with a loud *snap*. "By your own actions, I don't think this is a 'judgment-free zone.'"

"Oh." Amie vaguely remembered that. For David, it had been yesterday. For her, a bit longer.

"Okay, I'm sorry for that," she continued, cradling the plastic flamingo in her lap. "Can it be a judgment-free zone starting now?"

David snapped another two pieces together, glancing at her over his shoulder. He looked like he wanted to complain more about being teased for his lack of knowledge of slightly archaic texting acronyms, but there must've been something in her voice that made him nod instead.

Amie took a deep breath, holding her emotional support lawn flamingo a little tighter. "Do you know what a time loop is?"

David shifted on the floor to look at her fully. "Like in *The Bird Returns Again*?"

"In *what*?"

"*The Bird Returns Again*. 1987 sci-fi novel by Dana Malett."

"You know, most people would've just said, 'Like in *Groundhog Day*,'" Amie pointed out.

David waved a piece of the car track at her scoldingly. "The judgment-free zone didn't last long. SMH."

"Okay, you're right, sorry," Amie apologized. "Like *The Bird Returns Again*. I'm assuming. Did the person in that book keep repeating the same day?"

"I think the author called it a 'temporal loop,'" David confirmed, facing his track again. "It was the same nine hours, actually, but I think the general concept remains the same."

"I . . ." Amie tried searching for the right words. She was becoming increasingly more familiar with the reality that anything she said or did wouldn't have an impact that lasted beyond the next sunrise. Yet somehow she still felt it was important to get this right on the first try.

"Do you think that could really happen?" she finally asked. "That someone could get . . . stuck, repeating the same day over and over again?"

David had finished with the tracks and was on his feet, heading for the wicker basket.

"I suppose," he said, kneeling down and pulling the top of the basket open. "I don't have the scientific knowledge needed to say definitively what would need to happen to cause something like that, if it *was* possible."

He pulled a child-sized golf club out of the basket and let the lid fall, straightening as he turned back around. "Is this for an article?"

Amie shook her head silently, feeling her face begin to crumple. She knew she had to just let it out. But she didn't know what scared her more: that David might not believe her, or saying the words out loud for the first time.

Seeing her distress, David made his way to the couch, gingerly sitting down on the arm at the other end of it. "What is it?"

Amie took in a slow, shaky breath. "It's happening to me," she said, her voice cracking.

David's brow furrowed. "What is?"

"A time—" She cleared her throat, speaking a little louder. "A time loop. It's happening to me. This is Day 15. Not counting the original one. This is the third day I've visited you since it started. You wear the same gray T-shirt with the mustard stain and the blue sweatpants, and you always have Ella Fitzgerald on, and I don't know what to do. I don't . . ." She hugged the flamingo closer, staring at the floor. "I don't know what to do."

The silence was unbearable. Amie instantly wished she hadn't said anything. Even if he wouldn't remember it the next day, she hated to imagine what David was thinking of her at that moment. The only thing that kept her from dashing out the door was the row of dominoes that she'd feel bad about knocking over in a hasty exit.

After what felt like a thousand years (she briefly wondered if she'd eventually learn what a thousand years felt like), David let out a soft "Hm."

Amie's head whipped over to look at him. "That's *it*?" she burst out, her nerves bubbling over. "'Hm'? That's all you've got?"

"Give me a second," David said mildly, using his thumb to dab at the mustard stain on his shirt. "I'm getting old; I need time to process."

"Well, you have about . . ." Amie looked around. "Why don't you have any clocks in here?"

"It's close to 5:45," David said, looking at the window and somehow seeing the time there.

"You have about nine hours to process before the day resets," Amie finished, slumping back into the couch. "But take your time, I guess."

"The day resets at two forty-five AM?" David asked.

Amie gave him a wary look. "Do you believe me, or are you making fun?"

"I'm curious," he said simply.

Amie stared at him for another moment, but couldn't find any teasing in his eyes.

"Two twenty-two," she said cautiously. "I've stayed awake a few nights to see how far I could get. As soon as I see the clock hit two twenty-two AM, the next thing I know, I'm waking up, and it's September seventeenth again."

"Hm."

"Really?" Amie stood, her voice rising in pitch as she spoke. "You know what? Never mind. Forget I said anything. And you will. You and everyone else will forget everything that happens today. And I'll just be here, living the same day over and over again until the sun explodes or whatever. *Why am I still holding this fucking flamingo?*"

"Okay, okay," David held out a hand as if to block Amie from throwing the plastic bird across the room. "Take it easy. You're all right. Let's put down the bird."

Amie realized she was brandishing the lawn ornament over her head. She lowered her arm.

David gestured for her to sit again. She did.

"Now," he said, "are you feeling okay? Did you sleep last night?"

"You don't believe me," Amie said flatly.

David hesitated, clearly trying to figure out how to make his approach delicate.

"Kid, I'd . . . *like* to believe you," he said slowly. "It's just hard to—"

"Can we move past it?" Amie asked, suddenly feeling very tired. "We don't have to talk about it anymore."

She forced herself to smile as David continued looking at her with concern. "Really, I'm fine. It's fine. You're right, I just didn't get much sleep last night."

David's brows were knit together with concern, but he just shrugged, sliding off the couch arm. "If you say so. Why don't you help me with this next section? Take your mind off of things."

He held up the tiny golf club. "What should I do with this?"

Amie shrugged, aimlessly tracing the plastic feathers of the flamingo with her finger. David didn't usually pay much attention to any input she offered about his machines, much less solicited her for it. She knew he was just feeling bad for her.

"You could attach it to something that rotates," she offered, remembering this part of the machine from the last time she visited. "Don't you have that round necklace display that spins? Stick it onto that, then make it spin and hit the ball."

She'd stay for another twenty minutes, just long enough for David to stop worrying. It was silly of her to have tried to tell him. Sure, she could have probably dragged him out of the apartment and found some way to prove it. It was almost six o'clock, which was around the time that terrier got away from its owner outside of their building. She could call that just seconds before it happened and prove to him that she was telling the truth.

But what was the point, really? He was just going to reset the next day, same as everything else. And she didn't have it in her to keep going through this.

Besides, now that she was thinking about it, what would happen if she *was* able to convince someone of the existence of the time loop? What if it immediately made the day reset? What if it somehow added another millennia to her sentence for breaking some rule she was unaware of? What if it sucked David into the time loop too?

It wasn't worth it.

The silence became loud enough to pull Amie out of her thoughts. She assumed David would have gone rummaging for the necklace display and continued his tinkering, quickly forgetting about her outburst.

Looking back up, she instead saw him sitting back down on the couch arm with a soft *thump*. His expression had gone from worried to intrigued.

"What?" she asked, frowning self-consciously. "It's not a bad idea. It's literally what you were . . ."

She trailed off, nervously studying his face.

"It's literally what I was going to do," David finished, pointing at her with the golf club. "And I knew if you knew what I was going to do with this club, you wouldn't be able to resist telling me, because you knew I'd like that idea. Because it was *my* idea first."

"It was a lucky guess," Amie said, her worries of dragging her neighbor into the loop looming larger by the second. "I've seen you make enough of these by now; I know how you like to do things. Attaching it to the necklace display is an obvious answer."

"Aha!" David leapt up from the couch, startling her into almost dropping the flamingo (which she was *still* holding, for some reason). "But what you didn't know was that I just bought that necklace display at the yard sale this morning."

"I . . . you . . ." Amie shook her head. "You're confused. I've seen it before." She rolled her eyes good-naturedly. "You're getting old."

"Watch it," David said warningly, circling the couch as he headed for the back of the room. "Don't be rude."

"I was quoting *you*." Amie twisted around in her seat to look at him. "How come you can use that excuse, but I can't?"

"Aha!" David said again, grabbing a reusable grocery bag and holding it up for her to see.

"That's two 'ahas,'" Amie said, trying to distract him. "You only have one left for the rest of the day. Use it wisely."

David walked back over to the couch, holding open the bag for her to look inside. "See? My yard sale purchases from today. Toy truck. Bicycle wheel. Took some convincing to get them to sell it separately from the rest of the bike. And . . ."

"Yeah, I see it," Amie said softly, untwisting back around before he could pull out the rotating necklace display.

She heard the bag crumple as he set it on the floor.

"You were telling the truth, weren't you?" He walked around the couch to stand in front of her.

"I'm sorry. I shouldn't have brought it up. It doesn't matter."

"Sure it does." David was still holding the small plastic golf club. "This is . . . I mean, it's remarkable. And you're going through it alone? No one else has noticed the day repeating?"

"Not that I know of." Amie had spent the first few days of the time loop closely studying everyone she passed, trying to find the same stifled fear in someone else's eyes that she knew was visible in her own.

"And I'm just going to forget about it tomorrow." David scratched his chin, studying the ceiling. "Well, you're not gonna want to go through this every day."

Amie shook her head.

"Aha!" David snapped his fingers, pointing at her.

"That's your last one," Amie reminded him.

"That's fine; this is the best idea I'll have today." He began to pace, skillfully avoiding knocking over the dominoes. "We just need a code. Something that I can tell you to tell me that will immediately convince me of your situation. No ifs, ands, or buts."

He stopped pacing. "I've got it."

"What if I just mention the necklace display?" Amie suggested.

David visibly deflated. "Oh. That would probably work."

"Would you rather do your idea?"

"A little, yeah."

Amie gestured for him to proceed.

He sat down next to her on the couch. "When my niece was younger—"

Amie's eyebrows raised slightly, but she tried not to react otherwise. David didn't talk much about his family.

"—we had a code," he continued. "'Tell Genevieve I said hi.' Just something she knew she could say to her parents or me that would let us know she was in trouble and needed help. Thankfully, the worst time she needed to use it was when she wanted to leave a sleepover early."

"Who's Genevieve?" Amie asked.

"No one," David replied. "We didn't know a single Genevieve. That was the point."

"Ah." Amie had gone to elementary school with a Genevieve. She wondered what she was doing on this day, over and over and over again.

"So tomorrow," David instructed, "just say, 'I'm stuck in a time loop. Tell Genevieve I said hi.' And I'll understand."

"I don't want to bother you any more with this," Amie said quietly, her eyes starting to sting. She didn't like asking for help, and she *especially* didn't like asking for help when she didn't even know what help she needed.

David waggled the golf club at her in a faux-threatening manner. "If you show up tomorrow and don't tell me about this," he said, "or, even worse, don't show up at all, time loop be damned, I'll find out somehow, and I'll . . ."

"Force me to play golf?" Amie asked, blinking back tears as she nodded at the club.

"'Tell Genevieve I said hi,'" David repeated, giving her a look that made her miss her parents. "Promise me."

Amie tapped the golf club with the flamingo, sealing the deal with a plastic *thunk*. "Promise."

Chapter Three
A Disastrous Bagel Run

Day 1 A.L.

Getting dressed hadn't been difficult. Amie's outfits had been one of the few things she'd change on a daily basis in the time loop, though there hadn't been many in the rotation. There was a brief moment of confusion before she remembered that her favorite pair of jeans was still in the hamper and hadn't been supernaturally returned to their drawer. Grabbing a pair of shorts instead, she dressed before traveling a few doors down to see David.

Knock knock. Knock. Knock knock knock.

No response.

It was unlikely that he was still asleep, but there were a number of places he could have been: laundry room, hardware store, yet another yard sale.

I'll swing by later. Amie headed downstairs.

In the time loop, leaving her apartment building hadn't been the same exact experience every morning, although she had gotten into the habit of leaving around 9 AM on most days. But after seven hundred and sixty-ish goes of it, she had pretty much exited the building during every period of the day (and some of the night).

As she pushed open the front door of her building a little after nine o'clock, Amie knew logically that she probably wouldn't see the matching tracksuit couple, or the guy from 1A returning home with only one shoe, or the person with the mullet struggling to lock their bicycle to the lamppost. And yet she was still startled to be instead greeted by wet pavement and unfamiliar pedestrians.

The rain had stopped, but light gray clouds still hung overhead, diffusing the sunlight that was fighting to break through. September 17 had still felt like summer, but there was a slight chill in the air on September 18 that evoked a feeling of the approaching autumn.

Amie wrapped her arms around herself—because of the weather or a need for comfort, she wasn't sure—and began making her way down the front steps to the sidewalk.

She didn't notice the prickle of anxiety that had started to spread through her body until she reached the bottom of the stairs.

You're fine, she told herself. *It's a new day. You're free!*

Giving a shaky smile to a passing couple, Amie straightened her shoulders and began walking down the sidewalk toward Eons.

She made it about ten steps before a bicycle bell rang behind her, causing her to yelp and jump out of the way.

"Sorry," the bicyclist said, shooting her a concerned look as he rode past.

"Not a problem," Amie replied hurriedly.

You've made this walk hundreds of times. Just go to the coffee shop. It's not that hard.

She took in a slow, deep breath, tucked her elbows in close to her sides, and resumed her trek.

As she passed the delicatessen, instinct had her drifting to the left of the sidewalk. Someone in the neighborhood refused to pick up after their dog, and Amie had learned to hug the curb outside of the deli to save her shoes. Risking a quick glance to her right, she saw the spot was free of feces.

Right, she thought, chuckling to herself. *New day, no poop.*

The chuckle died in her throat as she moved her focus to the sidewalk in front of her, becoming even more cautious of where she walked.

After half a block, she felt her shoulders begin to relax. Allowing herself to look around, she started taking in the details of this new day. Her arms even began to swing a bit as she walked.

"Excuse me?"

Amie skidded to a stop, almost running into the person who had stepped in front of her.

"Uh . . . huh?" Amie asked. She felt her heart rate increase.

"I'm looking for 1670 North Grove Street," the man said, looking at a map on his phone as he spoke. "I'm a little confused by the numbers . . . do you know if it's over here, or . . ."

"Ah . . ." Her mouth had gone dry. *What's happening to me?* "I . . . I don't . . ."

The man sighed. "It's fine, I'll figure it out. Thanks anyway."

"Okay," Amie managed to get out as he passed her.

What the hell was that?

Amie was almost never the most sociable person in the room, but she'd never struggled to talk to people, especially those in need of assistance. She was the kind of person who'd jump in with an eager "Do you want me to take that for you?" any time she'd see a couple trying to take a selfie.

Still shaking off the dust. She gave her head a sharp jerk, as if that would somehow reset whatever was wrong with her brain.

She spotted a woman rounding the corner up ahead, walking down the sidewalk toward her.

All right, Amie thought, putting her shoulders back again as she resumed walking. *When you walk past, you're going to say, "Good morning!" Easy enough. Here we go.*

There was a rumbling behind her, and Amie looked over her shoulder to see a moving truck driving down the street. She turned back to see the woman veer to the other side of the sidewalk.

Get a grip, she thought to herself, forcing what she hoped was a pleasant smile onto her face. *You're being weird. People are noticing.*

As a cold shock of water hit the left side of her body, she realized why the woman had moved. The truck continued past her down the street, leaving her sopping wet from the puddle it had sped through.

"Rough luck," the woman said sympathetically as she passed.

"Ah, yeah, well," Amie stammered, frozen in place as water dripped from her clothes.

Remembering her self-appointed mission, she spun around, blurting out, "It's morning!"

The woman glanced back, giving her a confused smile before walking away. (Granted, that could've just been how the woman's regular smile looked, but there's really no other way to respond to a sopping-wet stranger yelling "It's morning!" at you than with confusion.)

Amie shook puddle water from her arm, wiping it on the drier side of her shirt. She briefly contemplated giving up and heading back to her apartment to hide under the covers for the rest of the day, or maybe forever. But the trip back to her building felt just as daunting as her remaining journey to the coffee shop, and at least the latter held the potential of a long-awaited blueberry bagel.

Steeling herself, Amie continued down the sidewalk. *Just be normal.*

The rest of her outing was not, despite her best efforts, normal. Amie found herself swerving away from people she passed on the sidewalk, heart jumping into her throat any time someone so much as looked at her. She almost bowled over a man sweeping in front of a store when a motorcycle roared down the street. An unsuspecting pigeon nearly got kicked in the head when it fluttered down to land by her shoes.

"Sorry," Amie whispered to the pigeon as she shuffled around it.

Just when she thought she'd overcome every obstacle between her and her destination, she was confronted by the final boss: police tape, blocking the sidewalk ahead of her. An officer stood by the building holding one end of the tape, which was wrapped around a telephone pole and street sign to cordon off the sidewalk in front of the café and the bookshop next door.

Amie stopped, her shoulders slumping with defeat as she kept herself from groaning out loud. She was so preoccupied with her disheartenment that she wasn't even startled when someone walked right past her and up to the cop. Thankfully, she wasn't so preoccupied as to not notice them exchange a few words before the officer stepped aside, allowing the person to enter the café.

Is it open or not? Amie wondered, taking a few curious steps forward. Then she stopped. She knew all she had to do was ask the officer if she could go inside or not, but for some reason she just couldn't come up with the words.

The cop finally saw her—which wasn't too impressive a feat, as she was standing frozen in the middle of the sidewalk with what she could only imagine was a very distressed look on her face.

"You gotta go around," the officer called to her. "Or are you trying to get to the café?"

Amie nodded, finding herself still capable of answering yes or no questions.

The cop stepped to the side, leaving a space for her to walk through. "Go ahead."

Amie's feet instinctually began moving, having been given a clear direction. She kept her gaze on the ground as she passed the officer, pulled the door open, and slipped inside.

Finally, she had made it to Eons Café. The line at the counter was much shorter than it had been on September 17, like a peace offering from the universe. (Although it was more likely due to the police tape that made it seem as if the business was closed.) Amie automatically made a beeline for the napkins before remembering that there probably wouldn't be a spill to clean up this time. Considering the trajectory of her morning so far, though, it wasn't completely out of the question.

As she took her spot at the back of the line, she exhaled heavily. *"Do you have blueberry bagels today?"* she rehearsed in her head, craning her neck to try to see the selection of baked goods in the glass display.

Moving up with the line, Amie spotted them—the blueberry bagels. A smile began to grow on her face. She knew she probably looked strange, smiling at a bunch of bagels, but she didn't care. It was like a beam of light was shining down from the heavens, illuminating the basket in the display that had been empty for seven hundred and sixty-ish September 17ths.

"Hey there," the barista greeted Amie cheerfully as she stepped up. Jess had short brown hair with matching brown eyes, had knowingly taken Amie's order over three hundred times, and had *unknowingly* taken it seven hundred and sixty-ish times on top of that.

"Go for a swim this morning?" they asked.

Amie's mouth hung open. She'd been ready to ask about the blueberry bagels, but this unexpected question swiftly undid all of her work in rehearsal.

"Uh," she said, chest tightening. "What?"

Jess gestured to her damp clothes.

"Oh!" Amie exclaimed, looking down at herself. "No, um . . . a truck. There was a truck, and a puddle. Water. On me."

She winced, but Jess seemed to follow the heavily abridged story well enough.

"Good news," they said. "We have blueberry bagels today. Sorry again we were out yesterday. Do you want that and a mint tea?"

Amie nodded emphatically, not trusting herself to speak. She'd already forgotten the line she'd been practicing but was pretty sure it was no longer applicable.

Oh! She knew something she could say.

"Do you know what's going on with . . . ?" Amie gestured to the door and the cop who stood on the other side of it.

Jess looked up as they finished tapping the screen. "Did you hear about Savannah?"

Amie knew exactly who they were referring to. Savannah Harlow, the owner of the bookshop next door, had a habit of making baristas redo her drink and loudly complaining about the "slow service." Amie had many times witnessed Savannah scolding Jess on September 17, which led to Jess knocking a drink off of the counter.

Savannah was also Amie's neighbor. She lived in the apartment directly above with her husband, Andrew, whose heavy tread was more familiar to Amie than her own. Savannah was infamous in their building for starting arguments, feeling personally attacked, and stealing packages. Amie had once accompanied David for moral support as he demanded that Savannah return his package of balloons that had gone missing from the mail room. Savannah returned the balloons, claiming that she thought the box had been addressed to her. Amie had quickly steered David away before he could comment on Savannah's poor reading skills or failing eyesight.

"No," Amie answered. She was getting the hang of this "holding a conversation" thing. "What happened?"

Jess leaned in and in a low voice said, "She died."

Amie frowned. "What? No. That can't . . . how do you know?"

"Someone got it out of one of the cops when they started taping the sidewalk off." Jess rested their forearms on the counter. "They found her dead this morning."

"In the bookstore?"

"Apparently. Do you have your rewards card?"

Taking a beat to recover from the conversational whiplash, Amie remembered the card sitting on her kitchen counter. She'd stopped bringing it to the café during the time loop, for obvious reasons. "Oh, I . . . no, not on me."

"I can look up your account if you'd like."

"Ah . . . sure." Amie gave the barista her email address.

"You're eligible for a free beverage on your next visit," Jess announced. "You can use that on tomorrow's breakfast!"

Amie had a vague memory of Jess saying the same words to her at the start of the time loop, back when Amie still thought the points her visit accrued might last into the next day. Finally, the statement was true.

As she slid her card into the reader, her mind floated away from the counter. She hadn't become completely defamiliarized with the concept of death during the time loop, though it had lost its permanence, as did all other things. Every evening, a mosquito would somehow manage to infiltrate her apartment, and Amie had eventually gotten the killing of it down to a science. But each day it'd be back, blissfully unaware of its impending demise via flyswatter.

But Savannah was dead. Permanently. She wasn't coming back.

"You can remove your card," Jess said, breaking Amie out of her thoughts as she became aware of the shrill beeping coming from the card reader.

"Did she, um . . ." Amie's brain raced to gather her thoughts enough to create a coherent sentence. "Savannah. Was it a medical thing, or . . . ?"

"Not sure." Jess printed out the receipt and handed it to her. "I think the cops are considering murder. You want your bagel toasted, right?"

Amie blinked at them. "Uh . . . yeah."

"Great. It'll be ready for you at the end of the counter." Jess pointed at the pickup spot. "Have a great day!"

"Thanks, you too," Amie replied automatically, drifting away.

Dead. Savannah is dead. Savannah might've been murdered.

She obviously hadn't *liked* the woman. But she had a terrible feeling in her stomach, something akin to guilt. Amie had wanted so badly to be free of the time loop. And as soon as she was, this woman died. If the time loop had continued, Savannah would have still been alive.

Don't be silly. She looked at the ceiling of the coffee shop, trying to regulate her thoughts. *This isn't your fault. Just because she would have continued living the same day on repeat doesn't mean she would have lived any longer.*

Her logical thoughts did little to appease the queasy feeling in her stomach. She hoped the bagel would do a better job.

The walk home started out easier than the walk to the café, and Amie felt a confidence returning to her stride. That is, until she was faced with a quartet of joggers heading in her direction. Amie stepped off the curb to get out of their way. She leapt back onto the sidewalk as an ambulance barreled down the street, choosing that moment to turn the siren on. Tea splashed onto her shirt, and she almost crashed into a man pushing a stroller.

"Sorry, sorry," she apologized to the man, stumbling back as she kept a death grip on the paper bag in her hand. She might not make it back to her apartment in dry clothes, but she was determined to protect her long-awaited blueberry bagel.

As Amie stepped back, she felt her left sneaker hit the pavement softer than the right. She winced, slowly looking down.

Dog poop.

* * *

Amie sat at the kitchen table, damp hair wrapped in a towel. She gnawed on her bagel, which had gone chewy as it waited for Amie to shower. But absence makes the heart grow fonder, so despite the toughness, it was still a very good bagel.

Unfortunately, Amie was barely tasting anything as she absently ran her finger over the cover of her planner, which featured the green-and-pink waves of the aurora borealis. Sighing, she flipped the book open. Tasks from earlier in the week were crossed out with straight, crisp lines. Plans for the rest of the week that she'd written over two years ago were penned in neat, careful letters.

The ink was too fresh. She felt like she should have been blowing dust off of the thing. The planner had sat untouched on her desk for ages, all of its boxes for the different days rendered purposeless in a life that was the same date on repeat.

An empty box at the top of the page was titled "My Goals for the Week." A few times, early in the loop, Amie had opened her planner and scribbled phrases into the box like "WHO CARES" and "WHATEVER I DID YESTERDAY I GUESS." One time she wrote so hard the pen ripped through the paper, and the planner ended up in the trash can.

Now it was sitting open on the kitchen table, showing no signs of past scribbles or rips, much more vulnerable to a lasting impact from either.

"'Mammogram piece due,'" Amie muttered to herself, reading the notes in the September 18 box. She'd planned on finishing that article the day before, then looking it over the next day before filing it. Obviously, that didn't happen, seeing as the day before she had no idea whether or not September 18 was ever going to come.

Amie was employed by a lighthearted online magazine, writing about health and science trends targeted at women over the age of forty. Many of the articles were listicles, and most were shared by people who didn't read past the catchy title, but Amie worked hard at the job. She'd never missed a deadline before, but she had a good relationship with her editor. After adding *Email Vivian for extension* to the September 18 box, she looked to see what else she had originally planned to get done that day.

Pitch vitamin C piece. Water plants. Test lotions.

The corner of her mouth quirked up as she recalled how she'd been planning on trying out a variety of "de-aging" facial lotions for an article. She could picture the final paragraph:

> **While the Celina Facial Cream had the best results of all these lotions, the most effective way of ensuring your face doesn't age for two years is getting stuck in a time loop! Tried and tested!**

She moved the pitch to the 19th, watering the plants to the 18th, and crossed out the lotion test.

At the bottom of the 17th she'd written: *Ziya friend date @ Fork and Egg (8pm).*

She suddenly remembered the text she'd received that morning. The first indication that she was free from the loop. Ziya.

Amie jumped up so quickly her left knee slammed into the underside of the table.

"AGHHH. Ow."

Limping, she crossed the apartment and retrieved her purse from its hook near the front door. After fishing out her phone, she returned the bag to its hook and hobbled back to the kitchen table to reread the texts from her ex-girlfriend:

Ziya: Hiya, feeling better this morning?
Ziya: Lmk when you're free to reschedule our dinner
Ziya: Unless you're not ready. Totally fine!!

Amie stared at the texts as she tried to formulate a reply, thumbs twitching with anticipation before she began tapping at the screen.

Good morning! she typed. **I'm feeling much better, thanks for ask—**

She deleted the message. Boring, basic. And it was perpetuating a lie, which she'd rather avoid, especially since her actions now had consequences.

I'm totally ready for this.

Amie stared at the message. Added a smiley emoji. Deleted the whole thing.

Shit, she thought. *What if she sees me typing?*

She swiped out of her messages and opened her notes app, then spent the next ten minutes of her newly linear life composing the perfect response.

Amie: Hey, good morning!

"Good" was a stretch, considering how she spent fifteen minutes of her morning scrubbing dog poop off of her sneaker, but she felt confident with that opener.

Amie: Thanks for checking in, I'm feeling great

Also a bit of a half-truth, but she could live with that. Time to bring it home.

Amie: Definitely down to reschedule. Free any time

Amie set down her phone with an exhale, mentally patting herself on the back. This was going well. Everything was getting back on track. Soon the time loop would be a distant memory, something she'd think back to at eighty and wonder if it had just been a bad mushroom trip (if she ever decided to try mushrooms).

She was finishing up planning the rest of her week when the phone lit up with a reply from Ziya:

Ziya: How's tonight?

The ticking from the clock that hung over her stove seemed to grow very loud, as if someone had cranked up its volume. Amie looked away from the text and down at her planner.

Tonight . . . tonight . . .

Amie had expected Ziya to suggest a date a week away, maybe more. Her ex-girlfriend liked to pack her schedule as much as humanly possible. It wasn't like her to have a free evening the day of. Granted, when they were dating, many of those evenings had been reserved for Amie, but Amie had assumed that a byproduct of being broken up was that Ziya would find other activities to occupy that time.

Amie *was* free that night. Technically. But was she ready to go out again so soon? Despite successfully completing her quest to acquire her first blueberry bagel in over two years, the journey to and from the coffee shop had been more treacherous than she'd expected.

"Reacclimation," she said out loud, looking down at the goals box in her planner. Amie picked up her pen to write down the word. It took her about thirty seconds, as the pen was running out of ink and she didn't want to take the time to track down another one.

With some difficulty (and a lot of scribbling in the margins to get the ink going), the word "Reacclimation" filled the goals box. It was time to get back to normal.

But as she closed the planner, her hand drifted over the cover again. An ominous feeling swept over Amie as she reached for the phone to confirm with Ziya. She paused, hand hovering over the device.

I need a second opinion, she thought.

Chapter One

Third First Friend Date

Day 2 I.L.

Determined to keep pretending that Everything Was Normal And Not Exactly The Same As The Previous Two Days, Amie once again got ready for her friend date and took the bus to the restaurant. The pretending was made difficult as she watched the same people board the bus, heard the same podcast blasted by a guy who refused to wear headphones, and smelled the same horrible blend of cheap cologne of the teenagers walking past as she arrived at her destination at 6:55. Same as the day before, and the day before that, and, unbeknownst to her, many days after as well.

Ziya Mathur arrived at 7:08, right on schedule (technically eight minutes late, but right on schedule for her established timeline).

"Hiii," Ziya sang, shifting gears into a skip as she closed the distance between them.

"Hi," Amie echoed as Ziya hopped to a stop in front of her. The butterflies in her stomach from seeing her ex-girlfriend again did little to distract from the larger issue at hand. By the time she'd gotten to this moment the day before, she'd managed to convince herself that she was dealing with a temporary glitch, and had a very pleasant second first friend date with Ziya.

It was harder to stick with the glitch theory on the third go-around.

"I love that outfit," Ziya commented, as Amie knew she would. "Is that a new skirt?"

Amie was wearing a brown sleeveless turtleneck and a dark plaid skirt. When she'd first dressed for this date two days before, she'd told herself that a T-shirt and jeans, even her nicest pair, were fine to wear. It was just Ziya, after all.

She'd forgotten how it felt to see an ex for the first time since a breakup. The jeans were an instant regret. Through the haze of confusion that had surrounded Amie on her first day in the time loop, she'd somehow managed to take the opportunity to choose a different outfit. Part of her even believed that the universe had given her a second chance solely for this reason. After once again waking up on the 17th the following day, she discovered that she might have overestimated the level of investment the universe had in her choice of wardrobe.

"Thanks," Amie replied, much more prepared to take the compliment this time than when she'd first received it two days before (Ziya had still complimented her then, despite the jeans). "Nah, this is old. Don't wear it much. Nice dress."

"Thank you!" Ziya did a spin, showing off her outfit. She was wearing a long-sleeved orange dress with a high neck and a cutout in the front. A matching orange headband stood out against her black hair, which fell down her back in thick waves as she completed her spin.

"No pockets." Amie's comment was only a few decibels above a murmur.

Ziya gave her a delighted smile at their seemingly shared thought. "I was about to say! It doesn't have pockets, but I'm willing to make the sacrifice."

Amie nodded, realizing she'd accidentally stepped on Ziya's line. It was like she'd watched the same movie two days in a row, and could now recite memorable lines along with the characters.

"Earth to Amie."

Amie looked up with a start, having zoned out. A pair of gold bangles clinked cheerfully on Ziya's wrist as she waved a hand in front of Amie's face. The bracelets had been recently sent to her from India by an aunt—though, as far as Ziya knew, she hadn't told Amie that yet.

At least Amie's distractedness had prompted an unfamiliar line from Ziya. The change in dialogue was comforting, and for a moment she was able to pretend that everything was normal. (As normal as one can be having dinner with their ex three months after the breakup.)

Having Amie's attention again, Ziya smiled, said, "Let's do this," just as she had the other two nights, and led them into the restaurant.

Ziya chatted with the host as they waited to be seated, giving Amie time to collect her thoughts. She promptly squandered this opportunity, allowing her thoughts to continue rattling around in her brain as she watched her ex-girlfriend talk.

Everything about Ziya made a person feel special when she looked at them. Amie knew she wasn't the only one who felt this way; she could see it in everyone Ziya spoke with. The same mix of mild surprise and delight on their faces as Ziya gave them her attention. Amie supposed it was because Ziya had the energy of someone who lived a very interesting and exciting life, and if she was giving her attention to someone, it could only be assumed that she saw them as interesting and exciting.

And it was true. Ziya found almost everyone and everything to be truly captivating, and was always eager for more. But while she liked to fill her life with different interesting experiences, she had always been more than happy to come back home to Amie.

Ziya turned to look at her, catching her staring. Amie jerked her gaze away, which is hands-down the worst thing to do when you're trying to pretend that you weren't staring at someone right after they've caught you very clearly staring at them. When Amie dared to glance back over, Ziya had returned to talking to the host, who was looking at Ziya with a very familiar mix of surprise and delight.

They were seated at the same table with the same seats next to the same older couple who looked vaguely like Amie's grandparents. Amie put in the same order—fettuccine alfredo—and didn't touch any of the table bread. She had been too nervous on the first day to go for the bread, too preoccupied with her situation to do so on the second, and was now circling back to nervous. After all, their last two dinners were good: Conversation was pleasant, food was fine, and Amie managed not to do anything embarrassing like spill her wine or say, "I'm still in love with you."

So, clearly, it was in her best interest to keep this meal as close to the previous two as possible.

This turned out to be easier planned than done. Ziya loved to focus in on the smallest mentions of things, so Amie had to work hard not to bring up anything that would send the conversation careening into unexplored terrain.

Her first mistake was bringing up *Float City* fifteen minutes too early. She said the name of the TV show in passing, realizing too late that Ziya would latch on to the mention.

"Oh my god, have you been keeping up with the new season?" Ziya asked eagerly, her eyes sparkling. "It's gone so far off the rails, but I kind of love it even more."

During their previous dinners, Amie had brought up *Float City* by casually mentioning that she was *so* busy with her successful job and numerous social engagements that she just hadn't the time to start the new season yet. This was, of course, a lie, but she definitely wasn't going to tell Ziya that the only reason she loved *Float City* was because Ziya loved it, and that she couldn't watch the show without her, and, for that matter, didn't want to.

Amie could have still gone with the lie. But she was so thrown off by the subject coming up early that all she could muster in the moment was, "Ah . . . no, I haven't. Because . . ."

It's remarkable how leaving a sentence unfinished can be even more damning than finishing it with the most unbelievable lie imaginable. Because not finishing a sentence allows the listener to fill in the blank with whatever they think the speaker wouldn't want to say. And as Amie watched the light in Ziya's eyes dim, she could tell that the assumption being made wasn't that Amie had too busy a social life to watch television.

"Right. Sorry." Ziya looked down at her plate, and Amie's stomach clenched.

It was downhill from there. Amie recalled their server struggling to maneuver their dinners onto the table the last two times. On those days, she and Ziya would hurry to move their glasses out of the way, but Amie's instinct to help overtook her internal directive to Keep Everything The Same. As a result, she burned herself on Ziya's plate while trying to help him set it down.

"Let me see," Ziya said after their server left. She plucked an ice cube from her water glass as Amie rested her stinging fingers on the table between them.

"It's fine," Amie said as Ziya applied the ice cube to the burn. She flinched at the sudden cold, then relaxed, appreciating the relief. The stinging subsided, but the warmth remained where Ziya's fingers were touching hers. The heat crept across her palm and up her arm—

Amie jerked her hand away, the force of her action causing Ziya's bangles to jingle with alarm.

"Did that hurt?" Ziya asked, withdrawing the ice cube.

"No, that helped, thanks. Sorry. I just . . ."

Ziya once again filled in the rest of Amie's sentence. "I'm sorry," she said. "I shouldn't have—"

Amie began shaking her head. "No, you didn't do anything wrong—"

"I know, I just . . . sorry."

"Don't be." Amie was feeling more terrible with each passing second.

The rest of the evening was agonizing. Amie didn't think it could get any worse until they were outside of the restaurant.

On previous days, they'd hugged goodbye—albeit a little awkwardly—and agreed to hang out again in the near future.

This time, Ziya's arms were stuck firmly to her sides as she glanced down the street. Her thumbs were rubbing the sides of her fists, a subconscious self-soothing motion she did when she was upset.

"I think . . ." she started, then stopped. She was still looking away from Amie, and didn't seem to be in any rush to look back.

This time, it was Amie's turn to fill in the blank, and she didn't like what she came up with. But she didn't know how to protest without sounding pathetic, so she just said, "Yeah."

Ziya finally looked back, smiling sadly. "Maybe we can try again in a couple months. Give it more time."

"Yeah," Amie repeated. Her throat had begun to feel tight, and she hoped Ziya didn't say anything else that would require her to try to choke out more than a single-word affirmation.

They parted ways soon after that. Amie caught the bus home, where she washed her face, brushed her teeth, changed into pajamas, had a quick cry into her pillow, and fell asleep.

* * *

Day 3 I.L.

Amie stopped the alarm, eyes darting to her phone screen. Of all the mornings she would wake up in the time loop, she would rarely ever again feel such relief at seeing the date remain unchanged.

Chapter Four
Last First Friend Date

Day 1 A.L.

It took Amie eight whole minutes to convince David that she had actually been stuck in a time loop.

"You can say it was a prank. I won't be mad." He was sitting at his kitchen table, a box of miscellaneous batteries at his elbow. Someone he'd found online had sold him the box for five dollars, and he was using a voltmeter to test the juice on each of the batteries. So far, none of them were the least bit juicy.

Amie briefly closed her eyes, trying to find patience. The text from Ziya had been sitting, unresponded to, for fifteen minutes. The more time she let pass, the more opportunity Ziya had to say, "Never mind, you lost your chance! Bye forever!" (She knew that would be very uncharacteristic of Ziya, but that knowledge didn't do much to ease her worry.)

"Again," she said, "*why* would I prank you?"

David shrugged, extracting another battery from the box. "I dunno. Nutty old man living alone in his apartment gets convinced that his neighbor is stuck in a temporal loop. Hilarious."

"Does that sound like something I'd do?"

David sighed heavily. "No," he admitted.

"Besides," Amie added, planting her hands on the table, "how else would I have known about Genevieve?"

She'd used David's code phrase regularly during the time loop, giving her regards to the fabled Genevieve any time she needed to convince him that what she was saying was true. He'd been right; the line always worked. David would stare at her for a moment, nod slowly, then ask if she wanted to change the music.

"Yeah, you did know about Genevieve, didn't you?" he grumbled. She knew the grumbling was less toward her and more toward the voltmeter, which was once again showing an unwelcome result. He tossed the battery into the bag at his feet and reached into the box again.

"How else would you expect a time loop to end, anyway?" Amie pressed, wanting to make sure he was convinced before moving on to the next order of business. "It's not like you would've noticed anything different. I was the only one who was aware of it."

"Could've been a big flash in the sky," he said. "Or an earthquake or something."

"Okay, well," Amie said, "I'll pass on your critique for the next time loop."

"That's all I'm asking for. Damn. This one's dead, too." Another battery dropped into the bag.

"Sooooo . . ." Amie slid into the chair across the table from him. "Now that we're back on the same page, I need your help."

David was busy pressing buttons on the voltmeter, but momentarily flicked his eyes up at her to indicate that he was listening.

"Ziya wants to hang out tonight, but I'm not sure if I'm ready." Amie paused. "Are you listening?"

"You only said one sentence."

"I know, but you don't really look like you're listening."

David cursed as a battery slipped from his hand and rolled across the table. "Weren't you supposed to get dinner yesterday?"

"Yeah, but I canceled."

He paused. "Did you ever go?"

"Sometimes." Amie had stopped the runaway battery and was absently rolling it under her fingers. "I tried to keep it the same every time. Doing things differently based on how it went in previous loops felt . . . unethical."

"Because you want to win her back."

Amie's mouth fell open in shock. "No I don't."

David rolled his eyes, returning to the batteries.

"I *don't*," Amie repeated. "I'm very determined to make this friendship work, and so is she, clearly, since she made time to reschedule our dinner to tonight."

"How do you know she 'made time'?" David asked, tossing another faulty battery away.

"You know how Ziya is. She's always booked up at least two weeks in advance. No way she just happened to have tonight free."

David nodded sagely. "So she's trying to win *you* back."

"I really feel like you're not listening to me."

"I am, only just barely. Say something that requires a little more mental stimulation and I'll listen more." David grabbed a handful of batteries from the box and held them out to her. "In the meantime, pass these to me as I check them."

Amie accepted the batteries and set them down on the table, passing one back.

"There's just a lot of pressure for this to go well," she continued. "And I've seen it go badly. People say, 'What's the worst that can happen?' I can give a play-by-play. I just don't want to mess it up."

She paused as he dropped a battery into the bag and held out his hand for another one.

"I was kind of . . . not great this morning."

David glanced up as she passed him a battery. "'Not great' how?"

"Like . . ." Amie looked up at the ceiling as if it held answers. ". . . a complete mess? I was jumpy and panicky. I could barely talk to people. Spilled tea on myself, stepped in dog poop. It was like I had such a cemented idea of how things were supposed to go that I couldn't handle it when they were different."

Amie looked back down. "On one hand, I think it'd be good for me to live my life normally to try to move past the whole . . . time thing. But on the other hand, I don't want to risk ruining this friend date by getting back out there too soon. I could barely hold a conversation with the barista at Eons."

"You're not having trouble holding a conversation with me." *Thump.* "Battery."

Amie scowled. "It's pretty easy when all the other person says to you is 'Battery.'" She passed him one. "I think it's because you'd always have me start our conversations in the time loop, so we'd never talk about the same things. I don't have these expectations for how our conversations are supposed to go. I *know* how this date is supposed to go. So what if I freak out if it isn't the way I expect it to be?"

She stared at David as he put a new battery into the voltmeter, frowned at the screen, then held out an open palm as he extracted and dropped the offending battery.

After a few seconds of his palm remaining empty, he looked up.

Amie had crossed her arms, raising an eyebrow expectantly.

David dropped the hand. "Would you want to tell her about the time loop?" he asked, sitting back in his chair.

"No!" Amie said immediately, horrified. "God, no. I don't even know if she'd believe me."

There were many times during the loop when Amie had been tempted to tell Ziya. But after their disastrous third first friend date, she had been reluctant to say or do anything that might have ruined the evening, even if it was all due to reset in just a few hours.

"I think," she said, hesitant, "if we were still dating, that she'd believe me. But when you're broken up, it's different."

"Why?"

"It just *is.*" Amie could feel herself getting frustrated. "Look, maybe I'll tell her someday, but not at this dinner, so I need a plan B." She took a deep breath. "Please."

David looked up, the ceiling apparently being a popular spot for finding answers.

"What if you went somewhere else?" he asked.

"Like, a different restaurant?"

"Sure." David looked back down at her. "You said you couldn't handle it when things didn't go as you expected them to. But if you're in a completely different place, you won't have as many expectations. Takes some of the pressure off."

Amie tried to ignore the anxiety creeping up the back of her neck. "Yeah. Yeah, that could work."

"And," he added, reaching over to grab a battery, "if it gets bad, you can just leave."

Amie wasn't sure about that. She doubted there'd be a second (third? She was losing track) friend date if she suddenly ran out in the middle of it. She frowned at the memory of Ziya smiling sadly at her before suggesting they give it more time.

"Hey."

David's expression had morphed into what she'd internally dubbed his "dad face."

"You're the only one who knows what you can handle," he said. "If you don't think you can do tonight, that's fine."

Amie wasn't sure if she knew what she could handle. Her experience that morning indicated that she was incapable of even a short walk to get breakfast. One line of police tape could send her running for the hills. She didn't want Ziya to see her like that.

"Did you hear about Savannah?" she asked, needing a change of subject.

David had returned to his battery testing. "What poor soul was subjected to her foul misdeeds this time?"

"Um . . . God? Or Satan, I guess. Or no one. Depends who you ask."

David looked at her. "What are you saying?"

"She's dead?"

"Are you asking or telling?"

"I haven't confirmed it with anyone official, but I've historically found baristas to be pretty reliable sources, so . . ."

She trailed off. David's gaze had drifted past her face, eyes unfocused, face pinched.

"You okay?" Amie asked.

He blinked, then nodded. "Well . . . ding-dong, I guess."

"That's not very nice."

"*She* wasn't very nice." David reached over and rolled the batteries to his side of the table, having lost patience with Amie forgetting to pass them to him. "Just yesterday I had to stop her from tearing the head off of a grocery store employee."

"Right," Amie murmured knowingly. She hadn't joined David on his weekly Monday morning trip to the grocery store on the last day of the time loop, but she had on previous days. Like clockwork (which was how almost everything worked in the time loop), Savannah would show up and begin chewing out the employee working at the flower counter.

Amie had quickly learned how to keep David from intervening. He and Savannah had a history of public spats, and she'd known that letting him enter the ring would have just added fuel to Savannah's fire. This was confirmed any day Amie *didn't* join him on his trip to the store, as David would recount an explosive argument ended by a close brush with the store's security.

"Do you know what happened?" David asked, interrupting Amie's trip down memory cul-de-sac.

"My source said the cops are considering murder, but that could've just been someone jumping to conclusions." She frowned. "It's just . . . hard to wrap my head around."

"Why, because you thought she was an immortal imp of hell with the sole mission of making people's lives miserable?"

Amie rolled her eyes. "*No.*" She continued haltingly, this being her first time vocalizing these feelings. "I just never thought . . . I mean, when I was in the time loop, I thought a lot about *why* it was happening to me, sure. But I didn't want to . . . I don't know, mess anything up, I guess. It felt like something huge was at work, and I figured if I just kept my head down and rode it out, that one day I'd come out the other side."

"And you did," David said.

"And I did. But what if . . ." She trailed off, unable to bring herself to finish the sentence.

"You think you were put in the time loop to stop Savannah from being murdered," David finished for her, his tone matter-of-fact.

Amie shrugged.

"Hm. Could be."

"*Could be?*" Amie yelped. She'd been hoping for reassurance that she was jumping to conclusions, not validation.

"Well, I don't know!" David seemed indignant that his response was taken so poorly. "It's possible, but just as possible as a goddamn *time loop*, which most people would say isn't very possible. So, yes, that *could be* an answer."

"Oh, god." Amie covered her face with her hands.

There was silence from David. Then, in a gentler tone:

"But that doesn't mean it's your fault. If the universe wanted you to become a crime-fighting superhero, it could've left a few more tools at your disposal other than a repeating day. At the very least, it could've left you a note saying something like, 'Hey! Savannah's getting murdered. Would appreciate it if you tried to save her. Thanks so much!'"

Amie peeked at him through her fingers. "You make it sound like the universe hired me as a pet sitter."

David snorted. "We can't know what the reason was," he said. "If there even *was* a reason. All you can do now is move on with your life. Are you going to do that?"

Amie thought for a moment. She picked up her phone.

Amie: Tonight would be great! Would you be open to trying a different place?

She locked the phone and put it down before she could overanalyze her response.

David was staring at the voltmeter, eyebrows furrowed. The longer Amie looked at him, the more it seemed like he was staring straight through it.

"Are you sure you're okay?" she finally asked.

"No," he said, his eyes focusing on the device again. "I'm annoyed that none of these batteries are any good."

Amie leaned across the table to look at the voltmeter. "The screen's blank. Shouldn't it at least be showing zeros or something?"

David threw his hands up. "I don't know. I got it at an estate sale, and no one ever knows where the instructions are at those things. Got kicked out of one once for rummaging around in the kitchen drawers looking for a toaster manual."

"Does it have batteries?" Amie asked.

She watched him stare at the device for another moment, thinking. Then he flipped it over and removed a panel from its back, revealing two empty spots for batteries.

David dropped the voltmeter with an irritated growl and stood. "I need a cup of tea."

As he filled the kettle with water, Amie popped two batteries into the device.

"Well," she said cheerfully, holding up the voltmeter to show him the line of zeros on the screen, "we know two of the batteries work!"

David grunted.

* * *

Out of the Loop

Amie stood outside of the restaurant, back pressed to the wall in a way she hoped looked casual and not like she was desperately trying to stay out of the way of the world.

The trip over had been easier than her morning bagel excursion. David was right—it helped not to have expectations for how things were meant to go. Still, she had stood very far from the curb as she waited for the bus to arrive, and caught herself anxiously gripping her legs multiple times throughout the ride.

Not too late to cancel. She shook the thought away as fast as it arrived. *No. I want to do this.*

What if you freak out? came the response to that.

I won't, was her foolproof reply.

But what if—

The thought faded into the background as Amie caught sight of Ziya on the other side of the street. She was wearing the same orange dress that Amie had seen her wear multiple times before. Amie, for the sake of trying to change things up, had opted out of the brown sweater and skirt, instead donning a dark-green bodysuit and black palazzo pants.

She watched as Ziya approached the crosswalk, stopping behind a couple who were waiting for the walk signal. Glancing up and down the street, she slipped around the couple and stepped off the curb.

By the time Amie had fully processed what had happened, it was already over. A car zipped down the perpendicular street and rounded the corner. Someone yelled. Ziya leapt back onto the curb as the car jerked to a stop in the spot she had just evacuated.

"What the fuck are you doing?" the driver yelled at her. Clearly uninterested in receiving a response, he accelerated and sped away.

"There's a fucking speed limit, you know!" Ziya yelled after the car. She smiled wryly as she said something to the couple on the curb, whose expressions morphed from horror to relieved amusement as they chuckled in response. The walk sign flashed on, and Ziya began her second attempt to cross the street.

Heart racing, Amie jogged down the sidewalk to meet her.

"Are you okay?" she asked as Ziya arrived safely on the other side of the street.

"Hi!" Ziya said, her face splitting into a smile. Usually, that smile would have made Amie's heart ache, but it was already pounding too hard for anything else to have an effect.

"Are you okay?" she repeated.

"Why? Oh, the car." Ziya waved a hand dismissively. "I'm fine. It was my fault. He didn't have to be such a dick about it, though. How are you?"

Her question was tinged with concern as she glanced at Amie's hands. Only then did Amie realize she was shaking. She crossed her arms.

"Fine," she said. "I'm great. Are you sure you're okay? That could've been really bad."

"Could've been!" Ziya tugged on Amie's arm as she began walking to the restaurant. "Let's go; near death experiences make me hungry."

Amie followed. The thrill that had shot through her from Ziya's touch became overshadowed by a prickly, anxious feeling that ran up her spine and tickled the back of her neck. She was unable to resist the urge to glance over her shoulder to make sure another car wasn't careening toward them.

Once they'd been seated, Ziya gave her an amused look. "I feel like you still need me to confirm that I'm okay."

"Once more would be nice." Amie tried to throw in a chuckle at the end to make the request more lighthearted, but her breath caught on the chuckle, and she had to clear her throat to hide the weird intake of air

"I'm okay," Ziya said, smiling. "Are *you* okay?"

Amie nodded, clearing her throat again.

"Are we going to spend the rest of the evening confirming that we're both okay?"

"No," Amie assured her. "That would be a bad friend date."

"You can just call it a date." Ziya rested her chin in her hand, looking around the restaurant. "Friends go on dates."

"Sure," Amie replied, "but how would your friends react if you told them you were going on a date with your ex?"

"They're very happy about it, actually. They all love you. How did David react?"

"With a baffling mix of disinterest and way too much investment."

"Oh, that's cute. I miss him."

"He . . ." Amie faltered. ". . . misses you."

Ziya's brown eyes flicked back to Amie, her head tilting curiously. Amie assumed she was trying to determine if this was meant to be Amie's subtle way of saying that *she'd* missed Ziya, which was something Amie was trying to determine as well.

Before either of them could come to a definitive conclusion, the waiter came by to take their drink order. As he walked away, Amie felt the shaking in her hands cease. She looked around, taking in the restaurant for the first time. Being there felt like unlocking a new section of a video game map after being stuck in one area for ages. During the time loop, she never ventured far from her usual spots. The furthest she'd ever strayed from home during the previous two years was the handful of times she got on a plane to visit her parents for a few hours. And even then, she'd always visit the same Bar & Grill for a pre-flight drink (though she never managed to learn if "Bar & Grill" was the establishment's name or just a descriptor of its main offerings).

Ziya was watching her, and Amie knew that the other woman wouldn't be able to sit in silence for much longer. She took these last few moments to remind herself of her mission: Be cool. Be normal. Go with the flow.

"So," Ziya said, right on cue, "what've you been up to?"

Amie took a deep breath. "Oh, you know. Keeping busy." *Good, good. Very cool, very casual.* "Work's good, life's good. How're you? How's school?"

Ziya smiled sheepishly, wincing a bit. "I'm thinking about switching majors."

"Again?" Amie already knew this, of course, but her incredulous reaction felt real every time. Ziya was pursuing a business degree, after previously pursuing an English degree, a psychology degree, and a statistics degree. She'd also taken three nonconsecutive semesters off, two of which were for travel and one for an electrician apprenticeship. Her parents were supportive of her taking her time to figure out what she wanted to do (especially with three older children with successful careers to split their attention). The issue was that Ziya wanted to do everything.

"I *know*," Ziya said, laughing with self-deprecation. "It's just that I'm pretty sure all of my classmates are planning on going into consulting, and I'm not even sure what that is, and by this point I'm afraid to ask."

At this moment in the conversation Amie would always laugh pleasantly, then attempt to explain consulting with what little knowledge she had about it. Today, though, she was doing things differently.

"I very much doubt that," she said.

Ziya raised an eyebrow. "That they're all going into consulting?"

"That you're afraid to ask."

That got a smile out of Ziya. "Okay, yeah, I asked someone about it. Ask me if I remember anything she said, though."

"And you call yourself a good listener," Amie teased. A warm feeling was beginning to grow in her chest, like a popcorn bag in a microwave.

"I *am* a good listener!" Ziya protested. "I listened. It's just that, y'know, none of it really stuck." She covered her face with embarrassment. "Oh my god, then later she messaged me asking me out, and—" She stopped suddenly, uncovering her face. Eyes wide, she studied Amie's expression. "Sorry. I shouldn't have mentioned that."

Amie shrugged. The popcorn bag had deflated, leaving a bunch of cold, buttery kernels rattling around in her chest. "It's fine.

I'm . . . I mean, we can talk about stuff like that. If you're seeing someone—"

"I'm not," Ziya said quickly, waving her hands as if trying to stop a car from running into her.

Shit. Amie thought she was past that.

"I turned her down," Ziya continued. "I just thought it was just a funny story, because . . ." She looked pained as she trailed off. "It's actually not that funny. Never mind."

She fell silent, which was unfortunate for Amie, who desperately needed a distraction from the prickly feeling that had begun to climb back up her spine.

A couple feet and she would've been gone. Just like that.

Thankfully, the waiter chose that moment to return with their drinks and take their meal orders.

"Can I get the fettuccine alfredo?" Ziya asked.

"What?" Amie blurted out.

Ziya glanced at her. "Fettuccine alfredo?"

Amie flipped through the menu, trying to disguise her shock at Ziya requesting Amie's time loop restaurant order. "I . . . wow, I didn't even see that on the menu!"

"I never knew how much you loved fettuccine alfredo," Ziya said as the waiter walked away. "Or is this a new thing?"

Amie groaned, covering her face with her hands. She heard Ziya chuckling, and felt a single kernel pop in her chest.

Ziya's laughter died down as Amie uncovered her face. The prickly sensation wasn't letting up, and it apparently showed in her face.

"I was just teasing you," Ziya said gently. "You're fine. I'm nervous, too."

Now *this* was new information to Amie. "You're nervous?"

"Of course." Ziya fidgeted with her silverware. "I want this to go well. I want us to be able to be friends." She glanced up at Amie, brows knit together. "But if you need—"

"No!" Amie said, straightening. "I'm good. Great, even. I'm just feeling a little off, but not about this. I feel good about this."

She hoped they could move on to a new topic, but wasn't surprised when Ziya asked, "Why are you feeling off?"

Amie debated saying something about not getting a good night's sleep, or getting her period, or Mercury being in retrograde. But since she wasn't sure if Mercury was in retrograde, or what it even meant for Mercury to be in retrograde, she instead said, "You almost got hit by a car."

Ziya looked surprised, as if she'd already forgotten that had happened. "I wouldn't say *almost*. Sure, it was close, but I have amazing reflexes."

Her smile dimmed as she studied Amie's face. "It really got to you."

"Yeah." Amie stared at her napkin, feeling very vulnerable.

"Hm." Ziya folded her hands on the table. "Well, I have fifteen psychology credits, so let's put them to good use."

Amie smiled at that. She knew sharing the reason for her distress would be going against her mission to be cool and normal, but Ziya was looking at her in a way that made her want to say something honest.

"I, um . . ." She paused, trying to figure out how to phrase what she wanted to say. "I went through a period of time when I wasn't really considering . . . death. Or, like, really the permanence of anything at all. But recently it's been hitting me just how little we can actually control in general, and how most times we can't undo things, and death is, like . . . one of the biggest things we can't undo."

She shifted in her seat. "So . . . yeah. That's probably it. Sorry for being a bummer."

"You're not being a bummer," Ziya said softly.

"No, I am," Amie asserted. "And I think I'm gonna be like this for a while, so if you want to head out, I understand."

Ziya frowned. "Do you really think I'd just leave because you're feeling down?"

"No, I know you wouldn't," Amie said. Strangely enough, the prickly feeling had begun to lessen. "That's why I'm telling you that it's okay if you want to leave. I know you wanted to have a fun night, and I don't want to waste your time—"

"Okay, can you stop?" Ziya asked, annoyance tingeing her words.

Unfortunately, Amie was on a roll. "I'm just saying, I do want us to be friends, but I'm just not sure I can be a good friend right now—not just to you, but, like, to anyone. Thankfully, David doesn't really need much, so I'll be okay—"

"Oh, but I'm so high maintenance?" Ziya was definitely annoyed now, Amie could tell. Somehow everything she was saying was just making things worse.

"No, no no, you're not," Amie said. "I mean—"

"No, it's my turn to talk." Ziya's voice was sharp. "And since you seem so sure about what *I'm* thinking, I'll tell you what *you're* thinking."

Amie shrunk into her seat, chastened. "Okay."

Ziya stared at her for a long moment. Amie stared back, wondering, if Ziya looked hard enough, if she'd be able to see the effects of the time loop. Could she tell how many days it had actually been for Amie since they'd broken up? Was there any sign that Amie had been on this date before? Did she see how many times Amie had tried to get this right?

"What *are* you thinking?" Ziya finally asked, looking defeated.

Amie's shoulders slumped.

At the same time, they both became aware of the rising volume of voices nearby, and looked over to identify the source of the noise.

A group of people were sitting around a table, their attention on three members of their party who were on their feet, arguing with each other.

"—because you're a fucking liar!"

"Are you really gonna do this right now? *Really?*"

"Don't talk to me like that—"

The other occupants of the table were calling for their companions to settle down as a host rushed over to address the situation. The situation escalated to new heights as someone got pushed, a chair toppled, a waiter tripped, and a tray of dishes and glasses went crashing to the ground. The volume inside the restaurant skyrocketed as people stood to get a better look at the commotion.

Amie found herself glancing behind her, shoulders tightening like they were anticipating a tray of dishes to drop on her head any second.

Oh my god, breathe, she thought as her breaths came in fast and shallow.

"Dinner and a show," Ziya deadpanned, turning back around.

Her expression dropped as she saw Amie gripping the table, shoulders hunched. "Are you okay?"

Run.

She couldn't. Who knew what could happen between there and the door?

Stay.

She couldn't. Who knew what could happen if she remained in that spot?

"Can I touch you?"

Ziya's voice was surprisingly close to her ear. That's when Amie realized she had squeezed her eyes shut.

She nodded.

"Come on."

An arm wrapped around Amie's shoulders. The familiar sound of Ziya's bangles clinked near her ear as she let herself get pulled from the chair and led away from their table.

Amie's eyes snapped open as she felt fresh air hit her face. Ziya had led her all the way across the restaurant and outside.

"Sit here," Ziya directed, herding her over to a bench that sat along the building.

Amie obeyed, noticing both of their purses swinging from Ziya's shoulder.

"Sorry," she said quietly. No longer feeling like something was about to crash down onto her head, she began taking deeper, slower breaths.

"Enough of that." Ziya sat down next to her. "Water?"

She was holding a glass of water from their table. Amie accepted the glass and took a small sip.

"I've never seen you have a panic attack before," Ziya said, taking the water back.

Amie rested her forearms on her thighs. "Me neither."

She heard a rustle. Then:

"Gum?"

A stick of gum appeared in Amie's line of vision. She took it. "Thanks."

"It's cinnamon."

"I know." Amie unwrapped the gum. Next to her, Ziya did the same.

Amie chewed until she felt her heart rate begin to slow.

"What do we do now?" she finally asked, bracing herself as she left the safety of the comfortable silence that had settled between them. She had no idea what came next, and that terrified her.

Out of the corner of her eye, she saw Ziya look over. "What do you want to do?"

Call it off, came the unwanted thought. *This was too much, too soon. She doesn't need to deal with this.*

Amie opened her mouth to respond.

"Someone's calling you." Ziya was looking down into Amie's purse, taking it off her shoulder to pass it over.

Amie accepted the bag and reached inside, pulling out her phone.

"It's David," she said. "He never calls me. He almost exclusively uses speech-to-text."

Accepting the call, she angled slightly away as she lowered the phone's volume. She didn't want Ziya overhearing if David asked her how the date was going. How could Amie even respond to that? Seven hundred and sixty-ish days of waiting for a second date with her ex-girlfriend, and she'd blown it in under thirty minutes.

"Hello?"

"Hello!" David replied, his voice sounding cheerfully strained. "Sorry to interrupt your dinner. Just thought someone should know that I'm about to be arrested."

Chapter One
Hallie From The Park

Day 371 I.L.

Amie was stepping out of her comfort zone.

Maybe "step" was too big a word. She was shuffling out of her comfort zone. Sticking a toe in. Leaning slightly over the line.

She was sitting at a bus stop across the street from Willows Park, a folded newspaper resting in her lap. The newspaper had been purchased on the walk over—Amie had thought it could prove useful in her stakeout, to help avoid drawing attention to herself. Upon arrival, she decided that a twenty-eight-year-old reading a newspaper at a bus stop was far more suspicious than a twenty-eight-year-old looking at her phone at a bus stop. She'd abandoned the newspaper in favor of the phone.

Time check: 4:47 PM. Any second . . .

Amie spotted Hallie From The Park cresting a hill, power walking toward a grassy spot underneath a copse of sugar maple trees. Hallie had a plastic takeout bag hanging from one arm and a panicked look on her face as she stopped and stared intently at the grass below her.

Starting a timer on her phone, Amie sat back and tried to ignore the sour feeling in her stomach.

On her twelfth day in the time loop, Amie had begun subconsciously accepting her recurring fate. Breaking from her regular routine, she'd wandered aimlessly around town, feeling hopeless. Late in the afternoon she'd stumbled upon Hallie, who was frantically searching for a ring she'd lost during sunrise yoga that morning.

"It was a gift from my boyfriend," Hallie would always say as they combed through the grass together. "Not an engagement ring. He's such a commitment-phobe—I gave him a key to my place and keep dropping hints that he should give me a key to his. But so far he has *not* taken the hint. I left work early to surprise him with Vietnamese food. Do you like Vietnamese food? It's our favorite. I think—"

This was the point when, during that first meeting, Amie discovered the ring.

Amie returned to her routines, adding Hallie From The Park to them. She was well aware that even if Hallie couldn't find the ring on her own, the time loop made the lasting impact of that loss significantly less impactful. But Amie couldn't help but feel bad leaving the woman to search on her own, whether or not the results of that search were undone by the next sunrise yoga.

That uncomfortable feeling was now roiling inside of Amie as she pretended not to see Hallie scouring the grass for her jewelry. She glanced down at the timer on her phone, which had just passed the three-minute mark.

She'd visited David earlier that day. After telling him about the time loop and giving him Genevieve's regards to cement his belief in her story, she'd mentioned how she'd had a particularly bad time about a week prior. It had been the one-year anniversary of the time loop (or what she assumed was the one-year anniversary—she'd lost track once or twice, causing her to doubt if she had the exact number correct). She'd spent most of the day in bed, blasting sad music, ruminating on her situation, and soaking in hopelessness.

By the next day, she'd bounced back, but the experience had left both her and David wondering how the day had gone without her interference. A sort of "Ghost of Christmas Yet to Come" curiosity. This interest was what brought her to the bus stop bench, which she was very close to abandoning as the timer hit the twenty-minute mark.

"You've passed it twice now," she muttered under her breath, watching Hallie circle the spot where her ring sat hidden in a patch of clover. "It's *right there.*" She'd fully given up on subtlety and was outright staring, as if she could telepathically guide the target of her gaze to where she needed to go.

Finally, just before the time hit twenty-four minutes, Hallie let out a delighted cry as she picked up her ring.

Amie tapped the timer to stop it, sighing with relief. It wasn't a *great* result. She'd been hoping that Hallie would have been able to find the ring easily enough without Amie's help. But the woman had managed to find it on her own, even if it took a bit of time, and that was enough to put Amie's mind at ease. Maybe she could occasionally skip visiting the park with a clear conscience.

After stopping for a celebratory smoothie, Amie headed back home. Noting the movers as she arrived at her building, she slipped through the entrance and made her way to the emergency stairwell to avoid getting caught behind an ascending couch. She wondered if she'd ever get the chance to meet her new neighbors. By this point, she was *very* familiar with their taste in furniture (boho chic), as well as with the people moving it (well-muscled but painfully slow-moving).

The sound of a vacuum cleaner made her pause as she walked down the hall to her apartment. Amie backtracked, putting an ear to David's door. She checked the time on her phone, an uncomfortable sensation crawling under her skin.

Knock knock. Knock. Knock knock knock.

The vacuuming continued.

KNOCK KNOCK. KNOCK. KNOCK KNOCK KNOCK.

The vacuuming stopped. The door swung open.

"I'm vacuuming," David said, the aforementioned machine in his hand.

"You're napping," Amie replied, perplexed.

David stared at her, looked to the vacuum, then back at her. ". . . No?"

"You're supposed to be napping right now," Amie said, squeezing past him. "You're always napping at this time. Why aren't you napping right now?"

"I was, but I was woken up almost immediately. Once I'm up, I'm up. So I decided to clean." David shut the door behind her. "Is this a time loop thing?"

"I don't know." Amie sat on the couch, resting her near-empty smoothie cup on a coaster. "This has never happened before."

"Ohhh." David snapped his fingers. "You did things differently today, didn't you? The experiment we talked about. That must be it."

"That must be what?" Amie asked, still confused.

David unplugged the vacuum from the wall. "I was woken up by voices," he explained. "People arguing. Very inconsiderate to those around them who might have been trying to nap. According to you, that doesn't usually happen, or else you wouldn't be used to me being asleep during this time. Therefore, you must have done something differently today that triggered the argument."

Amie frowned. She'd done multiple things differently that day. In addition to leaving Hallie to search on her own, she'd also withheld her assistance cleaning up the coffee spill at the café that morning, avoided the woman trying to prop up her phone to take a photo of her outfit, and tried to let that stray cat cross the road by itself. (She'd eventually given in after the cat had a close call with a school bus, but she still counted the attempt.)

"But I didn't make anyone get into an argument," she said. "I wasn't even here."

"It doesn't necessarily have to be the direct result of your interference," David mused, standing and crossing the apartment. "Not to talk like a stereotypical 'Guy Who Builds Rube Goldberg Machines'—"

"I don't think that's a common stereotype."

"—but one little action on your part could potentially set off a larger chain of events." David picked up Amie's smoothie cup, placing it on his work table at the bottom of a small ramp.

"Let's say this cup represents your normal route to get breakfast." He picked up a small blue marble and dropped it down the ramp. The marble bounced against the cup and dove off the side of the table. "Marble falls onto the floor. That's it. As long as the cup is there, the marble will fall onto the floor." He removed the cup, retrieving the marble.

"Now let's say you take a new route to get breakfast." David dropped the marble down the ramp. It began traveling through the machine. "You're crossing a different street than usual, causing a car to stop for you. The woman in that car arrives eight seconds later to work, putting her in the perfect position to collide with a man carrying a box of files as she's rushing into the building. This causes the man to miss an elevator ride with his boss. The boss gets stuck in the elevator, and his employee isn't there with the big box of files that they could've used to climb up and out of the elevator.

"So the boss has to wait for the firefighters, and doesn't get to the office until an hour later. He walks into the office just in time to see one of his employees looking out the window, having just seen a loose piece of paper fly by—one of the files that had been dropped earlier by the other employee. The boss mistakes this for distractedness, so later, when he's giving out promotions, he doesn't consider that employee for one."

The marble fell into a plastic cup with a victorious *plunk* as it finished its journey across the room, having left a trail of fallen dominos and other miscellaneous items in its wake.

"And all because you took a different route to get breakfast," David finished.

"I think you just wanted a reason to show off your new machine," Amie said. "And telling me that I might've made someone miss out on a promotion isn't really making me feel better."

David waved a hand. "Don't worry about her. It made her decide that she deserves better, and now she's going to quit and get a job that pays her twice as much and has dental insurance. Things always work out."

"I guess." Amie crossed her arms uncomfortably. "I just don't like that my actions have so much power in this time loop."

"Your actions always have power," David said, resetting the dominoes. "You're just being reminded of them over and over again. The good thing is, the consequences aren't long-lasting. Also, I learned that the phrase 'you dipshit' is alive and well. I always forget about that one. Almost makes getting woken up worth it."

"Good" wasn't the word Amie would have normally used to describe the effects of the time loop, but in this case, it did bring her some comfort. Regardless, she still felt strange, and couldn't shake the feeling for the rest of the evening.

Chapter Five

Mac and Cheese

Day 1 A.L.

Ziya insisted on driving Amie back to her building.

"Should we call a lawyer?" she asked, speeding through an intersection just as the yellow light flashed to red. "Does he have a lawyer we can call?"

"I don't know." Amie gripped the inside of the door, her whole body tense. Ziya was, on paper, a good driver—she'd never caused a car accident, or gotten a ticket, or even been pulled over. But she definitely pushed the boundaries of traffic laws, especially when she had someplace to be (which, with Ziya, was almost always).

"What exactly did he say?" Ziya slowed momentarily at a stop sign, then stepped on the gas and zipped around the corner.

"He said he thought someone should know he was about to be arrested, and if he wasn't home when I got back, I should check the police station. Then he told me not to rush, and . . . and he hung up."

Amie decided at the last second to leave out David telling her not to let this get in the way of "winning Ziya back." He'd hung up before she could reply.

"Why would he be arrested?" Ziya asked. "Did I miss them outlawing Rube Goldberg machines or something?"

"I don't know," Amie repeated. She thought about the police tape outside of the bookshop that morning. How David seemed undisturbed by the news of Savannah's death.

She shook her head. That wasn't possible. It had to be something else.

Ziya glanced over at her. "You thought of something."

"Hm?"

"You shook your head like you do when you're trying to work something out and it doesn't make sense."

Amie wrinkled her nose. "I hate that."

"What?"

"That you know that about me. You shouldn't know that about me if we're not dating."

Ziya laughed. "Just because we're not dating anymore means I'm supposed to forget everything I know about you?"

"Yes. It's embarrassing. Wipe your memory."

"I'll try my best." Ziya shook her head with amusement as she turned down Amie's street.

"Thanks for driving me," Amie said.

"No problem. I want to make sure he's okay."

Amie paused, trying to figure out if she misunderstood. "You . . . are you coming in?"

Ziya gave her an incredulous look. "Of course!"

"You don't have to."

"I *want* to. Besides, if he's not there, you'll need a ride to the police station."

That was a strong argument. Still, Amie felt compelled to push back.

"I can take the bus. There aren't any open parking spots, anyway."

Ziya pulled up next to an open parking spot in front of Amie's building. She looked over, eyebrows raised.

"Oh." Just because there were no open parking spots on September 17 didn't mean there wouldn't be any on September 18.

Ziya expertly parallel parked, and the two exited the car.

Amie felt dazed as they entered the building. Even the most indulgent of scenarios she'd played out in her head hadn't ended with Ziya going home with her. Granted, even if she *had* allowed herself to imagine a scenario where Ziya went home with her, it likely wouldn't have been under these circumstances.

"Wait." Ziya grabbed Amie's hand as the latter raised it to knock on David's door. She quickly released her, then pressed an ear to the door, listening. Amie struggled to figure out what to do with her hand, which was tingling from the contact.

"I hear voices," Ziya whispered.

"David?"

"Can't tell. But they wouldn't be in there without him, right?" Ziya straightened, knocking on the door.

Knock knock. Knock. Knock knock knock.

A few moments later, the door cracked open.

"I told you not to rush," David said, scowling at Amie as he opened the door wider.

His face brightened as he saw Ziya. "Hello, stranger!"

"Hello to you!" Ziya replied, throwing her arms around him. David returned the hug, raising his eyebrows pointedly at Amie over Ziya's shoulder.

"What happened?" Amie asked, exasperated.

"I have a couple of visitors," David said drily as Ziya released him. "Come in." He stepped out of the way to let them into the apartment, gesturing to the men sitting on the couch. A bent spatula sat between the two police officers, one of whom looked like he'd recently discovered that he'd been sitting on a spatula.

"Officers Dell and Reiger," David said, "this is my neighbor, and her . . ."

He trailed off, an almost cartoonish expression on his face as he looked questioningly at the new arrivals.

"Friend," the women said in unison.

"What's going on?" Ziya asked as Amie glowered at David.

"The gentlemen had a few questions for me about Savannah Harlow," David explained as he closed the door behind them. "Mainly about an interaction I had with her yesterday."

"At the grocery store?" Amie asked.

"That's right," David said. "If I'm accurately reading between the lines—and, officers, please correct me if I'm not—I believe I'm a suspect for her murder."

Ziya gasped, looking at Amie. "Savannah's *dead*?"

Amie gave her a quick nod before turning back to the cops. "On what grounds is he being accused?" (She wasn't sure if those were the correct terms to use, but they sounded good to her.)

One of the officers stood, and the other one followed suit. "No one's making any accusations," the first one said. "We were given a tip to speak to Mr. Lenski."

"The officers heard about our argument," David explained.

"But that was nothing!" Amie exclaimed. "She was yelling at an employee. David was just trying to get her to stop."

"Did you witness the argument?" the second officer asked.

"Y—" Amie stopped. No, technically, she hadn't. Not on the specific day they were referring to, at least. She shook her head.

"I think we have everything," the first officer said. "Mr. Lenski, we'll be in touch if we need anything else from you."

David escorted the cops out the door. "'No one's making any accusations,'" he said in a mocking tone as soon as the door shut. "They were sounding *pre*tty accusatory before you two showed up."

"Are you really their main suspect?" Amie asked as Ziya crossed the room. "I know you two fought a lot, but I feel like she has to have bigger enemies than you."

"I couldn't say," David said. "When you told me earlier what had happened to her, I started thinking about how I was probably one of the last people seen arguing with her. But I just told myself that was my author brain getting carried away."

"Sorry, just to clarify . . ." Ziya raised a hand as she sat down on the couch. "Savannah's dead? By way of *murder*?"

"Does that surprise you?" David asked. "The murder part?"

Ziya shrugged, tilting her head in acquiescence. "Guess not."

"You're both terrible," Amie said.

David let out a scoff as he spotted the bent spatula sitting next to Ziya. "This is why I don't like visitors." He picked it up, sitting down next to Ziya as he looked mournfully at the kitchen tool.

"Maybe it should be why you shouldn't leave spatulas on your couch," Amie suggested.

David looked up from the wreckage to narrow his eyes at her. "So how'd tonight go?"

Amie let out a strangled yelp. "AHH okay," she exclaimed, avoiding eye contact with Ziya. "Let's focus on the issue at hand."

"Who told the cops about your argument at the grocery store?" Ziya asked.

David shrugged. "They wouldn't tell me." He sat forward, hands clasped between his knees. "What I don't like is that someone's making an effort to point a finger at me."

"You think you're being framed?" Amie asked.

"Either someone went out of their way to send the tip, or the police just happened to be talking to someone who witnessed the argument. Who could the latter be?"

Amie cast her mind back to all those trips to the grocery store. "There weren't that many people around," she said. "But Savannah was pretty loud, and the flower counter is by the entrance. Someone could've just walked by and noticed."

"How do you know that?" Ziya asked.

"I don't," Amie said. "It's just a theory."

"No, about there not being a lot of people around. You said you weren't there."

Amie felt her jaw go slack. If she was ever going to tell Ziya about the time loop, this wasn't how she wanted to do it. "Uh . . ." She glanced at David. "He . . . told me there weren't. Didn't you?"

"Right," David said slowly. "I did tell you that."

Ziya looked back and forth between them. "I don't know how *you* guys felt about that performance," she said, eyebrows arched, "but I've seen better."

"Savannah could've also mentioned the argument to her husband," Amie added hurriedly. "The police definitely would have spoken to him."

"That's true." David spread his hands, sitting back on the couch. "Guess there's nothing else the police can do, unless someone plants evidence against me. Or if they find all the threatening letters I've sent to Savannah."

"You did *what*?" Amie yelled. Ziya's eyes went round with horror.

"I'm *joking*," David said. "I only wrote them in my head."

"I bet you could figure out who killed Savannah," Ziya said as Amie rubbed her temples. "You've got the knowledge from—"

She stopped, covering her mouth as David gave her a wide-eyed stare.

Amie narrowed her eyes. "Knowledge from what?"

"You swore," David said, ignoring Amie.

"I know, I'm sorry," Ziya replied, her voice muffled by her hand. Despite the apologetic tone of voice, her eyes shone with amusement.

Amie tried to think of what secret David would have from her that Ziya could know about. It only took her a few moments to figure it out.

"You wrote mystery books!" she declared triumphantly, pointing at David.

He covered his face in confirmation.

"Why wouldn't you want to tell me that?" Amie asked. "I was starting to think you were a bestselling erotica author or something. Not that *that* should be embarrassing, but—"

"The books are garbage," David replied flatly. "I didn't want you reading them."

"They're really not," Ziya said, looking excited to finally be able to talk openly about the topic. "My dad's obsessed with them. He gave me one to read. That's how I found out—I recognized David from the author photo."

"And you didn't tell me?" Amie asked, pouting.

"He made me promise not to!"

"*Anyway*," David said loudly, "I will *not* be trying to solve Savannah's murder, thank you very much. Especially if someone's trying to make me look guilty. I think it's best if I stay as far from the situation as I can until it all blows over."

He stretched his arms out over his head, yawning. After a moment of silence:

"That was my polite way of saying 'Get out.'"

"Feel like there's something in between yawning and 'get out,'" Amie muttered as Ziya laughed. A cold wave of reality washed over her as the other two said their goodbyes. Just thirty minutes before she'd been trying to convince Ziya to leave, and now that she was faced with it, she . . .

Well. It didn't feel good.

"Did you eat?" Amie blurted out as the door to David's apartment closed behind them.

Ziya looked at her, amused. "No. Between leaving the restaurant early and coming here, I didn't get the chance."

"Right." Amie winced. "I meant . . . do you want to eat?"

"Good god," came David's muffled voice from the other side of the door.

"Go to bed!" Amie yelled, feeling her face growing warm.

Ziya was smiling. "Are you offering me dinner?" she asked.

"Depends on the contents of my fridge." Amie didn't know why she said that. She was *very* familiar with every single item in her refrigerator, down to the last slightly moldy jar of salsa in the very back corner. "I can't do fettuccine alfredo, but I have boxed mac and cheese. Or—"

"Say no more." Ziya lifted a hand to stop her. "Take me to the mac and cheese."

As they walked down the hallway, Amie frantically tried to remember the state of her apartment when she left earlier that evening.

"Hang on," she said, fishing her keys out of her purse as they stopped by the door. "Just . . . give me fifteen seconds."

"We basically lived together for months," Ziya said as Amie unlocked the door. She followed Amie inside. "Can't imagine how bad it'd have to be to top your towering pile of dirty laundry."

"It's not bad . . . I'm just making sure. Wait here, please." She ran down the short entrance hall, leaving Ziya by the door.

"You have until my shoes are off, and then I'm coming in." There was a grunt. "The straps are fucked, so . . . you've got time."

Amie ran through the living room, giving it a quick once-over before moving on to the kitchen. One plate in the sink . . . that was fine. She dashed across the kitchen and into her bedroom, giving herself a sniff test on the way. Not bad, but she still gave both armpits a preventative swipe of deodorant, just in case.

"Here I come!" came Ziya's voice from the other side of the apartment.

Amie took one quick glance in the mirror, ran her fingers through her hair, *immediately* regretted doing that, debated putting on a hat, realized Ziya might think she was waiting for her in the bedroom, and bolted out.

Ziya was standing in the living room, a teasing smile on her face as Amie shut the sliding door to her bedroom.

"All clear?" she asked.

"Yeah." Amie walked back into the kitchen. "I mean, I was just . . ." She gestured behind her toward the bedroom. ". . . trying to fix my hair." She hated admitting that, but the truth was better than her ex-girlfriend thinking she was preparing the bedroom for post-dinner activities.

"Mm." Ziya closed the distance between them, her fingers going to Amie's hair. She brushed a few strands to one side before leaning back to assess her work.

"Perfect," Ziya said.

"Hnghh," came Amie's strangled response.

Ziya laughed, pulling out one of the chairs at the kitchen table. "You're very cute when you're flustered."

"I'm not *flustered*," Amie said indignantly, turning to the cabinets and retrieving a pot to boil the pasta. "And you shouldn't be trying to fluster your friend. Especially if she's your ex-girlfriend."

Ziya propped her elbows on the table and rested her chin on the backs of her hands. "I wasn't trying to do anything," she said with faux innocence.

"Oh, sure." Amie stuck the pot under the sink, hitting the faucet. "You weren't trying anything when you put your face inches away from my face and played with my hair. That's just regular friend stuff."

"I wasn't *playing* with your hair, I was fixing it!"

"Next thing I know you're gonna show me how to make mac and cheese 'the right way' by standing behind me and guiding my hands."

"I'm not going to Swayze you."

"Well now you're not, because I've called you out."

"Your pot's overflowing."

"Oh, shit—" Amie shut off the sink and poured out the excess water. She deposited the pot onto the stove and switched on the burner.

"I'm sorry if I'm making you uncomfortable," Ziya said, growing serious. "I'm still . . . figuring out how to do this."

"I know."

"Would you rather I not touch you?"

"No, it's okay. It's just the flirty stuff. I mean, I know you kind of do that with everyone, but—"

"It's different. I get it." Ziya began counting on her fingers. "No flirty hair touching, forget everything I know about you—"

"Don't offer to feed me a bite of your food," Amie added.

"Well, okay, we'll be here all night if we're gonna make up scenarios."

Amie's instinct to defend herself outpaced the rest of her brain. "I didn't make that up. You did that!"

Ziya gave her a confused smile. "When?"

"To—" Amie stopped. No. Ziya hadn't done that tonight. That was during their time loop date.

"Are you okay?" Ziya asked as Amie buffered. "You keep saying strange things. And the panic attack at the restaurant—"

"I'm fine," Amie assured her. "Really. I just had a long day. I found out about Savannah, and then I was scrambling to finish an article before our friend date, and then David and the police . . . it's just, it's been a long day."

Ziya hummed with understanding. She reached over to where Amie's planner was sitting open on the table, pulling it to her. "So what are you reacclimating to?" she asked, tapping a pink manicured nail on the word Amie had written in giant letters.

Amie's shoulders stiffened. She'd been so busy looking for any mess to tidy up that her gaze had slid right over the planner during her lightning round apartment inspection.

"Do you feel like you need to reacclimate to me?" Ziya looked hesitant. "I know we gave it a few months, but if it still feels too hard, we could . . . we could give it more time."

"No," Amie blurted out, a memory flashing through her mind of Ziya standing outside of a restaurant on a day that didn't happen. "No," she said again.

"So why is this weird?" Ziya asked, her voice strained.

Amie lifted her hands in exasperation. "Well, you can't expect things to be perfectly normal right away, Z," she said. "It's not something you can rush; it takes time."

"It's been three months."

It was much longer than that, for Amie. "Right, but now we have to get used to actually being around each other again. I mean, I barely know anything about what you've been up to for the past three months. How was Iceland?"

It was a dangerous move, but she needed to get Ziya away from the topic of Amie's strange behavior.

Ziya's expression went cloudy. She closed Amie's planner, not looking at it as she pushed the book away. "I didn't go," she said. The mood of the room shifted to that of an audience watching a tightrope walker, as if one wrong step could lead to disaster.

"Oh," Amie said. This was news to her. On all the September 17ths she spent with Ziya, neither of them dared to bring up Iceland. "I just figured—"

"I got a partial refund, so." Ziya's shoulders slumped. "I know you think this has been easier for me than it's been for you, Ames. I *know* you do. And I don't know what it's been like for you, but it hasn't been easy for me. Okay? It's been really fucking hard."

Amie stayed silent.

"It's fine if we're weird for a while," Ziya continued. "I can live with that. And if Savannah's murder messed you up to the point of panic attacks, I want to be there for you. Can you let me do that?"

Amie's heart squeezed at the declaration. She spoke cautiously, giving herself as much time as she could to change her mind. "It's not . . . it's not just about Savannah. Or you, or David. Something happened to me."

Ziya watched her quietly, her dark brown eyes inviting Amie in.

"I . . . was stuck in a time loop."

They stared at each other, silent, for several long seconds. The silence was interrupted by a loud sizzling as the boiling pot of water began to overflow onto the stovetop.

"Shit!" Amie whipped around and lowered the flame. "Shit, shit, shit . . ."

When she turned back, Ziya was rubbing one side of her forehead, her eyes closed.

"Can you say something?" Amie pleaded.

"Put the macaroni in the water."

"But—"

"Don't make me Swayze you."

Comforted only a tiny bit by the joke, Amie returned to the stove and dumped in the noodles.

Ziya's eyes were open by the time Amie was done.

"So . . ." Amie prompted.

"I'm not sure what you want me to say."

"Do you believe me?"

Ziya laughed.

Nodding to herself, Amie clicked her tongue. "Guess not." She grabbed a spoon and gave the macaroni a stir.

"I'm sorry," Ziya said, still giggling. "But you'd be the *worst* person to get stuck in a time loop."

Amie was prepared for a variety of responses, but that had not been one of them.

"Why?" she demanded, feeling slightly miffed. She thought she'd handled the time loop pretty well. She'd gotten out of it, hadn't she?

Ziya was still smiling as she searched for words. "What would *you* do in a time loop, Amie?"

"What do you mean?"

"I mean," Ziya said carefully, "I think a lot of people would take advantage of being given infinite time to do as many things as they could with no long-lasting consequences. Do you really think you'd do that? Sorry—*did* you do that?"

Amie frowned. Somehow, even though Ziya clearly didn't believe Amie, she was still right.

"I did some things," Amie argued weakly. "I visited my parents a few times. Read at the library. Tried that new Thai place by the library." She struggled to come up with another example, preferably one that had taken her beyond a five-block radius of the library.

"God," Ziya said, shaking her head, "if I was in a time loop, I'd do so many things. I'd travel all the time, as far as I could get within a day. Learn another language . . . ooh! Skydiving!"

She was still going strong ten minutes later as they sat in front of steaming bowls of macaroni and cheese.

"Mm," Ziya said between forkfuls, "I'd run a marathon. Normally I'd feel like shit the next day, but in a time loop? No problem!"

"All right, I get it," Amie said, rolling her eyes. "You'd be amazing in a time loop. I'd be terrible. New topic, please."

"Seriously, though," Ziya said, chuckling. "What's with the time loop talk? What did you mean by that?"

Amie was too tired to deflect. "I was in a time loop," she repeated, stabbing a fork into her bowl. She didn't look at Ziya. She couldn't.

After a long moment, Ziya sighed. "Okay," she said. "New topic."

* * *

This felt like the longest day of Amie's life. And that was saying something, considering.

The previous hour and a half had gone surprisingly well. Ziya filled a lot of the time talking about various exploits from the intervening three months, and Amie was just happy to listen.

But as the night wore on, a creeping sense of dread began to make its way up the back of Amie's neck. At first she thought she just didn't want Ziya to leave. But it was more than that.

"You okay?" Ziya asked.

Only then did Amie notice she'd zoned out, not processing anything Ziya had been saying for the past minute. "Sorry."

"It's okay." Ziya pushed back her chair and stood. "It's late. I should get going."

Dread shifted to panic. "Wait," Amie said, a frantic edge in her voice. "Do you want dessert? I have ice cream, and . . . that's it. I have ice cream." She hurried over to the freezer, as if visual evidence of the ice cream would make the offer more enticing. "It's got these little cookie chunks . . . I've kind of gotten tired of it, honestly, but it's really good."

Amie didn't register her difficulty breathing until she turned too fast to deposit the carton of ice cream onto the table. The room spun, and she pressed her palms against the hard surface to steady herself.

"Whoa," Ziya said, rounding the table. "Take it easy. Deep breaths."

Amie sucked in a deep breath. The room stopped spinning, but the feeling of dread was still clamped onto her neck.

"Now what was that about?" Ziya asked gently. Her fingertips were almost painfully soft on the back of Amie's hand.

Amie squeezed her eyes shut. As long and difficult as this day had been, it was a gift. A reprieve after years of repetition. And now it was coming to a close, and Amie was beginning to doubt the permanence of this reprieve.

"Could you stay?" Amie whispered, staring at the table. Just asking the question seemed to dislodge dread's grip by a fraction. "I know you don't believe me about the time loop, but . . . this was my first day back, and I'm scared I'm going to wake up tomorrow and be right back in it. I'm really scared."

Ziya shifted next to her, the weight of her hand growing heavier on Amie's as she answered. "I can stay."

Once Amie had calmed down a bit, she began falling over herself to convince Ziya that this wasn't a gross ploy to get her to sleep over. Over Ziya's laughter, she insisted on taking the couch before running off to get fresh sheets for the bed.

"If you're not feeling well, you should sleep in your own bed," Ziya called after her.

"It's okay," Amie called back. "I think I'll feel better falling asleep in a different place. And hopefully waking up there in the morning."

Ziya didn't have a response for that, which Amie expected. She knew that Ziya wanted to be supportive, but a time loop was a difficult thing to wrap one's head around. It had taken Amie two weeks, and she'd been living in it.

She lay on the couch a while later, staring at the ceiling as Ziya slept in the other room. It was a strange combination of unsettling and comforting, this change of sleeping arrangements. Even when she'd visit her parents, she'd always make them stay up with her until 2:22 AM. This was her first time trying to fall asleep somewhere other than her bed since the last time she'd slept over at Ziya's place.

But she liked it. She liked the change. Especially with the comfort of knowing that Ziya was nearby.

The worst person to get stuck in a time loop, she had said. Amie thought back to her conversation with David, when he assured her that Savannah's death wasn't her fault. She knew it wasn't. But if someone other than her had been stuck in that time loop, could they have prevented it? Would they know who killed Savannah?

Determination filled Amie's body, but it was swiftly replaced with exhaustion. Whatever it was she was determined to do, she'd figure it out in the morning.

Chapter Six

Time Loop Maxims

Day 2 A.L.

If time loops were a common shared experience by a large enough fraction of Earth's population, there would probably be more maxims about them. *What happens in the loop stays in the loop*, perhaps. *Every change in the loop happens for a reason: you.* Put that on a plank of wood in a beach house bathroom. *Loop me once, shame on you. Loop me twice . . . well, let's hope it doesn't come to that.*

Thankfully, it didn't come to that. The good news was, for the first time in a long time, Amie Teller woke up somewhere other than her own bed. The bad news: Her secondhand couch was *not* comfortable to wake up on.

Back pain aside, Amie was feeling better. Until Ziya emerged from her bedroom, sleepily suggesting they get breakfast from Eons, and she was suddenly reminded of her Homeric quest to get a blueberry bagel the day before. (Replace Polyphemus with a moving truck and Scylla with a group of joggers and she and Odysseus *basically* went through the same ordeal.)

Out of the Loop

Another time loop maxim: *Life after a time loop is like riding a bike.* For Amie, a very mediocre bicyclist, this could be interpreted as "very shaky and potentially dangerous for herself and everyone in her vicinity." But it also meant that twenty-eight years of living a life that chronologists would call "normal" meant that she had deep-rooted instincts that two years in a time loop couldn't wipe out.

Despite that, there were still a few small moments of panic. An unthinkably obnoxious sports car roaring down the street. A passing jogger taking her by surprise. A plane flying overhead, so loud that even a non-anxious person might think, "Huh. That plane's kind of loud." But with Amie's determination to Get Back To Normal, Ziya's comforting chatter, and a merciful lack of trucks driving through puddles, they reached Eons Café so fast Penelope would've said, "Back so soon?"

Inside the café, Jess was back at the register. *Some things remain the same, even after a time loop.*

"Hey there," they said as Amie and Ziya reached the front of the line. "Haven't seen you in a bit; how's it going?"

"I'm great, good to see you," Ziya replied cheerfully. "Can I get a black coffee and cranberry muffin? And a blueberry bagel and mint tea." She shot Amie a sideways look to confirm.

"What did I say?" Amie said sternly as Jess rang up the order.

Ziya's eyes went wide with worry. "What?"

"You said you'd forget everything you know about me."

A choked laugh escaped Ziya's lips, relief washing over her face. "I said I'd try," she corrected. "It's a slow process. Plus, as I've gone on the record saying before: Blueberry bagels are weird. Have a more normal breakfast order and I'll have an easier time forgetting that."

Amie made a face as she dipped into her purse. Ziya stopped her.

"I've got it," she said, flashing her own card. "You covered dinner."

"I *ruined* dinner," Amie reminded her. "And I have a free beverage reward."

"Save it. That mac and cheese was better than anything I could've ordered at the restaurant. You rescued dinner." She tapped her card on the reader.

Amie glanced behind them. No one else was in line, so she turned back to the counter and asked, "Hey, Jess?"

"What's up?"

"Have you heard anything more about Savannah?"

The barista's eyes lit up. They glanced past Amie and Ziya, then lowered their voice and said, "Savannah went to the bookstore two nights ago and never returned home. Her husband found her dead in the store early the next morning. Bludgeoned in the head."

Amie's stomach lurched. "So she was killed Monday night?"

"Seems like it."

She hadn't been sure, but now it was confirmed: Savannah had died during the time loop. Every night, when Amie was eating dinner in her apartment, or at the restaurant with Ziya, or . . . well, that was about all she did. But every night, Savannah was murdered, and Amie had never known.

Jess gave Amie a concerned look. "You all right?"

Amie nodded queasily, taking in a deep breath through her nose.

Ziya had also observed Amie's distress. "Do the police have any suspects?" she asked, kindly taking over the conversational reins.

"That I don't know," Jess said. They looked around again, gesturing for Amie and Ziya to lean in. Once they did so, the barista whispered, "I wouldn't be surprised if they suspected Madeline."

There was a brief pause. The name rang a faint bell for Amie. She waited to see if Ziya had any reaction, assuming she was doing the same.

When neither of them said anything, Jess added, "Our owner?"

"Ohhh," said Amie and Ziya in unison. Madeline was the owner of Eons Café, and would occasionally greet and check in on customers whenever she was in. Amie hadn't seen the woman in a while, as she hadn't been in the café during any of Amie's trips to Eons on Monday.

"Why would she be a suspect?" Ziya asked.

Jess somehow managed to lower the volume of their voice even more than before. Amie pressed closer to catch their words.

"Madeline's been wanting to buy the bookstore from Savannah for ages," the barista said. "She wants to knock down the wall and make it one big business. But Savannah wasn't gonna sell, no matter how much the store was suffering or how much Madeline offered her."

"So you think Madeline might've . . . ?" Ziya dragged a finger across her throat, clearly reveling in the drama.

Jess shrugged, stepping back. "All I'm saying is that I'd be surprised if she isn't a suspect. But you didn't hear it from me."

"Of course," Amie said. "Is Madeline here now?"

Ziya gave her a strange look as Jess answered.

"No," they said, "she went next door for the memorial."

"A memorial?" Amie asked. "That's quick. It's barely been a day since they found her."

"Yeah," Jess agreed, scratching the back of their neck. "Honestly, I don't think the store can afford to stay closed for too long. Whoever planned it was probably trying to come up with a classy way to keep the doors open."

"Do you think—" Ziya began, but the barista's eyes were on the couple that had just entered the café and were heading for the register.

"Your order will be ready for you at the end of the counter," Jess said. "Have a great day!"

"What were you going to say?" Amie asked as they walked over to the pickup spot.

"I was gonna ask if they think Madeline will buy the bookstore now." Ziya lounged against the counter. She had borrowed clothes from Amie—a pair of flip-flops, black running shorts, and a tie-dye T-shirt she'd twisted and tucked into a crop top. "Whether or not she killed Savannah, if she wanted to buy the store before, she can probably do it now."

"We could ask her," Amie said. "She's right next door."

Ziya cocked her head. "I was wondering why you asked if she's here. Do you really want to talk to her?"

Amie shrugged, shuffling her feet self-consciously. She wasn't sure how to explain her guilt around Savannah's murder to someone who didn't believe her about the time loop. Then a thought crossed her mind.

"The police are suspecting David," Amie said. "And we know he didn't do it. So I was just thinking . . . maybe I could try to figure out who did. To keep David out of trouble."

As she spoke, she realized that she *was* worried about David. If there was a killer out there who had sent the police after her friend, who knew what else they might do to keep the cops off their tail and on David's?

Ziya rolled this over in her head. "Could be fun," she mused. "Okay, I'm in."

Amie gave a start. "Hang on. Who invited you?"

"Ha. Me, bitch." Ziya crossed her arms. "David's my friend, too. Just because you got custody of him in the breakup doesn't mean I don't want to clear him of murder."

"Okay. Fair." Amie thought this over. Having Ziya join her could be helpful. At the very least, if that morning's walk to the café was any indication, having her around would significantly shorten Amie's travel time. (Her effect on Amie's heart rate any time their arms brushed could be distracting, but Amie was willing to work through that.)

They thanked the barista who brought over their drinks and food.

"So," Ziya said, popping open the lid of her coffee, "let's chug these and go next door to interrogate Madeline." She took a sip of her drink, then winced. "Ah! Hot. Too hot to chug. Never mind."

After finishing their drinks at a rate that was somewhere between a chug and a slow sip, they stowed away their bagel and muffin and headed next door to the bookshop.

Amie was fully aware that their friend date was dangerously close to the sixteen-hour mark. She knew that spending so much time with her ex-girlfriend (who she still had unaddressed feelings for) was probably not the smartest idea. It was apparent to her that despite things going well between them so far, it could all easily fall apart at any moment. She was cognizant of the fact that—

The runaway train of logic that was barreling through her mind screeched to a halt as Ziya pulled open the door to the bookshop and flashed Amie a smile. "Time travelers first."

Amie paused, startled. She'd assumed Ziya had already forgotten she'd brought up the time loop, chalking it up to Amie trying out a strange metaphor. Apparently, whether she believed it or not, the time loop was still on her mind.

"I'm not a time traveler," Amie said, feeling shy. She didn't know how to talk to Ziya about it. "I didn't really do much traveling through time. I was more like a . . . time homebody."

"Yeah, that sounds like you." Ziya chuckled as she followed Amie inside.

Shelf Starter was a store that used almost every free inch for its merchandise. The space was packed with books, with aisles so narrow that one had to become physically intimate with a shelf of literary fiction in order to allow another person to squeeze by. The only items that came close to the books in quantity (though by a wide margin) were the fresh bouquets of flowers scattered about wherever there was surface space.

The business normally boasted about two or three customers at a time, but on this day there was an unusually large number of bodies packed into the store. Amie watched two people play a quick round of "Which Way Are *You* Going?" as they tried to pass each other in the romance section. A young woman was perilously balancing an armful of books while trying to wriggle through the crowd in the sci-fi aisle. Shelf Starter usually piped calm music through invisible speakers, but if the music was playing, it was drowned out by the ambient noise of a fire marshal's worst nightmare.

Ziya leaned in close to Amie's ear. "I didn't know Savannah was so beloved," she whispered.

It took Amie a beat to process what Ziya had said, her brain focusing instead on the proximity of her ex's mouth to her neck.

"Uh, yeah," she finally managed to get out. "Seems strange."

"Ah." Ziya pointed to a "50% Off All Books" sign that was taped to the end of one shelf, underneath another sign promoting the bookshop's printing services. "That makes more sense."

Amie looked around for Madeline. She knew the woman was blond, but couldn't quite remember her face. She hoped she'd recognize her on sight, but wasn't having any luck so far.

Her luck took a turn for the worse as they bushwhacked their way to the back of the store. A small spread of cheese and crackers had been set up on the counter next to a large bouquet of lilies by the register. A framed photo of Savannah was half-obscured by a near-empty pitcher of what appeared to be iced tea. A familiar figure was standing alone by the refreshments, building a sandwich with a slice of cheddar and two crackers.

"Ugh," Amie said, nudging Ziya. "My landlord is here."

"Gorgeous Benny?" Ziya asked eagerly, looking around.

"Don't call him that. What's he doing here?"

Ziya winced. "You're gonna be really bad at this mystery-solving thing, aren't you?"

"Why?"

"Well," Ziya explained, "this is Savannah's memorial. Savannah lived in your building. Benny is your landlord. Which would make him Savannah's landlord. It's elementary, Amie."

"I know *that*," Amie grumbled. "I'm just surprised to see him show up to something. Took him six weeks to come fix my radiator." She tugged on Ziya's arm, pulling her down an aisle of books. "I can't do awkward small talk with him right now."

They weaved around several more people who seemed far more interested in the discounted books than memorializing Savannah.

"Oh, there's Raina," Amie said as she and Ziya stopped by the nonfiction section. She nodded at the young woman standing at the end of the aisle, talking to someone she couldn't see. "She's the manager."

"Mm, big suspect, then," Ziya commented.

Amie frowned. "Why?"

"Based on the stories I've heard and my few interactions with her, Savannah was a nightmare to be around." She lowered her voice. "I think anyone who regularly spent time with her has a strong motive for murder."

"Hm." Amie wasn't sure she agreed. They likely needed to come up with a stronger motive than "spent too much time around Savannah."

A customer carrying a teetering stack of books was taking his balancing act to the other end of their aisle. Ziya stepped in closer to Amie, who flattened her back against the shelf behind her.

"You don't like my theory?" Ziya asked, keeping her voice low as she used one hand to brace herself against the books. Her hair tickled Amie's ear as she inclined her head to be heard over the hubbub of the store.

"I didn't say that." Amie clenched her hands into fists to keep them from going to Ziya's hips and pulling her closer. Her eyes were under strict orders to stay on Ziya's eyes and not drift any lower. "It's a good theory."

Her breathing grew shallow as her ex-girlfriend leaned in more. Their noses just barely brushed before Ziya pushed off the shelf, stepping away.

"It needs more proof to back it up," she declared. "Let's go get it."

"Mhm" was the best Amie could manage in response.

As they continued down the aisle toward Raina, Amie was finally able to see who the woman was talking to. The face she'd been unable to conjure was now crystal clear and in Technicolor: the owner of Eons Café.

"That's Madeline, right?" Ziya asked, noticing the woman as well. "Two birds with one stone. Let's eavesdrop."

Retracing their steps, they circled back around and hurried down the next aisle. Amie and Ziya stopped by a shelf of thick fantasy books, right around the corner from the two other women.

"You should ask him," came Raina's voice from the other side of the shelves. "I know it's soon, but I think he'd appreciate getting it off his plate."

"I do need to talk to him eventually," Madeline replied. "I just don't know if now is—oh, here he comes."

There was a pause as they waited for the subject of their conversation to join them. Then, a strained, baritone voice quietly demanded, "What are you doing here?"

Ziya snuck a peek through the shelf, with Amie following her lead. Andrew Harlow, Savannah's husband, was staring at the café owner. He had white hair, bright blue eyes, and a pale complexion that was steadily turning red from the barely contained rage that simmered beneath his weathered features.

"Andrew," Madeline said, sounding confused. "I'm so sorry for—"

"Get out," he said. He was still speaking in a low voice, but more anger spilled forth as he continued. "Get out of my wife's store and don't come back. I don't want to see you, and I don't want to hear from you. Do you understand?"

Madeline's curls bounced as she shook her head. "I . . . I really don't."

"Mr. Harlow," Raina started cautiously, "Madeline wanted to talk—"

"I said *get out*!" Andrew repeated, louder and sharper this time. "You are *never* getting this store. So get out. *Now.*"

Without another word, Madeline stepped past him and hurried away.

"Shit," Ziya muttered. "I'll try to catch her. You talk to Raina."

Amie spluttered. "What? Wait—" But Ziya was already rushing down the aisle before she could say anything more.

Andrew's voice brought Amie back to eavesdropping.

"I'm sorry about that," he said, his voice rough.

"Don't worry about it." Raina sounded concerned. "You don't have to stay if it's too much."

"No, no, I'm fine. I want to be here."

"Do you need anything?"

"Keep her out of the store, please," Andrew said firmly. "And . . . I think we're almost out of iced tea."

"I have another jug in the back," Raina said. "I'll go get it."

Amie froze as Raina passed the aisle she was hiding in, but the store's manager didn't notice her as she disappeared into the back room.

"Can I help you find something?"

Amie jumped, knocking a fantasy trilogy clean off the shelf as she whirled around.

The person who'd spoken knelt down to retrieve the fallen books. He looked to be in his early twenties, with a shock of red curls tied up in a short ponytail. Amie recognized him as one of the store's employees.

"I'm so sorry," she said. She shuffled backward awkwardly to give him room as he scooped the books up. As he straightened, she caught a glimpse of the name on his tag—Grayson.

"Nah, my fault," he replied, tucking the clipboard he'd been holding under his arm as he returned the books to their shelf. "Didn't mean to scare you."

"I've just been jumpy lately," Amie said. "Not your fault."

"Bro, same." Grayson hunched his shoulders, lowering his voice. "I didn't even wanna come in today. Since Savannah couldn't work, for obvious reasons, they needed the help. But there's a *murderer* out there." He shivered. "Any of us could be next."

Amie was taken aback by how indiscreetly this guy was speaking to her. Not wanting to discourage him, she hid her surprise.

"I'm sure you're not in danger," she said. "Especially not in a busy bookstore in the middle of the day."

"I dunno, man." Grayson shook his head. "Crowds can make it easy for someone to take out a knife"—he mimed drawing what appeared to be a dagger from a sheath, stabbing it into the air—"then slip away into the throng, undetected."

Amie suddenly felt less safe standing in a busy bookstore in the middle of the day. Especially with someone who was so adept with imaginary knives.

"It's even worse when there's hardly anyone around," Grayson continued. "Thank god they never leave me alone in here. It gets *spooky* quiet."

Considering how willingly he abandoned working to talk with Amie, she could understand why that might be a policy.

"Do you have a reason to believe you'd be in danger?" she asked.

"Not really." He tapped his right temple. "But some murderers kill for reasons we'd never be able to guess. It's scary. Like, what if this guy has a vendetta against people who work at bookstores, and I'm next?"

"I don't think that's the case," Amie said soothingly, though Grayson seemed more eager than scared by the prospect of being targeted by a bibliophobic serial killer.

"If anything," Grayson continued, "it'd probably be Raina, then me."

Amie was struggling to follow him through the conversation. "Sorry?"

"Order of death," Grayson explained. "If we're talking chain of command. Though, if the murderer had asked me, I would've told them to start from the bottom and work their way up. Me, then Raina, then Savannah. Builds suspense more that way."

"Bet you're glad they didn't ask you, then," Amie said weakly.

Grayson laughed. "Yeah, imagine."

They pressed their backs to the books as a couple of women squeezed by. Once they'd passed, Amie had finished processing what Grayson had said.

"What about the rest of the employees?" she asked. "Aren't there other people working here?"

"Nope, just me. Others got laid off."

Surprised, Amie asked, "When?"

Grayson looked up, doing the mental math. "Three weeks ago? A month? Something like that. Savannah kept me on because I've been working here the longest."

"Why'd the rest get laid off?"

Grayson rubbed his thumb against his pointer and middle fingers. "Why else? Store's been struggling as long as I've worked here. I felt kind of bad for the others, but it means I can more easily pick up extra hours when I need the cash, so I'm not complaining."

Out of the corner of her eye, Amie saw Raina emerge from the back room with a jug of iced tea. She gave Amie a small smile as she passed them.

"Did Raina complain?" Amie asked, lowering her voice. Through the shelves, she saw the store's manager veer down the next aisle, away from the empty pitcher she'd been on her way to fill. Benny was still standing by the refreshments, appearing to have single-handedly eaten half of the crackers.

"About Savannah laying off the other part-timers?" Grayson asked. "Nah, she was cool with it. Raina always goes along with whatever Savannah says. She's probably gonna take over the store once Savannah retires."

He winced, scratching the back of his head. "I mean, she was. Maybe not anymore."

Amie's heart picked up speed. "Raina wanted to take over the store?"

Grayson nodded. "She wants to own it one day, I think." Then, apparently catching on to Amie's train of thought, hastily added, "But she wouldn't have, like, *killed* for it. She loved Savannah. Or, at least, she dealt with her better than most people. Raina's been working here forever, but Savannah was probably only a few more years out from retirement. She wouldn't have killed Savannah just because she was taking too long to retire. Raina's, like, one of the most patient people in the world."

"I'd imagine you'd have to be, to work that much with Savannah," Amie said.

"You got that right."

"Did *you* get along with Savannah?"

Grayson snorted. "No one *got along* with Savannah. You'd either let her walk all over you, or get chewed up, spit out, and *then* walked all over. I usually opted for the first. I honestly wouldn't have minded getting laid off. I'm pretty sure the guys who did get the boot didn't care much."

He shrugged. "But it's just a job. I clock in, I take a super long lunch break, I clock out. Try not to take things too seriously. Plus I get an employee discount, so, not the worst use of my time."

"Savannah was killed here in the store, right?" Amie asked, wracking her brain for more questions to ask while she had such a willing subject.

"In the back room, yeah. Heard it happened after closing. Wasn't told much else."

"Was it a break-in?"

Grayson shook his head. "Not from what I saw. No broken windows or busted doors. It can get really stuffy in the back, so sometimes we prop the door open to get fresh air. My guess is Savannah forgot to close it, and they came in through there."

"Were you here when the store closed?" Amie asked.

"Nah, I worked open to three."

"Mm." Amie wracked a little more. "Did you see anything . . . suspicious that day? Anything unusual happen?"

"Not really." Grayson rubbed his chin. "I might've noticed more if I'd known there was going to be a murder that night. I've been working on my powers of observation today, in case there's another one."

He looked around. "Ask me . . . um . . . oh! Ask me how many bouquets of flowers are in the store right now."

"How many—"

"Seven," Grayson cut in. He paused. "But we get those flowers every week, so maybe that doesn't count. Ask me . . ."

The mention of flowers jogged Amie's memory. "Savannah was at the grocery store that morning," she said. "She got into an argument with a man named David. Did you hear about this?"

"Oh, yeah," Grayson said. "Didn't think much of it. It'd be more unusual if a day went by when Savannah *wasn't* pissed off about something."

"Who else did she tell about it?"

"She was grumbling all day about people sticking their noses into other people's business. If anyone bothered asking her what was wrong, she'd go off about how David started yelling at her while she was talking to the flower guy."

Amie's stomach sank. That meant anyone could have known that Savannah and David had gotten into an argument that day.

"Anyway," Grayson said, "I should probably get back to looking like I'm working. Oh!" He held out the clipboard he'd been clutching. "Would you like to sign up for our newsletter? You'll be notified about new releases through text or email."

Amie wasn't particularly interested, but since the guy had spent so much time answering her questions, she felt compelled to help him out.

Scribbling her name and email address onto the sheet, Amie was surprised to see Benny's name and phone number above hers. She suspected it was more likely he'd filled it out due to social pressure than a genuine love for books. In his defense, that had been her reasoning, too. It was likely Grayson would get a good amount of sign-ups solely from people who would feel bad saying no.

"Did you need help finding something?" Grayson asked as she finished.

"Oh, no. Just browsing, thanks."

"All right. Let Raina know if you need anything." He gave her a small salute, then wandered off.

Amie peeked around the bookshelf. Benny was still haunting the refreshments, the pitcher of iced tea sitting empty next to him. She drifted back down the aisle, looking for Raina in a way she hoped didn't seem like she was looking for Raina.

Stopping by a display of autobiographies, she peeked through the shelf to search for her target. Raina was standing in the next aisle, her back to Amie, the jug of iced tea resting in the crook of her arm. She appeared to be scanning the bookshelf for something, but Amie recognized the other woman's casual glances down the aisle. They were identical to the casual glances Amie had been casting less than a minute earlier. Raina was looking for someone.

Amie knew this could be her opportunity to talk to the store's manager, but curiosity kept her where she stood. She wanted to see who Raina was looking for.

As the minutes passed, Amie began to wonder what was taking Ziya so long. She hoped she hadn't confronted Madeline directly about Savannah's murder. If Madeline *was* the murderer, and suspected that Ziya was onto her . . .

Amie's anxiety began to spike. She was moments away from sprinting out of the store when Raina began moving down the aisle toward the counter.

Abandoning any subterfuge she'd been attempting earlier, Amie followed the manager down her parallel aisle, peeking out to see who she was approaching. To her surprise, there was no one. Raina had twisted the cap off the jug and was refilling the pitcher.

"Excuse me" came Andrew's voice from behind. Amie froze, then slowly turned, expecting to see the man glowering at her for spying.

But Andrew was walking over to Benny, who was standing by the door to the back room.

"Sorry, Benny," Andrew said. "Employees only."

The landlord's face was pink with embarrassment. "I was looking for the bathroom," he said awkwardly.

Andrew shook his head. "Normally I'd let you use the employee bathroom, but the police still have a section of the back room blocked off. No one can get to it right now. Sorry."

"Sure, no problem," Benny mumbled, moving away from the door. He shuffled past Andrew, disappearing down one of the aisles. Andrew watched him go, then entered the back room.

Amie turned back to find her view of Raina blocked by several people who had seemingly all in unison decided it was time to buy their books.

Raina must have also noticed the sudden line at the register. "Grayson!" Amie heard her call from behind the wall of people. "Register!"

Grayson jogged out of a nearby aisle, making a beeline for the back room. "I'm taking my lunch break!" he called, sliding his clipboard across the counter and slipping through the door.

A moment later, Raina appeared behind the counter. She retrieved the clipboard, shooting an annoyed glance at the back room door before smiling at the first customer in line.

Amie let out a frustrated huff. It'd be a while before the other woman was free to talk. Ziya could be dead by then.

ZIYA. Remembering her worry for her ex, Amie allowed her fear to rush her out the door of the bookshop so fast she collided with the subject of her concern.

"Ow," Ziya groaned, grabbing Amie's shoulders to steady them both. "What happened? Are you being chased?"

"No, I—are you okay?"

Ziya rolled her eyes. "That woman moves *fast*. I chased her into the café, but wasn't able to get to her before she went in the back. Had to stand in line and order a cake pop just to tell Jess I wanted to talk to their boss."

"Did you really have to order the cake pop?" Amie asked, smiling.

"Well, I stood in line for so long, I had to get *something*."

"You haven't even eaten your muffin yet."

"I got you one, too."

"Ooh!"

They sat at a small table outside of the café, neglecting their breakfast items in favor of the frosting-coated balls of cake on sticks.

"When Madeline came out," Ziya said, "I said I saw Andrew yelling at her and wanted to make sure she was okay. She looked kind of weirded out that I dragged her out of her office for that, but she said she appreciated me asking."

Ziya took a bite of her cake pop, then continued. "I asked if she knew why Andrew was so upset with her. She was still a little confused, but also seemed like she wanted to talk about it, y'know? Defend herself to someone, even if it wasn't him."

Amie nodded.

"Anyway, she figured he thought she was gonna ask about buying the bookstore. She said she would've never brought it up to him so soon after Savannah's death, but he didn't give her a chance."

"You think Andrew's a suspect, too," Amie said, reading Ziya's face.

"Well, *yeah*," Ziya said. "It's almost always the husband. If Savannah was refusing to sell the store, putting her and her husband into more and more debt, killing her would be one way to put an end to it."

"You have a twisted mind," Amie said.

"Thank you. That was all I got from Madeline. What did Raina say?"

"Couldn't get a hold of her. Thought you might be getting murdered, so I left."

"Oh, you're sweet."

"But I did talk to Grayson, one of the other employees," Amie said. "The *only* other employee, apparently. Savannah laid off the rest a few weeks ago. Grayson said he didn't think any of them were mad, but they could be suspects."

"Nah," Ziya replied. The last few bites of her cake pop threatened to fall off the stick as she waved it in the air. "Who's gonna kill someone over losing a part-time job?"

"You were the one who said someone might have killed her just from spending too much time around her!" Amie exclaimed. "That's even *less* of a motive."

"I was just being silly," Ziya said dismissively. "I know we'd need a stronger motive than that. What would the laid-off employees get from murdering their former boss?"

"Revenge?"

"Whoa," Ziya said, putting her hands up. "You're even more twisted than me. I wouldn't want to be your ex-girlfriend."

Amie fought hard to hold back the smile she was worried would expose her as enjoying Ziya's company more than she felt comfortable admitting. She filled Ziya in on everything else Grayson had told her.

"The Raina thing is interesting," Ziya continued, tapping her chin. "If Savannah was laying people off, Raina might've been concerned for her job. If she knew Madeline wanted to buy the bookstore—"

"And it sounded like she did," Amie cut in. "Based on what we overheard before Andrew showed up."

"Right. Then maybe Raina thought she had a better chance of keeping her job if the store was under new management."

Amie frowned. "But Raina's so nice," she said.

"All killers are," Ziya responded, her tone serious.

"I . . . don't think that's true."

"I know. It just sounded deliciously ominous." Ziya pushed her chair back and stood. "I have to get to class. Walk me back to my car?"

Amie stood as well, taking her time to do so. She'd had more than enough time to prepare for the two of them to part ways, and yet she still felt unprepared to say goodbye.

Stop being dramatic, she scolded herself as they began walking back down the street. *You're not saying goodbye forever. You'll see her again.*

"Ooh, they're setting up for the fall festival!" Ziya pointed at a pickup truck that was turning down a perpendicular street toward Willows Park. A tall strength-tester game was lashed to the back, the bell at the top repeatedly dinging as it bumped against the wall of the truck bed.

"We should go," Ziya said as they continued down the street. "I need my annual funnel cake fix."

"Mm," Amie murmured in agreement, her spirits lifting as Ziya made plans for their future (albeit a very near future with the main goal of acquiring deep-fried fair food).

"What're you up to today?" Ziya asked, slowing as they approached her car. "Working on anything?"

"Not really." Amie kicked a pebble off the sidewalk. "I asked Vivian if I could take a little longer on my next assignment. Just needed a break."

"And she was fine with that?"

"Yeah. Honestly, I think they're a few weeks away from replacing everyone with freelancers and AI. I doubt it'll make much of a difference if I don't log on to Slack for a few days."

Ziya stopped by her car. "I'm sorry."

"Eh." Amie shrugged uncomfortably. "It'll be fine."

"You could still do journalism school," Ziya suggested, her tone slightly teasing. This was not the first time she'd made the suggestion, and clearly she already knew what the response would be.

"Yeah, no," Amie said. "I'm not gonna waste my time going back to school just so I can *maybe* get a better-paying job. I'm almost thirty."

She paused, frowning. Was she already thirty? How had she never thought about this before? She'd been twenty-eight at the start of the time loop, but for her, over two years had passed since then. *Holy shit, am I thirty?*

"I'm twenty-seven, and I'm still in school," Ziya countered, unaware of Amie's internal crisis. "And it's not just about getting paid more. You should have a job that you enjoy."

Amie put a pin in her mental age debate. "A lot of people have jobs they don't enjoy, Z."

"But you could have one, if you just tried. You'd be a great journalist."

Exhaling through her nose, Amie looked up at her building. This was one thing that always bothered her about Ziya: how she would continue to push after Amie had already expressed her stance, usually on a topic related to how Amie lived her life. But what bothered Amie even more was how bothered she'd get by it. She knew Ziya only pushed because she wanted Amie to be happy. So why did Amie always get so irritated when Ziya was just trying to show that she cared?

"You left your dress and shoes upstairs," Amie said, ending the conversation. "I can run up and grab them."

Ziya's car unlocked with a *chirp* as she pressed her key fob. "It's fine, I'll get them next time I see you. I'll return these clothes, too."

"Ohh," Amie chuckled as Ziya circled the front of her car. "The old 'I left something at your apartment, so now we have to see each other again' trick. Very sneaky."

Laughing, Ziya said, "I can't risk letting you freak out and ghost me after I leave you alone with your thoughts for five minutes. Now I've given you a mission you won't be able to refuse."

"You got me there."

Ziya opened the driver's side door. "This went well, right?" she asked.

Seeing the expression on her ex-girlfriend's face, Amie felt her heart crack open. A mix of hope and nervousness danced across Ziya's features, her brown eyes big and questioning as she waited for a response.

Amie smiled softly. "Yeah. I think it went well."

She only got a brief glimpse of the megawatt grin that flashed across Ziya's face before she ducked into the car and turned on the engine.

Rolling down the passenger side window, Ziya called, "Don't solve any murders without me, okay? This is our new friendship thing that we're doing together."

Amie bent over to peer through the window. "You know, normal people would just watch *Survivor* or something."

"Boriiing!" Ziya sang as she put the car in reverse.

Stepping back, Amie watched Ziya ease away from the curb and zip down the street.

Chapter Seven
Gossip

Day 2 A.L.

And now to distract myself with this murder so I don't overanalyze every little thing I said to her, Amie thought as Ziya sped away. Letting out a small sigh, she turned back to her building and started up the steps.

Amie was focusing so hard on everything she'd learned in the previous hour surrounding Savannah and her death that she almost ran into the person standing at the top of the stairs.

"Ah, sorry!" she exclaimed, swerving to avoid plowing down the tiny woman in front of her. "Oh, hi Elena."

Amie's neighbor beamed up at her through large, plum-colored glasses. Elena Serrano was in her late fifties. She had a short brown bob streaked with gray, and standing at about four feet, eight inches, she was clothed in her usual outfit: a multicolored knit poncho over linen pants.

The woman did tarot and palm readings out of her apartment, a few doors down from Amie. She was also the self-appointed town crier of the building, seeming to consider it her sworn duty to stay up-to-date with everything that was going on with her neighbors and then share that information with as many people as she could. Amie was almost surprised Elena hadn't yet figured out that Amie had been stuck in a time loop.

"Hello, sweetheart." Elena patted her on the arm. "Was that Ziya I saw leaving just now? Have you two patched things up?"

Amie winced. She really didn't need the building gossip telling everyone about Amie's love life—or lack thereof.

"It was," she said with caution. "We're just friends now."

"Ah, I see." Elena nodded thoughtfully. "You know, my second husband—Charles, I've told you about him, the ginger who builds furniture—he and I reconnected after I divorced my third husband. And then he and I became lovers for a long while, even longer than we had been married. The sex was better than before, too. Sometimes you just need some time apart."

"That's really sweet, Elena," Amie said weakly. "We're kind of just taking things slow right now." *If you can call conducting a murder investigation "taking things slow."*

"Of course, of course. By the way . . ." Elena leaned in conspiratorially, and Amie braced herself for more romantic (or, god forbid, sex) advice.

But instead, the woman whispered, "Did you hear people think David might've killed Savannah?"

Amie reeled back. "Elena!" she scolded. "You know that's not true."

Elena shrugged. "I just share what I hear," she said, her eyebrows rising with innocence. "I know you're close to him, dear, but—"

"Come on," Amie said sternly. "I'm sure you've heard more stories than anyone about Savannah terrorizing half the people she comes into contact with. You really think David's the most likely suspect? He hardly leaves his apartment."

"You sound like you have your own suspicions," Elena said, her eyes brightening. "Who do *you* think did it?"

"Haven't really thought about it," Amie lied, pulling her key fob out of her pocket. "I just know it wasn't David."

"Interesting," Elena hummed as Amie held the fob up to the scanner by the door. "So what did Ziya mean when she told you not to solve any murders without her?"

Amie turned back to the woman, ignoring the *beep* and soft click as the door unlocked. "Were you standing here so you could eavesdrop on my conversation?"

Elena let out a theatrical gasp at the accusation. "Of course not! I was just looking for my key, and I happened to hear Ziya call out to you." Her expression morphed into curiosity. "So? Who do you think did it?"

"I don't know," Amie said firmly. "I'm not going to tell you my theories just so you can go around telling people they did it like you're doing with David."

"But you *do* have theories."

Amie huffed with frustration. "I'm just gathering some information in case David gets into hotter water than he already is," she explained. "He didn't do it."

"I know, I know," Elena said, raising her hands in surrender. "I just tell it like I hear it. But if you find out anything juicy about anyone else, you let me know, okay? You have my email, right?"

"Yes," Amie said, scanning her fob again. Elena had wrangled Amie's email address out of her within a week of moving in. "But not unless it's backed by fact. A real person has died. It's serious."

"Oh, of course, I know that." Elena followed her into the building, her sandals slapping on the tile floor. "Poor Savannah. She rubbed a lot of people the wrong way, but she was a spitfire. One of the strongest auras I've ever seen."

"That's a nice way to describe her." Amie stopped by the mailboxes, pulling out her key ring again.

"I read her cards just last week," Elena said. "If I'd known it would've been her last reading . . . well, at the very least, I wouldn't have charged her."

"I didn't know Savannah was into tarot," Amie said, unlocking her mailbox. She hadn't checked the mail in what felt like years, and she almost expected an avalanche of letters to fall out. But, chronologically, it had just been a couple of days, so the only item in there was a flier for a plumbing service addressed to "Our Friends" at Amie's address.

"Oh, yes, Savannah had her cards read every week," Elena said. "She told me it helped to focus her mind."

"Did she feel like her mind had been unfocused lately?" Amie asked, removing the flier and closing her mailbox. If Elena had spoken to Savannah recently, she might have learned something that could help point Amie toward the murderer.

"No more than usual," Elena responded. "I can't say anything other than that. Client confidentiality."

Amie groaned internally. Of course when she actually wanted Elena's gossip, *that's* when the woman decided to be unforthcoming. She crossed the lobby and pushed open the door to the stairwell. Elena followed close behind.

"Do you want to know who *I* think did it?" Elena asked as they ascended the stairs together.

"You said it was David."

"I said *people* think it was David. *I* don't think he did it."

"Okay. Who do you think did it?"

Elena stopped in the middle of the stairs, gesturing for the younger woman to lean in close. Amie backtracked down a step, crouching so that Elena could lean in and whisper in her ear.

"*Benny.*"

Amie's eyebrows shot up. Both women glanced around, as if their landlord could be lurking in the stairwell.

"Why would he kill Savannah?" Amie whispered back.

"The Harlows were struggling with money," Elena said. "Things had gotten a little easier for them, I think, but I still wouldn't be surprised if they were behind on rent payments."

Amie shook her head. "But that still doesn't explain why he'd *kill* her."

Elena huffed. "Well, I haven't had much time to develop the theory," she said, starting up the stairs again. "I only just saw him in the Harlows' apartment several minutes ago."

"Wait, what?" Amie hurried to follow.

"Oh, right." Elena stopped again as she seemed to realize she'd forgotten to mention a key part of her theory. "I was in my apartment, doing the crossword, when I heard yelling from out in the hallway. It was hard to make out what the person was saying, so I left to go investigate."

"Naturally," Amie said, not unkindly.

"By the time I opened the door, the yelling had stopped. I heard footsteps going down the stairwell, but I didn't see who it was. A couple of decades ago I might've gone after them, but . . ."

Elena bounced where she stood, as if to demonstrate the deteriorating strength of her limbs. "These knees probably wouldn't have survived the chase. So I went down the hall to see if I could find out who was doing the yelling, or who was getting yelled at. There wasn't anyone out there, but the door to the Harlows' apartment was open. I thought maybe Andrew had forgotten to close it when he left for the memorial—that reminds me, I need to go down there and pay my respects—but then I heard someone moving around inside.

"So I called out, 'Hello?'" Elena's hands flew to her chest. "And as soon as I did, my god, did my heart start pounding. Because I realized: that could've been Savannah's murderer! And there I was, calling, 'Hello? Hello?' Can you believe it? I could've died, too!"

"I'm sure you would've been fine standing in the middle of the hallway," Amie said. "But that *is* scary."

Elena seemed pleased that Amie understood the gravity of the situation. "But then I peeked through the door, and *Benny* was right on the other side, sitting on the floor." She whispered the name, as if saying it too loudly might summon the man. "He did not look well. Very discombobulated. He said, 'What's wrong, Elena?' And I said, 'I heard yelling. Is everything okay?' And he said, 'Everything's fine. I was just looking for something.'"

"What was he looking for?" Amie asked eagerly.

"I just assumed Savannah had taken one of his packages," Elena said, shrugging. "We've all been there. But I don't know what he was doing sitting on the floor, looking like someone had died."

She frowned. "Though, I guess someone *has* died. I just didn't think Benny cared that much about Savannah."

Amie nodded in agreement. "He seemed okay at her memorial. His appetite wasn't affected, at least," she added, recalling how much time the man had spent near the refreshments.

"Anyway," Elena continued, "I asked him if he wanted help looking for his package. Just as a kindness, you know?"

"Sure," Amie said drily. She knew Elena would never pass up the opportunity to snoop around someone else's apartment. "Did you find it?"

Elena shook her head. "Didn't even make it inside. He just stood up, said"—she deepened her voice to a rough growl—"'Doesn't matter anymore.'" She returned to her regular speaking voice. "Then he pushed past me and closed the door."

Tapping the side of her nose, the woman said, "Now, you'll notice that he didn't comment on the yelling. So I said, 'Did you hear the yelling?' And he said, 'No, I didn't hear anything.' Well, I knew that was a lie, since I'd heard it all the way from down the hall. But I couldn't just call the man a liar to his face, so I left to go call him a liar behind his back. And here we are."

"Hang on," Amie said. "If this was all several minutes ago, how did you end up outside of the building trying to get back in?"

A coy smile inched onto Elena's face. "All right," she admitted. "Maybe I saw you and Ziya out my window and thought I'd come say hi. Is that a crime?"

Amie rolled her eyes good-naturedly as they continued up the stairs. "Do you think Benny was really at the Harlows' apartment to look for a package?" she asked.

Elena grimaced. "Well, he certainly wasn't there to do any landlording. I find it hard to believe he's finally discovered a work ethic in his mid-forties."

They reached the landing for the second floor.

"Who was he yelling at?" Amie asked softly, almost to herself.

"Oh, Benny wasn't the one yelling," Elena said, once again realizing she hadn't finished her story. "The voice was much higher."

"You think it was the person you heard in the stairwell?" Amie asked.

"That's right," Elena confirmed. "My hearing isn't what it used to be, so I couldn't make out what all the yelling was about. But I was able to catch one thing."

"What?"

Elena lifted a hand, pointing a finger at Amie menacingly. "'*You did it.*'"

* * *

Amie stared at the blank document open on her laptop. The longer she looked at it, the faster the cursor seemed to blink. She'd thought that stepping back from work to recover a bit from the time loop would be a good idea. However, until she figured out how to explain her situation to a therapist without immediately getting referred to a psychiatrist, Amie didn't really know what to do while she "recovered." Opening a new document was her way of trying to jumpstart any sort of productivity, but it really only gave her a new thing to look at as she once again got lost in her thoughts.

It was unlikely she'd be able to figure out who'd murdered Savannah. If Amie had known about Savannah's death during the time loop, that would have been a different story. She was almost positive she could have prevented it. Hidden in the back room right before the store closed. Watched Savannah do inventory or pack up a delivery as someone came in through the back door. Then she'd . . .

. . . tackle them?

Amie wasn't exactly sure how she would have incapacitated the murderer. She supposed, given the nature of the time loop, she would've had the opportunity to learn from trial and error if she didn't get it right on the first attempt.

But she hadn't even gotten that far. She hadn't even known Savannah was murdered. If Amie had been put in the time loop to stop Savannah's death, the universe must have eventually lost patience with her and just given up.

She probably couldn't solve this murder. But she had to at least *try*.

Amie checked her phone. She'd messaged Ziya after her stairwell conversation with Elena, updating her on what the woman had shared about Benny.

She hadn't noticed how easy texting her ex-girlfriend had been until the initial messages were sent. During the months after the breakup and before the time loop, any texts sent to Ziya had been written, then rewritten, then deleted entirely, then written again with only slightly different wording than the rewrite. None of them had been sent. At the time, it had felt like one wrong word could destroy any possibility of the two of them reconciling.

But after the past twenty-four hours, that fear had all but vanished. Its ominous drumbeat of warning was drowned out by a university marching band performing the instrumental version of a song called "Talk to Ziya! (feat. Serotonin)."

Benny was turned away while trying to get into the back room at the bookstore, was Amie's final text of the updates. **He said he was looking for the bathroom, but now I'm wondering if he was looking for something else.**

That makes SO much sense, Ziya replied. **When he couldn't look in the store, he went to look in Savannah's apartment. SUSPICIOUS!!!!**

Then again, Amie texted, **it could just be that Savannah stole one of Benny's packages. Like, that's probably a more likely scenario than Benny murdering Savannah.**

Or maybe he murdered her for stealing one of his packages, Ziya countered.

Must've been a pretty important package if that's true.

Amie watched the three dots appear as Ziya began typing, then added, **Don't say anything about Benny's important package.**

The dots disappeared, then returned. **You know me too well.**

The university marching band hit a triumphant chord as Amie smiled to herself.

Halftime ended soon after when Ziya said her class was about to start. Amie was granted a final marimba trill when Ziya signed off with, **I'll text you later!**

That had been several hours ago. There had been no new texts from Ziya in the interim. Amie wasn't overthinking it.

Knock knock. Knock. Knock knock knock.

"Come i—"

"What would you define 'later' as?" Amie asked, barging into the apartment before David could finish granting her entry.

"I'll need more context than that. Also, hello." David was sitting cross-legged under his work table, setting up a ramp between two of the legs.

"Hi." Amie knelt next to the table, grimacing as her left knee throbbed with pain. A bruise had begun to develop where she'd slammed it into the table the day before.

Once, during the time loop, Amie had badly sliced her hand while opening a can of chickpeas. She'd cleaned the wound, bandaged it up, and by the next day, there had been no sign of any injury. The rest of the day she kept touching the palm of her hand, having difficulty processing how something so painful could have disappeared so swiftly and completely.

It'd been a while since her body had been given enough time to develop a bruise or scar from an injury. She couldn't honestly say she'd missed it.

Shifting into a squat, she said, "If someone says they'll text you later, when would you assume that to be? Four hours later? Five? Six? Stop me when I get there. Seven? Whenever you're ready. *Eight?* Please stop me."

"Did you drink seven cups of coffee?" David asked. "You sound unwell."

"Ziya said she'd text me later, but I don't know when that is. Am I allowed to text her first?"

"By whose rules?" David countered.

"I don't know!" Amie wobbled, trying to keep her balance. "Society's! How much time should I let pass before I can text her again?"

"What do you want to text her about?"

"Oh my *god*." Her legs were beginning to ache, so Amie sat down on the floor. "Can you answer any of my questions not in the form of another question?"

"Would that make you feel better?"

"Now you're just doing it on purpose."

David chuckled, ripping a piece of duct tape off a roll. "You shouldn't have to wait to text her. If you have something to say, just say it." He handed her the roll of tape. "Rip off five more pieces for me, will you?"

Amie accepted the roll, frowning. "I don't have anything specific to say," she said, picking at the tape with her fingernail. "I just feel like we're in a really good place right now, and I don't want to lose that if she gets too busy and forgets about me."

David snorted. "Yeah, okay."

"What?"

"Tape."

Amie dutifully ripped off a piece of tape and passed it over.

"Why don't you ask her if she wants to get dinner tonight?" David suggested, working to unstick the tape from his fingers.

"No, no no no," Amie said, shaking her head. "That's too soon."

"Why?"

"Because," Amie explained, "it's too eager. I don't want her to think I'm trying to get back together with her."

"That's ridiculous," David said flatly. "Who'd ever assume that?"

Amie chose not to respond to the clearly sarcastic comment. "Besides, she's busy tonight. She's going to the opening of some jazz-funk club because Lil Screw might be there."

"Who?" David asked, holding his hand out for another piece of tape.

"He's a rapper." Amie ripped off another piece and stuck it to his outstretched hand. "She doesn't really like him, or jazz, but . . ."

"That's Ziya," David said, finishing her sentence. "Always doing something."

"Yeah." Amie was quiet for a moment. "It's strange to know her so well."

"What do you mean?"

Amie spoke slowly as thoughts that had been lurking in the depths of her brain floated up to the surface. "It's just strange that you can build a relationship with someone, get to know them intimately, and feel like no one in the world knows you as well as they do. And then you break up, and then there's just this person who you spent so much time getting to know, and now you have to live your life with that person out there who you know so well but can't be with because you've ended that relationship."

Amie sucked in a deep breath, looking at David expectantly. David, in turn, was staring back at her, eyebrows raised.

"Was there a question in there?"

Amie flexed her fingers, as if trying to physically hold the question as she struggled to compose it. "How can you feel so close to a person, know them so well, and just . . . be friends?"

David returned to taping the ramp. "I think you know me pretty well," he said. "And we're just friends."

"Yeah, but I don't want to kiss you on the mouth."

"Aha!" David pointed a section of the ramp at her. "So you admit that you still have feelings for Ziya!"

"Ughhhh," Amie said in response, falling back to lie on the floor. "And I don't know you *that* well. I still don't know the titles of any of your books."

"I can't believe Ziya let that slip," David grumbled, retrieving the duct tape from the supine Amie.

"Why don't you want me to read them?" Amie asked, turning her head to look at him. "They can't be that bad."

"No," David acquiesced. "They're fine. I just don't particularly care for them. I'm sure you wouldn't either, but I knew you'd think you were being supportive by reading them. I didn't want you to waste your time."

"Too bad you didn't tell me on Monday," Amie said wryly. "I had a good amount of free time on my hands. Can't tell you how many times a librarian watched me pick up a book and start reading it from the middle."

"Ha."

"I might enjoy them." Amie propped herself up on her forearm. "If they're bestsellers, that must mean a lot of people like them."

"You sound like my editor." David finished taping the last section of the track, crawling out from under the table. "She keeps asking me to write another one."

"How have we never talked about this?" Amie asked in disbelief. "Do I talk about my own issues too much?"

"No, no." She heard him rummaging through a box on top of the table. "I don't like to talk about it. I already know what you'd say."

"What would I say?"

David pitched up his voice. "'You should do it! You'd make so many people happy, and it'd give you something to do other than building machines and haunting local yard sales! Hee hee!'"

"'*Hee hee*'?" Amie asked, indignant. "When have I ever said 'hee hee'? Is that really how I sound to you?"

David dropped the voice. "For the most part, yes."

Amie lay back down on the floor. "That's not what I'd say."

"What would you say, then?" David returned to the underside of the table, holding a Ping-Pong ball.

"I'd ask if you want to write another book."

Amie looked over after a few moments of silence. David was turning the ball over in his hand, his thoughts elsewhere.

"Possibly," he finally said. "When my niece was little, I thought I might like to write a children's book for her."

Amie gasped. "That'd be so cute!" she squealed.

David gave her a sideways look.

"Yeah, okay, I hear it now, I understand the voice. But if that's what you want to do, you should do it."

"Elle's starting high school next year. She's too old for children's books now." David released the Ping-Pong ball at the top of the ramp. It picked up speed as it rolled down, flying off the end and bouncing across the floor to the other side of the room.

"Too fast," he muttered to himself. "Need to adjust the angle." He began peeling tape off the ramp.

"I'm sure she'd still appreciate it." Amie stared at the ceiling. "I know you don't get to see her a lot. This could be a way to show you're thinking of her."

"I might've been able to pull it off several years ago," David said. "But nowadays I don't think Harry Jenkins would be able to sell anything other than a new Detective Richards mystery. Elle's going to have to settle for the usual fifty-dollar bill on her birthday."

"Fifty dollars? Pretty cheap for a bestselling author."

"I spend a lot of money on duct tape." Ramp adjusted, David went to retrieve the runaway Ping-Pong ball.

"You know you just told me your pen name, right?" Amie said.

"I've given up on the secret." David grunted as he reached under the couch to grab the ball. "Read the books if you want; I don't care."

"Yay. I will. Thanks, Harry." Amie sat up. "Maybe I'll learn something from your detective that'll help me figure out who killed Savannah."

David gave her a strange look as he returned to the table. "Why would you want to figure that out?"

"Aren't you curious?" Amie asked. "Especially since you might be a suspect. Don't you want to clear your name?"

"Unless they take me away in handcuffs, I'm staying as far away from the situation as I can." David sat on the table. "I've read—and written—enough mysteries to know that a suspect getting involved in a case only lands them in more trouble than they were already in."

"Well, it'd be pretty hard for you to figure out who did it if you got arrested," Amie pointed out.

"That's why I keep you around. My girl Friday, working on the outside." David tossed her the Ping-Pong ball, standing. "Drop that on the ramp, will you?"

Amie leaned over to deposit the ball. It descended the ramp at a much more leisurely rate than it had during the first trial. David stopped it with his foot as it reached the end of the ramp.

"Excellent." He bent over to pick up the ball.

"Elena thinks Benny did it," Amie said.

"Elena also thinks she can predict the future based on the phase of the moon," David countered, sitting on the table again. "She's a nice woman, but I wouldn't put my money where her mouth is."

"Okay, but listen to this." Amie told him about what Elena had observed, as well as Benny's interaction with Andrew at the memorial.

When she finished, David was scratching his chin, which Amie took as a sign that she was onto something.

"I wonder why he gave up when Elena arrived," David mused. "He could've just shut the door on her."

"Maybe he couldn't find what he was looking for," Amie suggested. "Or maybe he decided to go back when Elena wasn't hanging around, in case she'd see him leaving with whatever it was."

"But if he was just looking for his package, he'd have no reason to hide that."

"So what if it wasn't a package?" Amie posited. "What if it was something that would have pointed to him as the murderer? If he couldn't look for it at the bookshop, maybe he found it at the apartment."

"Then it'd probably be back at his place now," David said mildly. "Not for long, I'd assume, if it's incriminating evidence. He'd probably want to get rid of that as soon as possible."

A sense of urgency shot through Amie. "I need to search his apartment," she said, scrambling to her feet.

David laughed.

"I'm not joking." Amie crossed her arms. "Are you gonna help me?"

David's expression was frozen at the crossroads of amused and appalled. Finally, he rubbed his face. "Okay, sit down."

"There's no—"

"Sit."

In a tiny act of rebellion, Amie squatted instead.

"What's this about, really?" David asked. "It can't just be that you want to clear my name. There isn't enough evidence against me; I'm not in any imminent danger. Why are you so determined to get mixed up in this?"

Amie looked at the floor. She didn't want to tell David about her guilt. She knew what he'd say—they'd already had this conversation. He couldn't understand.

"Ziya seemed excited by the prospect of solving the mystery," she said instead. "I . . . I want to impress her."

Amie was almost insulted at how readily David seemed to accept this excuse. She wasn't *that* pathetic about her ex-girlfriend, was she?

"Fine." He heaved himself up off the table, sighing heavily. "For young love, I'll help you." He snapped his fingers. "And now you have something to text her about!"

"Maybe I should wait to see how successful we are," Amie said hesitantly.

"No, text her now." David headed for the door. "If you get us arrested for this, we'll need her to bail us out."

Chapter One

Alley-vous

Day 371 I.L.

Amie was in a weird mood.

She'd hoped that seeing Ziya would improve her spirits. However, she quickly realized her mistake as her unsettled mood leaked into the friend date, souring the vibes. Not wanting to wait for Ziya to suggest they "give it more time," Amie had faked a migraine and left early.

Awkwardly carrying the Styrofoam box of fettuccine alfredo Ziya had insisted she take home with her, Amie disembarked the bus and began the walk back home.

She might've missed the figure standing in the alleyway next to her building if it hadn't been for the dim glow of the cigarette he was smoking. Amie squinted through the shadows to see Benny leaning against the wall next to the emergency exit.

They made eye contact. Benny lifted his chin in greeting.

"Hey," he said sullenly. The man wasn't the most cheerful person Amie had ever met—in fact, she wasn't sure she'd ever seen him genuinely smile. But she'd also never seen him look this troubled.

"Hi." Amie slowed to a stop. She didn't have an established rapport with Benny, unless anyone would consider multiple unanswered texts about a finicky radiator a rapport. But something about his expression made her ask, "Everything okay?"

Benny shrugged. "Just some personal shit." He nodded at the box in Amie's hands. "What's that?"

"Fettuccine alfredo?" Amie popped open the top, as if Benny wouldn't believe her unless she showed the food. "I was out with my . . . my ex. Had to leave early. I'm honestly not that hungry, but she told me to take it, so . . ."

"I'll take it," Benny said, holding out a hand.

Amie gave a start. "Oh!" She struggled to secure the top back onto the box, walking over to him. "Sure, take it."

"Thanks." Benny accepted the food from her. "I was supposed to eat with my . . . ex, but she left."

Amie raised her eyebrows, surprised to find a commonality with her landlord. "You hang out with your ex, too?"

Benny dropped the cigarette, grinding it under his foot. "No. The ex thing is pretty new." He scowled. "Like, *today* new."

"Oh." Amie resisted the urge to wince. "Sorry."

"'swhatever," he mumbled. "Just sucks to get dumped, you know? I tried calling her to see if we could talk, but it went straight to voicemail."

"That sucks," Amie said sympathetically. "You just have to give her some time. And you know what they say about fish and the sea."

Benny stared at her blankly. "What?"

"That there's . . . there's plenty of fish," Amie said haltingly. "In it. The sea."

"Oh. Right." Benny looked like he was regretting putting out his cigarette so soon. "Yeah, I know. I'm already seeing this other girl, and she's all right."

"Oh!" Amie said. "That's . . . fast."

"Nah, we've had a situationship for a while."

Amie blinked. "And is the situation . . . polyamory?"

Benny gave her a strange look. "I was seeing her in secret. That's why my girlfriend broke up with me."

Amie didn't know why *she* was the one getting the strange look. "Right," she said, regretting staying in this conversation for as long as she had. "Well—"

"I'd had some close calls before," Benny continued, unaware that Amie was no longer the sympathetic audience she had been just seconds before. He jerked a thumb at the emergency exit. "A couple times I had to send the other girl out this way before buzzing my girlfriend up. It was hot, sneaking around like that."

Amie was trying desperately to rein in the sour look that was threatening to take over her expression. "Uh-huh."

"But she finally caught us." Benny's mouth twisted as he appeared to fight back a swell of emotion. "Whatever," he said, his voice rough.

Amie silently counted to five, which she felt was the appropriate amount of time to wait before making her escape. "Well," she said after the interlude, "I hope the pasta brings you some comfort. I'm gonna head in."

"Yeah, me too." Benny moved to follow her out of the alleyway. He stopped as he saw that Amie wasn't moving.

She looked pointedly at the cigarette butt squished into the pavement. "Are you going to . . . ?"

Benny grunted, crouching down to pick up the cigarette. He began walking to the back of the building.

Amie shifted back and forth, not knowing if she should wait for him to return or just leave. She opted for walking very slowly to the front door.

There was a deep *clang* as Benny opened the lid of the dumpster, then a louder slam as he let the top fall closed. By the time Amie reached the door, Benny had returned.

"I'm gonna check my mailbox," she said as they entered the lobby, trying to avoid an awkward walk upstairs. "Goodnight!"

"Night."

Amie listened to Benny's echoing footsteps, frowning as her stomach growled.

Darn, she thought. *Guess I* was *hungry.*

Chapter Eight
An Awkward Exit

Day 2 A.L.

Amie let David lay out the plan. One, because she knew he'd feel better if he got to make a plan, and two, she didn't really have one anyway.

"I will lure Benny out of his apartment," David said, twirling his keys on one finger as they stood by his door. "Once we're gone, you'll have ten minutes to search his place. Let's coordinate our watches."

"I don't have a watch." Amie said, waving her phone at him. "Our phones should have the exact same time."

David pulled his phone out of his pocket, intrigued. "Do they really?"

They spent the following twelve seconds silently waiting to see if the clocks on their phones changed at the same time. When they did, David let out a satisfied "Hmph."

"Great. By the ten-minute mark, you need to be out of there."

"Got it," Amie said. "Ten minutes and I'm out of there. What am I looking for?"

David stuffed his phone back into his pocket. "How should I know? You were the one who wanted to search his apartment!"

"Okay, okay." Amie frowned. "I'll . . . figure it out."

Apparently, there was something in Amie's expression that didn't give David much confidence in her figuring it out. He sighed. "Just look for anything that seems out of place. Check drawers and closets. And garbage cans. Definitely check the garbage cans."

Amie perked up at receiving instructions she could follow. "Garbage cans. I can do that."

"All right." David opened the door and gestured for Amie to exit. "Let's do this."

* * *

Benny wasn't home. Which would have been convenient for someone trying to sneak into his apartment, presuming that person had a key or knew how to pick a lock. After a quick inventory of keys and skills, Amie and David came to the conclusion that they were zero for two.

"He could've gone out for the evening," David said. They were standing in the stairwell, looking through the small window that faced the street. "We could be here for hours."

"It's only been thirty minutes," Amie said, resting her forehead against the window pane. "Just wait a little longer."

"You sure you don't have some time loop knowledge that can tell us where he is right now and when he's coming back?"

"I'm not *psychic*," Amie retorted. "Just because I know a lot about things that happened on Monday doesn't mean I'm supernaturally attuned to everyone's habits and whereabouts now."

"Worth asking." David leaned against the wall. "Do you know where Benny was Monday evening?"

"Why?"

"Well," he said, "if Savannah was killed that night, but you knew he was in his apartment watching football all evening, then that gives him an alibi. And it gives *me* the excuse to abandon this mission and get back to my machine."

Amie stepped back from the window, sifting through her memories of the time loop to see if Benny appeared in any of them.

"I'd see him in the morning, sometimes," she said. "He'd leave the building around eleven thirty AM and get into his car, which was parked across the street." She closed her eyes, thinking harder. "His car was back by mid-afternoon. I never saw him after—"

Amie stopped suddenly, a memory coming back to her.

"I saw him once," she said, struggling to remember. "I'd left my date with Ziya early. He was smoking outside the building." She recounted her interaction with the landlord to the best of her ability, including the fresh breakup, the cheating, and the regrettable gifting of leftovers.

"So he *was* home that evening," David said, pushing off the wall as he made to leave.

"Hang on!" Amie protested, grabbing him by the shirt sleeve. "We don't know what time Savannah was killed. He could've just come from killing her, or gone back out after!"

David sagged against the wall again with defeat. "Around what time did you see him?"

Amie started doing the mental math, then gave up and began doing the verbal math. "We were always seated at a quarter after seven. I think I bailed about thirty minutes in. It was just as the food arrived, I remember that. Say, twenty minutes to take the bus, five-minute walk home from the park. So . . . a little after eight?"

"Do you remember anything else?" David pressed. "Any other details?"

Amie squeezed her eyes shut, scrunching up her face, as if that would help sharpen the memory. "He was wearing Crocs," she offered.

"A clue!" David exclaimed, sardonic.

A loud *thunk* echoed through the stairwell as someone opened the door on the ground floor. They looked at each other.

"Have you been keeping watch?" David whispered.

"I *just* opened my eyes."

There was a brief, quiet scramble as they positioned themselves as two people casually conversing in a stairwell.

"That's so interesting," Amie said loudly. "Tell me more about that."

They had a silent, two-second-long argument as David mimed his protestation at being given the bulk of the effort in their simulated conversation.

"Sure, no problem," he finally relented as the footsteps grew louder. "Let me just think about where to start . . ."

Amie glanced over to see Benny trudging his way toward them. A takeout bag swung from one hand, a six-pack of beer in the other. His eyes were glued to the stairs as he climbed.

"Oh, hi Benny," Amie said, her voice a little too high-pitched. She cleared her throat as David visibly relaxed, saved from having to do any more improvisation. "How's it going?"

Benny looked up as he arrived on the landing. Dark circles hung under his eyes. "Hey. It's going."

"Have a good evening!" Amie called after him as he continued his ascent. She received a half-hearted wave over the shoulder in response.

They waited silently until the slam of Benny's apartment door echoed down the stairwell.

"Okay," Amie said, heading for the steps to the third floor. "Go time."

"Hang on." David put out an arm to stop her. "The man just got dinner. Shouldn't we let him eat first?"

Amie huffed impatiently. "He also got a bunch of beers. If he gets drunk before you show up at his door, he's just gonna tell you to come back tomorrow." She started up the stairs.

"If he gets drunk, he's probably not meticulously destroying any evidence tonight," David grumbled, following.

Amie hid in the stairwell as David knocked on the door to Benny's apartment. As the silence stretched on, she began to fidget nervously. *What if he's panicking and destroying the evidence?*

Finally, she heard a door click open.

"Hey there!" David said. His tone was so chipper Amie almost didn't recognize his voice. "Sorry to bother. Seeing you just now reminded me that I think I've got rats or mice or something in my apartment. Would you be able to set up some traps?"

"I'll give you the traps," came Benny's voice. "You can set them up yourself."

"Ah, right, that's going to be a problem." Amie assumed Benny had retreated into his apartment as David's volume increased to call after him. "You see, morally I'm against trapping animals, even with the catch-and-release ones. I think they should be allowed to roam free—but I'd prefer if they didn't roam free in my apartment. I'm fine with *you* setting up the traps, though. I just can't do it myself. Morally."

Amie winced. The excuse had seemed solid when they'd developed it back in David's apartment. Hearing it in action, however, was making her confidence in their plan plummet.

Thankfully, Benny seemed to have come to the conclusion that setting up the traps himself would make this interaction end faster than if he tried to argue.

"Thank you so much," David said in response to Benny's silent enlistment. "After you. We just have to move the oven away from the wall . . ."

As the two men approached the door to the stairwell, Amie squeezed herself into a corner. The door swung toward her as Benny pushed it open, just grazing her knees as she pressed her back against the wall. Once she was satisfied that the coast was clear, Amie leapt to her feet and slipped into the hallway.

Adrenaline shot through her body as she saw Benny's door was propped open by a singular Jenga block. *I can't believe that worked*, she thought as she retrieved the block and entered the apartment.

"Ten minutes," she said to herself, pulling out her phone and setting a timer.

Timer set, she walked into the apartment and looked around. It was surprisingly tidy. Amie wasn't sure what she'd expected, but considering the neatness came as a surprise to her, she supposed she'd been expecting Benny to have the same amount of care for his apartment as he seemed to have for those of his tenants (very little).

She thought back to David's advice: Look for anything out of place. Drawers, closets.

Running to Benny's bedroom, she slid open the door and made a beeline for his dresser.

"Sorry, sorry," she whispered as she searched for any non-clothing items. She didn't know why searching through someone's underwear felt so much more wrong than breaking into their apartment, but she felt a lot better once she was able to conclude that particular search.

Finding nothing of note in the dresser, she moved on to Benny's closet. Hoodie, hoodie, hoodie, hoodie, nice suit in a dry cleaning bag . . . the floor was carpeted with a variety of sneakers and sandals (and one familiar pair of Crocs). No intriguing boxes or other mysterious items stuffed into the back.

Amie ran to the kitchen. She began pulling open drawers and cabinets, searching for anything strange hidden among silverware or bowls or . . . six boxes of "Luke Legend's Alpha King Organic Protein Powder."

She closed the door to the protein powder cabinet, slumping against the counter in defeat.

What am I even looking for? she thought. *Maybe he didn't find anything in Savannah's apartment after all.*

Amie scanned the space, looking for anything out of place, anywhere Benny might've hidden something.

"Garbage cans. Definitely check the garbage cans." David's voice came back to her in a flash as her gaze alighted on the garbage can in the kitchen.

She ran over and stomped on the pedal of the can, peering in. There was barely anything inside: just a banana peel, coffee grounds, and a few other food remains.

Amie let the lid of the can fall with a dull *clunk* and sprinted back into the bedroom. A small wastebasket sat by the bed, and Amie steeled herself before looking inside.

The majority of the contents were tissues, plus a light blue sock that looked too small for Benny. The sock almost took the prize for most intriguing item, if there hadn't been several torn pieces of paper stuffed among the tissues. They were all seemingly parts of a whole, having been ripped up and shoved into the basket.

Delicately, she used her thumb and pointer finger to pick out the pieces. The paper was soft and wrinkled, as if it had been crumpled up at least once. There was printed text on one side and a photograph on the other. Amie began laying the pieces on the floor, text side up, trying to match the jagged edges to each other.

A loud, muffled voice in the distance caught her attention. Amie froze, two pieces in her hands, as she listened.

"—still think there might be a couple spots that would benefit from traps," David was saying. "Oh! Did I mention the weird sound my refrigerator's been making? Shoot, forgot to mention that. We might as well go look now while I have you. No?"

There was an unintelligible response from Benny.

"Ah of course, dinner." David's voice grew markedly louder. "MOST IMPORTANT MEAL OF THE DAY, I SAY. YOU HAVE DINNER WAITING FOR YOU, OF COURSE, I DON'T WANT TO HOLD YOU UP ANY LONGER."

Amie collected the pieces of paper and shoved them into the front pocket of her shorts. She hurried out of the room, wondering if she could pull off the "hide behind the door then slip out" trick a second time. The sound of a doorknob rattling sent her scrambling back into the bedroom, sliding the door partially closed as she hid behind it.

"Can I ask you something?" David's voice came from the other side of the apartment as the door opened. "Landlording. That must be a stressful gig. All the people in this building, only one you. How do you keep the pressure from getting on top of you?"

"Uh . . ." The door shut. "I dunno. I just do it, I guess."

"Just do it," David said. "Wow. What a motto. Someone should use that for something."

Amie heard a quiet *thump*, which she assumed was Benny sitting on his couch. Hoping she was right and that Benny's back was now to her, she risked a peek around the corner of the sliding door.

Benny was indeed sitting on the couch, digging through the takeout bag that sat on the coffee table in front of him. Off to the side, David was anxiously shifting his weight back and forth, eyes darting around the apartment.

"Want a beer?" Benny asked, seemingly trying to make the best of his uninvited guest.

"Oh, I should probably get—" David's sentence was cut off by a yelp as his eyes met Amie's.

"Whoa, what?" Benny asked, sitting up as Amie ducked back behind the door. "What's wrong?"

"Nothing, it's nothing," David said hurriedly. "Twinge in my back. When you get to be my age it'll happen all the time. Just gotta stretch it out."

"Did you see something?" Benny pressed. "Like a . . . like a ghost?"

"A ghost? No, I didn't see a ghost. Why?"

"I . . . never mind."

Amie's heart leapt into her throat as a loud chiming emerged from her front pocket. *The ten-minute alarm.*

Thankfully, Benny had chosen that moment to switch on the television. The sudden blast of sound drowned out the noise of the alarm (and the subsequent sounds of Amie frantically scrambling to shut the alarm off). She heaved a sigh of relief as she returned the traitorous device to her pocket.

"Oh, I love this show," David commented. "Incredible writing."

"That's a paper towel commercial."

"Ah."

Amie took stock of her situation. Benny's back was to her while on the couch, but he'd see her if she tried to sneak out the front door. She could wait until he needed to use the bathroom, but he'd have to walk through the bedroom to get there.

So . . . she'd hide!

Amie tiptoed over to the bed, lay down, and shimmied underneath. Her hand hit something soft, and she instinctively swiped it away from her. The item went flying out from under the bed, landing silently on the floor a couple feet in front of Amie. Squinting in the dim light, she saw it was the matching sock to the one she'd found in the wastebasket.

Maybe now he won't have to throw out the other one, Amie thought, shifting to a more comfortable position. (That was, as comfortable as one can get hiding under the bed of a man who may have been involved in the murder of one's neighbor while waiting for said man to go use the bathroom.)

She suddenly realized that David might have been trying to contact her, or that she at least should be updating him on her plan. Squirming a bit, she managed to extract her phone from her pocket and bring it up to her face.

There were, in fact, multiple messages from David, beginning with the **WE'RE COMING BACK** variety before transitioning to a general **WHAT ARE YOU GOING TO DO?** sentiment.

There was also a text from Ziya, received just a couple minutes before: **Where are you?**

Amie's brow furrowed as she read the message, then reread it (which was a pointless endeavor, seeing how it was only three words and therefore pretty difficult to misread on the first go).

Deciding that Ziya had probably meant to text someone else, Amie swiped the notification away and shot off a message to David:

Amie: I'm hiding under the bed. Gonna try to slip out when he uses the bathroom

Bubbles appeared to indicate that David was typing. About thirty seconds later (David was the slowest texter Amie had ever encountered), he responded:

David: Okay. I will try to get him to drink more. Hang tight.

"If the offer still stands, I will take that beer, actually," David said from the other room.

A studio audience burst into applause through the TV's speakers. There was a loud snap as a beer can was opened.

"You know, I used to be able to chug one of these in five seconds," he continued.

"No way," came Benny's half-interested response.

"Yes way. I was kind of a legend. Bet it'd take you more than twenty."

Benny's interest was growing. "Nah, I could do it in ten, easy."

"No way."

There was another snap as a fresh can was opened. "Time me."

Amie shook her head in amazement as David began counting. She couldn't believe that actually worked.

"—eight . . . nine . . . te—"

"Done!" came Benny's proud announcement, followed by an even prouder burp.

"Very impressive," David said.

"Now you go."

"Oh, no, I couldn't—"

"Dude, I went, now you have to go. Ready . . . set . . ."

Amie rested her chin on her folded arms as Benny began counting. Her phone lit up from where it sat on the floor next to her.

Seriously, where the hell is everyone?

Starting to feel bad that Ziya couldn't find her friends, Amie picked up the phone and tapped out a reply. **Wrong person!**

"—twenty-one . . . twenty-two . . . did you finish?"

"Intermission," David choked out between gasps for air. "I think I'm halfway through."

"Forget it, man." Benny was chuckling. "It's okay."

"Oh, thank god."

Hoping that Benny had a weak bladder, Amie reached down to her pocket to pull out the pieces of paper she'd retrieved from the wastebasket. Shifting her weight to one arm, she used her opposite hand to try putting together the photo side of the ripped-up paper.

"Can I be real with you for a second?" she heard Benny ask.

"That's one of my favorite ways for people to be with me," David responded. "Second only to 'not.'"

There was a brief pause.

"Anyway, you were saying?"

"I just, I thought you were kind of a weird dude, if I'm being honest. No offense."

"None taken."

"But my girlfriend broke up with me, and I really didn't want to be alone tonight. So thanks for hanging with me."

Another brief pause.

"Glad I could be here for you," David finally said, his voice strained. "Sorry to hear about your breakup."

"It's fine. Shit happens."

"Sure does."

"But you're all right, man. Even if you did kill Savannah."

Amie froze as the pause that followed stretched far beyond the definition of "brief."

"I . . . didn't do that," David finally said.

"Oh, sorry, I didn't mean it like that. I mean, I don't give a shit. She was a total bi—" Benny stopped. "Do you . . . believe in ghosts?" he asked tentatively.

"I guess I'm agnostic about it. Don't really believe or disbelieve. Do you think you're being haunted?"

"No. I mean, I don't know. I guess I'm acrostic about it, too."

"Has something happened to make you think—"

"Let's just watch the show."

Returning to her garbage puzzle, Amie put the final pieces into place. She'd immediately identified Benny. The rest of the pieces came together to reveal his lips pressed against the cheek of a laughing woman, who appeared to be the photographer of the selfie.

Amie deflated a bit. *Benny's ex-girlfriend*, she thought. He must have torn up the photo and thrown it out after she broke up with him the other night. Nothing to do with Savannah after all.

Remembering the text on the other side, she flipped over the top right piece to reveal the first few words: **Benny—**

The words were illuminated by Amie's phone lighting up again. Huffing with annoyance, she looked at it.

AMELIA TELLER. I AM IN YOUR BUILDING. WHERE ARE YOU?

Amie's eyes widened. *Ziya's HERE?*

Before she could begin to formulate a response (or even just move past thinking *Ziya's HERE?* over and over again), David's raised voice caught her attention.

"Hey! Where are you heading off to? They're about to . . . say who won . . . the . . . thing."

David clearly had not been paying attention to whatever they were watching.

"Gotta go piss. It's fine, I can pause it."

The apartment was plunged into an ominous silence as Benny paused the television.

Amie quickly gathered up the pieces of paper and her phone. She held her breath, watching the door to the bedroom slide open as Benny's socked feet entered the room. He closed the door behind him, then crossed the room into the adjoining bathroom.

As light from the bathroom flooded into the bedroom, Amie became aware of a detrimental flaw in her plan: Benny wasn't closing the door. Unless he had an extremely convenient habit of closing his eyes while urinating, he'd definitely see her if she tried to make an exit.

Heart sinking, she put down the papers and unlocked her phone. Underscored by the sound of Benny heeding nature's call, she texted David: **Not gonna work. He left the door open. He'd see me leave.**

"Goddammit," came David's voice from the other room.

"What'd you say?" Benny called from the bathroom.

"Nothing!"

Amie swiped on her phone, opening her messages with Ziya.

Amie: What are you doing here??
Ziya: You weren't answering your doorbell, so I tried David. He buzzed me up
Amie: My original question still stands
Ziya: I told you not to solve any murders without me!!

Amie looked up as the toilet flushed. She shot off a response before locking her phone again:

Amie: Hiding under Benny's bed. David's trying to distract him, but I have no way of leaving

The bathroom light switched off. Amie held her breath again as Benny emerged.

Her whole body tensed as his feet stopped right in front of where she was hiding. She had a grim, scientifically supported feeling that the rest of him had stopped as well.

"Where did . . . ?" Benny mumbled.

A hand came into view, and Amie squeezed her eyes shut, as if the man wouldn't be able to see her if she couldn't see him. After several painfully long seconds, she chanced a peek through her eyelashes.

The hand had disappeared, as did the sock Amie had flung out from beneath the bed in disgust. She silently cursed herself for being so careless, then applauded herself for her seemingly successful "if I can't see him, he can't see me" strategy.

"Hey, Hallie." Amie tensed again as Benny spoke in a low voice. "Um, just wanted to see if we can talk? Feel like things happened really fast, and I think . . . I dunno, I think we can fix this. You left your socks here, so if you want them . . . let me know. This is Benny, by the way. Um, you probably knew that. Okay. Cool. Bye."

Benny's feet slowly pivoted, and there was a rustle in the direction of the wastebasket. He walked out.

Amie let out a slow breath. Her mind, in contrast, was racing. *Hallie? Like "Hallie From The Park" Hallie?* That *Hallie?*

What were the odds? How many people were named Hallie? And if it *was* Hallie From The Park, who was the woman in the photo?

Moving to inspect the papers again, a new message on her phone caught her attention.

You're not gonna like this, Ziya said, **but I think you have to climb the balconies.**

Amie gave a start as the television blared again. She pinched the bridge of her nose as she considered this new plan. Ziya was right; she didn't like it.

Every apartment had a small . . . honestly, the word "balcony" was generous. Every apartment had a small ledge surrounded by a railing accessed by a sliding door in the bedroom. Each ledge was several feet wide and only about a foot deep. It was an architectural anomaly, mainly used by the occupants of the building for hanging wet clothes, storing dirty shoes, and not much else.

Amie winced at the thought of climbing from balcony to balcony. She didn't exactly have a fear of heights. A more accurate diagnosis would be that she had a fear of *falling* from a great height, even in situations where people assured her that it was very unlikely she would fall. Not to mention situations where she *was* very likely to fall, like *climbing across the balconies of the third floor of her apartment building.*

And where would she even go? Both she and David lived on the floor below. Did she have to climb *down* too?

As the minutes ticked by, Amie became more and more resigned. Her phone remained dark. Ziya was waiting for an update, and David had either become incredibly engrossed in whatever Benny had on the TV, or he was also lacking ideas.

What's happening? Ziya finally asked. **Did he catch you?**

No, Amie replied. She sighed, resigned. **I'm going to climb the balconies**.

She sent a similar text to David, then rolled out from under the bed. Climbing to her feet, she securely stuffed the papers and her phone into her pockets.

The television continued to blare in the other room as she picked her way across the bedroom to the sliding door. Amie touched the handle, pausing. The lock was already unlatched, but she knew these doors had a tendency for squeaking. She waited, listening for a swell in volume from the TV.

With extraordinary good timing, David's voice rang out from the other room.

"Well, I'd better head back to my place to check the traps," he said. "Thank you for the beer."

Amie eased the door open as Benny responded, wincing at the squeaking of rubber on plastic. She paused, listening, hoping that Benny's own voice in his ears would help to muffle the squeaks. After a few seconds of no one angrily storming into the bedroom, she slipped outside. There was a loud applause break from the television, and with that cue, Amie pulled the door shut behind her.

It was a muggy evening. The sky was full of pink clouds with dark-purple shadows, the glow of the setting sun illuminating the way as Amie sidled along the width of the balcony.

Amie never before had an issue being out on her own balcony (so long as she had a firm grip on the doorway), but the knowledge of what was to come made every moment she was out there feel ten times more perilous.

Stopping at the railing, Amie assessed her next obstacle. There was a gap about a foot and a half wide between Benny's balcony and the next. Against her better judgment, she looked down into the gap, her breath temporarily stalling as she saw the distance to the ground. Her vision swam as she took a hurried step back. She had to focus on her breathing for a full minute before she felt assured that her heart wasn't going to pound its way out of her chest, grow little legs, and go running back into Benny's apartment.

This was impossible. Who thought this was a good idea?

"Amie?" The hissed whisper cut through the ambient noise of distant traffic. "Amie!"

The whisperer's target audience looked out toward the source of the noise. From a balcony two doors down and one floor below, a hand shot out to wave at her.

"Ziya?" Amie whispered, squinting through the long shadows cast by the surrounding buildings. Her ex-girlfriend was standing on David's balcony, pulling up her dark red crop top as she leaned dangerously far over the railing to see Amie.

"It's okay, don't talk," Ziya replied, gold hoops swinging from her ears as she waved her hands. "Don't want him to hear you!"

"He has the TV on at max volume," came David's voice from out of Amie's line of sight. "So at the very least, he won't hear anything when Amie falls to her death."

"*Unhelpful*," Ziya said as Amie's stomach did a flip. "Hey. Don't listen to him. You just need to go two balconies over and climb down."

"Oh, just that?" Amie said, her voice jumping half an octave.

An even higher noise flew out of her mouth as Ziya threw a leg over the railing, straddling it so she could get a better view of Amie.

"Ziya!" Amie said as loud as she dared. "Get back on the balcony!"

"It's fine! This is a skort."

"That's *not* what I was concerned about."

"I'm gonna stay here until you make it down."

"David!" Amie said pleadingly.

"What am *I* supposed to do?" came David's frustrated reply.

"Hold her arm or something, at least!"

Amie watched Ziya extend an arm to the out-of-view David.

"There," Ziya said. "He's got me." To Amie's horror, she released the railing with her other hand and leaned out even further, waving Amie over. "Now come on!"

"Okay, okay!" Bolstered by her fear of Ziya taking a dive over the railing, Amie turned back to the balcony next door. Holding on tight to the railing, she lifted one leg and stepped over it, mirroring Ziya's straddle. Her second leg followed, and she found herself on the outside of the railing.

"How's it going?" Ziya called.

"Haven't heard any sickening thumps yet, so that's promising," David said.

"I'm revoking your speaking privileges."

Worried that replying might break her concentration, Amie squeezed her lips shut and focused on not falling. She transferred her right hand to the next balcony's railing, gripping it so tight her knuckles hurt. As she looked over to make sure she had a clear spot to relocate her right foot, she caught another glimpse of the ground below.

Amie's stomach once again did a flip. At this rate, she was considering entering it in the next Olympic gymnastics qualifiers.

Carefully, she took one step over to the next balcony. Without giving herself time to overthink, she unlatched her left hand, grabbed the other railing, and pulled the rest of her body over the gap. She clambered over the rail to the safety of the balcony.

Sucking in a deep breath, she sagged against the perpendicular railing.

"I see her!" Ziya was waving from below, as if Amie might have forgotten where she was since they last spoke a minute before.

"Can you get down from there?" Amie begged.

"I'll get down when you get down."

Amie groaned, stepping over a pair of mud-caked boots as she moved across the balcony. "What are you even *doing* here?"

"I told you!"

"You're saying you abandoned Lil Screw and jazz-funk because you didn't want to miss out on—" Amie paused, deciding it was probably not the best idea to say "me breaking into my landlord's apartment" while still in such close proximity to said apartment.

"On the mystery, yeah," Ziya finished. "I don't even like Lil Screw, anyway. I knew the real action was with you two."

"Hopefully that won't be true." Amie had reached the end of the balcony. Logically, she knew this gap couldn't be any wider than the last one, and yet it somehow seemed to stretch out farther than she could possibly reach. "I think I'm gonna call it here, you guys. I live on this balcony now. Feel free to visit any time."

There was a brief scuffle from below. Ziya and David appeared on the narrow side of David's balcony, looking up at her. Now that Amie was closer, she could see the glittery eyeshadow on Ziya's lids winking at her as she gazed up at Amie.

"Look at you! You're so close!" Ziya held her arms out over the railing. "I could literally catch you if you fell."

"I don't think that's true," Amie said weakly, clinging to the railing.

"Well, David could catch you."

"I don't think that's true," David echoed.

"Oh my god, I'm surrounded by pessimists."

The words "I prefer 'realist'" died in Amie's throat as she looked down at the ground, which had somehow remained the same terrifying distance from her as every other time she'd looked at it.

"Come on, Amie." Ziya crossed her arms, her tone growing serious. "Be a big girl and climb the railing."

"I can't." Like a tongue to cold metal, Amie felt her arms fusing with the railing. "I can't do it."

"I have some rope," David offered. "It's not very strong, but . . ."

"Amie," Ziya said, "if you come down, I'll tell you why I really came."

Interest piqued, Amie peered over the railing. "Why?"

"Come down and I'll tell you."

"No, tell me first."

"Get down here safely, and then—"

"Oh my *god!*" David burst out. "Just do it at the same time! The mosquitos are eating me alive. Let's keep this moving, please!"

Amie and Ziya looked at each other.

"Fine."

"Fine."

Amie took a deep breath, then pulled her leg up over the rail. She paused, giving Ziya a pointed look that read, *Now your turn*.

"O*kay*." Ziya sighed. "So . . . after we broke up—"

"Oh, this sounds personal." David covered his ears and turned away. "Let me know when you're done. Or if she falls. Whichever comes first." Despite his words, Amie saw him keeping her in his peripheral vision as she continued easing over the rail.

"After we broke up," Ziya repeated, speaking slowly, "I just started saying yes to everything. My schedule was *packed*. Like, think of the most random thing that you've made fun of me for doing, and I probably did something even weirder than that."

"Like what?" Amie asked, her voice strained. She'd managed to pull her other leg over the rail, and was working herself up to face the next balcony.

"Like . . . I dragged my friends to this art show where all the frames were empty. And you were supposed to read the description of each piece and then stare at the empty frame and imagine what the piece would look like based on its description."

Amie, who didn't like to judge other people's definitions of art, said, "That sounds kind of interesting."

"It had a thirty-dollar admission fee."

"Not *that* interesting." Amie successfully transferred her right hand and flattened her back against the railing.

"Oh, and tarantula yoga." There was a shudder in Ziya's voice as she remembered. "That was . . . rough. Didn't think white people could misappropriate yoga more than they already have, but they figured out a way."

She paused. "The spiders sucked, too. Anyway, it got to the point where I'd start double booking stuff just because I was worried someone might cancel and I'd be left without plans." There was a snort of self-deprecation. "My friends started getting pissed. Because of the double bookings, and the ridiculous admission prices. And the tarantulas. Come on, don't stop now, big step."

"I feel like you're just saying stuff to distract me." Amie's vision wobbled as she pressed her back to the railing. "Are you going anywhere with this?"

"Oh my *god*, okay. Basically, I was burning myself out and didn't know how to stop. It felt like my brain was blasting sped up over-compressed hyperpop twenty-four seven. My friends literally held an intervention that was just them forcing me to do an evening of self-care at home."

"That was nice of them." Amie unlatched her right hand and leaned forward, grabbing onto the next railing.

"Yeah, they're great, I love them to death. And then you and I had our incredibly drawn-out date—"

"Friend date," Amie said through gritted teeth, taking care not to look down as she stepped over the gap.

"And the whole time my brain was just . . . quiet."

Following her strategy from last time, Amie brought over her left hand and foot before she had the chance to freeze. She clutched the railing, breathing heavily.

"You did it!" Ziya cheered. "Now we just have to get you down . . ."

Who's to say why the bird chose that moment to dive-bomb Amie? It's possible it spotted one of the many mosquitoes David had been complaining about, hovering right by her head. Or perhaps it mistook her for a baby bird, reluctant to take her first leap out of the nest and in need of a push. Or maybe it had watched the entirety of Amie's precarious journey across the balconies and was disappointed that the most dramatic moment was when her ex-girlfriend not-so-subtly implied that Amie brought a calmness to her life that she had yet to find an equal replacement for.

Be it a natural predatory instinct or an incapacity to comprehend the nuances of human emotions (specifically those of the sapphic variety), a bird chose that moment to dive-bomb Amie.

Ultimately, it was Amie's anxiety-induced grip on the railing that saved her from plummeting to the ground. Even the sudden appearance of an animal zipping past her head wasn't enough to startle her out of letting go of the rail.

Her feet were another story. Instinct taking over, Amie stumbled back onto nothing but empty air, and gravity rudely refused to make an exception. (It didn't seem like a big ask, considering how *time* had been able to do it, but alas.)

Amie's body, now anchored only by her hands on the railing, crashed into the balcony. The cement floor slammed into her stomach, knocking the wind out of her. Through the loud ringing in her ears, she could hear Ziya and David making various noises of alarm from below. A hand grabbed her ankle.

"You have to slide down," came Ziya's frantic voice. "You need to get lower so David can grab you."

Amie could only manage a hybrid groan/whine in response. The railing gave its own groan/whine in turn as it struggled against the weight of something heavier than its usual burden of damp laundry.

"*Now*, Amie. Come on."

Hearing in Ziya's voice that she was about five seconds away from attempting to climb up and bring Amie down herself, Amie managed to gasp out, "Okay!"

With great difficulty (and while keeping an eye out for any more avian interference), Amie shifted her hands from the horizontal rail onto two of the vertical rails. She painstakingly began lessening and reapplying pressure to her grip, allowing her body to steadily lose altitude.

Just as the painful burn on her hands was becoming too much to bear, she felt arms wrap around her legs. She hadn't even realized her eyes were shut until she heard Ziya's voice say, "Let go. He's got you, let go."

Keeping her eyes closed, Amie obeyed the command. She felt herself get pulled down and deposited into a smaller pair of arms.

"Holy shit," Ziya said into her ear. "Oh, we're going down, okay, careful."

Despite having done very little work in the past minute, Amie's legs had decided to clock out early for the day. As her knees buckled, Amie felt herself being eased into a sitting position on the floor of David's balcony. She slumped into the arms wrapped tightly around her, cheek pressing against a warm collarbone.

"Look at you, daredevil," Ziya murmured. Amie could hear her heart sprinting. "Who are you, and what did you do with my Amie?"

A weak "ahh" was all the commentary Amie could muster.

"Are you okay? Give me one ahh for 'yes,' two ahhs for 'no.'"

"I'm okay," Amie said. After a few seconds, she added, "Was that the kind of action you were hoping for?"

"Honestly, I was just looking for something quiet." Ziya's voice vibrated against Amie's cheek and through the rest of her body, soothing Amie's jittering nerves. Both their heartbeats were slowing, matching each other's pace. "This is pretty nice."

"It is."

Gentle fingers skimmed across Amie's forearm in a comforting caress, sending sparks through Amie's body. The hand suddenly dropped as the door to the balcony slid open, then shut again. A glass of water appeared next to Amie's face.

"What's that?" She reluctantly pulled out of Ziya's embrace to look up at David. She hadn't even noticed him leaving the balcony.

"It's *water*. Did you hit your head?"

"I'm not thirsty."

"She's not thirsty." Exasperated, David straightened. "Well, that went terribly."

Amie reached for the glass. "*Okay*, I'll drink it."

"Not that." David pulled the glass away, as if he didn't want her pity acceptance of the beverage. "Your infiltration plan."

"*My* plan?" Amie exclaimed, dismayed. "That was *your* plan!"

David pointed up at the balconies Amie had just scaled across. "Spider-Amie wasn't anywhere in *my* plan."

"You were supposed to give me ten minutes! What happened to my ten minutes?"

"This one"—David pointed accusingly at Ziya—"distracted me with the doorbell. When—"

"You know the name tag next to your apartment number says 'Garfield'?" Ziya interrupted. "I almost didn't ring the bell."

"Good, that is by design," David answered. "I don't need strangers on the street knowing my apartment number *and* my last name."

"Only that he really hates Mondays," Amie deadpanned.

"Oh, great, a clever quip. At least we know you're probably not concussed." David gestured to Ziya again. "When I went to buzz her up, Benny finished with the traps and slipped past me."

"Well, you did a really good job keeping him occupied in his apartment while I figured out my escape plan," Amie said gratefully. "So thank you for that."

"Eh." David waved a hand dismissively, his curmudgeon act losing steam after being shown genuine appreciation. "Glad you're safe, kid."

The trio migrated inside.

"That might not have been a complete waste of time," Amie said, settling onto the couch. "I heard Benny leaving a message for his ex-girlfriend when I was hiding under the bed. I think I might've met her on Monday."

"And met her and met her and met her?" David asked from the kitchen.

Ziya looked at David with a curious expression, like she couldn't determine if he was joking or not.

"I think she was on her way to Benny's," Amie continued, ignoring the question. "I also found this."

She began extracting the pieces of paper from her pocket, placing them down on David's coffee table. Out of the corner of her eye, she saw Ziya stand and walk over, moving a plastic container of Matchbox cars off the table and onto the floor to make room.

"These were in Benny's wastebasket," Amie explained, once again putting the pieces together photo-side up. "At first I thought it was him and his girlfriend, but then I heard him mention Hallie on the phone, and this isn't Hallie. At least, not the one I know. His ex-girlfriend could be a different Hallie, but—"

"Seems like too much of a coincidence," Ziya finished. She made to return to her seat, but David had slipped past her and commandeered the chair.

"I need to tape these together," Amie murmured as Ziya sat down next to her.

"Here." David reached over the arm of his chair, grabbing a small cardboard box. He fished out a roll of tape and tossed it to Amie.

"Thanks." With Ziya's help, she began taping the pieces together.

"Do you think she's the other woman?" David suggested. "Maybe Hallie found the photo and ripped it up out of anger."

"That's what I'm thinking," Amie agreed, accepting a piece of tape that Ziya handed to her. "When I saw Benny on Monday night, he said his girlfriend had just broken up with him. Hallie had told me just a few hours before then that she was on her way to her boyfriend's place to surprise him with dinner."

"So that's probably when she caught him cheating!" Ziya exclaimed as Amie taped together the last two pieces.

"This is all very interesting," David said, leaning back in his chair. "I'm sure Elena would be thrilled by this gossip. But Amie went in there looking for something that might explain why Benny was in the Harlows' apartment, or at least something that might show that he had a motive for killing Savannah. I hate to be a killjoy, but based on all of this, the only thing Benny seems guilty of is being an asshole. And we already knew that."

Amie had flipped over the mended paper, revealing the message printed on the opposite side.

"There might be more to Benny than we thought," she said, scanning the note as Ziya scooched closer. David stood and circled the couch to read the message over their shoulders:

Benny—

I haven't forgotten about you. Here's something to motivate you to keep our arrangement going, or this and the other photos will be sent to Hallie. And keep an eye on your mailbox—the terms may be changing soon.

Chapter Nine

2:23 AM

Day 2 A.L.

"Okay," Ziya said slowly. "Okay, so . . . okay."

"My thoughts exactly," Amie murmured, reading the message for the seventh time.

Behind them, David shifted. "So someone . . ." He paused, as if collecting his thoughts. "Someone was *blackmailing* Benny."

"With a photo of him and the woman he was cheating on his girlfriend with," Amie finished. "But what was he being black-mailed to do? Was that why he was in Savannah's apartment?"

"What do you mean?" Ziya asked.

"Maybe whatever he was being blackmailed to do involved Savannah." Amie pointed to David. "Benny said that he felt like Savannah was haunting him. What if that was stemming from guilt about something he did to her? Like . . . murder?"

A bolt of adrenaline raced through Amie. She might've just broken into the apartment of a murderer. Sure, the pursuit of this discovery was the main reason she'd broken into the apartment in the first place, but now that Benny was confirmed as a very possible murder suspect, the reality of the situation was finally hitting her.

"Another option," David mused, "is that *Savannah* was the one blackmailing him with the photos."

Amie sat up, grabbing Ziya's arm with excitement. "Could *that* have been why he was in her apartment?"

"He was looking for the photos to get rid of them." David circled back to the front of the couch and picked up the paper.

"But why?" Ziya asked, looking back and forth between them. "If he'd already been broken up with, why did it matter if he got the photos back or not?"

Amie deflated, then noticed she was still holding on to Ziya's arm. She retracted her hand. "Sorry."

"It's fine," Ziya said quickly.

"Okay." David set the letter back down and returned to his chair. "Let's say Savannah was blackmailing Benny for something."

"That gives Benny a motive for killing her," Amie said.

"So even if he didn't necessarily *need* the photos back," David continued, "their mere existence in Savannah's store or home is enough evidence to draw attention to him as a murder suspect."

"Just to play devil's advocate," Ziya said, rubbing her arm thoughtfully as David stood to attend to the squealing tea kettle, "what if it was Savannah's husband who was blackmailing Benny?"

"For what reason, though?" Amie asked.

"Well, we don't know the reason Savannah would have been blackmailing him, either," Ziya pointed out, seeming determined to continue her pursuit of satanic litigation. "But it would still explain why Benny was searching their apartment."

Amie frowned, sorting through her very thin mental file on Andrew Harlow. Her strongest memory of the man was seeing him at Eons the afternoon of the time loop. She recalled the barista he spoke to going to the back, returning empty-handed with an apologetic expression. Unlike his wife, who would have absolutely made a fuss over whatever she'd asked for not being available, Andrew had quietly left.

"It's possible, I guess," she said, unconvinced. "Andrew always seemed like a pretty nice guy. Nice enough to make someone question why he was married to a person like Savannah."

"Tea, anyone?" David called from the kitchen.

"No, thanks," Amie and Ziya replied in unison.

"I'm just saying, we know the bookstore was struggling," Ziya continued. "Savannah wouldn't sell, so maybe Andrew was blackmailing Benny for money."

"You *really* want it to be the husband, don't you?" Amie asked wryly.

A smile split Ziya's face. "Well, I called it pretty early," she admitted. "It'd be very impressive of me if I ended up being right."

"Unfortunately," David said, returning to his chair with a steaming mug of tea, "really wanting a person to be the culprit isn't enough to determine their guilt. *Plus—*" He raised his voice, and only then did Amie realize she and Ziya were still chuckling with each other and paying very little attention to what he had been saying. She turned her focus back to David, feeling her face warm.

"—it doesn't really matter which Harlow was doing the blackmail," David continued, having regained his audience. "If Benny believed it was Savannah, that's enough motive for him to have killed her." He took a sip of tea to punctuate his point, then hissed with pain. "Ah, that's hot. Forgot I just poured that."

"I wonder if he got the photos," Amie murmured, flipping the message back over to look at the image on the back. "I didn't see any in his apartment."

"Have we considered that we're living in the twenty-first century?" Ziya asked. "If Savannah—or Andrew—had the photos, they could just be on a phone or computer somewhere."

"But how—" David snapped his fingers. "The printer."

"Explain," Amie requested.

David set his mug down on the coffee table, likely to avoid more absentminded tongue-burning. "How did the blackmailer even get access to the photos in the first place?" he asked. Then, answering his own question, he said, "The bookshop offers printing services."

"Benny went to the bookshop to print the photos," Amie said, following.

"More likely it was the woman he was seeing." Ziya sat back into the couch. "Doesn't seem like something a guy like Benny would do."

"Plus," Amie added, "this was the woman Benny was cheating on his girlfriend with. Why would he want any more physical evidence of that?"

"Good points all around," David said. "So the woman he was seeing went to the bookshop to get the photos printed. Savannah recognized Benny in the photos, somehow knew that the woman wasn't his girlfriend, and made extra copies for herself."

"Or she showed them to Andrew, and *he* made the copies," Ziya added.

"If Benny wasn't able to find physical photos to get rid of," Amie said, "then he could still be looking for digital copies. We need to find these photos."

"We need to turn this over to the police," David corrected her.

"*What?*" Amie and Ziya exclaimed.

David threw his hands into the air. "Am I the only one who remembers Amie almost *dying* twenty minutes ago? The sleuthing needs to stop before it gets any more dangerous."

"Come *on*," Amie pleaded. "You were just getting into it."

"And now I'm getting out of it." David picked up his mug, this time giving it a tentative sip before going for a bigger one.

"How is she supposed to explain to the police how she got this?" Ziya asked. "Breaking and entering is technically a crime, and last I checked, the cops don't super love people who do those. Even if they're done by someone trying to uncover a different, much worse crime. Unless that person is also a cop, which Amie is not."

David waved his free hand. "Just say you found it in the dumpster or something."

"The whole point of this was to try to get the police's attention off of you," Amie said, knowing this was a half-truth. "What're they going to think if you pop up in the middle of their investigation again?"

"And that's why I didn't want to be involved in the first place!" David exclaimed, his tea threatening to spill over the edge of the mug. "You can bring the letter to the police and leave my name out of it."

"And what if they fingerprint the letter?" Ziya asked.

Amie and David both looked at her questioningly.

"You think the blackmailer's fingerprints would be on the letter?" Amie asked.

"No," Ziya said, rolling her eyes. "Anyone with half a brain would wear gloves while handling a blackmail letter. That's, like, Criminal 101. I'm talking about *David's* fingerprints on the letter."

Amie flashed back to the very recent memory of David picking up the paper to look at it.

"Oh, goddammit." David rubbed the bridge of his nose. "Idiot."

Ziya continued over David's grumbling. "I'm pretty sure they'd see through the dumpster lie, anyway. No paper would come out of there without some mysterious substance on it."

"Just give me a couple of days," Amie said to David, who was sullenly sipping his tea. "If I can't find anything else, we'll take this to the police and try to keep your name out of it. Okay?"

David let out a long-suffering sigh. "I'm not going to sign off on any more dangerous snooping," he said. "But you can have your couple of days."

* * *

"Are your friends mad at you?" Amie asked as she and Ziya walked down the hallway.

Ziya looked up from her phone, the screen angled away from Amie as she tried to understand the question. "What?"

"For leaving them at the club. Are they mad?"

"Oh. No, they're not mad." She dropped her phone into her clutch, closing it with a definitive *snap*. "Just being annoying. They say hi."

"To me?"

"Yeah, to you."

"How did I come up?"

"I told them I was with you."

"Are they mad at me?"

"No, they love you. That's what they're being annoying about."

"How so?"

"Oh, look, we've reached the end of the hall. How time flies." Ziya pulled open the door to the stairwell. Amie's unanswered question was left hanging in the air behind them as she followed.

"Sorry you wasted your time coming here," Amie said as they reached the bottom of the stairs. "You probably expected a little more excitement than coaxing me down from the balcony like a cat stuck in a tree."

Ziya snorted. "Firstly, a cat would've been *way* easier and *way* less nerve-wracking to get down. Secondly, helping you escape a potential murderer and discovering a blackmail plot is *incredibly* exciting. Thirdly—"

"Hello, girls!"

Amie had just pushed open the stairwell door to the lobby. Elena was standing by her mailbox, a couple of envelopes in hand, beaming at the two of them.

Excellent, Amie thought with consternation as Ziya waved to the older woman. She braced herself for Elena to make things weird.

To her credit, Amie's neighbor wasted no time. "Two visits in one day," she observed cheerfully, closing her mailbox. "Just couldn't stay away from our Amie for too long, could you, Ziya?"

Ziya let out a stilted laugh, dropping her gaze to the floor. Amie blinked with surprise. Was Ziya *embarrassed*?

"She was just stopping by to get her—" Amie fell silent. When she began speaking, she'd been planning on saying that Ziya had returned to pick up her clothes from the night before. Two thoughts that she wished had come to her *before* she began that sentence were that Ziya wasn't holding any clothes, and that informing Elena that Ziya had stayed over the night before was *not* the direction Amie wanted this conversation to take.

"Purse," Ziya finished, holding up her clutch. She'd apparently recovered from her bout of embarrassment. "Amie borrowed it a while ago, and I needed it for tonight."

"Sure, sure," Elena said mildly, flapping her mail at them. "Any excuse you can find, I get it."

"Great seeing you as always, Elena," Amie said hurriedly, gesturing for Ziya to follow as she headed for the front door. "Goodnight!"

As they exited the building, Amie took Ziya by the elbow and pulled her over to one side of the door.

"She's absolutely going up to her window to spy on us," Amie explained to a wide-eyed Ziya. "She won't have a good line of sight if we stand here."

"Oh," Ziya breathed, her face relaxing. "Got it. Makes sense."

"Sorry about her."

"Pfft. It's fine. She's fun."

"That's one word for it." Amie looked up, just in case Elena was leaning out the window to get a better view of them. "I forgot I still have your clothes. I can run up and grab them."

"No, don't worry about it. I'll get them eventually."

Amie's heart lifted at the promise of eventually.

Ziya glanced up, then pressed closer to speak in Amie's ear.

"Let me know if you get any new leads," she murmured. Amie didn't think they needed to be *that* close to keep Elena from overhearing, but she wasn't complaining. "And give me a little more warning the next time you're gonna do some detective work." Ziya nudged Amie's foot with hers, which was clad in a black four-inch chunky heel. "I knew I should've worn my ratty bar sneakers tonight."

Amie swallowed, feeling her ears prickle with heat. "You got it."

"Good."

Amie's pulse quickened as Ziya's breath slid across her skin, its warmth having an almost intoxicating effect as it soaked into her body. Her head instinctively tipped away, leaving her neck open for—

—Ziya to step away. She cleared her throat, fingers dancing restlessly on her thighs. "Okay. Goodnight!"

Amie rubbed her neck as if all along she'd been trying to work out a painful muscle. "Yep, 'night."

She watched as Ziya descended the stairs and walked down the sidewalk. Her car's headlights flashed as she unlocked it, and Amie waited until she was safely inside before heading for the door of her building.

Turning around again, she walked halfway down the stairs, looking up to see Elena peering out through a stairwell window. The woman waved as Amie crossed her arms, then disappeared from view.

Rolling her eyes good-naturedly (she was in too good a mood to roll her eyes in any other way), Amie unlocked the door and returned inside.

* * *

2:09 AM

Amie blinked sleepily at the time on her phone. She was lying in bed, the sheets kicked to one side from the frustration of not being able to fall asleep.

The logical part of her brain had been pleading with the rest of her body for hours, desperately trying to convince herself that she wasn't going to wake up in a time loop again. She knew she should have just gone to sleep on the couch, since that had worked so well the night before. But Amie knew that if she started depending on the couch to get any rest, she was never going to sleep in her bed again. Plus, her massage bills would be through the roof.

(Besides, she had a strong suspicion that Ziya's presence in the other room had also contributed greatly to Amie being able to easily fall asleep the night before.)

She'd drank two cups of tea, taken a melatonin tablet, listened to rain sounds, gotten up to pee three times, finally turned off the rain sounds because they kept making her need to pee, and still, come two AM, she was awake. Sleepy, but unable to sleep.

In fact, as two AM rolled around, her anxiety kicked things up a notch. During the time loop, Amie had never been able to stay awake past 2:22 AM. Several times she'd tried to last the night, hoping that was her means of escape. Eventually, she was able to gather that no matter how awake she was, and no matter how hard she stared at the clock, she could never make it past 2:22 AM. Her last memory would be seeing the clock flip from 2:21 to 2:22, and then it would be morning.

Amie had even tried changing her phone's clock to Pacific time, as if time could be fooled by a quick settings change. (She'd be embarrassed to admit that she really thought she'd cracked it with that idea.) But as soon as the clock hit 11:22, Amie found herself once again opening her eyes on September 17, her phone reset to Eastern time and her mood reset to crestfallen.

And now here she was, actually *trying* to fall asleep but instead being kept awake by every cell in her body urgently insisting that something was *wrong* and she was in *danger* and she had to *pee again.*

Groaning, Amie rolled out of bed and went to use the bathroom for the fourth time that night. Returning to bed, she checked the time. 2:12.

What if I do get sent back? she thought. It was the kind of thought she'd been trying to keep at bay for the past few hours, hoping that if she didn't give it any attention it would go away. But as 2:22 AM neared, the unwelcome thoughts began to squeeze through her mental dam—first a trickle, then a stream, then a full-fledged torrent of *what ifs*.

What if I'm not working fast enough to solve Savannah's murder? she thought. *What if I'm supposed to be doing more, and if I can't figure it out, I'll get sent back to the 17th until I do?*

What if that's for the best?

The sheer force of the thought sent her into an upright position. *I could catch the killer. Maybe even prevent the murder. And then I'd be free again.*

The thought of returning to the time loop, even with a possible end in sight, made her feel nauseous. But if she was able to prevent someone from dying, shouldn't she? Shouldn't she want to go back and fix it? Actually make use of her time in the loop, instead of just waiting for it to end?

2:15.

As the minutes passed, Amie became more and more convinced that this was what needed to happen. She was giving the universe permission for this to happen. At 2:22, she would wake up again the morning of the 17th. She would find some kind of weapon, hide in the back of the bookshop at closing time, and try to stop the murderer. And she'd keep trying until she was successful. Now that she knew what she needed to do, she could finally make the best use of her time.

With this newfound confidence, a wave of calm passed over Amie's body, followed by a rush of excitement.

2:20.

She would tell David about the time loop, tell him Genevieve said hi, tell him she needed his help stopping a murderer. She'd text Ziya to postpone their date—or, hell, maybe she'd tell Ziya about the time loop. Prove it to her so she'd actually believe Amie once it all ended. Amie had been so scared to do so during the time loop, to say anything that might risk Ziya giving her that sad look again, even if it was only temporary. But now she knew Ziya wouldn't leave. She might laugh, tease a bit, not really believe, but she wasn't going away.

And in the time loop, Amie could prove it to her. Then Ziya could help her stop the murder. She could understand what Amie had been through. She'd know how long it had *really* been for Amie since their breakup, and how even after all that time Amie still—

2:23.

Amie did a double take as she stared at her phone. She'd become so engrossed in her thoughts that she hadn't seen 2:22 come and go.

"Oh," she said out loud. Her body suddenly felt very heavy as she came down from the sudden adrenaline rush of the past few minutes. Her mind reached for emotions that collided with one another as she tried them all on at once: disappointment, relief, vexation, confusion. Her throat began to tighten, and hot tears stung her eyes. She was back where she'd been before—having absolutely no idea what she was supposed to do next.

THUMP.

Amie looked up, startled by the loud noise above her. She was used to hearing heavy footsteps and the occasional vacuuming from the Harlows' apartment, but this sounded like someone had fallen.

She thought of Andrew Harlow alone in his apartment as she listened for any other sounds that might indicate movement above. All was silent.

Amie rubbed her fists over her eyes to clear away any excess moisture, then climbed out of bed and donned her robe. She stepped into a pair of flip-flops, grabbed her keys, and exited her apartment.

As she padded down the hall, it began to sink in that this was the first instance in a very long time (in her own timeline, at least) that Amie was awake after 2:22 AM. After entering the stairwell and reaching the first landing, she paused to look out the window, as if the world might look vastly different during this time she'd become so unfamiliar with.

To her mild disappointment, everything looked pretty much the same. This seemed to Amie like it should have been a moment of great import, but try as she might, she was having trouble mustering up strong feelings while wearing flip-flops and a robe.

Resuming her quest, she made her way up to the third floor and down the hall to apartment 3B. Amie knocked gently, pressing her ear to the door to listen for a response.

To her relief, there was a shuffling sound inside. At least she knew Andrew hadn't been knocked unconscious.

There was a muffled rattling of a chain lock, and then the door opened a crack.

"Hello?"

"Hi, Mr. Harlow." Amie spoke in a low voice so as not to wake any neighbors. "I'm Amie Teller. I live in the apartment below you? I heard a loud noise, so—"

"Sorry for waking you." Andrew still hadn't opened the door any wider. "It won't happen again."

"Oh, it's okay," Amie assured him. "I wasn't asleep. I just wanted to make sure you were okay. It sounded like someone fell."

There was a pause, and then the door opened wider. Andrew's white hair was mussed, and the corners of his eyes drooped as he scrutinized Amie. He too was wearing a robe, dark red with white vertical stripes.

"That's kind of you to check on me," he said. Amie hadn't even noticed the edge of caution that had been present in his tone until it disappeared. "I did fall, but I'm fine." He hesitated. "Were you having trouble sleeping as well? Or are you one of those young people who stays up through the night?"

Amie smiled. "Trouble sleeping," she said. "Just thinking too much."

Andrew nodded. "Me too." He pulled the door open even wider. "Would you like a cup of tea?"

In all honesty, Amie really wasn't interested in a third cup of tea. But something in her couldn't say no to the recent widower who seemed like he wanted some company. She stepped inside.

The apartment was dark, but Andrew flipped on the hallway light as the door shut.

"Watch out for that trip wire," he warned at the end of the hall. He pointed to a nearly invisible wire close to the floor. "Just step over it."

Amie silently followed his instructions. She gave the wire an inquisitive backward look as she trailed behind the older man as he made his way to the kitchen. The electric kettle on the countertop was already making noises as Andrew turned on another light.

Before Amie could question Andrew's archaic security system, he spoke:

"I saw you at the bookshop today." He gestured for Amie to take a seat. "I knew you looked familiar, but I couldn't put my finger on it. Oh, sorry for the mess."

The man began tidying a pile of papers and other miscellaneous items that were spread on the table, putting them in a cardboard box that sat on one of the chairs. "I got some of my wife's things from the store. Started to go through them, then . . . needed a break."

Amie handed him a business card that had fluttered off the top of the pile. "I'm so sorry about your wife." She clasped her hands in her lap. "She was . . ."

Why did I start that sentence? she wondered, panicking slightly.

"Thank you," Andrew said, rescuing Amie from having to come up with a nice thing to say about his dead wife. "It was very nice of you to come."

As Amie watched him open a cabinet, she thought back to the fury in his face as he ordered Madeline out of the bookshop. That man was almost unrecognizable now as he withdrew two mugs from the cabinet, placing them down on the counter with a soft *clink*.

"I actually, um . . ." She steeled herself, working hard to override the part of her brain that was ordering her not to pry into other people's business. "I saw you, at the memorial, yell . . . er, *speaking* to Madeline. The owner of Eons?"

"You heard that?" Andrew looked shamefaced. "I was trying not to ruin the memorial by making a dramatic scene, but I think I lost my temper a little bit."

"Oh, it's fine," Amie assured him, her people-pleasing tendencies automatically kicking in. "Honestly, it was the most calm I've ever seen someone be while losing their temper."

Andrew chuckled at that, opening a different cabinet. "Chamomile okay?"

"Yes, thank you." Amie was still reluctant to pry, but she could almost hear Ziya in the back of her head, pushing her to take advantage of the situation. "Can I ask what Madeline did?"

Andrew dropped the tea bags into the mugs, then moved to the other side of the table. He sat down with a heavy sigh, leaning back in his chair.

"She hasn't done anything, as far as I know for sure," he admitted. "She's been wanting to buy the store from Savannah for a long time now. Says she wants to turn it into an extension of her café." His jaw tightened. "When I saw her, it just . . . it made me realize that she's likely happy to have a chance now. Maybe it was petty of me, but I just didn't want her to feel hopeful. I'm not sure I can look at her again without getting angry, knowing she thinks she might benefit from my wife's death."

"That's understandable," Amie said gently. "Savannah didn't want to sell the store?"

"No," Andrew said, shaking his head. "God rest her soul, she was determined to keep that bookshop running, even when the costs were getting far higher than the profit. I tried to talk her into selling. Tried anything I could think of. But Savannah wouldn't budge."

Amie studied the man as her mind drifted back to the time loop. Some afternoons, before she'd go to the park to "find" Hallie's ring, Amie would sit in Eons and nurse a tea while doing a crossword puzzle on her phone. On numerous occasions she'd seen Andrew interact with the barista in a way that made her assume the café was out of whatever he'd been hoping to order. It was the sort of interaction that one would forget five minutes after seeing it, unless one saw it again and again and again. Amie herself never thought much of it, even after seeing it again and again and again. But with Savannah dead, and Andrew and Madeline's shared desire for Savannah to sell the store made clear . . .

"Did you ever speak with Madeline about her wanting to buy the bookstore?" Amie asked. "Behind . . . er, separate from Savannah?"

Andrew hesitated, a muscle in his forehead twitching.

"I . . . did," he finally said, sounding ashamed. "That's how I know how much she really wanted the store. Savannah wouldn't listen to my advice, but I'd talk with Madeline and encourage her to keep trying. Suggest ways she could possibly convince Savannah to sell."

"When was the last time you talked to Madeline about that?"

"Hm. A few weeks ago? I went to talk to her on Monday, just to check in, but she wasn't at the café."

Amie resisted a smile of self-satisfaction as her hunch was confirmed. Andrew hadn't gone to Eons on Monday to buy something. He'd been looking for Madeline.

The widower's eyes had gone dark as he gazed at a spot on the table in front of him. "Maybe that made me a bad husband, going behind Savannah's back like that. I don't know."

"I'm sure you were doing it in her best interest," Amie said reassuringly.

"It was in *our* best interest, I thought," Andrew said. "It wasn't just about the money. The store was her whole life. It took up so much of her time. She'd never accept my offers to help; it was *her* business. She'd come home every night too tired to even have a conversation."

He looked up at Amie, frowning. "I'm sorry. I shouldn't be talking about her like this."

"It's okay," Amie said. "It's clear you loved her very much. I'm sure she didn't want to make you unhappy."

"She didn't," he agreed, standing as the kettle let out a loud *click* to signal the completion of its job. "We figured out some compromises. Coming home by seven was one of them; she used to stay at the store even later before we agreed on that. She'd also agreed to not work on Sundays, let go of a few part-time employees, and feature more bestsellers in the window." He chuckled sadly as he poured hot water into the mugs. "She disliked modern romance books but couldn't deny that they sold the best."

Amie was slowly distilling everything he'd just said. "Did she come home at seven on Monday?"

The small smile on his face faded, and Amie squeezed her lips tightly together to prevent herself from adding, "I'm sorry! You don't have to answer that! Ignore me!"

"Yes and no," Andrew said. "It's very strange."

He turned toward the living room, eyes unfocused as he returned to the memory. "I was reading by the window. It *was* seven—I'd checked the clock just before looking out the window. I saw her walking up the steps of the building, so I went to set the table for dinner. When she didn't come in, I assumed she'd forgotten something at the store and went back. I ate without her, figuring she'd eat whenever she got home. But she never . . ." He stopped, clearing his throat. The circles under his eyes seemed to grow deeper.

"I fell asleep waiting for her to come home," he said. "And in the morning . . ."

"I'm sorry," Amie cut in, not wanting him to feel pressured to say any more. She already knew what came next. She instead moved backward through his story. "Do you know why she might've gone back to the store?"

Andrew picked up the mugs, depositing one in front of Amie before sitting back down with his. "I just assumed she'd forgotten to do something and went back. I think the police are leaning toward the theory that she surprised a thief mid-robbery."

This was news to Amie. "Were there any signs of a break-in?" she asked, remembering Grayson saying he hadn't seen any.

"No," Andrew said in a tone that indicated he was doubtful of the robbery theory. "But if she forgot to lock up, that might have been why she went back."

"Do you think that's what happened?"

A half-hearted shrug. "She hasn't done it before, to my knowledge," he said. "But her manager, Raina, left the store a little before her. She said Savannah seemed distracted; bothered about something. If that was the case, I suppose it's believable that she'd forget to lock the doors. Or the back door, at least."

"But do you think that's what happened?" Amie pressed gently.

Andrew dropped his eyes to the table. "I just don't know." Taking in a deep inhale, he straightened. "Anyway, that's what's been keeping *me* awake." He took a small sip of tea. "I'm sure I've had many people reach out with condolences, but I haven't looked at my phone since Tuesday morning. It all just feels too overwhelming right now. But you've been a good listening ear. Thank you."

Amie felt a stab of guilt. She hadn't been asking questions just out of the kindness of her heart. Then again, she *was* trying to figure out who killed his wife, which was something she assumed he'd appreciate if she was successful.

Pushing down the guilty feeling, she smiled. "Of course."

In the silence that followed, Amie scrambled for a way to lighten the mood. This man had invited her in for tea, saying he couldn't sleep due to thinking about how his wife was murdered, and there she was, making him think about how his wife was murdered.

"I'm sure she would've really appreciated the memorial," she finally said. "The flowers were beautiful."

"Thank you," Andrew said with a small smile. "Savannah chose them herself. That was one of the things I could never talk her out of—her weekly flower order."

Amie stiffened, remembering Savannah yelling at the flower counter employee. She'd never paid much attention to what the woman had been yelling about, despite hearing her so many times. But hearing Andrew say "weekly flower order" triggered a memory (multiple memories, technically) of her yelling that exact phrase.

"Care to share what's been keeping you awake?" Andrew asked kindly. "Could help."

Amie didn't know where she could begin to explain everything that had been keeping her awake, even if she wanted to. "My life's just kind of . . . a mess." She shrugged. "Nothing I can solve overnight, but my brain's still determined to try."

Andrew nodded knowingly. "Brains tend to have way too much faith in our ability to do things, huh?"

"Yeah." Amie folded her hands around her mug. The further the moment got in her rearview mirror, the more she had trouble believing that for a few minutes she had actually begun to wish she was back in the time loop. The notion frightened her, for some reason. She didn't want to think about it anymore.

"May I ask about the trip wire?" She tilted her head toward the front hall of the apartment.

"Ah," Andrew said sheepishly. "It's silly of me, I know. Savannah always used to say I was too paranoid. But with her murderer still out there and us not knowing why they did what they did . . ."

He trailed off, the corners of his mouth turning down as he wrestled with his emotions. Shaking his head, he said, "I just don't know what to expect. I don't like not knowing what's coming next."

"I know how you feel," Amie said. Then she added, "A trip wire is pretty smart thinking. What happens if it's set off?"

Smiling, Andrew stood. "I'll show you."

Amie followed him back to the hallway, where he pointed to a tall, pedestal-like table that sat near the corner. On top of the table sat a large white vase with blue floral designs, a fresh bouquet of flowers resting inside.

"Hold on to that vase, will you?" Andrew asked, crouching down.

Amie dutifully picked up the vase, the flowers tickling her nose as she did so.

"When someone walks through it . . ." As Andrew tugged on the wire, the table began to tip.

"The vase would fall and break," Amie finished, understanding.

Andrew released the wire, and the table thudded back into place. "Figured the mess of the vase breaking would be worth it if it manages to warn me of an intruder."

"Pretty smart," Amie commented. She returned the vase to its table as he straightened back up.

"If I was smarter," Andrew said, leading them back to the kitchen, "I would've remembered that I also set up a wire in the entrance to the bedroom. *That* one was meant to trip up anyone who might try to enter."

He chuckled to himself as they sat down again. "Instead, it caught me leaving my room to make tea. Not very smart of me."

"At least you know it works," Amie offered, to which Andrew laughed.

"That's a good way of looking at it."

Amie picked up her mug as she glanced around the apartment. She thought about Benny being in there earlier that day, looking for the photos. Where had he looked? Did he find them on a laptop and delete them? How could Amie possibly find them herself?

She sucked in a breath as a thought hit her.

"What is it?" Andrew asked.

Amie flashed him a smile. "Tea's hot," was the excuse she managed to get out. "It's very good though. Um, when did you set up the trip wire?"

"Before I went to bed," Andrew answered. "I haven't had much time to get used to it, hence me forgetting it was there."

Amie frowned. *Never mind then.*

"Oh, the bedroom one I did today," Andrew amended. "The one in the hallway I set up yesterday evening."

"Ah," Amie said, her mind beginning to race again. "Extra security. Smart."

She didn't even know what she was saying; she was too busy thinking. Elena had seen Benny in the Harlows' apartment earlier that day, sitting on the other side of the door. Had he tripped over the wire? No, the vase was still intact, and besides, he would've been further down the hall if he'd tripped.

So Benny *hadn't* made it far into the apartment, and didn't return later. If he still wanted those photos, he could be back.

"Very smart," Amie added, this time with added emphasis. "Has, um, Benny stopped by lately?"

"Here?" Andrew asked. "No, he hasn't. He came by the store to pay his respects."

"Just . . ." Amie scrambled for the right words. She didn't want to frighten the man. "The trip wire is smart. I'd keep using the chain lock on the door, too."

Andrew stared at her for several seconds. Then he gave her a slow nod. "I will."

They sat quietly for a minute, sipping their teas. Amie finally spoke, feeling a need to fill the silence.

"Your traps remind me of my friend David," she said. "I don't know if you've met him; he lives on the second floor. He loves building Rube Goldberg machines, you know, one thing causes another thing causes another . . ."

She trailed off as Andrew put down his mug with a heavy *thunk.*

"I know David," he said gruffly, still gripping the handle of the mug.

Uh-oh. Amie shifted uncomfortably, waiting for Andrew to say more. He didn't.

"I don't know what you might've heard," Amie said hesitantly, "but David wouldn't . . . I mean, I know him, and he—"

Andrew sighed, rubbing his face. "I know. I'm sorry. The police told me they were going to question him, but I know that doesn't mean much."

"So you weren't the one who told the police about the argument," Amie murmured, almost to herself. "Right. Because you didn't talk to Savannah that evening."

"I only heard about it from the police," Andrew confirmed.

"Did they tell you who tipped them off about the argument?"

Andrew shook his head, folding his hands on the table. "I know . . . my wife was often difficult to deal with. She had very strong opinions, was incredibly stubborn, and tended to . . ."

He paused, then finished tightly, ". . . put her own feelings above the feelings of others. But I just can't imagine . . . murder. Why would someone *murder* her?"

The question was not being posed to Amie, she knew that. Andrew was asking it not to be answered, but as a signal to the universe that to him, this Didn't Make Sense. Amie understood the small comfort in declaring oneself to the cosmos—if a person couldn't control their fate, the least they could do was make it known when they felt the narrative designed by the powers that be was frustratingly lacking in logic.

Andrew's question had a much higher likelihood of being answered than the ones Amie had posed to the universe during the time loop. But not by anyone in that room. Not that night, at least.

Chapter One
Golden Spiral

Day 112 I.L.

David was convinced that this was the day Amie would escape the time loop.

"One hundred twelve," he said as they walked past Eons Café. "You're familiar with the Fibonacci sequence?"

Amie wracked her brain, trying to summon memories from middle school math. She hoped she was just imagining things, but the longer she spent repeating the same day, the harder it felt to recall pre-loop memories (especially the ones she'd already made an effort to suppress, a category under which most of her time in middle school fell).

"Every number in the sequence is the sum of the two numbers that come before it," David continued mercifully. "Zero, one, one, two, three, five—"

"Bicycle," Amie interrupted. She pulled David to the curb a few seconds before a bicyclist rounded the corner and sped past them.

"Wear a helmet!" David yelled. Amie joylessly mouthed the words along with him.

They continued walking without further comment on the bicyclist. The novelty of Amie's prescience always swiftly faded for David. He was more interested in discussing the time loop itself than watching Amie continue to prove its existence.

"The Fibonacci sequence can be used to construct a Fibonacci spiral," he continued, "which is a golden spiral that repeats infinitely." He paused, giving Amie a pointed look.

"Like a time loop," she said half-heartedly. She was having difficulty finding enthusiasm for this theory, but didn't want to discourage him.

"Well, *hopefully* this time loop doesn't repeat infinitely," David said.

Amie grew nauseous at the thought.

"But," David added, "Fibonacci sequences are often found in nature. Fruits, flowers, shells. What if zero-one-one-two appears at the end of this loop?"

"Hey, from your lips to . . ." Amie waved her hand vaguely. ". . . ears."

"You don't sound convinced."

They paused at the corner, David looking up and down the streets for cars. Amie knew they had about fifteen seconds before a break in traffic, so she said, "It's just that yesterday you were *very* confident about one hundred eleven being 'the day.'"

She dropped the air quotes. "Something about magic and prime numbers. You said similar things about eighty-one, thirty-nine, twenty-seven, and . . ." Amie struggled to remember, ". . . fifteen?" She stepped out into the street as the red Jeep drove past, signaling the break in traffic.

"What's *your* theory, then?" David asked as they entered the grocery store. "I don't need that," he added as Amie headed for the shopping baskets.

"You will," she responded, pulling the top basket from the stack. "I don't really have a theory."

David often asked her this question. Every time Amie gave her answer, she wondered if she'd have a better one the next time he asked.

"Excuse me," Amie said, flagging down an employee as she and David exited the produce section. "There's a woman in aisle two who needs help reaching the top shelf."

"Have you ever tried picking the lottery numbers?" David asked. They passed aisle two, where a woman was thanking the employee for his assistance.

"Wouldn't last long," Amie said. "The money goes away as soon as the day resets."

"But if you do it every day, eventually—" David trailed off as he noticed Amie was copying him word for word.

"'—you'll get out of the loop and still have the money,'" Amie finished. "Yeah, I know. I just feel like I'll jinx it if I try to game the system." She grabbed a jar of peanut butter from an endcap.

"That must get tiring," David said as they turned down an aisle.

"It doesn't," Amie replied, knowing that he was referring to hearing people say the same things over and over again. "At least, not our conversations. But that's because I try to switch them up. Like . . ." She picked up a bag of pretzels, pointing at the cartoon mascot displayed on the front. "Doesn't this sort of look like Mr. Sanderson in 2A?"

David added a bag of chips to the growing pile in his arms. "Riveting conversation fuel."

"Well, some days are better than others." Amie returned the pretzels to their shelf.

Savannah arrived right on time. Her voice cut through the relative quiet of the late Monday morning grocery store lull as Amie and David reached the cereal aisle.

"Don't do it," Amie warned, watching her companion react to the voice. "You'll only make things worse."

"I wouldn't," David argued, reaching for a box on a high shelf. He struggled to get the height he needed without dropping the rest of his groceries.

"Trust me," Amie said, holding out the basket she'd been carrying. "You will."

David eyed the basket, then begrudgingly deposited his armful of groceries before retrieving the elusive cereal box.

Amie passed him the basket, grabbing a bag of granola off a shelf. "Be right back. Don't interact with Savannah."

She left behind a grumbling David as she exited the aisle. A woman was wandering toward her, looking frustrated as she peered down a different aisle.

"Raina!" Amie called.

The woman looked at her, brightening. "Hi, Amie," she said, abandoning her search and walking over.

"Did you see Savannah?" Amie asked. She already knew the answer, but she liked to start the conversation with something casual. The manager of Shelf Starter was always wandering the aisles on her morning off, and despite Amie knowing exactly what she was looking for and where to find it, she didn't want to unnerve Raina with her intimate knowledge of the other woman's grocery list.

"Yeah," Raina said, almost apologetically. "She'll run out of steam soon. Probably."

They both winced as Savannah's distant yelling crescendoed.

"Were you looking for something?" Amie prompted, wanting to get back to David.

"Ah, yeah. I ran out of granola—"

Amie held up the bag she'd grabbed. "I've got this granola if you want it."

Raina looked startled. "I don't want to take your—"

"Don't worry about it. I also just decided I don't want this peanut butter. Crunchy, not smooth." Amie shoved the groceries into the other woman's arms. "And if you need a can of pinto beans, make sure to take it from the top of the pyramid of cans, not the bottom. Gotta run, bye!"

Amie darted down the juice aisle just in time to intercept David, who was striding purposefully toward the flower counter.

"No you don't," she said, grabbing the back of his shirt and yanking him to a stop. "Leave it alone."

"But—"

"Go get your eggs," Amie said. "I promise you, by the time you get them, she'll be done."

David mumbled something about not having to take orders from her as he proceeded to follow her orders. While waiting for him to return, Amie helped Canned Peaches Man find the canned peaches and prevented Destroyer of Fruits from causing an avalanche of apples (his mother thanked Amie as she deposited the toddler back into her shopping cart).

Sure enough, by the time David returned with a carton of eggs, the grocery store had once again descended into blissful quiet.

"'The only thing necessary for the triumph of evil is for good men to do nothing,'" David said as they made their way to check out. "Edmund Burke."

"Edmund Burke didn't say that."

"Yes, he did!"

"No, he didn't. I looked it up after the fifth time you quoted it to me."

David didn't speak for several minutes after that.

Chapter Ten
A Flower Arrangement

Day 3 A.L.

"This was a good idea," Amie said as she and David walked down the street.

"Of course it was," David said breezily. "It was *my* idea."

Amie rolled her eyes, smiling. Unsure of how to proceed with Benny, she had the thought that morning to go to the grocery store in pursuit of the person who tipped off the police about David and Savannah's argument. If David was right about his suspicion that he was being framed, it was likely the tipster was at least involved with Savannah's murder, if not the murderer themself.

She also knew it was possible that whoever had pointed the cops David's way had just been innocently trying to assist with the investigation, but in order to determine that innocence, Amie first needed to find them. The man who had been working at the flower counter that day seemed like a good place to start. If he hadn't been the one to make the tip, maybe he'd seen who else had witnessed the argument.

The "good idea" had been David's.

"You haven't seemed to be struggling much with that post-loop anxiety you said you were experiencing," he'd commented earlier as they'd exited the stairwell into the lobby of their building. "Do you think you're better now?"

"Mm." Amie thought for a moment. "Yes and no. It's still easier to do things I didn't do during the time loop. Less expectation. The walk to the café this morning was a little better, though. I only a little bit felt like the sky could fall on my head any second."

"'Only a little bit' sounds like an improvement." They were descending the front steps when he suggested, "Should we try a different route to the grocery store?"

Amie paused at the foot of the stairs, considering this. "Oh." Her shoulders loosened at the thought. She hadn't even known how much she'd been dreading reprising their usual walk to the store.

"Unless you think it's better to push through," David added. "Exposure therapy and all that."

Amie winced. "I think I've done enough exposure for one day." She headed left, away from the more convenient path to their destination. "Let's try it."

And it had worked. Not only was Amie relaxed on their walk, she was enjoying the change of scenery. This street had many more trees lining the sidewalk, some of them with leaves that were showing signs of early senescence in the form of reds and yellows peeking out through the green. Amie was sure the leaves had already begun changing on Monday, but their promise of autumn was much more effectual when she knew the passage of time was operating as normal.

"So . . ." David said in the tone of someone attempting to speak casually and utterly failing at doing so, "how are things going with Ziya?"

"They're going," Amie said vaguely, pulling her attention away from the trees. "Thank you for your concern."

"I'm not concerned. Just curious. She left her friends to be with you last night."

"She left her friends because she didn't want to be left out of the investigation," Amie corrected him. "That's different."

"I don't think those two things are necessarily mutually exclusive."

"Did she, um . . ." Amie crossed her arms. ". . . did she seem, like, super worried about me, or . . . ?"

"She was very worried about you," David said. "She practically pushed me all the way back to my apartment when I told her what was happening."

"Hm," Amie murmured noncommittally. In case her response hadn't been enough to indicate that she wanted a change of subject, she decided to initiate one herself.

"Do you remember what Savannah was upset about?" she asked. "When she was yelling at the flower counter employee on Monday?"

David let out a half-hearted scoff. "Can't say I was paying much attention. She never proved to me that anything she had to say held much substance beyond furthering her own interests, so I've gotten used to drowning out her tirades."

"I think it had something to do with her weekly flower order," Amie said. "I remember her mentioning that. Plus she was at the flower counter, so . . ."

"Adds up," David finished. "Why do you ask?"

"I'm just thinking about something Andrew said last night. That he knew Savannah was . . . the way that she was, but he couldn't imagine what she could've said or done to make someone want to kill her."

When Amie had returned to her apartment after speaking with Andrew, she'd opened a note on her phone and typed out as much as she could remember from their conversation. She'd been noticing that some details of the previous couple of days were growing foggy in her memory. Typing out the events of their conversation at least assured her that there was a backup in case her memory continued to display signs of incompetence.

Amie looked over at David. "Yelling at someone about an issue with her flower order, that's regular for Savannah. She was an annoyance at best, and mean at worst. But *murder*? What could she have said or done to drive someone to *murder*?"

"Maybe she hurt someone so much that they felt they needed to hurt her back." David shrugged. "Or maybe she just wore them down over time, and they'd had enough."

"Sounds like I'd be a good suspect, then," Amie joked. "If she'd done something even mildly cruel to me during the time loop, two years of that might've been enough to drive me to murder."

David began easing toward the far side of the sidewalk, away from Amie.

"I'm *kidding*!"

"I know." He closed the gap between them again, chuckling. "I don't think you have it in you, anyway."

"But who does?" Amie asked.

"That's the million-dollar question."

They entered the grocery store, cold air greeting them as they passed the shopping carts and headed for the flower counter. Amie sucked in a breath as she caught sight of the employee at the counter.

"That's the same guy from Monday!" she whispered, patting David's arm with excitement.

"I'm very happy for you," he said. "I'm also going to make myself scarce to avoid implicating myself any further. Find me when you're done; I'm going to see if there's still a sale on condiments."

"Mkay," Amie murmured, not fully listening as she began crafting her game plan for approaching the employee. Then, processing what David had said, she called over her shoulder, "Sale ended Tuesday!"

"Damn it!" echoed his reply from the aisle he'd withdrawn to.

The man working at the flower counter was grimacing at several orange-and-red bouquets sitting in front of him, anxiously tugging at his hair as Amie approached.

"Hi . . ." Amie's eyes darted to the name tag on the man's shirt. ". . . Winston. How are you?"

Winston glanced up at her. "Fine, thanks," he said, his tone distant as he focused on his work. "How can I help you?"

"You were working here on Monday, right?" Amie asked. She knew he had been, but didn't want to startle him by opening with "DID YOU TALK TO THE POLICE?"

"Yeah. Do you mind walking with me?"

Amie blinked as the man stepped away from his post and headed into the labyrinth of flowers to the right of the counter. "Oh, sure."

She hurried after him, picking her way through buckets of lilies and irises.

"Customer's picking up this order in ten minutes," Winston explained, stopping by a bushel of aster. "What did you ask, again?"

"You were working here on Monday," Amie repeated. "You interacted with Savannah Harlow, right?"

Winston froze, giving her a defensive look. "Maybe. Why?"

"Sorry, I just . . ." How *was* she going to explain this? "I was just wondering if you spoke to the police about the argument she had with the man who came over. His name was David."

"Yeah. I caught his name somewhere in between her calling him a nosy idiot and a self-righteous asshole." Winston returned to the aster, still casting hesitant looks in Amie's direction. "The police didn't ask many questions when they came by. They just wanted to know what she was yelling about that made him come over, and what they said to each other."

"Sorry, the police came to talk to you? You didn't contact them?"

"Course not. Why would I contact them?"

Amie frowned. That meant the cops had already been pursuing the tip before they spoke to Winston.

"What *was* Savannah yelling about?" she asked.

Winston hesitated, and Amie got a sense he was trying to figure out how to ask "Why do you care?" in a customer-friendly way.

"David's my friend," she explained. "I think someone might have been trying to frame him by telling the police about their argument. I'm just trying to find out more about what happened."

She gave him a thin-lipped smile, hoping she looked sympathetic enough to help out.

The man sighed. "Savannah was upset because her flowers hadn't been delivered. She kept screaming at me as I tried pulling up her order, but I just started working here last week and our computer system is a million years old, so it was taking forever." He'd begun picking aster from the bucket, then paused. "Pussy willows," he murmured, returning the flowers. "Maybe that'd be better."

"Then what happened?" Amie asked as the man strode past her, not wanting him to lose his train of thought.

"The guy came over," Winston said over his shoulder. "David. He started scolding her, telling her to leave me alone. I appreciated the gesture, but honestly, I think it just made things worse."

"I told him it would," Amie muttered as they stopped by a group of buckets holding stalks of fuzzy-tipped pussy willow. "Did you notice anyone else watching the argument?"

"I was just trying to keep my head down," Winston said, examining the flowers. "Can't say I saw who else was around."

He glanced up. "Your friend didn't say anything threatening. Nothing like 'I'm gonna kill you!' or anything like that. Honestly, the police didn't seem very invested. They left pretty quickly."

Amie looked around to see if David was nearby. Between this and Andrew sharing the police's theory about the murderer being a thief, she had a feeling that David no longer had to worry about being a prime suspect. But seeing as how Amie wasn't ready yet to grapple with her primary, guilt-motivated reason for looking into Savannah's death, she decided to ignore that feeling for the time being.

"Were you able to sort out Savannah's order?" she asked absently, her mind already wandering as she tried to determine her next steps.

"Oh, yeah." Winston began picking out the flowers he needed. "The system glitched the day before and canceled her regular order. She had me put the order back in and schedule the next delivery for the following morning."

Amie recalled the fresh flowers scattered about the shop the day before. Little did Savannah know the flowers from that order would be used to decorate her own memorial.

"Then she called back later and rescheduled them to be delivered that evening."

Amie jerked her head up to look at Winston, who was still delicately selecting pussy willows from the bucket. "What?"

"She called back later to reschedule. I put in the change right before clocking out." Finishing his selection, he headed back to the front counter with an implicit invitation for Amie to follow. "I was just relieved she didn't come back in to do it. I don't know if I would've been able to handle seeing her twice in one day."

"Did she say why she was rescheduling?" Amie asked. "What time was this?"

"A little before three? And no, she didn't say." Winston reached the counter and began placing the pussy willows into the bouquets. "Just gave her name and said she wanted her flowers delivered at seven."

Amie's mind raced as she circled back around the front of the counter. This was why Savannah had returned to the shop that evening, to retrieve the rescheduled flower order. Andrew must have seen her outside of their building right before she remembered she'd changed the delivery.

Either that, or . . .

"What's that?" Winston asked, giving her a concerned glance as he continued arranging. Amie realized she'd been muttering under her breath.

"Sorry, um . . ." She took another moment to organize her thoughts. "Is there some sort of alert or something your customers get when their flowers are delivered?"

Winston nodded. "Yeah, they get an email confirmation when the flowers are dropped off."

"And would they have just been dropped off?" Amie continued eagerly. "Or did someone need to sign for the flowers?" Had the delivery person seen Savannah right before she died?

"That's above my pay grade," Winston said, shaking his head. "Or, at least, it's a lateral move from my pay grade. Either way, not my job."

The disappointment on Amie's face was seemingly effective enough to make him add, reluctantly, "I can see if I can ask someone about it, if you want."

Amie perked up. "Really?"

The man opened a drawer underneath the counter and began digging around. He extracted a pen and a sticky note, placing them on the counter in front of Amie. "Write down your contact info. I'll let you know if I can find anything out."

Amie frowned, picking up the pen. She was hoping he'd be able to go ask someone, like, *right then*. Not wanting to turn down what could possibly be useful information, she wrote her phone number and email address on the sticky note.

"Ooh, are those my flowers?" exclaimed a voice from behind Amie. A woman was approaching the counter, beaming happily at the arrangements sitting on it.

"Thanks for your help," Amie said to Winston before stepping out of the way. Relief washed over his features as the woman began cooing over the flowers. Amie felt almost proud of him.

She found David closely comparing the prices of two jars of salsa.

"All done?" he asked, pulling his gaze from the shelf as she walked up.

"All done," she confirmed.

"Success?"

"A little. Are you buying anything?"

David scoffed in the direction of the salsa, his disdain signaling to Amie that no, he was not buying anything at *these* prices.

As they exited the aisle, Amie nearly ran into what on first glance she could only describe as a pile of party supplies come to life.

"Whoa, sorry." She jumped out of the way, getting a clear look at the human behind the vibrant pile of plastic.

"Oh, hi!" Raina shifted slightly to prevent a pack of noisemakers from sliding out of her arms. "Sorry, I have very low visibility right now. Should've thought to grab a basket."

"I can get you one," David offered, setting off toward the front entrance.

"Oh, thank you!" Raina called after him, losing a stack of conical party hats in the process. "Shoot . . ."

Amie crouched down to retrieve the runaway stack of hats, their escape foiled by the very nature of their existence as they rolled in a lazy circle.

"Big party?" she asked, straightening. "Or is this all just for a chill night at home?"

Raina laughed. "Bachelorette," she explained. "For my best friend. We're going to this rooftop bar on Spring Street."

Amie held out her arms in a silent offer to take some of the items off of Raina's hands.

"Oh, thanks," Raina said gratefully.

"Are you the maid of honor?" Amie asked, careful not to knock anything over as she relieved Raina of four packets of balloons.

"You'd think, right?" Raina asked wryly, pointing her chin at her cargo. "Just a bridesmaid. I thought twenty-plus years of friendship would be enough to get me maid of honor, but she asked her sister. Who she only talks to, like, three times a year. Family pressure, I guess."

She sighed. "Unfortunately, the sister isn't really much of a planner. Which is how I find myself here, the day of the bachelorette, buying a white plastic sash that says 'Bride' and as many gold balloons as I can find. Next stop is the mall to see if they have any phallic-themed candy."

"They don't have that here?" Amie asked, widening her eyes in mock surprise.

Raina laughed again. "God, I wish. That'd make my life *so* much easier."

Amie decided to go for a third laugh. "At least you're already stocked up on granola."

Her stomach swooped as Raina's smiling face transmogrified into a look of confusion. It only took Amie a second to catch her error. She hadn't gone to the grocery store the last day of the time loop. To Raina, their interaction over the granola never happened.

As the other woman opened her mouth to question Amie's non sequitur, Amie's eye was drawn to movement over Raina's shoulder.

"Oh, there's David with a basket!" Amie exclaimed, steamrolling over the moment. *Maybe try thinking before you speak, for once*, she internally scolded herself as Raina turned.

The mental self-flagellation was pushed to the side by another thought. Raina had been at the grocery store the day David and

Savannah had their argument. And she worked at the bookstore—in fact, she was one of the last people to see Savannah alive. It was very likely the police had spoken with her. Had she been the one to point a finger at David? And if so, had it just been an innocent mention, or something more nefarious?

Amie cast her mind back to her conversation with Grayson at the bookshop, fighting through the growing fog in her memory toward a flickering light within. Grayson had said that Raina wanted to run the store once Savannah retired, maybe eventually own it. And he had appeared to be under the impression that Savannah saw this future for Raina as well. After laying off most of the staff, it didn't seem like she was planning on letting Raina go any time soon. So it wouldn't have made sense for Raina to kill Savannah . . . unless . . .

Raina had been encouraging Madeline to talk to Andrew about buying the store. If Shelf Starter became a part of Eons Café, Raina wouldn't be able to own it one day. But maybe Raina was more concerned about the financial future of the bookshop than one day owning it herself. If she'd thought Savannah was running the store into the ground, she might have figured she had a better chance at keeping her job if Madeline bought the place.

Could Raina and Madeline have been working together?

"—gotta get going. Thanks again. Bye, Amie!"

Amie automatically raised a hand in farewell as she emerged from her thoughts, realizing too late that she was saying goodbye to Raina, a person who she now had many questions for.

"Are you okay?" David asked, giving her a quizzical look.

"I . . . yeah."

"I only ask because I took those balloons from you a full thirty seconds ago."

Amie looked at her hand. Her fingers were gently curled around phantom packs of balloons.

She dropped her arm. "I was just thinking."

"Uh-oh."

"Ha. Let's leave."

As they exited the store, Amie summarized what she had learned from Winston at the flower counter.

"So that was why Savannah went back to the store that night," she said. "But here's what I think. I think—"

"—the person who rescheduled the delivery wasn't Savannah," David finished.

"Yes!" Amie exclaimed, glad that they were on the same page. "It makes sense, right? Whoever killed her wanted to make sure no one else was in the store when they did it. So they rescheduled the flower delivery. Savannah received the delivery notification just as she got home, when Andrew saw her arrive. She went back to the store, and the killer followed her inside and . . ."

She waved her hands to substitute saying the words "killed her," which in that moment was strangely difficult to say despite how similar it was to the word "killer."

"It does make sense," David agreed. "Though it's looking less and less like your prime suspect is this mysterious calculating schemer you've conjured up."

Amie frowned. "Benny? I mean, the timing works out. I saw him smoking a little after eight. Andrew saw Savannah outside the building at seven. If she went straight back to the store, that's enough time for Benny to kill her, return home, and go out to smoke in time for me to run into him."

"I wasn't talking about the timing," David said. "I was questioning if Benny has the capabilities to pull something like this off. I really can't imagine him meticulously planning all of this out. He seems more like an 'act now, think later' kind of guy. Besides, would he have known about Savannah's regular flower order?"

"Anyone who'd ever been to the store could see how much Savannah loved those flowers," Amie pointed out. "It wouldn't be difficult to figure out when and from where she had them delivered."

She gasped, a new theory hitting her. "What if Savannah *was* the one who rescheduled the order, and when she got back to the store, she caught Benny looking for the photos? Then maybe he lashed out without thinking and killed her."

"So you're dropping your first theory?"

Amie rolled her head back with exasperation. "I don't know. Benny seemed like the most likely suspect, but we don't really know who's blackmailing him. Or if *he* even knows who's blackmailing him. The only thing that made him suspicious was all his sneaking around, but maybe he *was* just looking for the bathroom at the bookshop. Maybe he *was* just in the Harlows' apartment looking for a package Savannah stole."

Amie's mind had returned to the bookshop, trying to remember how Benny had looked before infiltrating the back of the store. Had he been keeping a careful eye out for an opening? To her, it had seemed like he only had eyes for the cheese and cracker spread.

As she continued trying to sharpen the memory, the pair walked by Shelf Starter. Glancing through the window, Amie spotted Andrew sitting behind the counter, looking at his phone. In the aisle furthest from the cash register, Grayson was lounging against a shelf, also on his phone. A stack of books sat at his feet as he seemingly hid from Andrew to avoid doing work.

Hiding among the books . . .

"At the memorial," Amie said slowly, remembering, "Raina was supposed to refill the iced tea. But she stayed away from the refreshments until Benny had left."

"You think she was avoiding Benny?" David asked.

"Maybe. I don't know why. I'm not even sure she knows him. But the more I think about it, the more sure I am that she was avoiding him."

"Juicy drama," David commented drily, "but what does it have to do with Savannah?"

"I think there's more going on with Raina than we know," Amie said. "I'm not sure if it has anything to do with Savannah's death. But I'm gonna try to find out if it does."

Amie paused as David fully stopped in the middle of the sidewalk. "No more breaking and entering," he said firmly. "I'm not saying this for your sake. It's for me and my poor nerves."

Amie raised her eyebrows. "What if I do it and just don't tell you?"

"My poor nerves would still know. They'd sense it."

"I'm not going to break into her place," Amie assured him as they continued walking. "I'm going to crash a bachelorette party."

Chapter Eleven
Compliment Shower

Day 3 A.L.

Amie wasn't going to *crash a bachelorette party.* But she did want to talk more to Raina, and had failed during every attempt to do so thus far. She knew she could probably try to corner the woman at the bookshop, but wasn't sure how much Raina would feel free to say in the store's usual quiet atmosphere. Amie's plan required noise . . . and hopefully some alcohol in Raina's system.

Spring Street only had one rooftop bar, which thankfully meant Amie didn't have to do a bar crawl to track down her suspect. She could hear the sounds of music and conversation from where she stood on the sidewalk, waiting for Ziya.

Amie checked her phone again before nervously smoothing down the front of her sundress. They were going undercover at a rooftop bar, she had reminded herself as she got dressed earlier that evening. She needed to dress the part. Yes, it was true that Ziya had on multiple occasions expressed how attractive she found Amie in that particular dress. But this knowledge hadn't played a part in Amie's decision to wear the dress. In fact, Amie had almost

~~chickened out~~ opted for a different outfit for that exact reason. But the mission came first, and this was *definitely* the best outfit for the job. So really, thinking about it, it was incredibly brave and noble for Amie to wear this dress despite its history with her ex-girlfriend.

Satisfied that she had made an airtight argument to the jury that lived in her brain, Amie forced her shoulders to relax as she looked down the street for Ziya. And there she was.

"Hi," Ziya said, smiling as she approached. She was wearing cargo jeans and a V-neck olive-green tank top. Resting on the lace neckline of the top was a delicate orange citrine necklace that made her eyes look an even warmer shade of brown. A necklace which, most notably, *Amie* had gotten her for her birthday.

"Hi," Amie replied, resisting the urge to cross her arms as Ziya studied her outfit.

"I like your dress." Was that a smile tugging at the corner of her mouth? Did Ziya think Amie wore the dress for her? *I didn't!* Amie pleaded with the jury in her brain, who had begun to look like they didn't quite believe her. *I'm not wearing it for her!*

"Thanks," Amie said cautiously, not wanting her tone to indicate that she was mentally in the midst of a heated court case. Then, boldly, she added, "I like your necklace."

That was *definitely* a suppressed smile. "Thanks," Ziya said, tilting her head slightly as she maintained eye contact with Amie.

What was THAT? Amie yelled at the jury, gesticulating wildly. *How am* I *on trial here? Look at her! She wore that on purpose.*

We're a jury of your *peers, not hers,* said the foreman. *Also, just a heads up, this tension is only going to keep growing if you don't break the silence.*

"Okay!" Amie said loudly, her stomach fluttering from Ziya's gaze. She squinted skyward as if she could see the rooftop bar from where she stood. "Thank you for coming."

"Thank you for inviting me," Ziya said formally, gently mocking Amie's shift in tone. She too looked up. "Is Raina here yet?"

"Not sure. I assume so."

They both looked back down, then away from each other.

"And the plan is to just try to get her talking?" Ziya asked the sidewalk.

"Basically," Amie replied to a nearby bush. "I just feel like she has to know *something*. I mentioned the Benny thing when I texted, right?"

"Mhm. Weird vibes."

"Also, the way Raina was pushing Madeline to talk to Andrew," Amie added. "It makes me wonder—"

"If they were working together," Ziya finished.

"Exactly."

"Well . . ." Ziya gestured for Amie to lead the way. "Let's find out."

The sun was low in the sky as they arrived on the rooftop. Tables of various sizes were scattered about the space, surrounded by well-cushioned chairs. The bar sat in the center of the roof, an island where the bartender could take orders from any side.

Ziya nudged Amie, drawing her attention to one corner of the roof where a group of women in party hats were loudly cheersing with champagne flutes. Raina was among them, her party hat askew as she clinked glasses with the other women.

"Table for two?" the host asked, picking up two cocktail menus.

"Can we sit at the bar?" Amie asked quickly. Sitting across from Ziya at an intimate table as the sun set felt dangerously *date-ish*. After the incredibly charged dress/necklace moment, she was determined to keep this mission on the rails however she could.

"How drunk do they look?" Amie asked after thanking the host and climbing up onto their seats. "They're doing a champagne toast—I feel like that's a mid-party thing to do, right? Have a couple drinks, then break out the champagne?"

"Hard to tell." Ziya looked past Amie to assess the group. "All those feather boas are in the way; I can't see if there are any other glasses on the table."

They ordered drinks from the bartender—a Shirley Temple for Ziya and a watermelon mocktail for Amie.

"You're not drinking?" Amie asked.

Ziya shrugged one shoulder. "Thought it's probably best to keep a clear head. *You're* not drinking?"

"Same reason. Clear head. For the mission."

"Right. For the mission."

Laughter exploded from the direction of the bachelorette party, and Amie wrinkled her nose. "Did that sound like drunk laughter to you?"

"You know, there's an easy way to deal with this." Ziya smiled brightly at the bartender as he delivered her drink. "Can we also get a round of Fireball shots for the party over there?"

"Sure thing."

"Very smart," Amie marveled as he turned away to make Amie's drink.

Ziya flipped her hair over her shoulder. "I have my moments," she said modestly before taking a sip of her drink.

They watched the bartender begin pouring whiskey into a dozen shot glasses arranged on a tray.

"Should we be looking while they get delivered?" Amie asked. "Is it more or less suspicious if we're looking?"

"Well, the whole point of sending the shots was to get Raina drunker than she already is," Ziya pointed out, picking up her drink. "Do you want her noticing you and coming over now?"

"Good point. We can't let her see us yet." Only half-joking (though she'd deny any accusations that she was any percentage below 100 percent joking), Amie added, "We can do that movie thing where we kiss to keep her from seeing our faces."

Ziya coughed mid-drink, some of her Shirley Temple spilling from her glass and tap dancing on the countertop.

"Sorry, sorry!" Amie scrambled to grab a handful of napkins. "Bad joke, that was a bad joke."

"No, it was funny," Ziya croaked, accepting a napkin and dabbing her mouth. "I just"—she coughed again, then cleared her throat—"didn't expect it."

Amie mopped up the spilled drink. "Sorry," she said again. "I literally asked you to not say flirty stuff to me, and now I'm being a hypocrite."

Ziya laughed, her voice still slightly raspy from the coughing. "I can handle flirty."

Amie raised an eyebrow pointedly at the spilled drink. "*Can* you?" she teased.

"Is that a challenge?"

What might have turned into a record-breaking locking of gazes was interrupted by the soft clinking of glass as a waiter picked up the tray of shots and began walking it over to the bachelorette table.

"Let's move," Amie said urgently, balling up the damp napkins and grabbing her drink.

"I can't believe you've never been here before," Ziya said as they settled into their new seats on the other side of the bar. "It's such a nice spot. I'd come here more often if it wasn't for my 'no repeats' rule."

"I don't know how you stick to that rule," Amie said. "Remember when you found that restaurant you said made even better dosas than your grandma?"

Ziya made a show of glancing around, lowering her voice. "Yeah, and remember how I said we were to *never speak of that* in case Naani found out what I said?"

Amie grinned guiltily. "Sorry. But you never went back there again! After all the raving about how good the food was!"

"Life's too short to eat at the same place twice," Ziya stated. "But back to my original statement: How have *you* never been here before?"

"If you didn't take me, I probably didn't go," Amie said.

Ziya looked at her in disbelief. "What?"

"Have we met?" Amie held out a hand. "Hi, I'm Amie."

Ziya gave a playful moue, shaking her hand. "You *did* tell me to forget everything I know about you. And a lot can change in three months. Maybe you're a whole different person."

"Do I seem like a whole different person?" They had released each other from the handshake, Ziya's fingers coming to rest on Amie's wrist.

"I don't know," Ziya said, lifting her chin. "Not completely different. But you seem a *little* different." She studied Amie's face, brows furrowing. "Do you think you've changed?"

Amie *knew* she'd changed. It was ironic, considering the unchanging nature of the time loop, but she doubted that anyone could live through the same day for two years without coming out the other side a changed person.

"I think I'm a little different," she agreed. "I just don't know if it's a *good* different. Or different enough."

"Different enough for what?"

Different enough for you to be happy with me. "I . . . I don't know." Amie took a sip of her drink to give herself time to collect her thoughts before she said anything too incriminating. "You're a little different too. I mean, here you are, breaking your 'no repeats' rule."

Ziya chuckled. "Yeah, well, this was a special circumstance. An exception." She withdrew her hand, to Amie's great disappointment.

"We'll just have to find a suspect to talk to at that dosa place," Amie said. She was rewarded with another laugh from Ziya.

They chatted for another thirty minutes, occasionally sneaking peeks past the chalkboard to check on Raina. As the sky grew darker, tall lamps flickered on, brightening the rooftop. A perimeter of string lights contributed very little to the illumination, but did a lot of heavy lifting for the general ambiance.

"Ooh, bathroom trip," Ziya said, leaning back in her seat as she looked across the roof. "It's Raina and two other girls."

They both ducked their heads as the women walked behind them toward the bathrooms.

"I'll get her attention when she comes back," Amie said, straightening. Her drink was long gone, and though she appreciated having a clear mind, her nerves were jangling in a way that made her want something stronger than a watermelon mocktail. After a few minutes, she felt the need to occupy her mind by listing her objectives while counting on her fingers. "Okay, game plan. I need to find out if she talked to the police about David, how she feels about Madeline buying the bookshop, what's her relationship to Benny—"

Ziya put a hand on Amie's. "You need to have a normal conversation. If you try interrogating her point by point, she's gonna get scared off."

"I wasn't going to *interrogate* her," Amie protested. "I just need the bullet points to know what I'm supposed to say."

"You already know what you're supposed to say." Ziya once again committed the unforgivable sin of removing her hand from Amie's. "Go with your gut. If she starts to seem suspicious, I'll give her a compliment shower."

"Your compliment shower distraction tactic isn't as subtle as you think it is," Amie said wryly. "I was very aware of it any time you used it to avoid taking out the trash."

"The point isn't *subtlety*. The point is *distraction*. And did I ever end up taking out the trash?"

"No."

"And why was that?"

Amie fought a smile. "Because of the compliment shower."

"Exactly," Ziya said, smug. "I should really get the compliment shower trademarked. 'Hello, Sharks—'"

"Here she comes!" Amie whispered urgently, nearly toppling out of her chair with how fast she sat up. She lifted a hand to wave at Raina as the woman reemerged onto the rooftop.

"Hey!" Raina called, a huge smile splitting her face. She abandoned her friends, who spared only a passing glance as they returned to their table.

Raina's cheeks were flushed pink as she hugged Amie, who had not been expecting a hug and therefore spent the duration of it with her arms pinned to her sides.

"So good to see you again!" Raina exclaimed, releasing Amie. She narrowed her eyes playfully. "Are you following me?"

Barking out a laugh, Amie said, "No! No, of course not. I'm not following you. No."

Ziya cut in. "Hi, I'm Ziya. I love your top. Ooh, and your shoes! So cute."

Amie winced inwardly as Raina responded with enthusiasm. She hadn't taken long to need saving.

"You're Amie's girlfriend, right?" Raina was asking as Amie tuned back into the conversation. "I work at Shelf Starter. I remember you two coming by a few times."

Amie and Ziya immediately spoke over each other with different variations of "no, we broke up."

"Ah, sorry." Raina shuffled awkwardly. Then she brightened. "Nice that you can still be friends, though!"

"Can we buy you a drink?" Ziya asked, shifting over one seat and patting the now-vacant chair between them. "We saw you're with your friends, but I know I'd need a break from all the activities if I had the week you've had."

Amie raised an eyebrow. If Ziya had a boss who'd been murdered, she would *definitely* be out doing as many activities as she could to keep her mind off of things.

Raina glanced over at her friends, hesitating briefly. "Ah, sure," she said, climbing onto the chair. "Not like I'm the maid of honor. And everyone's too drunk to play the trivia game I planned, anyway."

"It looks like a fun party," Amie offered as Ziya waved down the bartender. "You did a good job."

"Thanks," Raina said, smiling sheepishly. "I'm sure I sound so bitchy complaining about the maid of honor thing. I'll get over it. What's important is that the bride has a good time, right?"

She leaned forward to study the menu as the bartender took Ziya and Amie's orders. A silent conversation took place behind Raina's back as they waited for the newcomer to decide on her drink.

It's going well so far, Ziya communicated with raised eyebrows.

Could still fall apart at any moment, Amie responded with a grimace.

It will definitely *fall apart with that attitude*, expressed Ziya with an eye roll.

Okay, okay, you're right, Amie agreed with hunched shoulders.

They snapped to attention as Raina finished ordering her drink and sat back in her chair with a heavy sigh.

"How've you been holding up?" Amie asked, interpreting the sigh as an open invitation to ask about Raina's emotional state.

"Just stressed," Raina said. "Weddings are exhausting, and . . ." She glanced at Amie, realization shaping her features. "Oh. Savannah."

"I mean, I was asking in general, but . . . yeah."

"Yeah." Raina folded her hands on the countertop, shoulders slumping. "It's been tough. When I left the store on Monday, I didn't think that'd be the last time I'd ever see her."

"You left the store before she did?" Amie asked, already knowing the answer. She caught Ziya's eyebrow twitching at the interrogative nature of the question, and hurriedly added, "I just ask because I know Andrew was wondering if Savannah had forgotten to lock the door to the shop when she left."

"You talked with Andrew?"

"We're neighbors," Amie explained. "He's having a rough time, understandably."

"I feel so bad for him," Raina said with a sad grimace. "He asked me that, too. About Savannah locking up. So did the police. She'd told me I could leave early, and that she would close up. I shouldn't have gone. She seemed preoccupied with something. I should've stayed to make sure everything was okay."

"You spoke with the police?" Ziya asked.

Nodding, Raina said, "They just asked me where I'd been, how Savannah had seemed when I left, if anyone suspicious had been hanging around the store, all of that."

"Did they happen to ask you about David?" Amie asked.

Raina frowned, trying to remember. "No, I don't think they did. Why?"

Amie was too occupied with her disappointment to answer right away, so Ziya stepped in.

"The cops found out that Savannah and David had a big argument earlier that day," she explained. "We're trying to figure out who told them about it."

"Oh, *right*," Raina said, her eyes widening. "Savannah was complaining about it for most of the afternoon. I never thought to mention it. She was always picking fights with people; it wasn't even her first fight with David. It didn't seem out of the ordinary."

Her expression went solemn. "You guys don't think . . . you don't think that *David* killed her, do you?"

"No!" Amie and Ziya protested in unison.

"We think someone might have been trying to frame David," Amie explained. "He'd never do that."

Raina looked unconvinced, and Amie regretted even putting the thought into her head. Thankfully, Ziya took over the reins of the conversation.

"Do you know what's going to happen to Shelf Starter now?" she asked as the bartender delivered their drinks. "We heard you don't have a lot of staff left."

"Andrew went in today to give me some time off," Raina said. "I really don't know what's going to happen." She picked up her glass and took a long drink.

"We were at the bookshop the other day during the memorial," Amie said, giving Ziya a look of appreciation for setting her up to address another one of her bullet points. "I heard you talking to Madeline about her possibly buying the store. Is that something you'd want?"

"You heard that?" Raina asked, lowering her glass.

Amie smiled apologetically. "Sorry. I was on the other side of the shelf, and I just—"

"No, it's okay." Raina shook her head, scoffing with self-deprecation at the memory. "I wish I hadn't told her to talk to Andrew that soon. He lost it as soon as he saw her."

"He sounded upset," Amie said.

"He was. Madeline's been wanting to buy Shelf Starter for a while. Andrew wanted Savannah to sell. I thought he'd be happy to talk to her about it."

Raina sighed. "But it was too soon. I should've known it was too soon. Now he won't even let her in the store. He won't talk to her at all."

"I assume you want her to buy the store," Ziya commented.

Raina grimaced. "I was really against it before Savannah died. I don't know why—maybe it was Savannah's stubbornness rubbing off on me. I wanted the store to survive on its own. But I know Andrew doesn't want to run a bookstore. Yesterday was the first time he worked at the store in years. I figured Madeline was his best bet for selling it."

"No one ever tried to buy the store other than Madeline?" Amie asked. "What are the chances he'd find someone else?"

Raina hesitated, thinking. "There was another person," she said. "Jonathan Oakland."

Amie perked up. "He wanted to buy the store?"

"Yeah. It's funny, I'd actually forgotten about him until yesterday. I found his business card while collecting some of Savannah's stuff in the back room of the shop for Andrew."

"Who is he?" Ziya asked.

"Some old rich guy who likes buying small businesses, I think. He stopped by a couple months ago and left his card. I didn't think

Savannah gave his offer a second thought, but she did keep his business card, so . . ." Raina shrugged.

The mention of a business card brought up a fuzzy memory. There had been a business card among the pile of things that had been dumped onto Andrew's kitchen table. She couldn't recall the name on it, but—

"Did you give the card to Andrew?" Amie asked.

"Yeah. Told him exactly what I told you about Oakland." She fidgeted with a corner of the napkin that sat under her glass. "If Andrew won't sell to Madeline, maybe he'll sell to him. I think Savannah would've wanted that."

"You do?" Amie asked, doubtful. From everything she had heard, it hadn't sounded like Savannah wanted to sell the store at all. Though she probably hadn't considered what she'd want to happen to the store in the event of her untimely death.

"Well, I know she didn't want it to become an extension of Eons." Raina rubbed her arm in a self-soothing motion. "I felt a little guilty encouraging Madeline, like I was dishonoring Savannah's memory. But she kept Oakland's business card. Maybe she would be okay with him buying it, wherever she is now."

Ziya looked pointedly downward behind Raina's back.

"Would *you* want to buy the store?" Amie asked before Raina could notice Ziya making her best guess as to where Savannah ended up.

Raina looked startled. "Oh, no. No, no, I couldn't afford it."

"I only ask because I was talking to Grayson," Amie continued. "He seemed to think you might take over the store one day."

Raina's expression went dreamy, her eyes focused on nothing as she stared across the bar. "I might've liked to own the store one day. Save up. Have Savannah appoint me as her successor. She felt the same, I thought."

"You thought?"

Raina turned to Amie, the unfocused look leaving her eyes. "Well, Savannah wasn't really the affectionate type. But we worked together well, and my presence didn't seem to grate on her as much as most other people's did, so . . . I had high hopes for the future."

She gently pushed her glass away as her expression soured. "But that's all ruined now."

"We're really sorry for your loss," Amie said softly.

"I should get back to my friends," Raina said, sliding off the chair. "Thanks for the drink."

Amie's mind had returned to her bullet points. She still hadn't asked about Benny. She had to be natural about it, like Ziya said. Just follow her gut and casually bring up—

"Benny!" Amie blurted out as Raina moved to leave.

Ziya covered her mouth, poorly hiding her wince (or her laughter—was she *laughing*? At a time like *this*?).

Raina paused. "Sorry?"

"Do you . . . know him?" Amie asked haltingly.

"I know of him," Raina said, brows furrowing. "He's the Harlows' landlord."

"Yes," Amie confirmed, nodding perhaps too emphatically. "Do you know if he and Savannah had . . . issues?"

"Savannah had issues with everyone," Raina said flatly.

"Right, right." Amie's mind raced as she tried to wrangle the conversation back in her favor. "But do you know if Savannah . . . I don't know, was, like, blackmailing him or anything?" The end of the sentence came out in a rush as Amie grasped how poorly she was handling this shift in their exchange.

"What are you *talking* about?" Raina asked, looking unsettled.

Amie looked to Ziya for help, not sure if a compliment shower could work in this situation.

Instead, Ziya said, "We think someone was blackmailing Benny because he was cheating on his girlfriend—now ex-girlfriend. Savannah, or maybe her husband. Some people think it could be her husband."

"*Ziya* thinks that," Amie clarified.

"We thought if Savannah was the one doing the blackmailing," Ziya continued, "or if Benny even *thought* she might be doing the blackmailing, that he could have potentially killed Savannah because of it."

Raina stared blankly at them for several long seconds. Amie could almost see the gears rotating in her head as she processed this information.

Then, without warning, her neutral expression crumpled, and she covered her face. "She *was* blackmailing him," she said through her hands, her voice shaking. "And it's my fault. It's all my fault."

Chapter Twelve
Guilt and Pizza

Day 3 A.L.

Amie and Ziya both leapt to their feet and ushered Raina back to the seat she'd just evacuated. Ziya asked the bartender for a glass of water while Amie urged Raina to take deep breaths.

"I'm sorry," Raina finally managed to get out after drinking some water. "I didn't want to lie to you. I've just been so scared of him, and scared that what you just said might be true, and—"

She'd begun to hyperventilate again.

"It's okay, it's okay," Amie said soothingly, rubbing her back. "Deep breaths."

"Talk when you're ready," Ziya added, earning her a glare from Amie.

What? Ziya demanded with a shake of her head.

Look at her! Amie silently retorted with a hand wave in Raina's direction. *We broke her!*

Do you want to find out what she knows or not? Ziya demanded with a widening of her eyes.

Before Amie could respond, Raina took a deep, trembling breath (which was a welcome interruption for Amie, who couldn't quite figure out how to use charades to communicate *We're not going to get anything out of her if she passes out from asphyxiation!*).

"It's kind of nice to finally be able to tell someone about this," she said, staring at her hands in her lap. "Savannah made me swear to secrecy, and when she died, I didn't want to risk Benny finding out that I'd been involved."

"Involved with what, exactly?" Amie asked gently.

Raina glanced at her, then back at her hands. "A woman came into the bookshop a couple months ago," she said. "She had some photos on her phone she wanted printed. There were some other customers in line behind her, so I had her AirDrop them to my phone and told her to come back in an hour.

"Later, when I was printing the photos in the back room, Savannah came by and saw them. She said that the man in the photos was her landlord, but she'd seen his girlfriend before and didn't think that was her. And these were, like, couple-y photos. They were kissing in one of them. Savannah was cackling to herself about how big of an idiot Benny was."

Raina took another sip of water. "Once she knew that Benny was probably cheating on his girlfriend, she started talking about how she could use it against him."

"Did that surprise you?" Amie asked. Savannah hadn't been a very nice person, but she'd never struck Amie as the conniving type.

Raina pursed her lips, thinking. "A little, I guess," she finally said. "But ever since the shop began really taking a nosedive into financial troubles, she started acting more and more out of character. Like when she ordered all those cookbooks and put them in the front window. Or like when she let go of everyone except me and Grayson. He'd been working there longer than the others, but he's a terrible employee. I think Savannah just found it easier to keep him than try to determine which one of the other employees was worth keeping more."

"She didn't ask for your opinion?"

"No," Raina replied, a small, wry smile tugging at her lips. "I was only the manager when Savannah needed me to be. Otherwise, she made all the decisions."

"So what happened with the photos?" Ziya prodded.

"Oh, right. I had to go back to the register, so that was the last I heard about it that day. Then, about a week later, I noticed that Savannah's personal email was open on the computer in the back room. That wasn't unusual; she was always leaving her email up. But I saw that the email open on the screen was from Benny, and since he'd just come up in conversation the week before, I was curious. It said that due to a recent law that had been passed about apartment buildings without elevators, all tenants living on the third floor would be seeing a five-hundred-dollar decrease of their monthly rent."

"*What?*" Amie cried with the indignance of a second-floor tenant.

"That law can't be real," Ziya said.

"It's not," Raina confirmed. "I looked it up. That's when I realized that Savannah must have blackmailed Benny into lowering her rent. She probably included the whole third floor to try to keep him from knowing it was her."

"Do you think he could've figured it out?" Amie asked. "The photos were printed at Savannah's store."

"That's what I've been afraid of," Raina said. "Even if he was as much of a moron as Savannah made him out to be—which didn't mean much, since Savannah called almost everyone she knew a moron—it'd only take him confronting the woman in the photos for them to figure out that Savannah was the blackmailer. And *I* was the one who was given the photos. He could have easily found out I was involved."

"But why then would Savannah bother including the entire third floor in her blackmail?" Amie wondered. "Since it was already so obvious that she was the blackmailer. It doesn't make sense."

"I can't imagine it was out of the goodness of her heart," Ziya said.

"My only guess is that she wanted to give herself as much distance from the blackmail as possible in case Benny brought it to the police," Raina said. "There wasn't any physical evidence that she'd ever come into contact with the photos."

Her shoulders slumped. "Anyway, that's the whole story."

Amie's mind had gone back to the torn-up letter she'd found in Benny's bedroom. "Do you know why Savannah might've been planning on changing the terms of the blackmail?"

Raina frowned. "No. Why?"

"We saw one of the letters," Amie explained. "It said . . ." She struggled to remember.

"It told Benny to keep an eye on his mailbox," Ziya finished. "Because the terms might be changing soon."

Amie flashed her a small smile in thanks. "Right. Do you think she might have been planning on asking for more money, or . . . ?"

"It's possible," Raina said slowly. "She definitely needed the money. But I couldn't say for sure what she meant by that." She looked at Ziya. "Do you really think Benny killed her?"

"Do *you* think he could have killed her?" Amie asked.

"I've been trying not to consider it," Raina said, wringing her hands anxiously. "I guess I thought that if he did it, that'd mean I helped cause her death, and that guilt . . . I, I . . ." She stammered for a moment, then fell silent.

"I understand," Amie said. Her own guilt surrounding Savannah's death churned sympathetically in her stomach.

"If he did it," Raina said quietly, "I'm scared of what he might do if he thinks I know too much. Please don't tell anyone about this."

"Why didn't you tell the police?" Ziya asked.

"I was worried there wasn't enough proof." Raina wrapped her arms around herself. "If Benny found out I'd talked to the police before they were able to arrest him . . ." She shuddered.

"What if we get more proof?" Amie asked. "Then would you talk to the police?"

Raina hesitated, then nodded. "I . . . yeah. I could do that, maybe."

"Okay." Amie looked at Ziya. "We need more proof."

Raina slid off her chair again.

"I need to get back to my friends," she said reluctantly, fixing her hair. "I'm not really in a party mood anymore."

"I'm so sorry," Amie said. "We didn't mean to ruin your night."

"No, it's okay." Raina rolled back her shoulders. "I'm glad to get it off my chest."

"Do you want to ditch them and come with us?" Ziya offered. "We're getting pizza."

"We are?" Amie asked.

"Uh-huh. You've had that 'I forgot to eat dinner' look in your eye all evening."

"That's nice, thanks," Raina said. "I really should get back to my friends. You guys take care."

Amie and Ziya bid her farewell as she crossed the roof to return to the bachelorette party.

"Wow," Amie said. "That was . . . a lot."

"It was." Ziya hopped off her chair. "But my brain's on strike until I feed it. Pizza debrief?"

"Pizza debrief."

* * *

"I appreciate you two wanting to update me on your investigation, but I'm not getting involved with this anymore." After opening the door to allow Amie and Ziya entry, David had already returned to his work table, where he was attempting to balance a series of ramps on one of his pegboards.

"Aren't you curious to hear what we learned?" Amie asked as Ziya cleared a space on the kitchen table.

"Absolutely not. I'm avoiding all curiosity on the matter. Trying to learn from the mistakes of the cat."

"You're not a cat, you're a human man."

"Cats are also afraid of vacuum cleaners," Ziya pointed out, putting the pizza box down on the table and flipping open the top. "Are you afraid of vacuum cleaners?" She lowered her voice as Amie passed behind her. "Does he even *own* a vacuum cleaner?"

"I can *hear* you. I own a vacuum."

"When's the last time you used it?"

David peered over his shoulder, giving the floor a critical glance. "What year is it again?"

Ziya crossed the apartment with a slice of pizza on a plate and held it near David's face. "If you come talk to us, you can have pizzaaaa."

"You brought food into *my* apartment," David grumbled, begrudgingly pushing his chair back and following Ziya to the kitchen. "I should be allowed to eat it wherever I want."

He took a seat at the table, picking up the slice of pizza as Ziya set the plate down in front of him. "I'll listen, but I won't participate."

Amie and Ziya took turns sharing what they'd learned from Raina. David silently consumed three slices of pizza as they spoke, and only broke his self-imposed "no participation" rule once with a loud "WHAT?" after hearing about the third floor's lowered rent.

"So we still don't know who told the police about your argument with Savannah," Amie said in summary once they'd finished. "But we know Savannah was the one blackmailing Benny. Before, it was just the question of whether Benny *thought* it was Savannah, but now that we know it was, that makes his motive even more solid."

"We just need more proof against Benny so Raina will feel safe going to the police," Ziya said.

"Mm," David murmured.

"What?"

"He doesn't think Benny did it," Amie explained.

"You got that from 'mm'?"

"We talked about it earlier. If someone used the florist to lure Savannah back to the store that night, it'd be a little . . . *elaborate*, for Benny."

"Mm." Ziya nodded. "Yeah, makes sense. But maybe he was working with someone. Remember Elena heard someone yelling at him the other day? Maybe that was his accomplice."

Amie sucked in a sharp breath. She'd been so focused on Benny being in the Harlows' apartment that day that she had completely forgotten why Elena had gone to investigate in the first place.

"What did the other person say to him?" Ziya asked.

Amie wracked her memory. "All she said she heard was 'you did it.'"

"Hm. Would've helped us more if they said, 'We did it.' Are we sure that wasn't his ex-girlfriend?"

"She'd just broken up with him two nights before," Amie said. "In my experience, you don't go to visit your ex so soon after a breakup."

"Gotta give it three months," Ziya agreed knowingly.

Or two years. "But it could've been her. Or his accomplice. Speaking of, since we learned that Raina hadn't wanted Madeline to buy the store before Savannah died, they probably didn't work together to kill Savannah."

David suddenly let out a low groan, wincing.

"Oh my god, what?" Amie asked, alarmed.

Ziya swiped his plate away. "No more pizza."

"No." David rubbed his face. "I'm fine. I just remembered something. I wasn't going to mention it because I knew it'd set you two off. And to reiterate, I don't condone continuing this investigation—"

"Sure, yeah, we get it," Amie said impatiently. "What is it?"

It was clear that David was trying his best to downplay the news, but there was a gleam of intrigue in his eyes that was impossible for him to disguise.

"I stopped by Eons on my way home from the hardware store," he said. "While I was waiting for my drink, I saw a man taking measurements of the wall across from the counter." He sat back in his chair, "my work here is done" scrawled across his face.

Amie and Ziya exchanged a look of confusion.

"Who was the man?" Amie finally asked, not sure if that was the correct question.

It was not.

"The man doesn't matter!" David exclaimed, apparently realizing that his work was not, in fact, done.

"That's harsh," Ziya said. "I'm sure he matters to someone. At the very least, he probably matters to whoever told him to take those measurements."

"And who would that have been?" David prompted.

"Madeline?" Amie asked. A thought struck her as she pictured the interior of the café. "The wall across from the counter is between Eons and Shelf Starter."

"Bingo." David crossed his arms, satisfied.

"You think she was getting measurements to combine the businesses?" Amie asked. "She still thinks she could buy the bookstore?"

"That'd be optimistic," Ziya commented drily. "Andrew hates her ass."

"Maybe she thinks he'll come around," Amie suggested.

"Do you think he would?"

"No. He hates her ass."

Ziya cackled.

"Andrew could sell to someone else," Amie said as David took his plate to the sink and returned to his work table. "Raina mentioned that man . . . John . . . something."

"Jonathan Oakland," Ziya said.

"Right." Amie hadn't had the chance to take notes like she had after her conversation with Andrew. She was grateful for Ziya's memory to back her up.

"He wanted to buy the store, too," she continued. "I think I saw his business card when I was at the Harlows' apartment."

"I've heard of him," David called from across the room. "He bought that pizzeria on Harvest Street."

"That's where we got this pizza!" Ziya exclaimed. "He owns it?"

"Brought it back from the brink of bankruptcy, I heard."

"It's thriving now," Amie said. "They were packed."

"I read an article about it a few weeks ago," David said. "Apparently, he loves buying failing businesses and turning them around."

"Makes sense why he was interested in Shelf Starter," Ziya said.

Amie stood from the table. "David, can I use your laptop? I want to look him up."

"What's wrong with your phone?"

"This is a big screen task. Please?"

"Fine. It's on the couch. Don't disturb my track."

A minute later, Amie and Ziya were sitting side by side on the couch, scrolling through search results for Jonathan Oakland. They were both leaning forward to avoid disturbing the wooden track David had set up on the back of the couch, and Amie was leaning to the side to avoid the accelerant to her pulse caused by Ziya's body heat.

They skimmed through the news article David had referenced, as well as a couple other interviews with websites centered on business and entrepreneurship.

"He just seems like a normal rich white guy," Ziya commented as Amie navigated back to the search results. "As normal as one of those can get, at least." She snickered, pointing at one of the results. "He calls himself 'The Dream Saver.'"

"Oh!" Amie sat up straight, the title jostling a memory loose. More than one memory, as her sojourn in the time loop tended to produce those in multiples. "The Dream Saver. I heard someone listening to a podcast he was on. I spent the whole bus ride to our dinner listening to these guys talking about business because the person was blasting it from their phone."

"Nightmare," Ziya said as she took over scrolling. "Here's his website."

"He was talking about his entrepreneurship course," Amie murmured, remembering. "And then he started telling a story about . . ."

Her breath caught as the familiar tale was suddenly cast in a new light.

"A while back, I began talking with a woman whose business I was interested in acquiring," Oakland had said. *"I'll call her 'Susannah' for her privacy."*

"And to keep your lawyers from calling," cracked one of the podcast hosts.

They'd all laughed.

"'Susannah rejected my offer to help with her struggling business,'" Amie recited.

Ziya glanced over at her. "What?"

"That's what he said on the podcast," Amie explained. The words came to her like a well-loved song. "'I wasn't bothered at all—in fact, I offered her a generous discount for my entrepreneurship course to encourage her to keep fighting for her dream. Since then, Susannah has visited me three times under the guise of friendship. I immediately realized that she was trying to attain my hard-earned knowledge for free.'"

Amie waved a hand. "And then one of the hosts says something about Oakland's good business sense, blah blah—"

She continued with the story. "'Instead of turning her away, I began giving her bad business advice. She—I know, I know, but she wanted to learn, didn't she? I was just teaching her a lesson. No such thing as a free lunch. Anyway, she took the advice to heart, believing that I was unknowingly giving her my entrepreneurship course for free. It was easy to convince her to take the poor advice, because I was validating and building upon concerns and ideas she's already had for her bookstore.'"

In her periphery, Ziya had gone very still, likely coming to the same conclusion Amie had come to.

"The hosts joke about his lawyers calling him for sharing too many details," Amie recalled, "and then Oakland says, 'My point is, some businesspeople can be easily convinced, often by their own minds, that everything they are doing with their business is correct, and that *everyone else* is the problem, not them. Susannah is without a doubt one of those people.'"

She looked at Ziya. "And then they cut to an ad read. But he's gotta be talking about Savannah, right?"

"How did you do that?"

Oh, fuck. Amie's stomach dropped as she realized that Ziya's stunned expression wasn't due to the story, but because of Amie's delivery of it.

She wasn't ready to try to have the time loop conversation again. Things had been going so well between them.

"I . . . I have good recall for these kinds of things" came Amie's weak excuse.

Ziya wasn't buying it. "Since when can you perfectly recite—"

"It wasn't perfect," Amie hurriedly interrupted. "Sorry, I made it sound like that was word-for-word, didn't I? It was just something like that. Not perfect at all."

"It does sound like he was talking about Savannah," David called from his work table in a merciful attempt to rescue Amie. He waved three conjoined toilet paper tubes like a lecturer's pointer stick. "Someone who owns a bookstore and believes that everyone other than her is the problem? That has 'Savannah' written all over it."

"And Raina said she'd been making strange decisions lately," Amie added, giving him a grateful look. "This must have been why."

"Do you think Oakland was doing it on purpose to tank the bookstore faster so she'd sell it to him?" Ziya asked.

Amie relaxed, relieved that they were moving past her uncanny feat. "He said he wasn't bothered by her rejection," she remembered. "But maybe. Could have been an added bonus to the lesson he was trying to teach her, at least."

A twinge of pity sparked in her chest. Amie summoned a memory of Savannah screaming at a barista to keep herself from feeling too bad for the woman. "I wonder if he knows she's dead."

"I wonder if Andrew will try to sell to him," Ziya added.

"I wonder if one of you will come hold this while I finish taping it," David said.

Ziya leapt to her feet. "Me! I'll help."

"I doubt Andrew would sell to him if he knew how Oakland was treating his wife," Amie said as Ziya went to assist David. Oakland's website was open on the laptop screen. She clicked on the large Contact button in the top-right corner. A page popped up with a contact form, showing spots for a name, an email address, and a message.

If "Susannah" was Savannah Harlow, that meant Oakland had spoken with her at length multiple times. Would she have mentioned blackmailing Benny, seeing it as a savvy move to save money she could put into her business? Could this man help prove that Benny had a motive to kill Savannah?

She knew she was grasping at straws. In fact, it felt like she was grasping at those paper straws that get soggy and lose their structure the longer they're left in liquid. Before the straws could completely dissolve, Amie typed:

I'd like to ask you some questions about Savannah Harlow.

Resisting the urge to add "whenever you get the chance," she typed out "Amie T." in the name spot. She added her old email address from high school that didn't include her full first and last name, and sent off the message just as David clapped his hands together.

"All right, that's it," he declared. "Want to do the honors?"

"Yes!" Ziya squealed.

Amie closed the laptop, putting it down next to her as she twisted around to watch David toss Ziya a Ping-Pong ball and point her toward the start of the machine.

"Should I do a countdown?" Ziya asked.

"I don't usually—"

"Three . . . two . . . one!"

The moment Ziya dropped the ball down the first ramp, Amie felt her phone buzz in her pocket. She pulled it out to see a new email notification on the screen.

At first glance, it looked like spam. The sender's address was a string of numbers and letters, and the subject line read: **be aware**

Swiping the notification, she opened the email. There was no text, only two photos. Amie tapped on the first one to enlarge the image.

It was a hallway in their building. There was an odd texture to the photo that Amie realized was a reflection on glass. Whoever took the photo had shot it through the little window in the door to the main stairwell at the end of the hall.

The image showed Benny standing at a door. His hands were on the knob, as if unlocking it. She opened the second photo, which was shot from the same location. The door to the apartment was open, and Benny was halfway inside.

Amie checked the subject line again, then the email address, trying to find a clue as to why someone had sent this to her. She looked at the photos once more and finally saw it.

Two apartments down from the one Benny was entering, a dark-green welcome mat sat in front of the door. The person who lived two doors down from Amie had that same welcome mat in front of their door.

Benny was entering Amie's apartment.

She sprung up off the couch, vaguely acknowledging a clattering sound from behind her.

"Amieee!"

"Huh?" Amie turned to see that she'd knocked over the wooden track on the back of the couch just as the Ping-Pong ball was rolling past.

"Easily fixable," David said, patting the shoulder of a pouting Ziya as he headed for the wreckage. "I've done worse. One time I knocked into a table and sent five hours of work crashing to the ground."

He paused, raising his eyebrows at Amie before kneeling behind the couch. "Everything okay?"

"Look." She climbed onto the couch and leaned over the back to show David the photos on her phone. Ziya hurried over to look as well.

"It's my apartment," she said. "Some anonymous email just sent me these photos of Benny going into my apartment."

"Is he still there?" Ziya asked.

The room fell silent as they all looked at each other for an answer.

Ziya moved first, scrambling around the couch and bolting for the door. Amie launched off the couch and followed, hearing David's footsteps close behind her. They all came to a stop outside of the closed door to Amie's apartment. Ziya tried the knob.

"Locked," she announced. Then, after a beat: "Open it!"

"Oh!" Amie patted herself down, searching for her keys.

"Purse," Ziya said.

"Ahhh." Bolting back to David's apartment, Amie grabbed her keys from her purse and ran back, unlocking the door. She grabbed Ziya's arm before the other woman could go charging in. "Hang on, Z."

"Let me go first," David said, his voice low as he pushed open the door and stepped through. "Hello?"

No response. Aside from a car alarm blaring in the distance, the apartment was silent.

Amie released Ziya's arm as they followed David inside.

Ziya immediately split from the group, peering behind Amie's couch as David went to check the kitchen. Amie lingered in the front hallway, looking around for any sign that Benny had been there (or still was).

Her left foot slipped a little, and she looked down to see a folded piece of paper under her shoe. Crouching down to pick it up, she unfolded the paper. Scribbled messily in black ink were six words:

Stop now before it's too late

"I don't think he's here, guys," Amie called, her heart rate increasing as she read the message again. "He left a note."

She handed the paper to David as he and Ziya hurried back over to her.

"This is getting dangerous," David said grimly, passing the note to Ziya.

"I think it was already dangerous when a woman got murdered," Amie said.

"I meant dangerous for *you*."

"I think we should confront the motherfucker," Ziya said. Her eyes were bright with fury. "He wants to break into your home and threaten you? I can do that too. But I'll threaten him to his face, fucking coward."

"In fairness, I already broke into his home," Amie pointed out, gently removing the paper from Ziya's grip before she could tear it in half.

"Why are you so calm right now?" Ziya demanded.

Amie frowned. She didn't feel calm. Her heart was still racing. The piece of paper in her hand could have been a bloody knife for how anxious it made Amie just from looking at it.

But if Benny was telling her to stop looking into Savannah's death, that meant he was genuinely concerned that Amie was capable of doing that. It was almost as if the note said, "Keep going, you're on the right track." And Amie loved being told that she was on the right track.

"There's nothing we can do tonight," she said. "He left a warning, which probably means he's going to wait and see if I keep looking into Savannah's murder. As long as I stay under the radar, everything will be fine."

"You're not seriously going to continue?" David looked appalled. "This has gone far enough. It's gone farther than it ever should have gone. The police haven't contacted me since Tuesday. We've seen no indication that they're still considering me as a suspect. Kid, this needs to end."

Amie was confused for a split second, having nearly forgotten that David still believed she was trying to clear his name. After her conversation with Winston at the grocery store, she'd been almost completely assured that David was no longer under serious investigation. No, now she was running solely on guilt. Guilt and pizza.

"I'll sleep on it," she said. "I'll think it over. I promise."

She *would* think it over. She just already knew the conclusion she would come to.

* * *

Ziya insisted on staying the night.

Despite Amie's repeated assurances, neither Ziya nor David could be convinced that Benny wouldn't return and make clear to Amie when "too late" would be. She finally agreed to let Ziya stay over, promising David they'd set up a makeshift alarm system using materials he brought over from his apartment.

"He really does have everything, doesn't he?" Ziya commented. The wrist bells in her hand jingled cheerfully in response as she waited for Amie to lock and chain the door behind David.

"Yup. You can just hang those on the doorknob. I don't think we need to set up the whole pulley system."

Ziya ripped the Velcro of the wristband open, wrapping it around the doorknob and securing the ends back together.

"Voilà." Ziya stepped back, examining her work. "Now we just need to heat up the doorknob and set up a paint can to swing down if it opens, and we can sleep safely tonight."

Amie snorted. "I think the chain lock and bells will do, but thanks, Kevin McCallister."

She suddenly felt shy as they walked into the living room. "Um, you can take the bed again, if you want."

Ziya waved a hand. "No, no. I'm here to protect you; I'll take the couch."

Amie was quietly relieved. As difficult as falling asleep in her bed had been the night prior, the experience was much more comfortable than when she'd slept on the couch the night before that.

"Feel free to grab whatever you want to sleep in from my dresser," she said, going into her bedroom to get sheets for the couch. "And I still have the toothbrush you used the other night."

"Knew I'd be coming back, huh?"

Amie felt her face flush with embarrassment. She'd tried to throw the toothbrush away, but in the end she'd just left it in the cup by the sink. It wasn't that she thought Ziya would be back. She just couldn't stand to throw out another one of her toothbrushes, even one that had barely been used.

"I'm teasing," Ziya called from the other room. "That was a joke."

"Ha, yeah. I know." Hoping her cheeks weren't as pink as they felt, Amie returned to the living room to make up the couch.

Half an hour later, she was lying in bed, imagining that she could hear Ziya's slow, measured breaths as she slept in the other room.

"Amie?"

Or, as she also lay awake in the other room.

"Yeah?"

"Who do you think sent the photos?"

"I don't know." Amie sat up in bed, grabbing her phone and pulling up the email. "I got so caught up in the Benny thing, I didn't even think about who sent them. Maybe I can check the metadata . . . that would at least tell us what kind of phone it was taken on . . ."

She saved the first photo to her camera roll, then opened her photos app and swiped up on the image.

"Did you find anything?"

Amie jumped. Ziya was standing in the doorway, one shoulder hidden by the door frame as if she wasn't fully committing to entering yet.

"No." Amie referenced her phone again. "I think any data about the photo got wiped when it was emailed. Either that, or the sender really knows how to cover their tracks."

"Can I see?"

Amie held out her phone as an invitation. Padding across the room, Ziya took the phone from her, sitting on the end of the bed. Amie pulled her knees to her chest, watching Ziya analyze the photo.

"Hm. Yeah. Nothing there," Ziya confirmed, handing the phone back to Amie. She folded her hands in her lap, looking around the darkened room.

Amie locked her phone and returned it to her bedside table, looking at Ziya with amusement. "So . . . what's up?"

Ziya looked at her. For a moment it seemed like she debated feigning ignorance. Then her expression shifted into a grimace. "Your couch is incredibly uncomfortable."

Amie laughed. "I know."

"I don't remember it being so uncomfortable. Was it always that bad?"

"I think it turns evil at night. I really do." Amie scooched over, silently patting the other side of the bed.

"Thank you," Ziya said, sounding relieved. As she returned to the living room to retrieve her pillow, Amie grabbed one of her pillows and stuffed it under the sheet in the middle of the bed.

Ziya reentered, clutching the pillow to her chest. "Actually, I need that side."

"Why?"

She huffed. "I'm supposed to be protecting you. It's gonna be harder to stand between you and a murderous landlord if I'm the furthest from the door."

"*Fine*," Amie grumbled, relocating.

"What's this?" Ziya patted the extra pillow as she climbed into bed.

"You know what that is."

"I mean, a pillow, duh. But what's it doing here?"

"It's a . . . y'know. A boundary."

"A boundary."

"Yes." Amie moved her arm to indicate the tall, invisible wall signified by the existence of the pillow. "Boundary wall. You stay on your side, I'll stay on mine."

Ziya snorted. "Did you think I was gonna jump your bones unless you put a single pillow between us?"

"I didn't say it was for you."

The weighted silence that followed made Amie rush to stammer out, "I-I mean, it's a mutual boundary. For all parties. It's for the best."

"For the best," Ziya echoed, lying on her back. Amie did the same, even though she could never fall asleep in that position. She didn't want to turn her back to Ziya, but she also couldn't face her.

She was trying to determine whether it was too late to say goodnight when Ziya spoke again.

"Do you think it was for the best?"

"Hm?"

"Do you think it was for the best?" Ziya repeated. She clearly didn't think Amie needed more context, and she was right.

"That we broke up?" Amie asked.

"Yeah. Now that some time has passed. Do you think it was the right move?"

Amie folded her hands on her stomach, twisting her fingers anxiously. "I don't know," she finally admitted. "You can't . . . really *know*, right? We don't know how things would have continued if we'd stayed together. We can judge how things are now, but if this is the *best* result?" She shrugged. "Yeah, I don't know."

"Hm."

"Do *you* think it was for the best?"

"Um. Well . . . no."

Amie sat up, her pulse quickening as she looked down at her. "No?"

Ziya continued staring at the ceiling. Her brows were drawn together, her mouth twisted into a frown.

"No," she repeated. "I mean, you're right, we don't *know*. And up until a few days ago I was able to convince myself that I was living my best life, even though I knew deep down that I was exhausted and lonely and miserable. I thought it was just one of those 'time heals all wounds' kind of situations."

She finally met Amie's eyes. "And time probably would've healed my wounds, eventually. I mean, it was only three months." A small laugh. "But I've gotta admit, being with you has felt a lot better than sitting around waiting for time to start doing its fucking job on these wounds."

Amie felt like she was teetering on the edge of a ravine, one that she so badly wanted to fall into.

"So what are you saying?" she asked quietly.

"I'm answering your question. I don't think it was for the best. Maybe it was good at the time, because we learned from it, I don't know. But I can barely remember why it happened in the first place. It doesn't feel . . . important anymore."

Ziya sat up as she began to speak faster. "But those three months were hell for me and I don't . . . I can't go back to that. I want you in my life, in whatever way I can have you. If this is just how things are now, I'll take it. If we need to have a pillow between us at all times, that's fine with me. Two pillows, three pillows, I'll even go back and sleep on your evil couch if it means that we can still—"

Amie leaned over the pillow and kissed her.

Chapter One

?

Day ? I.L.

Two years had passed in the time loop. During the seven hundred and twenties, Amie had come to the decision that she'd stop keeping count after hitting two years. Deep down, she was hoping that such a large milestone would indicate the end of the time loop. But Day 730 came and went, and like clockwork, Day 731 followed, identical to all its predecessors.

It had been harder to stop counting than she'd expected. Amie woke up on Day 732 and thought, *Day 732. Wait. No. Stop that.*

The next day, it was, *Day 733—HMMM HMMMM HMMMMM*, as if humming loudly in her head would distract herself from remembering the number.

It took about a week (not that she was paying close enough attention to confirm this). Once she stopped trying to remember, the numbers became jumbled in her mind.

She'd finally lost count.

It was both freeing and terrifying. Freeing, because she could no longer be disappointed by milestones that brought no change.

Terrifying, because the growing number of days had been her only way to keep track of the passing time she alone was experiencing. Without that number, she was floating in space, with no tether to the world as she'd once known it. She'd been fossilized alive in a way that no one else had ever been before (as far as she knew—even in the very depths of despair, Amie wasn't going to make everything about her). And despite that stagnancy, she felt deeply, irreparably lost in time.

Three days later, Tuesday came.

Chapter Thirteen
Something Quiet

Day 4 A.L.

In the time loop, Amie's dreams were often very mundane. She'd just be going about her day, either in her apartment or walking down the street. Most times she'd be alone, but sometimes she'd be with her parents, or David, or Ziya, or a random acquaintance from high school dredged up from the depths of her subconscious. Then, almost always, she'd have a sudden moment of realization that things were different, and that she was no longer stuck in the time loop. She'd laugh at herself for taking so long to notice, and celebrate her freedom.

Then Amie would wake up. And she would still be in the time loop.

She'd cried the first few times. Eventually, she'd learned to move past it and on with her day without a second thought.

This dream was the opposite of that. Amie was back in the time loop, and she recognized it immediately, somehow, as soon as she sat up in bed. She felt it. She just knew.

After a brief moment of panic, Amie remembered Savannah. Savannah was going to die that day.

Hope sparked within her. She'd wanted this, hadn't she? This was a blessing, not a curse. She could use the time loop to save Savannah. This had been Amie's purpose all along. She was just getting a second chance to fulfill it, now that she knew what she had to do. She wouldn't be stuck for long; she just had to save Savannah.

Amie ran out of her bedroom and into the lobby of her building. She walked outside, down the street and around the corner to the bookshop. It didn't matter the time of day, or that she wasn't at all prepared to stop a murderer from killing Savannah. She just knew that she had to get to the bookshop.

She pushed open the door to Shelf Starter and entered her bedroom. No, that wasn't right. She had to get to Savannah. She was running out of time. She ran out of her bedroom and into the lobby, out the door and down the street, into the bookstore and back into her room. Into the lobby and out the door and down the street and through the door into her bedroom and into the lobby and out the door and down the street and through the door into her bedroom and into the lobby and out the door and down the street and through the door into her bedroom and into the lobby and out the door and down the street and through the door into her bedroom and into the

There was a sick feeling in Amie's chest as she awoke with a shudder. The room was dark and silent. There was a warm weight on her right hand, and she turned her head to see Ziya, face squished into the pillow in a way that made Amie wonder how she was able to breathe. Her hand was resting on Amie's open palm, gently gripping it, even in sleep.

Amie's heart squeezed. She'd spent so many friend dates with Ziya wondering if there was still the possibility of a future together if the time loop ever ended. And there she was, out of the loop, lying next to a woman she loved so much it scared her to think about. She didn't want to ruin it again. She would do anything to keep things the same as they were before.

"Z," Amie whispered. It was so quiet; the sound hardly passed through her lips. But Ziya's eyes fluttered open, her long lashes brushing the pillow as she moved her head to receive air through both nostrils instead of just the one.

"Hm?" she asked sleepily. Her hand on Amie's tightened as she settled into a new position.

"I . . ." Amie had so many things to say. She had nothing to say. What should she say? "I had a bad dream."

"Mmm," Ziya groaned sympathetically, blinking as she grew more awake. "Do you want to talk about it?"

"Yes. No. I don't really know how."

"What happened?"

"I was . . . in the time loop." She gave Ziya a timid glance. "Remember how I told you about the time loop?"

"Yeah," Ziya said. "Not a time traveler, a time homebody."

Amie huffed a nervous laugh. "Right." She studied Ziya's face. "I know it's hard to believe, but—"

She stopped as Ziya gasped.

"*That's* how you memorized the podcast." Ziya propped herself up on her forearm, the teasing humor draining from her expression.

Amie nodded wordlessly. She felt like she could cry with relief to see Ziya, eyes bright, finally believing her.

"Oh my god." Ziya's eyes flickered across Amie's face. "You were in a time loop."

"I didn't want to lie to you," Amie said, her voice soft. "I wanted to tell you about it so badly. But you didn't believe me the first time, and I didn't want to scare you off by—"

"*Amie.*" Ziya shifted over, resting her head on Amie's shoulder as she pulled Amie's arm around her waist. "You should know by now that I'm not so easily scared."

Amie gave her a gentle squeeze. "I know."

I'm the one who's scared, she thought.

"Tell me about it."

"What?"

"The time loop." Ziya curled closer to Amie, as if settling in for a story. "You said you wanted to tell me about it. I'm ready."

So Amie did. She told her about how long it took her to accept that she was in a time loop. How she first told David about it. All the grocery store trips and the friend dates. How she'd stopped counting the days after two years.

"Two years," Ziya said softly. "And I thought three months felt like forever. How did you stay . . . I mean, *did* you stay—?"

"Sane?"

"I was gonna say 'optimistic.' I just feel like I'd give up. But I can't imagine you doing that."

"Well, I had a couple of nihilist phases. I'd sleep a lot. Wouldn't brush my teeth. Barely ate. Didn't even text you to say I wouldn't make our date."

"For how long?"

"How long what?"

"How long did these phases last?"

"Oh, never more than a day," Amie admitted sheepishly. "They were some of the only times I woke up relieved to still be in the loop. I'd feel terrible about not texting you. Also, my mouth would taste so bad by the end of the day, I'd have to brush my teeth just from the memory of it alone."

"I would've forgiven you for not texting me, you know," Ziya said, kissing the underside of Amie's jaw. "I'm not *that* needy." Her hair tickled Amie's neck as she shook her head. "I don't think I could've stayed that optimistic."

"I thought you said you'd be incredible in a time loop," Amie teased, tilting her chin down to look at her. "What about all those marathons you'd run?"

Ziya grinned. "I *would* do so many things." Her smile slowly faded. "But I think the novelty would fade pretty quickly." She was quiet for a few seconds. "You kept going on our date? And just said the same things every time?"

"It was a good date," Amie said. "I didn't want to risk ruining it."

"But didn't it get boring?"

"I was with you," Amie said simply. "I couldn't be bored with you."

Ziya's gaze had wandered off to a spot past Amie's head, and Amie suddenly had the feeling that she'd gone somewhere far away. Desperate to bring her back, she said, "I think I might be thirty."

Ziya's eyes flicked back to her, a smile tugging at her lips. "You're not thirty."

"I think I might be. I was twenty-eight when the time loop started. I spent over two years in there. That makes me thirty."

"The time loop doesn't count. It's the same day on repeat. Time is basically frozen."

"But it wasn't for me! My brain was still taking in information, even if my body wasn't changing. I was still living for those two years."

"Were you?"

"What?"

Ziya's eyes had taken on that faraway look again, though they remained on Amie's face. "Were you living in the time loop? Did that really feel like you were living?"

"I . . . yeah. Of course. I was alive. I was breathing."

"But were you *living*?"

Amie felt frustration creeping over her. "My heart was beating, so by definition, yes, I was living the whole time."

"You know what I mean."

"Okay, no, I wasn't embracing every day like it was my last, Z. Is that what you want me to say? We've already established that I'm the worst person to get stuck in a time loop, I get it. You're right. I spent two years doing a whole lot of nothing. Par for the course for me. But what I need to know is *am I fucking thirty*?"

Ziya laughed, and Amie's frustration rushed away like a receding tide. "Do you want to be thirty?"

Amie untensed, resting her head against Ziya's as she thought about it.

"No," she finally said. "I don't think so. Not yet."

"So you're still twenty-eight," said Ziya with the confidence of someone who had read the oh-so-elusive time loop rulebook that Amie had so desperately wished she could get her hands on. "Simple as that."

"Simple as that," Amie echoed. "You make it sound easy."

"It *can* be easy," Ziya said softly. Her fingers curled against Amie's waist, as if she was having trouble catching hold of her. "You make things so hard for yourself sometimes. It doesn't always have to be so hard, Ames. It can just be easy."

Amie wasn't sure what to say to that, and Ziya once again looked like she'd gone somewhere far away. So she didn't say anything, just held Ziya close, pressed a kiss to her forehead, and hoped that she'd come back to her soon.

Chapter Fourteen

The Sacred Rule of No Take Backsies

Day 4 A.L.

Ziya had managed to silently remove the bells from the doorknob and slip out. It was also possible that the bell removal was not silent, and Amie was a heavier sleeper than she'd thought. Either way, silently or not, Ziya had left.

Amie tried not to read into it as she climbed out of bed and got dressed. She tried not to read into it as she went into the bathroom. She tried not to read into it as she picked up her phone and read the text from Ziya, which just said: **Had to get to class. Talk later!**

She wasn't reading into it. Everything was fine. It had to be. And Amie was capable of being alone with her thoughts and emotions without feeling like she needed some sort of distraction to—

Knock knock. Knock. Knock knock knock.

"Oh, good," David said upon opening the door. "You're alive."

Amie gave his retreating back an indignant frown. "After all your freaking out last night, that's what I get?"

"Well, I figured I would have heard about it by now if you were dead, so it wasn't all that surprising."

Lingering in the doorway, Amie said, "Do you wanna go to Eons? Get some breakfast?"

"I already ate." David was breaking down his machine from the day before. He seemed to be taking meticulous care to decide where to store each item, which was ironic considering half of his storage boxes were simply labeled "Miscellaneous."

"Oh. Okay." Amie stayed where she was, closely studying a chip in the paint of the doorframe.

"Where's Ziya?" David asked, lowering the tube of toilet paper rolls into a box.

"Gone." Amie sighed heavily, trying to garner sympathy. "Kind of felt like we got somewhere last night, and then she just left."

David stopped what he was doing to raise his eyebrows at her. "You 'got somewhere'?"

Amie suppressed a smile. "I don't kiss and tell."

"Thank *god.*" David rubbed his face with both hands like he'd just been through an exhausting ordeal. "Took you two long enough. All your pining was *killing* me."

"I wasn't *pining.*"

"You were pretending not to pine, which was even worse than if you'd just been doing it outright."

Resisting the urge to roll her eyes, Amie said, "But this morning she left without a word. Well, she texted. But still. No goodbye or anything."

She pretended to have a sudden thought. "If I went to Eons to get a blueberry bagel and a tea, that might take my mind off of things. But I don't know if I can handle the journey alone." Slumping against the door frame, she added, "Maybe I'll just stay here and pine on the couch. You don't mind, do you?"

David shook his head, using his foot to push a box under the work table. "Everyone thinks you're so nice and sweet," he said accusingly, pointing at her. "But you are *manipulative*. I'm being *manipulated*."

"I'll buy you a cake pop."

"*Fine*." David stomped across the apartment, grabbed his keys from where they hung near the door. "Anything to keep you from pining. Let's go."

"Yaaaay."

* * *

Amie insisted they take her normal route to Eons. Despite Ziya's hasty departure that morning, she was feeling good. It was Friday, her fourth day out of the time loop. She'd had three whole days A.L. to refamiliarize herself with experiencing a new day every twenty-four hours. Granted, she'd spent a significant part of those days investigating a murder, but she was still refamiliarizing while doing so. And other than almost walking into the path of a bicyclist and refusing to jaywalk (David waited patiently on the opposite curb until the crosswalk light turned white), she handled the trip like someone who'd done it seven hundred and sixty-ish times before.

"Well?" David asked as they sat down—him with his promised cake pop, Amie with her bagel and tea. "Did you think it over?"

"Yes."

"And?"

"Are you sure you want me to answer that?"

David looked unsurprised. "I guess not."

"I'm gonna be careful," Amie insisted. "You saw how I was back at the crosswalk. I'm not taking any more risks."

"Until you find yourself dangling from a balcony three stories up," David reminded her.

Amie scrunched up her nose in acquiescence. "Okay, fair point."

"I really do believe I'm not a suspect anymore," David said, unwrapping his cake pop. "Elena tracked me down to inform me that the police think Savannah interrupted a robbery."

"Yeah," Amie said absently, splitting her bagel in half.

David narrowed his eyes at her. "Did you already know this?"

"Huh?"

"Did you already know that the police think Savannah was killed because she interrupted someone mid-robbery?"

"Oh, uh . . ." Amie couldn't see any way of getting around it. "I might've . . . heard something about that."

Not seeming to notice (or, more likely, care) about Amie withholding information from him, David gestured at her with his cake pop. "Then there's nothing to worry about. I'm in the clear. You can drop this investigation with a clean conscience. I'll be okay."

Amie took a bite of her bagel to avoid responding.

"Unless you have another reason to be doing this," David said, studying Amie's face. "Is it Ziya? Are you still trying to impress her?"

"Wub?" Amie asked through a mouthful of bread and cream cheese. She swallowed. "No. I'm not trying to impress Ziya."

"So what is it? Why won't you let this go?"

Amie shrugged. "I'm . . . bored?"

David made an incorrect buzzer sound. "Try again."

"Why do I need a reason?" Amie demanded. "Maybe I just want to figure it out for my own curiosity!"

"That's even more difficult to believe, somehow." David's shoulders slumped. "You still feel guilty."

"No," Amie said, far too fast to be convincing.

"I thought we talked about this."

"We did." Amie put down her bagel, crossing her arms self-consciously. "You told me it wasn't my fault that I never managed to stop Savannah's murder despite being given *two years* of attempts, and I appreciated you saying that, but realized it's an undeniable fact that I was given far too many chances to save her and because I am the way that I am, I didn't take any of them."

David laughed with disbelief. "You can't call it being given a chance if you didn't even know what you were being offered! Kid, be serious."

"I'm being serious. I know the past is in the past, and I can't fix my mistakes now, but if I have a chance to at least bring Savannah's murderer to justice, I should take it, right?"

"But why *you*?" David asked.

"I don't know, because I know things!" Amie waved her hands, gesturing at the vague "things" she referred to. "I lived the day of the murder over seven hundred times. If anyone's qualified to figure out who did it, it's me."

"But how much of the day are you familiar with, really?" David asked.

"What do you mean?"

"I *mean*, you went to the park every day to help a woman find her missing ring. You weren't exactly exploring every nook and cranny of the town."

"I didn't go *every* day," Amie mumbled.

"Were you ever even near the bookstore when Savannah died?" David asked pointedly.

Amie was silent.

Sighing, David said, "I'm not trying to be harsh. I'm just saying—"

"Shh." Amie held up a finger, her memory kicking into high gear.

"I'm just saying that—"

"No, seriously, shh. Please. Just—give me a second." Amie buried her head in her arms, her hippocampus straining to separate individual memories from the blurry mess in her brain.

Through the self-imposed darkness, she heard David let out another sigh. "If it's really that important to you . . . fine. I'll help. There's no need to get upset."

Amie popped back up. "I'm not upset. I'm just trying to concentrate." She hesitated, then added, "I . . . I feel like my memory's gotten worse since leaving the time loop."

"Hm." David nodded. "That makes sense. You were barely absorbing any new information during that time. Now everything is new again, and it's a struggle to hold on to it all."

"I guess," Amie said, less concerned with *why* this was happening and more with how to improve it. "Remembering stuff from the time loop is a mixed bag, too. A lot of things are crystal clear, but pinpointing specific individual moments . . . agh, it's hard to explain. Anyway, I accept your help, no take backsies. I just need a couple minutes of silence." She returned to her arms, David muttering something about being manipulated again before obligingly falling silent.

After a full minute of thinking, Amie popped back up, her eyes still closed as she struggled to retain her thoughts.

"Okay," she said. "Hallie From The Park is also Benny's ex-girlfriend Hallie."

Receiving no response, she opened her eyes. David was absent from his chair, leaving behind only a bare cake pop stick to indicate he'd ever been there. Amie twisted in her seat to see him at the cash register, purchasing a muffin.

He looked defensive as he returned with the muffin, Amie's expression apparently giving away her impatience. "You said I had a couple minutes. That cake thing was too sweet for me."

"You ate the whole thing."

"I wasn't going to waste it." David settled back into his chair and took a bite of the muffin. "Go ahead."

Amie spoke quickly, concerned she'd lose her grip on a crucial memory if she didn't get her thoughts out fast enough. "Hallie From The Park is also Benny's ex-girlfriend Hallie. Correct?"

"You tell me," David said. "You know better than I do."

"All right. Hallie From The Park is also Benny's ex-girlfriend Hallie. We know she caught him cheating and broke up with him on Monday, sometime after when she'd leave the park and before I talked to Benny outside of our building that one time. So between four fifty-ish and eight-ish."

"I would've thought living the day so many times would mean your timings would be a bit more accurate than 'ish,'" David commented drily.

"Well—" Amie huffed. "Hallie didn't always leave at the same exact time, depending on how fast I 'found' her ring. But I never let it go on for more than, like, five minutes. So at the latest, she was leaving at . . . four fifty-two. And I only talked to Benny that one time, so I can't get more exact about that timing. May I continue?"

"Please."

Amie inhaled deeply. "Hallie had food she was bringing to her boyfriend's place," she said, "so let's assume she went straight there after the park. It's a five-minute walk from the park to our building, so she'd get there at four fifty-seven at the latest. How did she get in?"

David's brow furrowed. "She had a key?"

Amie shook her head. "Nope. Hallie told me she didn't. She'd say, 'He's such a commitment-phobe—I gave him a key to my place and keep dropping hints that he should give me a key to his. But so far he has *not* taken the hint.'"

"Is that a direct quote?"

Amie pointed to herself. "Time loop."

"Right."

"And why would he give her a key?" she continued. "I remember he'd said something about having close calls when Hallie almost discovered his cheating before. Giving her a key would just make it easier for her to surprise him. Without a key, she'd have had to buzz Benny's apartment for him to let her in, which would have given him time to evacuate the other woman before Hallie arrived upstairs. So, again I ask: How did she get in undetected by Benny?"

“Someone was walking in or out of the building when she arrived?” David suggested.

“Very possible. The thing is, like I said, Hallie didn’t always leave the park at the same exact time. So what are the chances that every time she left the park, no matter the time, she managed to arrive at the same moment someone was coming in or out of our building?”

“You’re suggesting there were versions of the day when Hallie *didn’t* catch Benny cheating on her.”

“Yes.” Amie folded her hands on the table. She began speaking slower, worried the thoughts that had made sense in her head wouldn’t make as much sense when put into words. “Like I said: I didn’t help Hallie find her ring *every* day.”

“Riiight.”

“After I’d gotten into the habit of helping her look for the ring, the first day I *didn’t* help her was on this day that I tried *not* doing a bunch of stuff, just to see what would happen.”

“One of your wildest days,” David deadpanned.

“Sure,” Amie begrudged. “Anyway, I went to the park to watch Hallie, but didn’t help look for the ring. I just wanted to see if she could find it without me. And she did, but it took her more than twenty minutes. Brutal to watch, but it was nice to know that she wouldn’t leave the park without it if there was ever a day I didn’t go to help her.”

“Even though it was likely the day would just reset and none of that would matter anyway,” David pointed out.

“Yeah, whatever. *So*, on the days that Hallie had to find the ring herself, she would’ve gotten to our building around five fifteen.”

“Okay . . .”

“On Monday, the door to our building was propped open from five ten to five fifty-five.”

David’s eyebrows shot up. “Why?”

"Someone was moving in," Amie said. "Movers were going back and forth for forty-five minutes. They made the stairs a nightmare, so I learned to avoid the main stairwell during that time. You didn't know?"

"No." David shook his head. "I would've been napping."

"You didn't hear the movers, or anything else?"

David thought for a moment, then shrugged. "Don't think so."

Amie corralled her thoughts again.

"So that's how she got in," David said before she could speak. "Movers had the door propped open."

"Except the timing doesn't work for the days I helped her," Amie pointed out. "Remember? At the latest, she'd arrive at the building before five. The door would have still been closed."

"Maybe she made another stop on the way," David suggested.

Amie hesitated. "That's possible," she said, frowning. Her growing theory was seeming a lot less airtight.

Seeming to clock the doubt in her face, David offered, "There aren't many places to stop at between the park and our building, though. It's mostly residential. So that's not very likely."

"Yeah. Yeah, that's true." Amie shook away her doubts, deciding she might as well lay everything out before completely writing the theory off as a stretch. "Okay, so, yeah. She would have always arrived too early for the propped door. *Except* for the days that I didn't help her look for the ring. Those days, she would have arrived during the window of time when the door was propped open, making it easy for her to surprise Benny."

"Fascinating." David dusted crumbs off his hands. "So it's more likely she caught Benny cheating on the days when you *didn't* assist her with searching for her ring. Not sure what kind of message that sends to the kids, but it's interesting all the same."

"It also means that there were probably days she *didn't* catch him cheating," Amie said. "Days when she got to the building before the movers arrived and buzzed his apartment to be let in, warning him of her arrival. Which means that she wouldn't have broken up with him, which means that she probably would have been with him that evening, which means that he probably wouldn't have gone to murder Savannah."

"That's a lot of probablys," David said doubtfully. "Hallie could have still figured out he'd just had someone over. If she smelled perfume, or spotted lipstick on a glass—"

"Sure, maybe," Amie said, interrupting before David could come up with more examples. "But here's the thing: That day I talked to Benny and gave him my pasta? That was the 'wild day.' It was the first time in a while I wasn't there to help Hallie find the ring, and more importantly, it was the first time I didn't help her since I started visiting you in the time loop.

"Up until that day, you'd always be napping from four thirty-ish to six thirty-ish. I never got an exact start and end time, didn't want to disturb you. But on the wild day, you were up and about. You said you were woken up from your nap by someone yelling."

If David had been intrigued before, now he was truly fascinated. "You think the yelling was Hallie breaking up with Benny."

"At the time I wasn't sure *what* it meant. I knew it had to have been because of something I'd done—or didn't do—but I'd done so many different things that day I wasn't sure which caused the change. I never tried to have a day like that again, I was so freaked out afterward. Which was why I left my date with Ziya early that night, leading me to run into Benny when I got home. That was all *the same day*. I think that any time your nap went uninterrupted, that meant Hallie didn't catch the cheating and didn't break up with Benny that day."

David pondered that, then shook his head. "That doesn't work, though. My nap went uninterrupted on Monday—the *last* Monday, in your experience—but we know she broke up with him."

"Correct," Amie said, her words speeding up again as she approached the final stretch of her theory. "But I think she might have broken up with him after Monday. Wednesday morning, to be more exact.

"Elena heard someone yelling late Wednesday morning, and found Benny sitting in the Harlows' apartment, looking upset. She said all she had been able to make out from the yelling was 'You did it.' Ominous, right?"

"Very."

"But," Amie continued, "Elena also admitted that her hearing isn't very good. Maybe she misheard it as 'you did it' from the start, or maybe her brain filled in the blank once she'd seen Benny in the Harlows' apartment, making her suspicious of him."

"What else could it have been?" David asked.

"When you were complai—talking about being woken from your nap—"

"I'm sure I was complaining, I don't take offense to that."

"You said the person yelling called the other person a dipshit." Amie nodded, reassuring herself. "I remember, because after that I started using the word when that guy on the bus would listen to his podcast on full blast. In my head, of course."

David had rested his elbows on the table, templing his fingers in front of his face. "Dipshit . . . did it . . ."

Leaning back in her chair, Amie covered her mouth with both hands. "You dipshit," she said, her voice muffled. "You *dipshit*."

"Okay, enough, I'm sensitive." David scraped his teeth along his bottom lip, thinking. "Sure," he finally said. "I hear it. And like you said, if Elena already had her suspicions about Benny, 'you did it' is a lot juicier than 'you dipshit.'"

"So I think the yelling on Wednesday was the same breakup that would wake you up from your nap when I didn't help Hallie look for the ring on Monday," Amie said. "Only delayed a couple of days."

"Okay," David said. After a pause, he added, "Is that all?"

Amie frowned. "Yeah. Why? You don't buy it?"

"I can definitely buy it." David grimaced. "But I'm still not sure if it exonerates Benny from having possibly killed Savannah."

Amie's shoulders slumped with disappointment. "Why?"

"You're saying that on the last day of the time loop, Hallie didn't catch Benny cheating, didn't break up with him, and was with him all evening, if not all night. But you don't *know* that. He could have still ducked out to kill Savannah. You'd have to talk to Hallie to get a firm alibi for Benny."

"I guess I could try to do that . . ." Amie pressed her hands on the table. "But, wait. Why would he kill Savannah Monday night if his girlfriend hadn't broken up with him yet?"

"Because she was *blackmailing* him?" David suggested. "It's possible he didn't want to wait around for his girlfriend to discover the cheating before exacting revenge on the woman who was extorting him."

"If he'd already been broken up with, why did it matter if he got the photos back or not?" Ziya's words popped into Amie's head, which wasn't really helping her efforts to distract herself from thinking about Ziya. She moved her thoughts away from the speaker and focused on the words.

"We thought Benny was searching for the photos because if the police found out Savannah was blackmailing him, that would make him a suspect," Amie said. "But . . . imagine he wasn't smart enough to actually realize that."

"Done," David said immediately.

"If Hallie broke up with Benny on Wednesday instead of Monday," Amie continued, "it makes more sense why he had been looking for the photos before then. Because Savannah was dead and no longer blackmailing him, and he had a chance to destroy the evidence before Hallie could find out."

Another memory emerged at the front of her mind. "I was wondering why Benny never returned to the Harlows' apartment after Elena found him there. He could've easily gone back as soon as Elena had left, but he didn't. We know he didn't, because Andrew's alarm system hadn't been triggered.

"Elena said that Benny had been looking for something, but when she offered to help him find it, he said it didn't matter anymore. I just assumed he was saying that to get her to leave, but what if he really meant it? What if Hallie had *just* broken up with him, just as he was going into the Harlows' apartment to search for the photos, and he really believed it when he said it didn't matter anymore? As far as he knew—or cared—the photos couldn't harm him. The secret was out. It really didn't matter anymore."

David stuffed the rest of the muffin into his mouth, chewing thoughtfully. Amie waited, feeling like a student watching her teacher finish grading her work.

"It's believable," David said, swallowing. "Especially considering your theory about the murderer changing the flower delivery time to lure Savannah back to the bookshop. That didn't seem like something Benny would have thought to do."

"Agreed."

"But where does that leave you?"

"Without a prime suspect." Amie ticked off her fingers as she spoke. "It's not Benny, not Raina, probably not Andrew—"

"Why not Andrew?"

Amie paused, not quite sure why she'd been so quick to clear Savannah's husband from suspicion. "I guess . . . he just seemed really sad?"

David gave her a flat look.

"Okay! It could be Andrew. Or . . ." Amie turned in her seat, casting about the café in search of its owner. "Do you think Madeline's around?"

"I can ask," David said, pushing his chair back.

Amie gave a start, nonplussed by the offer. "Really?"

"I have to throw this trash out anyway."

"I was preparing myself for another lecture about leaving things alone."

"I said I'd help," David said, heading back to the counter. "I'm bound by my honor and the sacred rule of no take backsies."

* * *

After learning that Madeline had gone to the park, then buying a second muffin for David, the duo left Eons Café in pursuit of Amie's new top suspect.

"Here's a question," David said as they walked down the street. "If Benny didn't kill Savannah, why'd he leave that note in your apartment last night?"

Amie hummed into her bagel. She hadn't had much time to eat while she was monologuing in the coffee shop, so she was trying to get in a few more bites between locations.

"Maybe he didn't leave the note," David continued, scratching his chin. "It makes sense, honestly. How would he have known you were looking into Savannah's death?"

"I thought maybe Elena mentioned it to him," Amie admitted. "Though now that I'm saying it out loud, Elena probably wouldn't have done that, considering she suspects Benny." She took another bite of her bagel.

"You found the note relatively close to the door, right?"

Amie hummed again in confirmation.

"So," David said, "it's possible that whoever left the note slid it under the door."

"But what was Benny doing there?" Amie asked—although, with the bagel in her mouth, it sounded more like, "Bub wub wuz Bene dun ner?"

Apparently fluent in Mouthful of Bagel, David answered, "That's still up in the air. Also, who sent you the photos? Were they the one who left the note?" David snapped his fingers, pointing at Amie. "Maybe they didn't slip the note under the door at all. Once Benny unlocked it and entered, they could have thrown the note inside." David snapped his fingers again. "Or *maybe* they somehow managed to attach the note to Benny's shoe with some sort of release mechanism that was remotely activated once Benny entered your apartment."

Amie swallowed, snapping her fingers and pointing back at David. "I don't think I know anyone other than you who could figure out how to turn Benny into a living Trojan horse. Are you confessing?"

"It's so ingenious I'm almost tempted to take credit. But I can't."

"Didn't think so." Amie wrapped up what remained of her bagel. "I think you're right that whoever sent the photos is probably more involved than just being an accidental bystander, whether they left the note or not. Why else would they want to be anonymous?"

"Maybe Benny was right," David said, "and Savannah *is* a ghost, haunting us all, sending you photos of Benny going into your apartment for some reason."

"It'd be a lot more helpful if she sent me photos of the person who killed her," Amie said as they crossed the street.

David scoffed. "Since when was Savannah ever *helpful*?"

Setup for the fall festival was in full swing as they arrived at Willows Park. A sea of white tents flooded the grass. Hay bales were being loaded off a truck and constructed into a child-size maze. On the far side of the park, a Ferris wheel curved out over the lake. Several workers in hard hats swarmed the base of the ride as they attached the benches for people to sit on.

Amie and David wove through the park until they reached the culinary section, where local businesses were setting up booths across from a line of food trucks. David was first to spot the bright-blue banner that read "Eons Café" close to the end of the aisle. Madeline stood on one side of the booth, arms crossed as she scrutinized it.

"What's your plan of attack?" David asked as they approached.

"I'm just gonna ask her if she thinks she might buy the bookstore."

David pulled her to a stop. "Terrible plan."

"Why?" Amie asked, indignant. "If she's already getting measurements for the renovation, she must know something we don't."

"Or she's delusionally optimistic. Either way, do you really think she'd just freely share her plans with a stranger who has cream cheese on her face?"

Amie wiped her mouth with the back of her hand. "How about now?"

"Still a terrible plan."

"I meant the cream cheese."

"Oh. You got it."

"Trust me." Amie started toward the booth. "She'll talk. I'm very personable!"

"Maybe you two can bond over your delusional levels of optimism," David called from behind her.

Not waiting to see if he was following, Amie strode confidently up to the Eons booth. She could see now that Madeline was directing two workers hanging up a banner at the back of the tent.

"Hi, Madeline!" Amie chirped, rounding the side of the booth to where the other woman stood. "I'm Amie. Big fan of your establishment."

It was remarkable to consider how much difficulty Amie had experienced speaking to people on her first day out of the time loop. Despite having yet to easily fall asleep alone in her bed, the occasional bouts of anxiety, and struggling to make her memory operate as it used to, she was finally starting to feel like herself again.

Madeline gave her a quick glance before returning to supervising the hanging of the banner. "Hi. Blueberry bagel, right?"

Surprised to be recognized, Amie said, "Yeah! That's me."

"I almost took it off the menu about a month ago." Madeline's gaze was still on the banner. "Once word got around, I had three different employees mention you. Ended up keeping it on. A little higher on the right, guys."

"Wow." Amie was amazed. "Well, thanks for that."

"We love our regulars." Madeline circled back to the front of the booth to supervise the banner-hanging from there. Amie beamed at David as he caught up to her.

"I'm a beloved regular!" she whispered, shaking his arm.

"Congratulations," he replied, gently removing himself from her excited grip. "Is she no longer a murder suspect now that she's flattered you?"

"Oh. Right." Amie cleared her throat, approaching Madeline once more. "I just wanted to ask . . . you know, as a faithful patron . . . I'd heard rumors that Eons might be expanding into the bookshop next door. Is that true?"

Madeline gave her a look so sharp Amie almost took a step backward. "Who told you that?" she asked. Her voice was calm, as if she was reining herself in after her initial reaction to Amie's words.

"You know . . ." Amie waved her hands vaguely. "The rumor mill. Hard to keep track of who said what to who."

"Sure." Madeline gave a thumbs-up to the people hanging the banner, who descended from their stepladders. "I don't discuss private business like that, sorry. You'll hear about any changes being made to the café once that information becomes public."

Fighting her instinct to politely back off, Amie continued to press. "So there *are* changes being made?"

"Again—"

"What my intern means to say," David interrupted, stepping in, "is that there are other parties interested in the store next door to yours." He held out his hand to Madeline. "David Lenski, pleased to meet you."

Madeline shook his hand, looking at him warily. "Hi. I've seen you at the café."

"Yes! I'm one of the interested parties." He clapped his hands on Amie's shoulders, who resisted grimacing in response. "Apologies for my intern. She's still learning the ropes when it comes to conversing with other business owners." He gave Amie a little shake. "Gets a bit too optimistic that folks will want to drop everything to speak with her. But you and I know that a successful business owner doesn't have free time for small talk."

Still looking dubious, Madeline said, "That's right. And speaking of, I do have to get—"

"The thing is, Madeline—may I call you Madeline?"

"Sure."

"Fantastic." David dropped his hands from Amie's shoulders, who stared at him, feeling both impressed and slightly unnerved by whatever character he'd slipped into. A slight Southern drawl had begun leaking into his voice, and he was smiling so wide Amie was worried his face might crack in half. Hoping his accent wouldn't get any stronger, she tried her best to look like an intern, assuming that "impressed" and "slightly unnerved" were both appropriate emotions to display for the role.

"So, Madeline," David continued, "I've been very interested in acquiring the bookshop next door to your lovely café. The thing is, I don't want to waste my time and resources if it turns out you've already locked down a deal."

He placed a hand on his chest. "So I'd greatly appreciate it if you'd save an old man some time and just give it to me straight: Are you acquiring the business?"

Madeline rubbed her hairline, looking around as she thought. "I bought the bookshop, yes."

"You've already bought it?" Amie exclaimed, shocked. "How?"

"*So* sorry for my intern's outburst," David said, stepping to the side to put himself between Amie and Madeline. "She should be *silently taking notes right now.*"

"I sound more like an assistant than an intern," Amie grumbled, taking out her phone and opening a new note.

"Absolutely not," David said over his shoulder. "Then I'd have to pay you."

He turned back to Madeline. "I was under the impression that the current owner was a bit reluctant to sell. So soon after his wife's passing, especially."

"He was," Madeline said, grimacing a bit. "Or, he is. But Andrew didn't sell the store to me. His wife did."

"Savannah Harlow sold her store to you?" David chuckled. "I heard she was even more opposed to selling than her husband."

"Slow down, cowboy," Amie murmured as the drawl thickened.

Madeline looked around again, not seeming to notice David's oscillating accent. The workers who she'd been directing to hang the banner had walked off to a van parked a few yards behind the booth.

"I'd appreciate it if you don't share this wide," she said, lowering her voice as she did so. "The news will come out soon, but I haven't had the chance to speak with her husband yet, and—"

"He doesn't know?" Amie asked, standing on her toes to speak over David's shoulder.

Madeline shook her head. "I'd been trying to get Savannah to sell to me for a while," she explained. "She was never interested. But a few weeks ago, she reached out. She said she was done trying to keep the bookstore afloat, and asked if I still wanted to buy. I said yes, and we began discussions.

"When I heard she'd passed, I figured I'd lost the deal. I'd signed the paperwork on Friday and was waiting to hear back. Then, Tuesday afternoon, my lawyer told me she'd received the finished paperwork from Savannah's lawyer."

Shuddering, she said, "It felt like a message from beyond the grave. I was happy, of course, but I felt so terrible for her. And for Andrew, of course. Savannah had told me she wanted to surprise him with the finished paperwork. She'd asked me not to tell him about the deal until it was done, but she died so suddenly, I didn't know if she'd gotten the chance to tell him."

Behind David's back, Amie frowned. If Savannah signed the paperwork on Monday, she would have probably been planning on telling Andrew about the sale that evening. But according to Andrew, Savannah never made it home.

"He'd been wanting her to sell the store for a long time now," Madeline continued. "I went over there on Wednesday to speak with Andrew and find out if she'd gotten the chance to tell him."

"I saw you at the store that day," Amie said, stepping around David. "He was very upset."

Madeline winced. "When I asked the manager if he was around, she clearly assumed I wanted to speak to him about possibly buying the store. I didn't correct her. I wanted to make sure Andrew knew about the sale before anyone else. I should have known that if Savannah hadn't gotten the chance to tell him, he might make the same assumption about why I was there. I don't blame him for how he reacted. I probably would have acted the same if I thought someone was trying to buy my dead wife's store so soon after her passing."

"So he still doesn't know?" David asked.

Madeline shrugged. "I have no idea. I assumed Savannah's lawyer would tell him, but I haven't heard anything. I thought it was best just to give him space for a few days, so I haven't gone back to the store. Contractually, the place doesn't become mine until the start of next month, so he has a little time to tie things up before then. And of course I'd be willing to give him some more time if he needs it. The guy's in mourning, after all."

"That's mighty kind of you," David said, inclining his head in thanks. "And I appreciate you sharing this with us."

"It's fine." Madeline picked up a clipboard and pen and went behind the table to the back of the tent. "You weren't the first to ask about this, so I guess the rumor mill is doing its job. Andrew's bound to find out one way or the other, if he hasn't already heard by now."

"Someone else talked to you about buying Shelf Starter?" Amie asked.

Madeline had opened one of the cardboard boxes. "Yeah. Oh, what was his name? It was that rich guy who's always buying struggling businesses. He left his card with me; it's somewhere on my desk, I think."

"Jonathan Oakland?" Amie and David asked in unison.

"That's the guy." Madeline pointed her pen at them. "He came into the store Tuesday afternoon and asked to talk to me. Intense energy, a lot of eye contact. He wanted to know if I owned the bookstore yet."

"Did he say where he'd heard that from?" Amie asked.

"He said Savannah told him." Madeline opened another box. "Apparently he knew she was going to sell to me, but just didn't know if the sale had been finalized or not. I told him I wasn't sure—I *wasn't*, at that point. He tried to talk me into selling to him, but sort of lost steam once I told him I was planning on knocking down the wall and combining the businesses. Guess he knew he probably wasn't going to convince me. Just said something about businesses failing when they expand too fast, then gave me his card in case I changed my mind."

"You're not considering his offer, I take it?" David asked.

Madeline laughed. "No. I'm good. I do have to take inventory, though, so . . ." She returned to the boxes and began counting their contents.

"Thanks for your time," Amie called as she and David walked away. Once they were out of earshot, she asked, "What was *that*?"

"Huge surprise," David agreed.

"I was talking about your Oscar-worthy performance as 'Man Who Mistreats His Intern.'"

"Oh." David rubbed his chin sheepishly. "Thought I could channel Detective Richards."

"Who?"

"Protagonist from my books." Frowning at her, he added, "I thought you were going to read them."

Amie threw her hands into the air. "I've been a little busy! And I thought you didn't want me to read them."

"I mean," David huffed, "if you're going to, I'd rather you get it over with."

"Well, Detective Richards definitely knows how to get information from people." They stopped under a tree that was removed from the hustle and bustle of festival setup. "If Savannah sold the bookstore to Madeline, that means Madeline didn't have a motive to kill her."

David leaned against the tree. "Do you think Madeline was correct in assuming that Andrew didn't know about the sale?"

"I think so." Amie cast her mind back to her late-night visit to the Harlow residence as a memory fought its way to the front. "When I talked to Andrew the night after the memorial, he said something about not checking his phone because he was feeling overwhelmed. He might have missed a call from a lawyer telling him about the sale."

"Or," David suggested, "he might know by now and just be too embarrassed about his outburst to reach out to Madeline."

"Sure. Or he doesn't want to be reminded of how his wife was planning on surprising him with the sale and then died before she could tell him." Amie looked up at the leaves of the tree, thinking. "So Savannah told Jonathan Oakland that she was going to sell to Madeline. Oakland still wants to buy the store. Could he have killed Savannah hoping to stop the sale, not knowing that she'd already signed the paperwork?"

"Possibly." David checked his watch. "I'm done for the day, though. I'm meeting a guy in thirty minutes who's selling me a box of old windup toys."

"Okay. I'll try to figure out what to do next." They began walking out of the park. "You should probably keep a low profile anyway, just in case."

"Why?"

"Did you consider that you just told Madeline that you're interested in buying Savannah's store?" Amie asked. "Which gives you a motive to have killed her?"

David's eyes narrowed as he rolled her words over in his mind. "No, I did not consider that. That is, Detective Richards didn't consider that. So I can't be blamed here."

"Well"—Amie sighed—"now we *really* need to figure out who killed her, before your bad Southern accent gets you back on the police's radar."

David rubbed a hand over his eyes, nodding in silent agreement. Then: "Hang on. Was I doing a Southern accent?"

Chapter Zero
Iceland

Three months before the time loop began

Eons was short-staffed, and the line for the cash register showed it. Madeline had joined the ranks behind the counter to make up for the missing manpower. Even worse, the café's AC was broken, and the industrial fan that had been placed near the doorway was doing little to appease the sweating patrons impatiently waiting for their iced coffees.

"This isn't worth the wait," David complained, wiping sweat off his forehead with the sleeve of his T-shirt. "A five-dollar iced tea isn't worth heatstroke. Actually, now that I think about it, a five-dollar iced tea isn't worth it, period."

"I told Ziya I'd get those brownies she likes," Amie said, attempting to fan herself with a napkin she'd grabbed on her way in. "And we've already been waiting for ten minutes. We can't give up now."

"Sure I can. Easily. Observe." David stepped out of line and began walking to the door, then pivoted 180 degrees as it opened.

Rejoining Amie in line, he said, "Never mind. Evil forces are preventing my escape."

Amie peered around him to see Savannah beelining it to the pickup counter, Raina following close behind.

"Are you still mad that she stole your balloons?" Amie asked.

David huffed. "It's not just the balloons," he explained. "It's that she had the gall to pretend it was an innocent mistake when she's a notorious package thief. That'd be like Al Capone going, 'Whoops. Didn't know that guy was going to *die* when we shot him with machine guns.' We all know what you thought, Al!"

"You're being dramatic." They both shuffled forward with the line. "She's not *that* bad."

"Hmph." David glanced over his shoulder, jerking a thumb in the direction of the pickup counter. "Then why is she picking a fight with the barista right now?"

Savannah's voice was steadily rising above the ambient café noises as the two looked over.

"—put in the order *hours* ago. I have twenty people arriving in an hour for a book club, and you're saying you don't have a single chocolate croissant?"

The barista held out their hands helplessly. "We didn't do chocolate croissants today," they explained. "When you called earlier, I told you—"

"You told me you could make it work," Savannah said accusingly, pointing a finger.

"I said we had a variety of other baked goods for you to choose from. And we still do. If you'd like to come look—"

"This is ridiculous!" Savannah exclaimed, looking to Raina for validation. The younger woman, who had Styrofoam trays of drinks in both hands, shrugged uncomfortably.

"We can just get something else for the book club," she suggested.

"But I ordered *chocolate croissants*."

"Jess, can you cover the register?" Madeline exchanged places with the barista as she gave Savannah a tight smile. "Savannah."

"Madeline. Your employee's incompetence has ruined my book club."

"I'm sure we can still make things right. Can I interest you in—"

"Hi, what can I get you?"

Amie's attention was pulled away as she and David arrived at the front of the line. Jess was waiting for her response, their shoulders still visibly tensed from interacting with Savannah.

"Oh, hi, um . . ." Amie pointed at the glass display case. "Four of those brownies, please—actually, five, let's do five. And an unsweetened iced tea."

She braced herself for David to protest her buying his drink, and was surprised when she received no response. Turning, she saw her neighbor heading over to the pickup counter, his shoulders set determinedly.

"Oh no." Amie dipped into her wallet, slapping a few bills onto the counter. "You can keep the change."

By the time she'd caught up with David, he'd already inserted himself into the interaction.

"No, you don't deserve a discount on your order just because you couldn't take no for an answer," David was saying to Savannah. "As a small business owner yourself, I'm appalled you'd try to take advantage of another small business like that."

"I don't remember asking for your opinion," Savannah spat back.

"Please, folks," Madeline said. "I'd rather us handle this amicably—"

"I was being more than amicable before *he* jumped in!" Savannah exclaimed.

David scoffed. "You were yelling the moment you came in here—"

"Hey," Amie said, gently patting his arm. "Let's let them figure it out, okay?"

Taking her cue from Amie, Raina said, "Savannah, we need to get back."

David begrudgingly allowed himself to be pulled away. "A little kindness goes a long way!" he called over his shoulder. Savannah flipped him off in response.

"Stay here," Amie said once they'd exited the café. "I need to get my order."

"But—"

"Stay."

Amie gave Savannah a wide berth as she returned to the pickup counter. Raina gave her an apologetic smile as the bookstore owner continued to berate Madeline for the poor service.

Savannah paused as she saw the bag in Amie's hand. "What's that?"

Amie froze as if she'd been caught stealing. "Uh . . . brownies? I bought them."

"Hm." Savannah rolled her eyes at Madeline. "Fine. I'll take a dozen brownies with that discount you offered."

"Great," Madeline said, sounding relieved. "I'll get those for you right away."

Amie was attempting for a second time to make a subtle exit, but Savannah faced her as the café owner hurried away.

"Tell David he's lucky you were here to talk sense into him," the woman said. "He thought that was me yelling? He wouldn't want to see me actually angry."

"I'll tell him." Amie grabbed the iced tea and hurried out the door.

"Did she say anything to you?" David asked, too distracted by Savannah to notice Amie putting the drink in his hand.

"Nope," Amie lied. "Let's go."

* * *

Ziya was brimming with energy when she arrived at Amie's apartment for dinner that night. She said she was excited for the brownies, but Amie knew that couldn't be the whole reason. The brownies were good, sure, but Ziya was practically bouncing off the walls.

"Are you done?" Ziya asked, whisking away Amie's empty plate before she could respond. She sped to the kitchen and placed their dishes in the sink before bounding back to the table.

"I'll get the brownies," Amie said, starting to push her chair back.

"Wait." Ziya stood across the table from her, bouncing on the balls of her feet. "In a bit. First, I have something to tell you."

Amie felt nervous, though she wasn't entirely sure why. Things had been feeling a little off between her and Ziya lately, but it wasn't anything either of them had been able to put into words, so it had gone unaddressed. She thought maybe Ziya was about to address it, but her girlfriend was clearly suppressing a huge smile, which didn't seem like the correct energy to precede, "Hey, why do you think we keep sniping at each other for no clear reason?"

"Okay." Ziya took a deep breath. "I . . ." She drummed on the table with her hands. ". . . got tickets to Iceland!"

Amie blinked. "You . . . okay. Cool!" Ziya didn't usually make such a production out of announcing her trips, but Amie supposed after dating for nine months that maybe she felt these things needed more of a formal announcement.

Ziya looked equally surprised. "Wait. Really?"

"Really what?"

"You're cool with this?"

Now Amie was *really* confused. "Why wouldn't I be cool with it?"

Ziya stared at her, as if trying to determine if they were talking about the same thing. "You understand that I'm saying I got tickets for *us*, right? For us to go to Iceland? Together?"

Amie frowned, processing this unexpected twist. "Why?"

"Because I love spending money on exorbitant trips," Ziya said sarcastically. "No, actually, the prices weren't too bad. It'll be late

August, which is the start of the season, so less expensive but also less of a chance we'll see anything, but—"

"Wait." Amie shook her head, as if that would fix whatever was making her brain struggle to follow what Ziya was saying. "What are you talking about? What's happening?"

"I got tickets for us to go to Iceland," Ziya said. "Oh, to see the northern lights. Sorry, I didn't mention that part. I got too excited."

"Haven't you already been to Iceland?" Amie asked.

Ziya shrugged. "Yeah. But you haven't. And you talk about seeing the northern lights, like, all the time."

"I don't think I talk about it *all the time*."

Wordlessly, Ziya walked over to the counter, picked up Amie's planner, and held it up, displaying the image of the aurora borealis on the cover.

"I thought it looked pretty," Amie said.

"Ames." Ziya returned the planner, running back to the table and taking the chair by Amie's. "You've mentioned it *dozens of times*."

"Sure, I guess," Amie said. "I just . . ."

She knew she was being unnecessarily argumentative. She just didn't like when Ziya got like this, acting like the Tasmanian Devil, whirling around her, turning Amie's eyes into black and white spirals as she struggled to follow. This was all too fast, too soon.

". . . I can't," she finished.

"What do you mean, you can't?" Ziya asked.

"I can't. I have work—"

"We're not going tomorrow, silly," Ziya said. She was smiling, but some of the excitement had left her eyes. "I know you well enough not to do that. You can take a week off, and it'll be right before classes start up again, so we can both—"

"No," Amie interrupted. "I mean, I just . . . I don't want to."

Ziya's smile faded. "You *do* want to, though," she said. "You said you did."

"I mean, it's just one of those things you say, right?" Amie said. "It's on my bucket list, or whatever. Like, sure, I'd like to see the northern lights *someday.*"

She took Ziya's hand. "This was so sweet of you, really. I know you don't like going to the same place twice, so I really appreciate it. I just, I can't go."

"But why *not*?" Ziya insisted.

"Because . . ." Amie explained, ". . . it's something I want to do *someday*, but I just don't have time right now."

"So make time."

"I will!" Amie said, laughing a bit. "Someday!"

Ziya didn't laugh with her. "I really don't understand you sometimes."

"I just want to save some things for later," Amie explained.

Now Ziya laughed. "When's 'later'? *When?* When will you start doing things you want to do? When you're sixty?"

"Maybe!" Amie exclaimed. "I don't know!"

Ziya pulled her hand away. "I just want more for you."

"What does that even mean?"

"It *means*," Ziya said, "that nothing good is ever going to be worth your time if you don't think you deserve anything good. And you deserve *everything* good, Amie. I want you to live your life."

Amie bristled at her last statement. "I'm just fine with my life as it is."

"Yeah, that's your life," Ziya mumbled, leaning back in her chair. "Just fine."

"Oh, I'm sure you'd rather I live my life more like yours," Amie shot back. "Packing every waking second with *experiences*, most of which you don't even actually want to be doing."

"That's bullshit."

"Is it? So you enjoyed going to paintball with your study group two weeks ago?"

"It doesn't matter if I enjoyed it or not," Ziya argued. "At least I was living my life."

"What kind of life is that if you're not even enjoying it?" Amie exclaimed. "Jumping from job to job and major to major, never going back to places you liked because there might be something even *better* out there?"

"At least I'm *trying* to enjoy it!" Ziya pushed her chair back and stood. "You're never gonna see the northern lights if you don't even try to go."

"I'm gonna go," Amie repeated. "Someday. It just has to be the right time, and the right circumstances, with the right people—"

She stopped, wishing she could shove her words back into her mouth, or that maybe Ziya tuned her out and hadn't even heard it.

"Wow." Ziya's expression was pained.

"I didn't mean that," Amie said, standing.

"Yes, you did."

"No, I—" Amie rubbed her forehead. "I *did*, but I didn't mean you're not the right person. I'm just saying the time isn't right."

"And when will it be right?"

"I don't know." Amie shrugged weakly. "I think I'll just . . . feel it."

Ziya exhaled. "I just worry that one day you're going to look back at your life and realize you never did anything you wanted to do."

"I worry, too," Amie said. "I worry one day you're going to realize how much of your life you wasted doing stuff you hated because you're too scared of missing out on things."

"I'm happy with my life."

"So am I."

"So why are we fighting right now?"

"I don't know."

Ziya slumped back down into her chair. "Me neither."

Despite their agreement, the tension in the room didn't dissipate. Amie walked away from the table, resting against the counter with her arms crossed. Ziya stared at the ceiling. They sat in silence for a long, long time.

It was Ziya who finally spoke.

"Are we breaking up?" she asked in a small voice.

No, Amie thought.

"I don't know," Amie said. "Maybe we should."

"Why?"

You're right, bad idea, Amie thought.

"I don't know," Amie repeated.

"Should we try to figure it out?"

Yes, Amie thought.

"I don't know," Amie said for a third time. "I don't . . . I don't want to waste any more of your time."

Ziya took a deep, shaky breath. "Right."

Wrong, Amie thought.

Amie stayed silent.

They exchanged a few more words after that, but nothing of value. Soon after, they agreed to end things. Then, about three months later, Ziya reached out, asking if Amie wanted to get together for dinner, as friends. Amie instantly accepted, and on multiple occasions caught herself counting down the days until their first official "friend date."

Monday couldn't come fast enough.

Chapter Fifteen
How to Save This

Day 4 A.L.

Amie was writing (and pretending not to notice that Ziya still hadn't texted her).

The writing had begun with Amie putting all her notes about Savannah's murder into one document, and typing out anything she hadn't already recorded. This effort to combat her weakened memory led her to searching for memory tests online, and ended up occupying a full two hours with cognitive training. By lunchtime, her mind was swimming with strings of letters and grids of symbols. She was glad she'd written down all of her Savannah notes before taking the tests, worried that she might have somehow managed to make her brain worse in the process of attempting to strengthen it.

After lunch, she returned to her laptop, scrolling through everything she'd typed out. Savannah, Benny, Madeline, Andrew, Raina, Jonathan Oakland. The bookstore, the grocery store, the coffee shop. Money and blackmail and cheating and murder. Savannah was *murdered*. Why? Who would do that?

Amie rolled backward in her desk chair, as if staring at her laptop from a distance would somehow reveal a crucial piece she'd been missing. She closed her eyes, taking herself back to the time loop, trying to think of anything she might have missed, anything that was different or stood out. Unfortunately, there was very little from Amie's experience in the time loop that could be described as "different" or "standing out," as far as she could remember (which, if the multiple memory tests she'd taken earlier were any indication, wasn't very far).

Deciding she needed a step back to give her brain a rest from the murder investigation, she turned her attention to a more calming task—brainstorming article ideas for her job that was probably going to lay her off before the end of the month.

If she was being honest with herself, Ziya's gentle suggestion the other day about applying to journalism school had stuck with her more than it had any of the previous times the suggestion had been made. Going back to school, to Amie, always seemed like a step backward. She preferred to grind at these low-paying writing gigs in hopes that one of them would one day lead to something better.

"You make things so hard for yourself sometimes. It doesn't always have to be so hard, Ames. It can just be easy."

Amie glanced at her phone, caught herself, then flipped it over to hide the screen. She opened a new window and typed *journalism programs* into the search bar.

* * *

An email notification was waiting for Amie once she finally flipped her phone back over that evening. She'd gone down the rabbit hole of tertiary education research and only noticed how much time had passed once her head started hurting from staring at the laptop screen for so long.

Rubbing her exhausted eyes, Amie picked up her phone and swiped on the email notification. Her breath hitched when she saw the sender's name:

Dear Ms. T.,

I am emailing in response to the message you submitted through my website regarding Savannah Harlow. While I don't tend to respond to vague meeting requests from people who only go by their first name and last initial, I have to admit, my curiosity is piqued.

My address is below. Come by tomorrow at 6 PM. I will give your name to the doorman.

Regards,

Jonathan Oakland

Click here for my entrepreneurship course

Amie gaped at the email, skimming over it twice more before putting her phone down. She hadn't expected a response, and that was before she even suspected that Jonathan Oakland could have been Savannah's murderer. If he *was* guilty, why would he invite over someone who wanted to ask questions about his victim? Did he want to steer Amie off course? Was he planning on killing Amie, too?

She shook off the second thought, rolling her eyes at herself. If this was the person who seemingly lured Savannah to be murdered in her own store by impersonating her on the phone, inviting someone over to his own apartment to murder them would be a significant downgrade in the murder strategy department.

Picking up her phone again, Amie opened her texts with Ziya. She had been trying to play it cool and let Ziya take the lead on their romantic reconciliation, but she figured this was reason enough to reach out first.

Amie: I've got a lot of new Savannah info to fill you in on. Are you free tonight?

The typing bubbles from Ziya popped up almost immediately. Amie waited. The bubbles disappeared. In the interest of her own sanity, Amie put down her phone and walked away, looking for something to occupy her while she waited for Ziya to reply.

Finding nothing of interest, she ended up doing a lap around her apartment before returning to her desk and retrieving the phone. To her relief, there was a response:

Ziya: I have plans tonight, sorry

A sick feeling began to bloom in Amie's chest. She was used to Ziya having plans; that didn't bother her. It had been a long shot to expect Ziya to be free that night. What bothered her was the lack of a follow-up, or even any interest in—

The bubbles popped up again.

Ziya: What did you find out?

The sick feeling withered on the vine, and Amie took a deep breath. Everything was fine. Ziya wanted to hear from her.

She typed out a summary of what she and David had learned from Madeline and sent it, walking away again. This time, she attempted to occupy herself with making dinner, only getting as far as preheating the oven and removing the burger patties from the freezer before giving in to the siren call of her phone.

Ziya: Wow. So Madeline probably didn't do it then
Ziya: Oakland guy sounds suspicious
Amie: Yeah. I have a meeting with him tomorrow at 6. Can you come?

This time she stayed at her desk, staring at the phone for a full minute before Ziya began typing.

Ziya: I might have something. Can you bring David?

After "Detective Richards" accidentally gave David a motive for killing Savannah, Amie thought it would be best to keep her neighbor away from anyone else who could mention to the police that David Lenski was asking questions about Savannah Harlow. That, and Amie didn't want to go with David. She wanted to go with Ziya.

Amie: He can't go. If you're not free, I'll just go by myself.
Amie: Alone
Amie: To talk to a potential murderer
Amie: Who might murder me
Amie: Dead

Ziya's response came faster than any of her others:

Ziya: Okay, I can meet you there
Ziya: Send me the address

Amie texted the address Oakland had listed below his email signature. Her thumbs hovered over the screen, multiple follow-up messages running through her mind. *How was your day? What are your plans tonight? Can we hang out tomorrow night? Are we okay?* She considered scrapping all of those options and pressing the call button, just so she could hear Ziya's voice.

In the end, she settled for:

Amie: Great! See you then

Coward, she thought, locking her phone and returning to the kitchen.

* * *

Day 5 A.L.

Amie knew that being free from the time loop meant she should have been cherishing every fleeting moment of her newly mortal life. However, she ended up spending the majority of her Saturday researching colleges and scrolling through social media, the latter being an addiction she thought had been beaten by the time loop, but turned out to have just been—as was everything else—put on hold.

She also talked on the phone with her parents. Amie had been avoiding calling them, mainly because she was worried they'd be able to tell, even through the phone, that things were . . . different. But her mother called her Saturday morning after Amie forgot to phone the night before (a Friday night ritual she'd forgotten about after 700+ Mondays). Amie wasn't sure if her parents entirely believed her when she said everything was fine, but regardless, she was happy to hear their voices, and promised to call back soon.

Then she moved her bed.

Alone in her apartment the night before, she'd once again had trouble falling asleep, until she'd pulled her sheets out from under the mattress, grabbed her pillows, and soon after fell asleep with her head resting at the foot of her bed. After waking up late in the morning, Amie had a quick breakfast before getting to work rearranging the layout of her bedroom. Her primary focus was moving her bed against the opposite wall.

It wasn't the cleanest fit—her dresser was partially blocking the door to the closet, and she had to remove her hanging watercolor of the aurora borealis to push her bookshelf against that wall. But in the end, her bed was in a completely different place than it had been for the entirety of the time loop. Amie hoped that would be a big enough change to allow her brain to let her fall asleep without hours of anxiety-ridden torment.

Amie gave her room another once-over while preparing to leave late that afternoon. She wondered if Ziya would like it. Ziya was always moving furniture around in her apartment, often to her roommates' dismay. Amie, on the other hand, hadn't changed anything after moving in, not even the way her mom had arranged her chairs around the kitchen table, even though Amie was always squeezing past the one at the end to get to the sink.

But she liked it. It was different. A little awkward. But nice.

The bus dropped her off two blocks from her destination. As Amie walked, she checked the time on her phone. 5:50.

Ziya had given Amie's **See you soon!** text a thumbs-up, with no other response. Amie had to remind herself that this was normal behavior for Ziya. But that was back when Amie was secure and confident in their relationship. Now, after sleeping with her ex, telling her all about her experience in a time loop, and then waking up in an empty bed the following morning, Amie wasn't sure she wanted "normal."

Her wish was granted as she turned the corner and saw Ziya standing outside of Jonathan Oakland's building.

"You're early!" Amie called, surprised.

Ziya looked over and smiled. "I'm always keeping people on their toes," she called back. "Never let them know your next move."

Amie relaxed. Ziya was smiling at her, making jokes. Everything was fine.

As Amie closed the distance between them, Ziya gestured to the revolving door of the building. "Shall we?"

Amie thought she might say something else, like "Sorry I ran out yesterday," or "It's good to see you," or "Let's define the relationship right now, before we go in to talk to this potential murderer." She would have even settled for just a kiss. Actually, she was moving that to her first choice. If Ziya kissed her, she'd have zero complaints.

But as Ziya headed for the door, leaving Amie unkissed, Amie realized that was probably not in her near future. Which was fine. Ziya was focusing on the task at hand, and so was she. They could talk (and kiss? Hopefully??) later.

"I'm so bad at these," Amie mumbled self-consciously as she emerged from the revolving door, having taken several long seconds before she managed to successfully hop in.

"I think they're fun," Ziya said as they approached the desk to their right. "Regular doors are way too easy to walk through. Why not make them unnecessarily complicated?"

"Hi," Amie said to the man sitting behind the desk. "Amie T. for Jonathan Oakland?"

"IDs."

Amie and Ziya pulled out their IDs, handing them to the man. He scanned the cards and returned them, giving Amie an additional card.

"Scan this in the elevator," he said. "Make sure to return it when you leave."

Amie looked at the card, which had the word GUEST printed on it in bold letters. "Sorry, what's this?"

The man had already returned to his computer. "Penthouse access," he said, not looking at her. "Scan it and press the button with a P."

"Got it, thank you."

Ziya's eyes were comically wide as she mouthed, *Penthouse?*

As soon as the elevator doors shut, Ziya exclaimed, "*Penthouse?*" as if Amie might have had trouble reading her lips fifteen seconds prior. "So he's *rich* rich."

"I'm sure a penthouse in South Jersey runs less than a penthouse in an actual city," Amie pointed out.

"Sure, but living in a penthouse is inherently *rich* rich-person shit," Ziya countered. "Normal rich people buy, like, a house."

"I think he has some of those, too," Amie said, having done some more research on the man the night before.

"Whoa."

The elevator fell silent. Then Ziya said, "I think I'd prefer a house. Penthouse is too high up. What if the elevator breaks?"

Amie hummed a laugh in response while suppressing a concerned frown. Ziya's tone had shifted. It was too bright, almost forced. It was as if she was just trying to fill the silence. They'd never had a problem with silence before.

She didn't have time to overthink any more than she likely already was. The screen above the elevator doors flashed the letter *P*, and the doors opened with a cheerful *ding*.

The two women stepped out into a foyer that, if it was an escape room, would be themed "sensory overload." The wood floor was carpeted by two Persian rugs. A chandelier that looked like an explosion of glass frozen in time hung from the ceiling. The walls were covered with paintings and tapestries of varying size and styles, almost completely swallowing the patterned wallpaper underneath. Among them were little shelves holding a variety of knickknacks, vases, masks, musical instruments—

"Hey!" Ziya exclaimed with recognition. She pointed at a hanging tapestry of a woman in a saree standing underneath a tree. "My aunt and uncle have that in their house."

"Likely a copy," came a voice from the doorway. "Either that, or my art dealer cheated me out of a significant sum of money."

Jonathan Oakland looked to be in his late sixties or early seventies. His white hair was neatly trimmed, with thinning gray eyebrows that were raised with amusement over dark-blue eyes. His blue polo shirt was tucked neatly into an ironed pair of khaki pants.

"Mr. Oakland, hi, I'm Amie," said Amie, crossing the foyer to shake the man's hand. "This is my friend, Ziya." She'd practiced the introduction in her head on the bus ride over, primarily to avoid any stammering over the second half.

"Amie, Ziya, pleasure to meet you." He returned the handshake, shaking Ziya's hand as well. "And just 'Oakland' is fine. I'd say Mr. Oakland is my father, but the son of a bitch died when I was four, so I can't say for sure what people are calling him these days."

Amie and Ziya both chuckled politely as Oakland let out a belly laugh.

"Come, join me in the sitting room." The man led them down a short hall to a room that was somehow even more decorated than the foyer. Amie sat down delicately on a dark red fainting couch, utilizing her experience from David's apartment to avoid knocking over a small statue of a rabbit that sat on a wooden table to her left. Ziya sat beside her, gazing around the room.

"Your place is . . ." Ziya began, then paused, starting again. "You have a lot of beautiful things."

"Thank you!" Oakland sat down on a leather lounge chair, which had a name that escaped Amie but did, she knew, cost thousands of dollars.

The man gestured to a ceramic teapot that sat on a low table between them. "Can I offer you some tea or other refreshment?"

"We're good, thanks," Amie said. She didn't think Ziya would have accepted the tea anyway, but she figured it was better to err on the side of caution while speaking to a murder suspect.

"So . . ." Oakland sat back in his chair. "You said you wanted to talk about Savannah Harlow?"

"Yes," Amie said, giving him a tight smile. "I heard you talking about her on a podcast. Or, about Susannah."

Oakland chuckled. "Wasn't very subtle with that name change, was I? It was more to avoid legal trouble than a genuine attempt at obfuscation."

"So Susannah *was* Savannah."

"Of course! You seem like smart girls; I'm not going to insult your intelligence by pretending she wasn't. If that was my intention, I could have just as easily ignored your email."

"Why didn't you?" Ziya asked. She'd crossed her legs, folding her hands on one knee. "A stranger emailed you about a woman you have no public connection to. Why the interest?"

"For exactly that reason," Oakland said, looking at Amie. "Clearly you had some reason, some knowledge that connected me to Savannah Harlow. I was curious to know what you'd heard."

Amie now knew what Madeline had meant when she described Oakland's intense energy and excess of eye contact. She moved her gaze to the table in front of her to avoid his piercing stare.

"You'd been interested in buying Savannah's bookstore," Amie said to the ceramic teapot. "She turned you down. Then, according to your story, she tried to get free business advice from you."

"And instead of turning *her* down," Ziya jumped in, "you fed her bad business tips and shared the story to promote your entrepreneurship course."

Amie winced. Ziya's tone was neutral, but the criticism behind the words was clear to her. Thankfully, Oakland didn't seem to notice—or care.

"You seem to have most of the story," Oakland said, raising an eyebrow with amusement. "What brings you to me, then?"

"Did you hear about Savannah's murder?" Amie knew, from Madeline, that he had, but wanted to see his reaction.

To his credit, Oakland sobered. "I did," he said, carefully sitting up. "Terrible tragedy. She had a lot of life left in her."

"How did you find out about it?"

"Heard it reported on the radio."

"On Tuesday?"

"I believe so. She was found that morning, wasn't she?" Oakland tilted his head, chuckling lightly. "This is starting to feel like an interrogation, Amie. Am I being interrogated?"

As Amie hesitated, he continued:

"Oh." He nodded knowingly. "I see. Doing a bit of amateur sleuthing, are we? I wanted to buy the bookstore, but she refused, therefore I have a motive to have killed her." He rubbed his chin thoughtfully. "It's a good deduction. A little weak, considering I didn't want the bookstore *that* much, but I suppose I have no way of proving that."

"You did go out of your way to punish her for trying to use you for free advice," Ziya pointed out. "Seems like you had a good amount of malice toward her."

"Ah." Oakland waved a hand dismissively. "That wasn't malice; just me having some fun. She thought she was being so sneaky, speaking in hypotheticals and acting like we were good friends. It was amusing, and I got a good story out of it, that's all. I certainly didn't wish her any ill."

He leaned forward in his chair. "Also," he added, "it wouldn't make much sense for me to have killed her, seeing as how she was planning on selling the store to me."

Amie and Ziya glanced at each other, confused.

"That's interesting," Amie said slowly, turning back to the man. "Because I was told that the store was sold to Madeline, the owner of Eons Café."

Oakland narrowed his eyes. "Who told you that?"

"Madeline. She said the final paperwork came in after you visited her on Tuesday."

"Damn." Oakland snapped his fingers, looking mildly disappointed. "I lied to the man for nothing. Strange he didn't know . . ."

"Who did you lie to?" Amie asked, overlapping with Ziya saying, "Did you just lie to *us*?"

"Yes, my apologies," Oakland said, responding to Ziya's significantly louder query first. "All's fair in business, I always say. I knew Savannah was planning on selling to the young café owner." He winced. "She told me herself, very angrily and at an ear-piercing decibel."

"Why was she angry?" Amie asked.

"She heard the podcast." Oakland let out a half-hearted sigh. "I didn't expect the game to last forever. It was fun while it lasted. What I hadn't predicted was that she'd change her mind about selling the bookstore. She told me she'd decided to sell, and had been considering me as a buyer, but no longer wanted anything to do with me."

A wry smile crossed his face. "I have to admit, it *was* a poor business move on my part. Never good to burn bridges, even if you're having fun doing so. I tried to reason with her, but it was clear she'd only come by to yell at me, so I just let her tire herself out before she finally left."

"When was this?" Amie asked.

"Two, three weeks ago? When I heard of her passing, I went to speak with Madeline to try to find out if the sale had gone through. Thought I might still have a chance to buy the place off of Savannah's widower. Especially when he came by today."

Amie straightened. "Andrew Harlow visited you today?"

"He called me," Oakland said. "Found my business card in Savannah's effects. Said he was told I might be interested in buying the store. I invited him over this afternoon to chat."

"And you lied to him, too," Ziya said, accusatory. "You told him Savannah was planning on selling the store to you."

Oakland shrugged, an unconvincingly bashful look on his face. "All's fair," he repeated. "Not my fault Savannah didn't communicate with her husband."

"She wanted to surprise him," Amie said, surprising herself with how vehemently she was defending Savannah Harlow. "And he's in *mourning*. You tried to manipulate a man who just lost his wife."

"A man in mourning came to *me* to talk business," Oakland shot back, poking his own chest. "I didn't go to him, he came to *me*. If he wasn't ready to play the game, he shouldn't have stepped onto the court."

Ziya scoffed as Amie worked to suppress her own temper.

"What did he say?" she asked, her voice flat. "When you told him Savannah was planning on selling to you?"

Thinking back, Oakland said, "Not much. He let me do most of the talking. Told him what I'd told Savannah back when I first offered to her: I could get the bookstore back on its feet, even sell it back to him once it started turning a profit again—at a much higher selling price, of course."

Oakland chuckled. "He didn't seem very interested in that part of the offer. He did ask if anyone else knew that Savannah had been planning on selling to me. I suspected there was a good chance Madeline would speak to him at some point, so I told him that she knew about it."

His tone shifted, as if he was giving a lecture to a rapt audience instead of two women glaring daggers at him. "Planting seeds of doubt about your competition to a seller can give you a leg up when the time comes for them to make a decision. If Madeline tried to claim Savannah wanted to sell to *her*, but I'd already told him she wanted to sell to *me*, he's more likely to believe the person he heard from first."

"Not necessarily," Amie said, feeling argumentative.

"No? You were so quick to believe Madeline when she said Savannah sold the store to her. Did she show you any proof?"

"No," Amie admitted. "But—"

"You believed her because you heard from her first," Oakland said. "In business, timing is everything. First impressions can be more valuable than an already-signed check. I wasn't given any time to try to plead my case; you'd already concluded that I was the liar."

"You also gave up pretty much right away," Ziya said drily.

Oakland pointed at her. "That's fair, I'll give you that. Once you said the papers had been signed, I realized there wasn't much more I could say." He spread his hands. "Can't win them all. Madeline won out this time. I'll just have to keep myself busy with my eight other flourishing small businesses and various other investments."

He sat back in his chair, looking pensive. "I suppose this means I've returned to being a suspect. Who else is on the list?"

Now it was Amie's turn to scoff. "I'm not telling you!"

"Fine, fine." Oakland chuckled again. Amie hated how enjoyable a time he appeared to be having. "Oh, to be young and unemployed with all the time in the world to run around trying to solve a mystery."

"I'm not unemployed," Amie said, knowing the truth of that statement had a looming expiration date.

"Really?" Oakland studied her. "I usually pride myself on my ability to read people. It's a big reason why I'm as successful as I am. You work from home?"

Amie frowned. "Yeah."

"Do you enjoy your work?"

"Not really, no."

"I could tell," Oakland said. "People who enjoy what they do have a certain . . . well, it sounds cheesy, but the best way to describe it is a *glow*. You don't have that glow."

"It's been a rough week," Amie deadpanned.

"You know," Oakland continued, "I could give you a discount on my entrepreneurship course."

"Really."

"Of course! In just a few short weeks, you'll—"

"God, do you ever *stop*?" Ziya scowled at the man. "Seriously, give it a fucking break. We came here to ask you about a woman who was murdered, and all you've done is treat everything like it's a game."

Oakland seemed unaffected by the outburst, with the unflappability of someone accustomed to being yelled at. "Have I been unforthcoming with my answers?" he asked calmly. "I'll admit I made a small fib, but otherwise I believe I've answered everything asked of me with truth." He looked at Amie for confirmation.

"I . . ." She didn't really want to validate the man, especially if it would seem like she was siding with him against Ziya. Opting for a change of subject, she said, "Is there anything else you can tell us about Savannah? Any concerns she had about anyone, worries she expressed . . . ?"

"She was worried about a lot of things," Oakland said breezily. "Though she pretended not to be. She was worried about losing the store, worried about her incompetent staff, worried she was doing everything wrong. But if you're asking if she told me about any enemies, or expressed a fear for her life, then no, she didn't mention anything like that."

He spread his hands. "Any other questions?"

"Are you having fun?" Ziya asked coldly.

"Immensely. My life would be significantly more boring if I didn't find fun in everything I do. That's how people waste their lives away, when they don't allow themselves any fun. That was Savannah's problem, I suppose. She took everything far too seriously. Can you imagine how different her life might have ended up if she just had more fun with it?"

"You're saying Savannah was murdered because she wasn't having enough *fun*?" Ziya asked, aghast.

Oakland rolled his eyes with amusement. "Well, maybe not. But she was letting herself be bogged down with worry and stress and anger." He knocked on his chest with a closed fist. "That does something to a person. Makes it so you can never really live life to its fullest. It rots your soul."

"You're a bad person."

Oakland and Ziya both looked at Amie with surprise, who would have given herself a similar look if she was physically capable of doing so.

"Sorry," Amie said quickly. "Or, not. I—" She winced, rubbing her temple. "I just, you're talking like you're some paragon of living life, but you're not a nice person. You used Savannah, you lied to Andrew, you lied to *us*—"

Oakland shook his head. "When you're playing the game—"

"I don't want to play your game!" Amie stood up. "None of us want to play your game. You might be having fun, but when it's at the expense of other people? That's a terrible way to live your life. You're a terrible person."

"Do you know how much I've done for other people?" Oakland chuckled, although the laughter sounded more forced than it had previously. "How many small businesses I've saved? How many jobs I've saved, how many *dreams* I've saved?"

"I don't . . ." Amie shook her head. "I don't think any of that really matters if you hurt people to get there." She wasn't even trying to convince him of anything. She knew she wouldn't be able to. She just had to say it. "I'm sure there are lots of people who are grateful for you and your money, but that doesn't negate the way you treat everyone as competitors or pawns. I think life is about more than just making sure you're having the best time. I don't know."

She crossed her arms, looking away from the man in the chair as she finished.

"Well . . ." Oakland cleared his throat. "Word of advice: Ending your passionate speech with 'I don't know' can significantly detract from its effectiveness."

"Shut up," Ziya said tiredly, standing as well. "Let's go. He's just wasting our time."

"I wouldn't be wasting your time if you'd ask the right question," Oakland said. "I've been waiting for you to ask it."

Amie huffed with annoyance. "Ask what?"

"If I have an alibi for when Savannah was murdered." Oakland's eyes gleamed. "Monday night, wasn't it? I flew in from Boston early Tuesday morning. Red-eye flight. I can show you my boarding pass, if you'd like."

"You couldn't have led with that?" Ziya asked through gritted teeth.

"That wouldn't have been as fun for him," Amie said before he could respond. Oakland shrugged in silent acknowledgement, the ghost of a smile on his face.

They left him sitting in his thousand-dollar chair.

"Sorry," Amie said once the elevator doors closed.

"For what?"

"For . . . that." Amie gestured to the doors, as if Oakland was still sitting on the other side. "I didn't think I'd change his mind or anything. I was just mad."

"I snapped at him first," Ziya said. "And I'm not surprised he made you mad. He's, like, the anti-Amie."

"Because I'm a young woman with very little savings?" Amie joked.

Her companion stayed silent as the elevator continued to descend.

"What?"

Ziya sighed. "Amie . . . I—"

Ding. The elevator settled to a stop, and the doors slid open.

"What?" Amie asked again as Ziya walked into the lobby. She stood there until the doors began to shut. Realizing Ziya wasn't pausing, Amie put out an arm to stop the doors and followed her.

"Miss!"

Amie stumbled to a stop as she watched Ziya push through the static exit next to the revolving doors. She turned to see the man at the desk holding out a hand.

"The card?" he prompted.

"Oh." Amie scrambled to remove the elevator key card from her pocket, practically throwing it at the poor man before running to the exit. "Sorry. Thank you!"

Pausing at the revolving door, she watched it for a moment before jumping in. Its speed had seemed too quick as she waited to enter, but once inside, she urged the doors to move faster, visualizing Ziya disappearing around the corner as she finally emerged onto the sidewalk. Amie looked around wildly to see where Ziya had gone, only to find the subject of her search standing off to the left, arms crossed as she gazed at the darkening sky.

"Need a ride home?" Ziya asked. She looked away from the clouds above, though still not at Amie. "Seems like it's about to rain."

Amie had been eagerly awaiting her first post-loop rainstorm. The light sprinkle on her first day had only left her wanting more. But now the impending weather was the last thing on her mind.

"Is everything okay?" she asked. "We haven't talked about last night, and I know I'm probably overthinking it, but . . ."

She trailed off as Ziya glanced at her, brows knit with sadness as their eyes locked for a brief moment. Then she was gone, looking away down the street as she dropped her arms, thumbs rubbing the side of her fists.

"Oh my god," Amie said softly. "I'm not overthinking it, am I?"

"Ames . . ." Ziya said, her voice heartbreakingly gentle. She had that expression on her face, that look that Amie would never forget, no matter how much time passed, no matter how poor her memory got. The look that haunted Amie so much she'd become determined never to ruin things with Ziya again, even if it meant going on the same exact date day after day after day.

"No," Amie blurted out, shaking her head. "No. That's not fair."

"You don't know what I'm going to say."

"Yes, I do. You're going to say we should give it more time." She stared at Ziya, willing her to say she was wrong, to laugh and tell her not to be silly.

Ziya didn't do any of those things. She just sighed. The sound ripped through Amie as frustration and desperation welled up inside of her.

"What did I do?" Amie asked in a small voice, horrified as her voice cracked a bit.

"You didn't do anything," Ziya said quickly. Her hand lifted as if to reach out for Amie, but she pulled it back to her chest in one fluid motion. "I'm sorry. I wanted to think about this some more, and then talk and maybe figure things out together. But then you said you were coming here, and I didn't want you to go alone—"

"I just don't understand what there is to think about." Amie felt a petulant whine creeping into her words. Her mind was racing to figure out how to save things. There would be no restarting. If Ziya walked away, she could be gone forever. "Last night you said you wanted this. I thought we both wanted this."

"We did. *I* did."

"So what happened?"

"The time loop."

Amie's stomach dropped. "You don't believe me."

"Oh!" Ziya's eyes widened. "No, of course I do. I . . . admittedly didn't really know what to make of it at first, but last night, when you told me everything . . . of *course* I believe you. You went through something that was so . . ." She shook her head in disbelief. "I don't know what I would have done. And I know you did what you felt like you had to do to keep going."

"I'm okay," Amie said, her insides warming from the confirmation that Ziya really did believe her. She knew what this was about. She *could* save things. "I understand. You feel like I need some time on my own to recover, but I'm really okay. For now I have to take a different route to the grocery store, and last night I moved my bed, and I'm still not convinced that I'm not technically thirty, but eventually I'll be back to normal. Everything can go back to how it was."

She gave Ziya a tentative smile, holding out a hand. Ziya took it, her eyes not leaving Amie's face as she studied it.

"Why didn't you do anything?" Ziya asked.

Amie gave her a puzzled look. "When?"

"In the time loop."

"I did things in the time loop. I told you."

"You did the same things. Over and over again. You were the only person who could change their actions each day, and you hardly ever did."

Amie nodded. "I do regret that."

"You do?"

Exhaling heavily, Amie said, "I think . . . I think maybe I was supposed to prevent Savannah from being murdered. If I had just known, I would have done something about it. I don't really think David's in danger of being arrested. I just feel so guilty for letting Savannah die so many times."

"Oh . . ." Ziya squeezed her hand. "It's not—"

"I know you're going to say it's not my fault." Amie set her shoulders, giving Ziya a half smile. "It's fine. All I can do now is try to make things a little better by figuring out who killed her. And I need you with me to do that." She laughed. "I mean, imagine how different things would have been if you were in the time loop with me, telling me what to do. I *need* you, Z."

Ziya's eyes flicked away. "Amie . . ." She gave Amie's hand another squeeze, then released it. "That's the problem."

Amie blinked with surprise. She didn't know there was still a problem. She thought she'd fixed it. How was there still a problem?

"I was thinking about why we broke up," Ziya continued. "I missed you so much that it made everything in the past feel so small. I thought maybe after three months apart we could figure out how to make it work. I saw how invested you were with Savannah's murder, and sure, you said it was for David, but I knew you weren't telling the whole truth. I just thought the truth might be that in those three months, you'd finally figured out how to try something new for a change. To follow a passion instead of staying the course."

She took a shaky breath. "And then I found out that for you, it'd been more like *two years*." Ziya looked desperate for Amie to understand what she was trying to say. "And you didn't . . . you didn't do *anything*."

Amie scrambled for words. "What exactly was I supposed to do? I was in a *time loop*. It didn't come with instructions. I was just trying to keep some sense of normalcy in a very not-normal situation. I'm sorry I didn't go to every club within eighteen hours of here, or try not to go to the same restaurant twice even if I loved the food—"

"I don't want you to do those things!" Ziya exclaimed. "I don't want you to be like me. I don't want you to do anything you don't want to do. But you never do anything you *want* to do, Amie. Nothing new, nothing different. You hardly ever do anything for yourself, especially if no one is telling you to do it."

"What are you *talking* about?" Amie asked, dumbfounded. "I spent two years going on the same date with you, having the same conversations, eating the same fettuccine alfredo, just so I could see you and know for certain that at the end of the night, you were gonna smile at me and say, 'Let's do this again soon.' I didn't do that for *you*; you never even remembered it happening."

"You put yourself through the same motions because you know they're safe," Ziya argued. "You're so afraid of wasting your life that you never do anything more for yourself than what you already have."

"Going to see you was me doing something for myself!"

"You already had me!" Ziya burst out. "You *had* me. I wasn't going anywhere. But you're always just going through the motions until someone asks you for help. If someone suggests you try something different for yourself, you twist yourself into knots trying to calculate if it's worth risking your time for. And by doing that, you're letting your whole life pass you by without doing anything for yourself, and it *killed* me to watch you live like that."

"I did things," Amie insisted, her mind racing for examples. "Concerts. Paint and sip. Diwali—"

"Those were all things for *me*," Ziya cut in. "You'd only ever do things I wanted to do. I knew you'd be hesitant about going to Iceland, but I thought, *Maybe if I ask this of her, then she'll do it.*

"But you couldn't. Because even though I was asking, you knew it was for you, not for me. Even when I bought the tickets and planned everything for you, you just couldn't do it. And I don't love how I handled it, and some of the things I said, but I realized that even if you had gone, it still wouldn't have fixed things. Because I can't spend the rest of my life telling you how to live yours, Amie. I can't do it. I have my own shit to figure out, my own life to lead. I want us to be in each other's lives, but I can't be in charge of both of them."

Ziya wrapped her arms around herself. "So after you said no to the trip, I decided that as much as I loved you . . . no, *because* I loved you so much, I couldn't stand to watch you do this to yourself. And none of that's changed. I thought maybe it had, or that maybe I could make you understand . . ."

She gave Amie a pleading look. "*Do* you understand?"

A drop of water hit the tip of Amie's nose, and only then did she notice it was raining. She wanted to say, *Yes, I understand,* just to make Ziya stop crying, because Ziya had begun to cry, silently, tears joining the raindrops that had begun to speckle her face as she waited for Amie's response.

"I'm looking at colleges," Amie said, her voice tight with emotion as she made one final attempt to save things. "I'm going to go back to school. Getting a degree in something I'm passionate about—maybe journalism, maybe something else, I don't know yet."

Giving her a watery smile, Ziya asked, "Are you doing that for you, or because I told you to?"

Amie paused, her mouth moving around silent words as she carefully deliberated which ones to vocalize.

"I don't know," she finally said. "But is that really so bad?"

Ziya took her hand again, squeezing it with both hands. "I didn't come here thinking I was going to suggest we give it more time," she said. "Honestly, I hadn't even gotten there when *you* said it. But I think that might be for the best." Her voice climbed in pitch on the final words, shaking as she spoke.

"Okay," Amie said dully. She didn't know what else to say. Ziya seemed to know exactly what she wanted from Amie, and as much as Amie wanted to give it to her, she didn't know how. She didn't know how to save this.

"Please let me drive you home." Ziya released her hand. "The rain's getting harder."

Shaking her head, Amie took a step back. "I'll get the bus."

"I drove by that bus stop, it doesn't have a covering. Just let me—"

"It's fine."

"Amie, please—"

"It's *fine*." Amie didn't want to yell. Ziya looked sad enough as it was, and the rain dampening their clothes clearly wasn't improving either of their moods. But Amie was angry. Not really at Ziya, she knew, but at herself. How, *how*, after having been given so many chances to get Ziya back, had she managed to ruin it again?

"You wanted me to make decisions for myself," she said flatly. "This is me doing that. Drive safe. Don't stop too fast, you always stop too fast, you'll hydroplane if you do."

She forced herself to walk away, even as Ziya continued to call her name behind her.

Amie hadn't taken notice of it when she first arrived, but Ziya had been right—the bus stop didn't have a covering. She sat on the wet bench, her jeans already soaked enough that more water wasn't going to make a significant difference.

Shielding it from the rain, Amie took out her phone, swiping away notifications for a spam missed call and voicemail. A red icon popped up as she opened the bus app, signaling delays, and she determined that the next bus wouldn't be arriving for another thirty minutes.

She could have probably caught Ziya before she left, but she couldn't do that. Amie didn't want to talk anymore, and she even less so wanted to sit in silence as Ziya drove her home.

Her eyes began to well up with tears. She'd *just* gotten her back. And now she couldn't see her anymore. Just like that, Ziya was gone.

A sob wracked through her, shaking her body so hard it startled her. Amie covered her mouth as hot tears stung her eyes. She lifted her phone again and made a call.

"Hello?" David's voice was barely audible over the sound of rainfall.

Amie opened her mouth, but all that emerged was another sob. She barely had any idea what had just happened, much less how to explain it to David.

"Amie? What's wrong? Are you okay?"

"Tell—" Amie gulped, wiping her eyes with the back of her hand. "Tell Genevieve—" Her throat closed again as another sob commandeered her vocal chords.

"I'm on my way. Where are you?"

* * *

Upon arrival, David had begun to scold Amie for sitting out in the rain, saying he would've brought her a towel if he'd known . . . no, don't worry about the seat, just get in, get in . . . what on Earth were you think—oh, you're crying, oh, no. Okay, it's okay, make sure that vent is pointed at you, I'll crank up the heat . . . do you feel the air? Good. Don't worry about the seat, it's okay, just buckle up. Do you want the radio on? I can see you're having trouble speaking. I'm just going to turn on the radio. If you start crying harder, I'll turn it off.

Which was how Amie found herself shivering in the passenger seat of David's car, listening to classic rock on the radio, body tensed as if that would keep the car seat from getting any more wet.

Several minutes later, after she'd visibly calmed down, David lowered the volume of the radio. "Do you want to talk about it?" he ventured with caution.

"No," Amie replied miserably.

"All right then." He turned the volume back up, and they didn't speak again until they were walking up the stairwell of their building. David kept shooting worried glances at her.

"Are you hungry?" he asked. "I have leftover lasagna. Or I could order something and subject a delivery person to this rain."

"I'm not really hungry," Amie mumbled. "Thanks, though."

David opened his mouth to say something else, but instead let out a high-pitched scream. Wait, no, that hadn't come from David. The scream was muffled and originated from a point above them.

Amie and David looked at each other with wide eyes, then thundered up the stairs. They passed the second floor, up to the third floor, pushing through the door into the hallway just in time to see Madeline burst out of the Harlows' apartment, screaming for help, hands smeared with blood.

Chapter Sixteen

Voicemail

Day 5 A.L.

Amie sat on the floor in the corner of the lobby, waiting for David to finish talking to the police. Her clothes had gone from uncomfortably wet to uncomfortably damp, and the ends of her hair had begun to curl up as they dried.

"I think he's dead!" The memory of Madeline's screams still gave Amie goosebumps. She'd been hoping someone might give her one of those shock blankets when the EMTs arrived to take Andrew (who was not dead) to the hospital, but none was offered. In fairness, she wasn't really in shock. Just cold. And damp.

The lobby was full of building residents milling around, exchanging information and shooting concerned looks at the cops as they interviewed Amie, David, and a few other neighbors who had heard raised voices from the Harlows' apartment prior to Madeline's dramatic exit.

Amie had told the police what she'd encountered—Madeline running out of the apartment, blood on her hands. Madeline screaming and pointing into the apartment. How Amie and David had looked inside to see Andrew lying unconscious on the floor, a fresh wound on his head. David ordering her not to touch anything as he checked Andrew's pulse, then telling her to call an ambulance. Running downstairs to wait for the ambulance. The ambulance arriving with the police—

That was when the officer interviewing her said she could stop narrating what had happened. Then he'd asked if she'd noticed anything unusual in the apartment.

"Other than the unconscious, bleeding man?"

"Yes."

Amie had shaken her head. It was true. Not so much because there wasn't anything unusual to notice, but between worrying that Andrew was dead or that Madeline might pass out, she hadn't left much time in her schedule for calmly investigating the apartment.

Madeline had been briefly interviewed by the police before being escorted away—to the hospital or the police station, Amie wasn't sure.

She stared at Benny, who was standing in one corner of the lobby, typing on his phone. Amie hadn't encountered her landlord since receiving the photos of him entering her apartment the other night. Since she'd convinced herself of his innocence, it had become a tiny mystery that felt like a distraction from the bigger, more important one at hand. She was tempted to just walk up to Benny and ask him about it, but if there was still even a small chance he'd been the one to leave the threatening note, Amie felt safer with him not knowing she suspected him.

Catching sight of a familiar multicolored poncho, Amie raised a hand, attempting to get Elena's attention. The older woman hurried over as soon as she saw her.

"How're you holding up, sweetheart?" she asked, brows knit with sympathy.

Amie started to get up, but her neighbor waved her back down as she eased herself onto the floor.

"I'm all right," Amie said. "Better than Andrew. Or Madeline." She cast a sideways look at Elena. "Do you know what happened?"

"The police were very adamant about people keeping their distance while they conducted their interviews," Elena said.

"But . . ."

Elena straightened her glasses. "I might have overheard a few things." She leaned in to Amie, who met her halfway. "According to Madeline, Andrew invited her over to 'talk business.' Did you know Savannah had just sold the bookshop to Madeline?"

"Yeah, Madeline told me. Did she say that to the police?"

Elena nodded. "But I also had a feeling. The last time Savannah came over to have me read her cards, there was a recurring message about new beginnings that seemed to resonate with her. I sensed that the time might have finally come for her to sell."

She stretched her legs out, flexing her feet in her sneakers. "So, Madeline thought Andrew wanted to talk about her taking over the store. But when she arrived, he began filming her, and told her to admit that she'd killed Savannah."

Amie's stomach dropped. "*What?*"

Elena seemed pleased by her reaction. "Mhm. Madeline denied it, of course. Wouldn't you?"

"Sure, I guess," Amie said. "Mainly because I didn't kill Savannah, but—"

"Well, I don't know what Andrew had been expecting." Elena sniffed, as if unimpressed by Andrew's approach to his interrogation of Madeline. "Guilty or not, anyone would be an idiot to admit it under those circumstances."

"So then what happened?"

"Andrew got angrier," Elena reported. "According to Madeline, she tried running away. For some reason, Andrew had a wire strung out across his front hall. She said he'd had her step over it when she first arrived. Madeline remembered to avoid it, but Andrew tripped and slammed his head on the floor."

Amie winced. Andrew's attempt to protect his own life had ended up endangering it.

"Madeline tried to stop the bleeding. She thought he was dead, so she screamed and ran out. It's all very strange." Elena folded her hands in her lap to conclude her story. "If Savannah had already sold the store to Madeline, why would Andrew think Madeline had killed her? What reason would she have had to kill Savannah?"

"I lied to the man for nothing. Strange he didn't know . . ."

* * *

"Andrew still doesn't know Savannah sold the store to Madeline," Amie said. She was sitting on the couch in David's apartment, once again hugging her favorite plastic flamingo while David prepared the leftover lasagna she'd decided she was in fact hungry for.

"Oakland told me and Z—" *Ow.* "Oakland said he lied and told Andrew that Savannah had been planning on selling the bookstore to him. If Andrew believed him, he might have also believed that Madeline killed Savannah to try to get him to sell the store to her instead."

"This is assuming Madeline was telling the truth," David said over the beeping of the oven as he preheated it. "Or, for that matter, Elena."

"Why would Elena lie?" Amie asked.

"I don't think she'd *lie*. I just wouldn't put it past her to stretch the truth in pursuit of a juicier story."

"Did you see a shattered vase on the floor of the apartment when we were in there?" Amie looked over the back of the couch at David.

"Sure did. I had a look around while you went to meet the ambulance. Seemed like the table it was sitting on got tipped over. Was that what the wire was attached to?"

"Yeah." Amie turned back around. "Andrew rigged up the trip wire to the vase as an alarm system." She used the flamingo to gesture across the room at the finished (she assumed it was finished, though she could never really tell) machine that covered the surface of David's work table. "I think you two would get along."

He snorted. "I'll make sure to schedule a play date if he survives that head smash."

There was a pause. Then:

"Sorry. You've had a long day."

Amie shrugged. "Not my longest."

She braced herself as David went to sit in his armchair, not knowing how to answer if he asked what had happened with her and Ziya.

"How's the adjustment going?"

Amie frowned, confused. "The what?"

"To post-time-loop life."

"Oh!" She hadn't expected that question. "It's . . . fine. I tried some memory exercises yesterday. And your method of doing things differently has been working well. I moved my bed today because the only way I could fall asleep last night was by sleeping upside down."

"Like a bat?"

"Horizontally. Feet where my head was, and vice versa."

"Ah. Interesting."

Amie traced the plastic feathers of the flamingo's wing with her finger. "It's strange how leaving the time loop made everything that felt comfortable *un*comfortable. Now I have to do things differently to avoid the discomfort. But I assume that'll go away with time."

She glanced at David. "Do you think I don't do anything?"

"What do you mean?"

"I . . . guess I don't really know." Amie hugged the flamingo closer, sighing. "How do you know if you're happy enough with your life to not want anything more?"

David shifted forward in his chair. "I feel like these questions are all connected to one thing."

"They are, but I'm not ready to talk about that."

"Okay." David got to his feet, crossing the room to fidget with his machine. "I guess I don't know. Can't imagine anyone's happy one hundred percent of the time. I think anyone who'd claim that would be lying to themselves."

"But how—" Amie rubbed her face, feeling her frustration mounting. "How do you know you're spending your time in a way that will give you the best version of your life? How do you know that the choices you're making now are going to pay off later?"

"Kid." David pulled a silver concierge bell out of a box. "I think you know the answer to that."

"You don't?" Amie asked miserably.

David tapped the bell, then scowled at it as it failed to let out the *ding* he'd apparently been hoping for. "Piece of junk," he muttered, tossing it back into the box.

"That sucks." Amie flopped over onto the couch, flamingo still in her arms.

"That's life," David said. "Look, you know I love to haggle. Got that bell down to fifty cents from the original two-dollar asking price. But if you treat your time like money, and are always trying to haggle to get the most for it, you're gonna leave the yard sale with nothing."

"Hm."

"I lost you with the metaphor, didn't I?"

"A little, yeah. It sounded nice, though." Amie sat up. "You spend a lot of your time building these machines that you just take down a day or two later. Do you feel like that's a worthwhile use of your time?"

David narrowed his eyes. "Is this an intervention?"

"No! Sorry, that sounded harsh." Amie gestured to his machine. "I just mean, you seem pretty happy. But you spend most of your time doing this, over and over again. You don't even film it and put it online or anything."

"Would it be more worthwhile if I put videos online?"

"I dunno. Maybe? Don't you ever want to share your creativity with the world?"

"Been there, done that. It was fine. Speaking of, have you started my books yet?"

Dodging the question, Amie asked, "You're enjoying yourself, right?"

"In this conversation? I could go either way."

"In *life*."

David adjusted a domino that had gotten knocked out of line. "Sure. I feel like building these machines is worth my time because I enjoy it. So I suppose that means I'm happy with my life. But we're not talking about me, are we?"

"I just think that if it works for you, then it can work for me."

David whipped around so fast the movement sacrificed a row of dominos.

"Oh no," he said, holding up a finger. "Do not try to make a role model out of me. I'm not perfect."

"I didn't say you were *perfect*," Amie retorted. "You're far from perfect."

"Now hang on, 'far' is—"

"I'm just saying that we lead similar lives." She held out her hands palms-up. "I get the same bagel from the café every time I go for breakfast. You go grocery shopping at the same time every week. We stick with what we know. And we're happy!"

David ran a hand down his face, wincing. "Sure, but . . . I've lived a lot more life than you have, kid. I know what I like best because I've tried a lot of things. Can you say the same?"

Frowning, Amie stared at the flamingo. "I guess not," she mumbled. "But, okay, that brings me back to my first question. How do you know when you're happy enough? How do you know that you're spending your time in the best way possible?"

The oven beeped, indicating that it was finished preheating. David returned to the kitchen, put the lasagna in the oven, and disappeared into his bedroom.

Amie pulled out her phone, then stuffed it away again without looking at the screen. She wasn't sure what would make her feel worse: seeing a text from Ziya, or seeing that Ziya hadn't texted.

"Here." Her vision was overtaken by a short stack of papers being waved in front of her face. She took the papers as David retreated to his work table once more.

"What is it?" Amie placed the plastic flamingo on the couch next to her and flipped through the pages. They displayed rough sketches of what looked like people and animals, with words that were even more difficult to interpret.

"I started working on that children's book," David said, resurrecting the domino casualties from the Great Table Bump of Two Minutes Ago. "You were right—even if Elle is too old for it now, it's still something I want to do for her. And she'll still appreciate it, even if it's ten years overdue. I could agonize over what could've been if I hadn't waited so long to do it, but . . . why spend the energy on that?"

"This is *so* sweet." Amie held up a drawing of what looked like a lion/car hybrid playing volleyball. "But you're going to get an artist for this, right?"

"Okay, fuck off."

"No!" Amie laughed. "I'm sorry. These are really great."

"Eh, you're right." David turned, crossing his arms. "I can't draw to save my life. Clearly. I'll stick with the writing. I think it's a cute story, so . . ." He shrugged. "I don't know, I need to work on it some more."

He cleared his throat uncomfortably. "I never considered that it was something I could still do. But I did it because you gave me the push to try something different. So thanks for that."

"This is amazing." Amie flipped to another page as David abandoned the domino rescue effort to sit with her on the couch. "Ziya . . ." *Ow.* ". . . gave me the push to try something different, too. And then I did it, and she was still unhappy. But I think that's because I only push myself when someone else tells me it's the right thing to do. And she didn't like that I couldn't do that for myself. She wants 'more' for me."

"Mm." David laced his fingers together, resting his forearms on his thighs. "Do you think you could start doing that for yourself?"

"Probably not." Amie straightened the papers in her lap. "I spent two years in a time loop and almost never pushed myself to do anything. I think that might have been why I was in there for so long. I thought I just needed to keep my head down, but I was probably supposed to actually try something different."

David was quiet for a moment.

"I don't . . . think it matters what you think you were supposed to do," he finally said. "What matters is that you understand that you're . . . important. You spend a hell of a lot of time doing things for and worrying about other people, kid, but you don't treat yourself the same way. That's why you just kept your head down in the time loop. You were the only one impacted by it, the only one who needed help, but you don't consider yourself important enough to be worthy of your own help. Sometimes, Amie, the most important person you need to consider is *you*."

Amie pressed her lips together as her eyes started to prickle.

"I think," David continued, "if you were in Ziya's shoes, you'd want more for you, too."

"Yeah," Amie said softly. She passed David's papers back to him before any tears could fall on them and make the drawings look even more strange than they already did.

"Lasagna time!" David sprang off the couch, taking his pages with him. "Come and get it."

Amie wiped her eyes as she joined him in the kitchen. "The timer didn't go off yet," she pointed out.

"I know," David said, donning oven mitts, "but the energy was getting a little too touchy-feely for me, so I thought it'd be best to nip that in the bud."

He opened the oven door and removed the lasagna. Once it was set down safely on the stovetop, Amie gave him a hug.

"This was the bud I was trying to nip," David grumbled, patting the top of Amie's head with an oven mitt. "There, there." He gave her a one-armed squeeze before extracting himself from the embrace. "Come on, grab a plate."

* * *

Once she'd returned home for the night, Amie finally gave in and checked her phone. Her heart leapt into her throat when she saw the red notification bubble indicating an unplayed voicemail, until she remembered the spam call she'd ignored earlier that evening.

Poised to delete the message, Amie pressed play to listen:

> *"Hey, it's Winston. From the flower counter. Sorry this took so long—my manager was out yesterday, and today we were flooded with this huge last-minute order for the fall festival . . . anyway, doesn't matter.*
>
> *"So, I think you said you wanted to know if a delivery would've been left at the door if no one was there to accept it. The answer I got was yes, it would've been. My manager showed me how to access the notes on an order. I know you were asking about Savannah Harlow's delivery, so I checked the notes for that. The flowers were delivered at seven on Monday and left outside the address."*

Amie sat down at her kitchen table, turning up the volume on her phone. So the delivery person hadn't seen Savannah return to the store that night. Not that Amie had been wishing Savannah's wrath on an innocent delivery person, but she'd hoped there might be someone out there who could tell her if the bookstore owner had been upset about the change in delivery time. If so, it would have confirmed that someone had impersonated Savannah on the phone, changing the time to lure her back to the store to be murdered.

"I noticed something else," Winston continued. *"I thought the reason Savannah came in on Monday was because the system glitched and canceled her order. But after looking at her order notes, it looks like Savannah called in on Sunday herself to cancel it. Not sure why she took it out on me the next day. Guess she forgot."*

Amie stilled.

"That's all I got. Have a good weekend. Bye."

Chapter Seventeen

Fall

Day 6 A.L.

The new furniture arrangement worked. Amie slept well that night, despite the roller coaster of a day she'd had (or maybe because of it—by the time she got into bed, she could hardly keep her eyes open).

Sundays had always been her time to prepare, physically and emotionally, for the week ahead. Despite not having experienced a Sunday in quite some time, Amie easily fell into her pre-loop routine. She cleaned her apartment. Did the laundry. Stocked up on groceries. Finally replaced her failing pen and filled out her planner as best she could. (All she ended up writing was "Find new job," "Look at schools," and a bunch of doodles while she tried to come up with something else to jot down.)

Though it had been almost a week since the time loop, it felt odd dedicating a whole day to her future. But the feeling was comforting. And strangely exciting. Amie never thought she'd find doing laundry exciting. It was like the opposite of the Sunday scaries. Sunday . . . cheeries? No, never mind, it didn't need a name.

As she went about her day, she found her thoughts repeatedly drawn to Winston's message.

"But after looking at her order notes, it looks like Savannah called in on Sunday herself to cancel it."

That had immediately felt off to Amie. Savannah always seemed to relish taking her anger and annoyance out on other people, but canceling the order only to yell at Winston about it the next day didn't seem realistic. Nor did Savannah forgetting she'd canceled the order herself. Of all the people Amie had spoken to about the dead woman, no one had mentioned her struggling with her memory. Unless Amie, who *had* been struggling with her memory, had forgotten about that. But this seemed unlikely as well.

Especially once her memory helpfully served her a piece of information that almost made her topple off the chair she'd been standing on to dust the top of her bookcase.

"We figured out some compromises. Coming home by seven was one of them; she used to stay at the store even later before we agreed on that. She'd also agreed to not work on Sundays, let go of a few part-time employees, and feature more bestsellers in the window."

Amie remembered feeling surprised when Andrew told her this. Savannah never struck her as someone willing to compromise, but her widower had seemed confident that she had been sticking to her word. Would she have made a call canceling her flower order on the one day of the week she'd promised her husband she'd take off?

Despite the strengthening feeling that Savannah hadn't been behind either of the calls made to the flower counter at the grocery store, the reason for the first call continued to stump her. If the same person (presumably the murderer) had made both calls, what was the point of the first? They could have simply had a second order of flowers delivered to the store Monday evening to get Savannah to return. Why cancel her regular order as well? It felt like—Amie winced—overkill.

She was still thinking about it as she and David arrived at the fall festival that evening. The outing had been David's suggestion.

"Really?" Amie had asked, amused. "I feel like you're not really a festival guy."

"Not a big fan of fall, either," David admitted. "I like pumpkin spice as much as the next guy, but too much of a good thing is too much of a good thing. But we should still go. Trying new things. Doing something for yourself. All that."

Amie knew he was just trying to take her mind off of Ziya (though he still didn't know exactly what had happened). And she found it difficult to resist the allure of an apple cider donut once the idea was presented to her.

"It just feels like I'm missing something," Amie said. They walked past a couple sticking their heads through a painted board that made them look like two scarecrows in a cornfield. "Why the initial cancellation of the flowers? The person who did it must have known Savannah would go to the store to complain as soon as she realized the flowers wouldn't be delivered. What was the reasoning?"

"Maybe they wanted Savannah out of the bookstore," David suggested.

"Hm." Amie's mind raced as she tried to make sense of that. "If it had been Benny, maybe he wanted her gone so he could look for those photos. I still don't know what he was doing in my apartment. But like we've said, it seems overly complicated for Benny."

"Sometimes overcomplication can indicate a lack of logic." David ducked to avoid getting whacked in the face with a balloon as a child ran by. "But you also believe Benny had an alibi."

"Yeah." Amie crossed her arms as a breeze made its way under her cardigan. "For when Savannah was murdered, at least. He could've gone to the store earlier that day to look for the photos. Do you think it's possible that two people sabotaged Savannah's flower order for unrelated reasons?"

David shrugged. "It's possible. But if he was back there searching for the photos on Wednesday, that means something went wrong with his plan on Monday. Maybe he was interrupted."

"I wonder if Grayson saw someone," Amie mused.

"Who?"

"He works at the bookshop. I talked to him on Wednesday. He was pretty eager to talk, so I feel like he would have mentioned it if he caught Benny sneaking into the back room that day."

Why else would someone want Savannah out of the store?

They passed the Eons Café booth, where more people were lining up for hot drinks to fight off the dropping temperature as the sun set behind the Ferris wheel. Jess was taking orders at the front of the line, flashing Amie a quick smile as they made eye contact.

A thought struck Amie as they continued past. "Madeline said Savannah had signed the paperwork selling the store right before she died," she said slowly. "But what if it wasn't Savannah who signed it? What if Madeline snuck into the store to forge her signature and send it off to the lawyer?"

David scratched the back of his head, eyebrows scrunched together with doubt. "You think Savannah was never going to sell?"

"Well, no, because she told Oakland she was. But, I don't know, maybe she was getting cold feet or something." Amie began speaking faster as her excitement mounted. "Maybe Madeline canceled the order so Savannah would go to the grocery store, giving her the chance to sneak into the back of the bookshop and sign the contract. Then she killed Savannah before Savannah could find out."

Amie's eyes widened as she stopped short. "Maybe that's why Andrew attacked her. Maybe he knew something that we don't."

"That's a lot of maybes," David said, pulling her out of the flow of flannel-clad pedestrian traffic. "Do you have any time loop knowledge about Madeline? Anything that could solidify this theory?"

"No. I didn't see her at all on Monday. But that doesn't mean she wasn't around. And her café is right next door to the bookshop; she could've easily known about Savannah's regular flower delivery."

Amie bounced on the balls of her feet, looking around. "I need to find Grayson and ask if he saw Madeline that day. He's gotta be here."

Sighing, David said, "Look, I know by now that it's no use trying to deter you from this. How about we walk around some more, get some apple cider donuts, try to enjoy the festival, and if you see the guy, great. Interrogate away. If not, you'll still have a nice night, and you can talk to him tomorrow."

Amie tried to hide her disappointment. She'd been about to suggest they comb every inch of Willows Park until they found the guy. But she knew David was just worried about her, so . . .

. . . she'd send him off for donuts while she searched for Grayson herself.

"It'll be faster if we split up," she said. "You get the donuts, I'll get us hot chocolates."

"Okay," David said, seeming reassured by Amie's embracing of the fall festival spirit. "We'll meet back here. See you soon."

Amie headed back to the Eons booth, then veered off between two tents toward the carnival games. She weaved through the crowd, craning her neck as she searched for Grayson's auburn curls.

Unfortunately, her search required her to look a lot of people in the face, which is how she ended up locking eyes with Benny. He was walking away from a ring toss game, shoulder to shoulder with the woman from the infamous blackmail photos.

Too late to pretend she hadn't seen him, Amie gave him a tight smile and a nod, assuming he'd give her the same. Instead, he put up a hand to grab her attention before she could look away.

"Hey!" he said, looking annoyed. As he paused to let a group of teenagers pass, Amie briefly considered running away. Before she could make a decision, her landlord was standing in front of her, arms crossed.

"What happened with the 'flooding emergency' in your bathroom?" he demanded. "Was that just a dumb prank, or . . . ?"

Amie's mouth fell open with surprise. She didn't know what she'd been expecting, but it wasn't *this*. "I, uh . . . what?"

"You called and said you had a flooding emergency in your bathroom that needed to be dealt with ASAP," Benny said. "Then—"

"No, I didn't," Amie said, catching up to what must have happened. "Did someone call you and say that?"

Now Benny looked surprised. "Yeah. That wasn't you?"

"No." Amie felt jittery, like she'd downed three cups of coffee. "Did you go to my apartment?"

"Yeah," Benny said, studying her face as if to determine if she was telling the truth. "No one answered, so I let myself in. When I saw that there wasn't any flooding, I left. You didn't answer when I called you back."

"Was it my phone number?" Amie asked.

Benny shrugged.

"Do you not have my number saved in your phone?"

"No. I usually just ask people for their apartment number if they need something from me."

Amie closed her eyes so he couldn't see her rolling them. "Okay, well . . . that wasn't me."

"Huh. Weird."

"Ben." The woman rubbed Benny's arm as Amie opened her eyes again. "Can we go on the Ferris wheel now?"

"Sure." Benny gave Amie an awkward shrug. "No harm, no foul, I guess. Enjoy your night."

"You too." Amie gave a stiff wave as they walked off.

A third imitation phone call. That explained what Benny had been doing in Amie's apartment that night. Whoever made the call must have photographed Benny entering, then sent them to Amie to make her think he'd left the message.

Amie shivered, this time not from the autumn breeze. Was it Savannah's murderer? And if so, why would they want Amie to think Benny had wanted her to stop looking into Savannah's death? If it *was* Madeline, she had no connection to Benny, as far as Amie knew.

One thing at a time. She was looking for Grayson.

Not wanting to keep David waiting, she decided to finish her quick scan of the carnival games area, then head over to the

Eons booth. She could stand in line and look to see if Grayson walked past.

Thankfully, the line for the café's booth had shortened by the time Amie arrived. She took her spot at the end, turning around so she could scour the crowd of people walking past.

"Hi!"

Amie ignored the greeting, assuming it was for someone else. Then:

"Amie?"

Raina stepped into Amie's line of sight. She was wearing a green windbreaker and holding a white paper bag in one hand. A few autumn leaves were painted on her cheek, which danced as she smiled tentatively.

"Oh, hi!" Amie flashed her a quick smile before returning to her surveillance. Realizing this new arrival could be of assistance, she added, "Have you seen Grayson tonight?"

"Grayson?" Raina looked surprised. "Yeah, I saw him a little while ago by the rides. Do you guys know each other?"

"Not really. I just need to ask him something."

"I can text him for you," Raina offered, pulling out her phone. She sent off the text as Amie thanked her profusely.

"Fried Oreo while you wait?" Raina offered, holding out the white paper bag. "My friends went on the Zipper, so I got these to keep me occupied until they're done."

"I'm good, thanks." Amie had returned to keeping an eye out for Raina's coworker. "I'm picking up hot chocolates for me and David."

"What do you need Grayson for?" Raina asked, noticing Amie's preoccupation. "You don't have to tell me, of course."

Amie hesitated. She didn't want to go around accusing Madeline without stronger proof, especially so close to a handful of her employees.

"I'm still looking into Savannah's death," she said in a low voice. "And I had some questions for him about Madeline."

"Because of the incident with Andrew?"

"That, plus a few other things. I think there's a chance she was lying about Savannah selling the store to her."

Raina's eyebrows shot up. "Madeline said Savannah sold the store to her?"

Amie winced. She hadn't meant to share that. But if it turned out Madeline had lied, she supposed it wouldn't matter. "You didn't know anything about it?"

Raina shook her head slowly, returning to her phone as it dinged. "Grayson says to meet him at the lake. He's by the paddle boats."

"Great." Hopefully Grayson would stick around long enough for Amie to get the hot chocolates, find David, and head over there.

They reached the front of the line. Jess took Amie's order.

"Do you know how Madeline's doing?" Amie asked as the barista took her money.

"Not sure," Jess said, grabbing two cups and writing on them. "But she said she was going to try to stop by this evening, so sounds like she's okay." They smiled, passing off the cups to another employee. "They'll call out your name when it's ready."

"Thanks." Amie made a mental note to keep an eye out for Madeline. What she would do once she saw her . . . that was still being workshopped.

"So what does Grayson have to do with this?" Raina asked, opening the paper bag as they moved off to the side. She fished out a fried Oreo and popped it into her mouth.

Amie tried to think of the most abridged way to explain things to Raina. "Basically," she said, "I think whoever killed Savannah wanted her out of the store the morning before she died. If Madeline thought Savannah was getting cold feet about selling the store, she might have snuck into the back and forged the paperwork with Savannah's name." The more she said this theory out loud, the better it sounded. "So I want to ask Grayson if there's any way someone could have snuck into the back room without him noticing."

"Oh!" Raina dusted powdered sugar off her hands. "I can answer that for you. The store was pretty quiet that morning, so it would've been hard for someone to get back there without one of us noticing. But I guess if she somehow managed to sneak in the back door—"

"No, I'm talking about Monday morning," Amie clarified.

"Yeah. Me too."

Amie frowned. She'd been struggling with some memory issues, sure, but she was positive that every time she'd gone to the grocery store with David on Monday morning, Raina had been there. "You weren't at the bookshop then. You said you had the morning off."

"No, I didn't," Raina said, confused. "When did I tell you that?"

"When—" Amie stopped. *When we talked at the grocery store on a different version of the same day* would have probably led to more follow-up questions than Amie was willing to deal with at that moment.

"I . . . must have gotten confused," she said haltingly. "I thought Grayson was alone at the bookshop while Savannah was at the grocery store."

Raina snorted. "Absolutely not. We never leave Grayson alone in the store. I'm working full time now that Andrew is out of commission."

"Two hot chocolates for Amie!"

Amie vaguely acknowledged the announcement as she fell into her thoughts. Raina's words had dragged a memory to the front of her mind. Grayson had told Amie that he'd never been left in the store alone. He said nothing unusual happened on Monday. Raina was telling the truth; she'd been at the bookshop that morning on the final day of the time loop.

So why did Amie see her at the grocery store all those other times?

"Sometimes, Amie, the most important person you need to consider is you."

"How familiar are you with the grocery store?" Amie asked.

Raina looked puzzled by the non sequitur. "What?"

"The grocery store. The one where Savannah had her regular flower order delivered from. Do you go there often?"

"Yeah." Raina seemed concerned, which made sense. Amie knew she probably looked and sounded unusually eager for a conversation about a grocery store. "I do all my food shopping there."

"That's strange," Amie murmured.

Raina chuckled lightly. "Why?"

It was clear to Amie that Raina had lied to her, even if Raina herself didn't know. Amie had become so accustomed to her time loop habits at the grocery store that she'd nearly forgotten what had happened the first loop day she'd accompanied David there.

It had been a couple days after she'd finally told her neighbor about the time loop. She'd gone to visit him early, catching him right as he was leaving his apartment. He'd told her on a previous day that he'd nearly gotten escorted out by the store's security for arguing with Savannah, so Amie wanted to see if her presence could possibly prevent that from happening.

They heard Savannah start to yell as they reached the cereal aisle. David had needed a basket for his groceries, so she went to fetch it to keep him away from Savannah.

Then she'd run into Raina. Raina said she had the morning off. Raina needed help searching for granola. And peanut butter—crunchy, not smooth. Then she'd knocked over a display of pinto beans, and Amie helped her clean it up.

By the time Amie was finished assisting Raina, David and Savannah were at each other's throats, Savannah's original grievance long forgotten as she screamed at David to stay out of her business. Amie managed to drag David away before security arrived.

After that day, she quickly learned how to keep David away from Savannah. She could never convince him to go to the store at a different time (mentioning Savannah only made him more determined), but she knew how the timing worked. She knew to get a basket as they arrived. She knew to collect the groceries Raina needed as they shopped, so she could swiftly give them to her and return to David before he could make his way to the flower counter. She managed to change the story of what happened that day, because in the time loop, anything that changed was because of Amie.

Raina was at the bookshop Monday morning. So why was she at the grocery store all those other days during the time loop?

Because of Amie. Because Raina knew David was going to the grocery store that Monday, as he did every Monday. She'd see him walking past the bookshop. And when Amie was with him, she'd see Amie, too.

"You didn't want me to stop David and Savannah from arguing," Amie said, her words slow and careful. She gazed at the bright lights of the carnival rides in the distance as she worked through her thoughts. "You knew I could. You'd seen me do it before. You wanted them to fight. To be seen fighting. You—" *Oh my god, David was right. Someone was trying to frame him.*

"I what?" Raina asked. Her eyes were searching Amie's face. She still looked concerned, but something in her expression had shifted. She was no longer concerned for Amie. She was concerned *because* of Amie.

"You . . . should probably get back to your friends." Amie suddenly felt like she very much needed to leave. "David's waiting for me . . ."

"Sure, of course." Raina balled up the white paper bag, tossing it into a nearby trash can before digging into her purse. "Are you still going to meet Grayson?"

"No," Amie said, trying to appear calm. "I mean, yeah. I should talk to him. But don't let me take up any more of your time. It was nice seeing you!"

"You too!" Raina gave her a hug, and Amie felt a wave of relief wash over her. Now she just had to find David—

At first she thought the breeze had penetrated her cardigan again. Her relief rapidly ebbed as she registered the cool metal pressed against the small of her back. Raina pulled one arm away, leaving the other wrapped around Amie's waist.

"Or we could spend some more time together," Raina suggested. She seemed nervous, and without any other context, Amie could have been convinced that the other woman was flirting with her. But by now she was almost positive Raina had murdered Savannah, which was supported by the knife she seemed to be threatening Amie with, so Amie assumed Raina had more pressing matters on her mind than trying to ask her out on a date.

Amie stammered out something that was just as unintelligible to her as it was to Raina.

"I'm gonna take that as a yes," Raina said, pulling Amie into the throng of people passing by. She lowered her voice, speaking into Amie's ear. "The alternative option is that I stab you here and leave you bleeding on the ground. Which you *might* survive, but it'd be painful. I think we can figure out an easier way to deal with this. Would you prefer that?"

Amie nodded, trying to keep up with Raina's quickening pace. She was worried one trip, one jostle, any sudden movement might provoke Raina to opt in for the alternative option.

"Where are we going?" Amie asked as she was led around a corner.

"I need to think," Raina replied. "Just keep moving while I think."

Trying not to move her head, Amie glanced around, hoping to catch sight of David. They were already moving away from the food area, so unless David had taken a detour to get his face painted, she knew her chances of running into him were lessening with every step.

"Amie?"

"Shit," Raina muttered. "Act normal. Be quick."

How does one say "actually, I'm not feeling ready to talk to my ex-girlfriend who just re-broke up with me yesterday" to someone holding them at knifepoint? Amie couldn't come up with an answer fast enough as Raina turned them around, which is how she found herself face-to-face with Ziya and two of her friends.

"Hey," Amie said weakly, hoping that any strain in her voice would just be chalked up to their recent re-estrangement. "Enjoying the festival?"

Ziya was looking at Raina's arm wrapped around Amie's waist, which for multiple reasons was something Amie did *not* want her attention on.

Seeming to realize Ziya wasn't going to say anything, her friend Alison spoke up.

"Yeah!" she chirped. "We made sure to hit all the rides before getting food. Last year I got sooo sick on the Gravitron. No one wanted a repeat of that."

"Totally," Amie agreed, still watching Ziya.

"Hi, I'm Alison," Alison said to Raina, glancing at her friends as if to say, *Why am I the only one talking?*

"Raina. Hi."

Ziya's other friend, Jamilah, elbowed her. "Did you want to tell Amie something?" she prompted.

Finally looking away from Raina's arm, Ziya blinked at her. "Huh?"

"You called Amie's name," Jamilah said. *And everyone is wondering why you've put us in this awkward situation*, her expression added.

"Oh. Right. Um . . ." Ziya looked at Amie. "I just, uh, wanted to make sure you were okay." She glanced at Raina, giving her a tight smile. "But looks like you are."

"Yup," Raina said before Amie could speak. "We were actually just about to ride the Ferris wheel. We should probably go before the line gets too long."

"Right," Amie said, her heart starting to pound at just the suggestion of riding the Ferris wheel. Of course, she wasn't about to try to argue with Raina. Not while Ziya was within stabbing distance of that knife, at least. "It was good seeing you guys."

Ziya had an odd expression on her face, but Amie was too concerned with getting Raina away from her to decipher it. She wanted to alert Ziya to what was happening, but she couldn't think of a way of doing that without endangering her and her friends.

"Good seeing you, too!" Alison said, smiling.

"Yeah." Ziya attempted the tight smile again. "Tell David I said hi."

"I will." Amie was being pulled away. As they turned, she had a thought.

"Tell Genevieve I said hi, too," she added, trying to keep any urgency out of her voice.

"Who's Genevieve?" Raina asked, suspicion staining her voice as Amie hurried them away.

Amie stiffened. Maybe she hadn't sounded as casual as she'd hoped.

"Her . . . dog," Amie stammered. "Genevieve's her dog."

"You told her to say hi to her dog?"

Now Amie couldn't tell if the negativity in Raina's tone was from doubting her story, or just a general disdain for dog people.

In an attempt to distract her captor from the attempt to signal Ziya, Amie asked, "So *did* you know Savannah was selling the store? Is that why you killed her?"

She felt a pinch as Raina pressed the knife closer. "Keep your voice down. Jesus."

Amie straightened her back to try to avoid further contact with the weapon. It turned out being threatened at knifepoint was incredible for one's posture.

"I knew," Raina continued, her voice so low Amie had to lean in to hear her over the ambient noise of the festival. "That she was planning on it, at least. I made her an offer—it was low, I knew. I'd been planning on saving for a few more years before she was ready to sell, but I'd hoped . . ."

She scoffed. "I was an idiot. That woman didn't care about how many years of my life I gave to that store. She laughed when I told her what I was willing to offer. *Laughed.* God, I could've fucking killed her right there. But I didn't. I kept my cool."

"Yeah, you seem really chill and levelheaded. Ow." Amie winced as the knife pricked her back again. "Sorry."

"I *was,*" Raina insisted. "I'd waited that long, I knew I could wait a little longer. Try to buy it off of the next owner. I could be patient. But then I found out that she was considering selling to Madeline. That wasn't gonna work."

"Because she was going to combine the businesses," Amie said. "You'd never have a chance of buying it in the future."

"Right."

They stopped at an intersection, waiting for a break in the foot traffic.

"But if you didn't want the store to go to Madeline, why were you pushing her to talk to Andrew after . . . oh." Realization hit Amie like a truck. "You wanted her to upset Andrew so that he wouldn't sell to her."

"You got it." Raina pushed Amie through the intersection. "I knew it was too soon for her to bring it up at the memorial. She knew, too. Luckily, it didn't take much work, especially when I kept validating Andrew's suspicion of her over the next few days. He was grieving, and he needed someone to blame. I just offered him Madeline."

"And then you offered him Jonathan Oakland," Amie said. "You gave him Oakland's business card and told him you thought Savannah would've wanted to sell the store to him. Did you know that wasn't true?"

"Oh, yeah," Raina said. "She was trying to figure out if she could sue him for giving her bad advice. But I knew she hadn't told Andrew. I think she was embarrassed."

As they turned a corner, Amie suddenly noticed that they were, in fact, heading for the Ferris wheel. Before she could submit a formal complaint, Raina spoke again:

"I figured the old guy was better for my long-term plan than Madeline. He'd told Savannah he'd be willing to sell the store back to her at a higher price once it began making money again. I knew Andrew wouldn't take that offer, so I thought maybe Oakland would sell to me instead. I was willing to wait. But then Savannah said she was going to sell to Madeline. That was a problem."

"So you came up with a plan to kill her." Amie watched the Ferris wheel appear to grow in size as they approached. "And found a scapegoat for your crime."

Raina huffed. "I knew nothing was going to happen to David," she said, as if annoyed Amie had even implied such a thing. "There wasn't enough evidence against him. I just needed someone for the police to put their attention on long enough for my trail to cool. I'd see David walking to and from the grocery store every Monday morning, so I knew he'd be there. I just needed to set Savannah off about something and send her in his direction."

"So you canceled the flower order," Amie said. "And after she rescheduled, you rescheduled it *again* so it'd be delivered that night, to make her go back to the bookstore, where you were waiting."

Raina actually looked surprised. "You really *have* been investigating," she said, sounding impressed. "Yeah. I convinced Savannah to wait when the flowers didn't arrive first thing Monday, but as soon as I saw David go by, I told her they must have canceled the order. That was enough to get her going."

They stopped at the end of the Ferris wheel's line, which was shorter than Amie would've liked.

"What are we doing here?" Amie asked, as if there was a chance they were going swimming in the lake beyond instead of getting on the very obvious ride in front of them.

"I need time to think without worrying about you running away." Raina dug into her windbreaker pocket with her free hand, pulling out an accordion of tickets. "Rip off two."

Amie obliged, ripping off the tickets from the end. Raina returned the rest to her pocket.

"Why David?" Amie asked as Raina took the tickets from her. "Savannah was literally blackmailing Benny. He had a motive. *You* were even trying to get me to suspect him." Another truck of realization struck her (by this point, Amie was wishing the realizations would come to her a little less violently).

"Did you send me those photos?" Amie asked. "The ones of Benny going into my apartment. You left the threatening note. You set that all up."

"Yup." Raina didn't sound particularly proud or ashamed of herself. She was just stating facts. "I left the bar right after you. My friends were pissed, but I wanted to give you more motivation to look into Benny. Or to scare you away. Either one would've worked for me.

"I knew you lived in Savannah's building, so that was easy. Your name and apartment number were on the buzzers outside; that was easy, too. Benny had given his number for the updates thing we have for the store, so I called him and said your bathroom was flooding. Photographed him entering, emailed them to you."

"Which you also got from the updates thing," Amie said, making a mental note to never give out her contact info to anyone ever again. Assuming she survived the night.

"Mhm. Then I slipped the note under your door after he left."

"But still, why David? Why not Benny from the start? Savannah was blackmailing him—"

"*I* was blackmailing him," Raina said, sounding tired. "Savannah had no idea it was happening."

"*What?*" Amie struggled to make sense of that. "Then why did you tell me about it?"

"I wasn't going to," Raina explained. "But then you guys told me he and his girlfriend broke up, so I knew I couldn't blackmail him any more after that. I figured if you were already suspecting him, I might as well lean into it."

Amie was still working to catch up. "So everything about the rent, that was all made up?"

"No, that was true. I wasn't ready to buy the store yet, but I knew the Harlows were struggling with money, so I was hoping having their rent lowered would keep her going longer. Covering the whole floor wasn't Savannah trying to throw off Benny, it was—"

"—you trying to throw off Savannah," Amie finished. "So she wouldn't find out she was the only one with a lowered rent and start asking questions."

"I was going to keep blackmailing him for money after Savannah's death," Raina said. "But that wasn't going to work with him broken up, so I threw him under the bus."

Amie thought back to Benny sitting with David, talking about ghosts. The letter Amie had found in the wastebasket must have arrived after Savannah's death, leading Benny to feel like he was being haunted. Maybe that was even how Hallie had ultimately discovered his infidelity—he'd let his guard down after Savannah's death, thinking he was free from the blackmail letters. Until one arrived after her death, mentioning a possible change in terms.

"David, Madeline, Benny," Amie said quietly. "You had everyone looking everywhere except at you."

"That was the plan." They moved forward to the front of the line as the people ahead of them got on the ride. "I still don't know how you figured it out."

"You wouldn't believe me if I told you." Amie had been so invested in following everything Raina was saying that she'd only just become aware of how quickly the line had moved. She looked up at the Ferris wheel, then averted her eyes as her stomach lurched. "Isn't there somewhere else you can think? Maybe someplace on the ground?"

Raina shot her a sideways look. "Are you afraid of heights?"

"I'm not afraid of *heights*. It's more like—"

Amie was interrupted by the ride operator swinging open the gate. Raina pulled her through, handing over their tickets.

"It'll be fine," Raina said, walking her up the steps to their seats. "Remember the alternative."

Amie allowed herself to be lowered onto the seat, briefly considering the alternative as her body began shaking.

The ride operator lowered the bar down to their laps. Once they began rising over the lake, Raina removed the small pocketknife from Amie's skin. She closed it with a *snap*.

"I started carrying this with me after Savannah died," Raina said, resting the knife in her lap. "I was worried Benny might figure out it was me who was threatening him. I was sort of relieved to find out I couldn't blackmail him anymore. It had begun to feel like something I *needed* to do. Like, I'd gone so far, I couldn't just stop because Savannah was dead."

"Because you killed her," Amie said. She was still trembling, keeping her eyes fixed on Raina to avoid processing the heights they were reaching.

Raina's face twitched. "What?"

"You keep saying 'Savannah's death' and 'Savannah died.' She was *murdered*. You *murdered her*." Amie wasn't sure if it was the absence of the knife on her back that was giving her the confidence to say those things, but the words continued to spill out of her. "For what? A bookstore? You killed her over *a bookstore*?"

"IT WASN'T—" Raina reeled herself in, inhaling sharply. "It wasn't just for the bookstore," she said, her voice low and measured. "It was for *me*. For all the years I let her walk over me, all the time and energy I gave her, all for her to laugh in my face when I suggested that she sell the store to me. I said, 'To keep it in the family.' And she *laughed* at me."

Raina sat back in her seat, tilting her head to look up at the sky. "All those years, for nothing. I was nothing to her. So she became nothing to me. Just an obstacle in the way of getting what I wanted, so all that time didn't have to go to waste."

She let out a dry chuckle. "You know, it's been kind of nice to finally be able to tell someone about all of this. I hadn't realized how lonely I'd been feeling this week."

They were quiet for a full rotation of the wheel. Or maybe two or three. No longer able to avoid noticing their distance from the ground, Amie had closed her eyes, focusing on her breathing.

"Okay," she heard Raina finally say. "Here's what we're gonna do."

She nudged Amie's shoulder. "You still with me?"

"I can hear you, if that's what you're asking."

"Good. We're going to get off the Ferris wheel."

Amie was liking the plan so far.

"We're gonna go back to my place, and you're going to give me something from you—a video, an email, I'll figure it out when we get there—saying that David killed Savannah."

Amie wasn't liking the plan anymore.

"I'm not doing that," she said, opening her eyes to glare at Raina.

"Calm down. I'm not going to do anything with it. As long as you don't tell anyone anything about me and Savannah. A fair trade."

"I wouldn't exactly call it a fair trade." Amie stiffened as they slowed to a stop at the top of the wheel, gripping the lap bar as the seat swung gently. "On my end, an innocent person isn't accused of murder. On your end, a guilty person gets away with murder. How is that fair?"

"You're not really in a position to negotiate." Having come up with a plan, Raina seemed more cheerful. She leaned over the side, looking down over the festival. "I'd say you probably have about a minute to make your decision."

"Do I have a choice?" Amie looked out over the dark lake in front of them, finding its quiet stillness more comforting than looking at the people below.

"Sure. You can leave here with me to do my plan, or I can . . . oh! Perfect. Look at that."

Amie kept her eyes on the lake.

"Amie. Look."

Not wanting to disobey the woman holding a knife, Amie reluctantly looked over, following Raina's gaze to the ground. At first she thought Raina was looking at the magician introducing himself to a small crowd, and wondered if she was going to volunteer Amie to be sawed in half. Then she saw Ziya and David making their way through the crowd toward the Ferris wheel.

"Come with me," Raina said, "or I'll stab whichever one gets to us first."

"You're not gonna do that," Amie said shakily. "Come on. You're a planner. You created this whole scheme to kill Savannah. This can't end with you just stabbing someone out in the open."

"No," Raina argued, "this can't end with me getting caught. But if it does, I'm taking one of them with me."

She turned to look Amie in the eye. "You can't sit here forever. Either way, we're walking off this Ferris wheel. I'm offering you an easy choice: Sacrifice one of them to take me down, or leave with me, give me what I want, and we can all go on with our lives."

The Ferris wheel began to move again, this time in the opposite direction. The lake rose to meet them as they descended.

"You've got one and a half more rotations to decide," Raina said, settling back into her seat. "I feel like the easy choice is obvious."

"Neither of them are easy," Amie murmured. She looked over just in time to see Ziya and David reach the line for the ride before she was lifted past them back up into the sky.

"But one is easi*er*." Raina was beginning to sound impatient. "I'll help you. Pick option one. Happy ending. Everyone lives."

"Except Savannah." A small glimmer of an idea had appeared in Amie's mind. Like a tiny flame in the middle of a dark lake.

"Oh my *god*." Raina reopened the pocketknife as they reached the top and began their final descent. "Time's up, Amie. Decision time."

"Okay." Amie took a deep breath. "Decision time."

She fell silent for several seconds, waiting.

"Well?" Raina demanded. "What's your de—"

Amie pulled her legs up from under the lap bar and lunged for the knife. Raina clearly hadn't been expecting Amie to make a move while still on the ride, so her light grip on the weapon made it easy for Amie to grab it. The blade sliced her hand, but Amie held on, standing up on the seat.

Before Raina could fully react to what was happening, Amie leapt off the Ferris wheel, screaming, into the dark waters of the lake.

Chapter Eighteen
Fell

Day 6 A.L.

Not that Amie had wanted the Ferris wheel ride to be longer than it was, but if it had been, she would have had some time to ask herself a few questions. Like, "How deep do you think this lake is?" or . . . no, that would have been the primary one, probably.

Amie crashed through the surface of the water, her scream cut off as she clamped her mouth shut to preserve oxygen. A lightning bolt of pain shot up her ankle as her left foot hit the lake bed. (That answered that question.)

The sudden quiet under the water was startling, even more startling than the pain in her ankle or the freezing cold of the lake. For a moment, Amie floated in place as the water shielded her from the dull thrumming of the world above.

Her survival instincts checked in as her chest began to tighten. Limiting movement in her throbbing ankle, Amie kicked with her other leg and swam upward.

The noise felt almost deafening as she broke through the surface, gasping for air. The din grew even louder as onlookers spotted her and began shouting.

"—over there!"

"I see her!"

"David!"

Amie searched for the source of the last voice as she wiped water out of her eyes, struggling to stay afloat with only one leg in operation. Ziya stood in her socks on the lakeside, one boot in her hand, the other lying in the grass behind her. David was already wading into the lake, water up to his knees.

"I'm—" A fit of coughing interfered with her assurances that she was okay, so she demonstrated instead by paddling to shore. David met her in the shallows.

"Are you hurt?" he asked, hauling her upright.

"No—ow." Amie winced as she stepped with her left foot. Her hand stung from where she'd grabbed the knife, which she'd lost her grip on somewhere between jumping into the lake and resurfacing.

"Those are mutually exclusive responses. Which one is it?"

"Ow," Amie repeated, putting her weight on her right foot. "Final answer."

David helped her hop through the shallow water and onto dry land, depositing her into Ziya's arms.

"You're gonna smell like lake," Amie said half-heartedly, hoping she didn't sound too convincing as Ziya hugged her.

"I don't care. You scared the *shit* out of me." Ziya pulled away, looking her up and down. "Your hand is bleeding!"

"Is it bad?" Amie asked, examining the wound. It was deeper than it felt. She supposed she would feel it more once the adrenaline wore off.

"We should wrap it—"

Amie pulled off her cardigan. "I've got it," she said, swathing it around the wound. It wasn't until the act was done that she realized she hadn't considered the long-term stain ramifications. Despite her reacclimation efforts that week, she was still at times operating on the assumption that things would reset the following day. She wondered how long it would take until she no longer had moments like that.

Ziya's jaw was set with anger as she watched Amie wrap her hand. "Did Raina push you?"

"No. I jumped."

"*What?*" Ziya and David exclaimed.

"Shh!" Amie glanced around as David dropped his jacket over her shoulders. The onlookers were thankfully keeping their distance as they watched with curiosity. "She killed Savannah. She knew I knew, and gave me two choices. I didn't like either of them, so I grabbed her knife and jumped."

"Why didn't you just toss the knife?" Ziya asked, appalled.

"I wanted to make it seem like she pushed me," Amie explained, her teeth beginning to chatter, "so people will finally suspect her. And I needed to get you two away from her. Is she still here?"

"I see security coming," David said, glancing over their heads. "Looks like someone held on to her." Slipping his shoes back on, he said, "You take a second. I'll make sure she stays put."

He turned to leave, then hesitated, giving Amie a look of concern that made her heart squeeze for worrying him.

"I'm okay," she said. "Promise."

David nodded, giving her a silent pat on the shoulder before heading back to the base of the Ferris wheel.

"I knew the name Genevieve sounded familiar, but I couldn't put my finger on it," Ziya said, watching him leave. "I told the girls I thought something was wrong, but they told me I was just being jealous. I'd just left them when I found David looking for you. He locked in as soon as I told him about the Genevieve thing."

"How did you know something was wrong?" Amie asked, pulling David's jacket tighter around her as the breeze picked up.

"Raina said you were going to the *Ferris wheel,*" Ziya scoffed. "In what world does Amie Teller, famously afraid of falling from a great height, voluntarily get on the *Ferris wheel*? Idiot. Her, not you."

Amie watched Ziya as she continued to wax poetic about Raina's intelligence, a warm feeling battling the chill that had begun creeping through her body. Everything was going to be okay. Ziya was still there. And Amie was going to take as much time as was needed to keep her around.

"What did I say?" Amie asked softly.

Ziya stopped mid-epithet. "What?"

"I told you," Amie said, fighting a smile, "to forget everything you know about me."

"Oh my *god.*" Ziya's shoulders relaxed as she pulled her back into a hug. "I'm still working on it," she mumbled into Amie's shoulder.

"It's just that, you know, you've had four whole days since I asked, and it seems like you're really struggling—"

"I was supposed to forget everything about you in *four days*?"

"I would've preferred two, but I was trying to be reasonable."

"I give up. If it hasn't happened yet, it's probably not going to happen."

"Darn."

They pulled apart, Ziya's hands still resting on the sleeves of David's jacket.

"Hey," Amie said. "Tell me what you think I should do now."

Ziya gave her a curious look. "I think . . . you should talk to the police. And then let me take you home."

Amie hesitated, an automatic "okay" resting on her lips. She hadn't been expecting *that.*

"No," she said instead, holding strong. "David can take me home. I want to shower and go to sleep."

"Oh." Ziya stepped back, looking chagrined. "Of course, yeah."

"But can I see you tomorrow?" Amie asked tentatively. "I've been thinking about everything you said, and—"

"Yes," Ziya cut her off, eyes sparkling. "Tomorrow sounds great."

Tomorrow did sound great.

Epilogue

Day 188 A.L.

It turned out that putting all of one's effort into framing other people for their crime left a person with very little remaining time to cover their own tracks if the cops eventually decided to look in their direction.

Raina had previously informed the police that she had been at home at the time of Savannah's murder. She'd even secured an eyewitness to confirm her arrival home, with whom the police had not even bothered to speak until they were encouraged to do so by Amie's accusation. Raina had not, however, accounted for the eyewitness who saw her exiting her apartment soon after via the fire escape. Her story quickly fell apart after that.

Madeline dropped her assault charges on Andrew, with an agreement that he would attend grief counseling. Shelf Starter was closed for the rest of the month. (Reportedly, Grayson arrived at the store the next day, looked through the window, shrugged, and left.) On October 1, Madeline began renovations to incorporate the bookstore into Eons Café.

About six months after the fall festival, Amie and Ziya flew to Iceland.

"I'm gonna want to do a bunch of stuff you've already done," Amie warned. "Is that okay?"

"I can handle some repeats," Ziya assured her. "Watching you experience it all for the first time will be worth it."

"It'll be worth it because you'll enjoy it," Amie corrected her.

"That, too," Ziya conceded, rolling her eyes good-naturedly. "Especially if we see the northern lights."

By the night before their departure, Ziya's confidence was clearly wavering as they looked at the weather forecast for the week ahead.

"We could get a partial refund," she offered as they looked sadly at the line of cartoon clouds. "Try again next month."

Amie shut the laptop. "No," she said firmly. "We're doing this. Northern lights or no, this is going to be a good trip."

The sky was overcast for almost the entirety of their time in Iceland. A brief, hopeful Monday of sun had gone cloudy once more by the time evening arrived. But that didn't deter the two from enjoying themselves.

They were preparing to go out on their final night when David called.

"I just wanted to say there's no rush to look at the pages of the new book draft I emailed you," he said. Amie put him on speaker-phone so she could finish pulling on her boots. "Also, I sent you two newer versions in the past three hours. So ignore the first two. And possibly the third if I send another within the next hour."

"I received every version," Amie confirmed, shoving her foot into the snow boot. "We just finished reading the last one. It was great! I would have called you, but I thought you were with your family."

"Everyone's out of the house for the afternoon, thank god," David said. "I've been using this beautiful peace and quiet to edit."

"Don't act like you haven't been enjoying yourself," called Ziya from across the hotel room. "You sent us, like, a hundred photos of your niece at the zoo."

"I didn't say I wasn't enjoying myself," David argued. "I can enjoy my family while still appreciating some silence when I can get it. How's the weather looking tonight?"

"Clearest it's been," Amie reported, pulling on her other boot. "We're keeping expectations low."

"Just remember," David said, "there are thousands of photos and videos of the aurora borealis online that you can look at for free—"

"Noted," Amie said, cutting him off. "Thank you so much as always for your sage wisdom."

"Happy to help. Have fun, kid."

They left the hotel soon after saying goodbye to David, getting on a shuttle that drove them and several other people out to a location that advertised a near guarantee for viewing the northern lights.

Two hours later, the word "near" held a lot more weight than when they'd first seen it.

"Last shuttle leaves in ten," Ziya said, returning their empty thermos to her bag. "We can go now, or we can wait and risk getting honked at by the driver."

"I'll risk a honk," said Amie, shifting in her camping chair. She'd had her eyes glued to the sky as soon as they sat down, occasionally stretching her neck to avoid keeping it in one position for too long.

"I'm sorry," Ziya said. "I should've taken us more north. Or booked the trip earlier in the season. Or—"

Amie took her hand, keeping her eyes on the sky (she wasn't going to let sentimentality get in the way of her mission). "Z. This was the best trip I've ever been on. Thank you."

Ziya squeezed her hand, her thumb running over the scar on Amie's palm. "You haven't actually been on a lot of trips."

"Okay, well—" Amie stopped, squinting at the sky. "Do you see that?"

"You saw a light?"

"I mean, it's just . . ." Amie framed the sky with her hands. "Doesn't it look kind of pinkish to you?"

Ziya was quiet for a moment. "It's definitely pinkish," she confirmed. "And you're gonna think I'm making this up, but I see a little green, too."

"No, I see the green."

They stared at the sky for another few minutes, waiting to see if the whispers of color would grow any louder.

"I think that counts," Amie said finally.

"Oh, that for sure counts." Ziya reached over and squeezed Amie's face between her gloves. "We saw the northern lights!"

Amie echoed her cheer, pulling Ziya into a hug that caused them to topple backward off their chairs and into the snow, screaming with laughter. They kissed under what may or may not have been the northern lights, it didn't really matter, until the blare of the shuttle's horn sent them both scrambling to gather their belongings.

"So now what?" Ziya asked, pulling the strap of her chair over her shoulder. "What's next?"

Still breathless from the laughter and the kiss and the lights, Amie took Ziya's gloved hand in hers as they trudged through the snow. The words on her lips filled her with a tingling anticipation—still a little uncomfortable, but not at all unpleasant.

Amie smiled. "I don't know."

Acknowledgements

One day I was talking to my literary agent Melissa Jeglinski about this time loop mystery I was working on, telling her that I just didn't have a title for it yet. No more than FIVE SECONDS passed before Melissa went, so matter-of-factly, "Out of the Loop." Melissa, thank you so much as always for all your hard work, guidance, and support. Five seconds. Cannot emphasize enough how fast she said it.

Thank you to my editor Jess Verdi, whose care and enthusiasm for this book was already through the roof on Day One and somehow continued to ascend to even greater heights with every passing milestone. I was also lucky to have, in Jess' words, two editors for the price of one! Thanks as well to Rebecca Nelson, who was faced with a multiple timeline mystery and returned it to me with incredible kindness and insight.

Thanks to my copyeditor, Madison Schultz, and to all the wonderful folks at Crooked Lane who've worked on this book, including Thai Fantauzzi Pérez, Dulce Botello, Mikaela Bender, Stephanie Manova, and Megan Matti. And thank you to Michel Vrana for bringing your incredible artistry to the cover!

Thank you to Leona at Maple Intersectionality Consulting, whose thoughtful suggestions for Ziya helped to ground her in reality and make her a character worthy of the friends I wrote her for. Any mistakes are my own!

Acknowledgements

Some more thanks:

Thank you to Brian Murphy for that last scene with Oliana in the NADDPod Campaign Three finale, causing my jaw to drop with a sudden epiphany that had me running to the last chapter of this book to make changes two weeks before my deadline.

Forever thank you to Shannon Plackis, without whom none of this would exist.

Thanks to Nicole and Jamie, my early readers, and to Divya for feedback on Ziya's name, even though you tried to guilt me into just changing a couple letters and naming her after you. Thank you to all my other friends and family for the endless support and excitement and photos of *Charlotte Illes* in bookstores and libraries.

Echoing my dedication, thank you to all the booksellers who are always so fantastic and lovely. Savannah is the most fictional of all the fictional characters I've ever written. Absolutely the most unrealistic part of this book, and that's including the time loop.

Thank you to all my readers, whose outpouring of love and enthusiasm for Charlotte made me go, "Oh okay, I think I should keep doing this."

And thank you always to my parents, without whom ~~I~~ David wouldn't exist. Dad, because I think the best parts of him might be you a little bit, and Mom, because of your repeated demands that I "write more older people."